Kingdoms
of the
Savanna

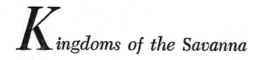

*K*ingdoms of the Savanna

JAN VANSINA

The University of Wisconsin Press

Published 1966
The University of Wisconsin Press
Box 1379, Madison, Wisconsin 53701
The University of Wisconsin Press, Ltd.
70 Great Russell Street, London

Printings 1966, 1968, 1970, 1975

Printed in the United States of America

ISBN 0-299-03664-2; LC 65-16367

Preface

This book grew out of a set of three Knaplund lectures in Tropical History given at the University of Wisconsin in the fall of 1961. I was asked to publish them and promised to do so, but I felt that more detail and a small bibliography might be useful. By the time the present version was completed, I came to wonder if I should have kept that promise at all, for the gaps in the data are little short of appalling and because of that any synthesis is out of the question. This indicates how little work has been devoted to the history of Central Africa. On the other hand, reports keep coming in about fieldwork (especially among the Lozi, Bemba, and Lunda) and archival research is also being pushed, which is a sign that historians are becoming aware of the task which awaits them there. Because of this situation, a work like this cannot be more than a modest introduction to the field, a tool for the convenience of other historians.

Apart from place names, for which the official spelling has been retained, an attempt has been made to unify the spelling of all other Bantu words by the use of the African alphabet. In this spelling the letter *c* stands for the English sound *ch*. The other symbols are close to standard usage in English. The combination *ng* should always be uttered as *ng* in English at the end of a word, for example, as in si*ng*.

Without the persistent interest of Dr. Philip D. Curtin in the fruition of this study, the work would never have been written. I am also grateful to M. F. Crine, M. le Chanoine L. Jadin, and Fraulein Dr. E. Sulzmann for their help in providing materials from their unpublished research about the Lunda, the Kongo, and the Bolia. Miss L. Marmor has been my research assistant on this project, and I wish especially to thank her for her unstinting cooperation. Finally, I also want to thank the staff of the Memorial Library of the University, which has been of great help in locating some published materials in foreign libraries.

The Rockefeller Foundation, the Graduate School, and the Institute for Research in the Humanities of the University of Wisconsin have provided the necessary funds and created time for research. I am grateful to all of them for their support.

J. Vansina

Gooreind, 1963
Madison, 1964

Contents

List of Maps and Charts

*Kingdoms
of the
Savanna*

Introduction

Relatively little is known about the history of Central Africa in precolonial times, and even today this part of the continent is the stepchild of African historiography. One reason for this seems to be that the sources at our disposal are often not the familiar written documents, and that even when written documents are available—for instance, as in the history of the coastal peoples during the eighteenth and nineteenth centuries—they were not always exploited. Because the sources are unfamiliar, the unfortunate result has been an unspoken feeling that there are no sources for a history of Central Africa, that such a history cannot be written. This is of course not true. Actually, the overriding reason for this state of affairs is the general lack of interest in African history, as distinguished from a history of European endeavors in Africa.

The ultimate justification for this book is to break with the tradition of neglect, to counter the vague feeling that nothing can be done. It is true, certainly, that because of the lack of data it is not possible at the present time to write a well-rounded book on the early history of Central Africa; in fact, this work will remind the reader very often of a Swiss cheese—all holes with enough

3

cheese to keep the holes together. But it is possible to write an exploratory work, an introduction to the history of the area and its problems, to arouse interest, and to orient beginners in this field. This study should be considered, then, as a workbook. Every chapter is but a summary of the known major events, and a substantial bibliography is intended to be a first guide for future research.

This work does not cover the history of the whole of Central Africa, but is limited to the savannas north of the Zambesi and south of the equatorial forest. This arbitrary limitation is based on a remarkable fact: all or almost all the peoples in this area have developed kingdoms or chiefdoms—that is, they have developed political systems which have a centralized political structure and which are ruled by a single person. In the surrounding area most populations are stateless: they have no centralized political structure and very often no single leader. (The exceptions to this are the areas around Lake Leopold II and Lake Tumba, where some few groups are organized into small states; however, very little is known about them. Also, in the southeast there are, or there have been, states in the sense in which I am using the term, but historically they belong in the great East African rather than in the Central African tradition.) This book, therefore, is first a political history, a history of states, and mainly of Central African states.

There are drawbacks to focusing on political history because political structures and developments are only part of the history of a culture. And in this case such a focus is also regrettable because so much of African history, indeed nearly all of it, has been almost exclusively political history. It would have been good to break with this pattern in historiography, yet there are cogent reasons for stressing political history at this stage. Most of our written and oral sources deal with this aspect of history more than with any other, and this is so true that we know very little today about the early history of all those peoples in Central Africa outside of the area chosen for discussion; they are not formed as states, there are no written sources, there are few oral sources.

and the anthropological materials which are available for a cultural history have not been studied well enough as yet to enable one to outline even the major facts of the history of those peoples. Also, the structures of the states seem to have influenced the cultures to a very high degree. The existence of kingdoms quickened the pace of change in many different aspects of culture: traders were protected, items of material culture and economic techniques became widespread, languages of conquerors were diffused, social and political ideas as well as religious rituals and myths were disseminated, etc. There is almost a political determinism to cultural change in Central Africa from 1500 to 1900. Finally, while it remains true that a political history is a severely limited one, history with only occasional reference to political structures and developments would be most confusing; it is the political history which provides a chronology, and history without chronology ceases to be history.

The development of the major states—Kongo, Luba, Lunda, Kazembe, Lozi, and the colony of Angola—profoundly influenced the history of all the surrounding peoples. This is the main reason why a non-African state such as Angola has been included within the scope of this work. Although the facts do not warrant speaking of these major states as a political hegemony, the kingdoms exercised a profound influence on other political structures and other cultures, as well as on each other. In fact, it could be said that the history of the peoples in the savanna in the five centuries preceding 1900 is the story of the development of a Luba-Lunda culture in the east and of a Kongo and colonial Portuguese culture in the west. In between these areas the regions known as Kwango, Kasanje, and Ovimbundu, influenced both by Western and by Eastern cultures, produced a number of mixed cultures. Along the lower Kasai, around Stanley Pool, and around Lake Leopold II in the north, and on the upper Zambesi in the south, marginal cultures and societies can easily be delimited. Although such a general view is an oversimplification, it will be a convenient guide for the student of the area, and in addition it has the virtue of being correct to a high degree in the more limited field of political developments, which is the major theme of this book.

This general idea has guided the outline of the work. Generally speaking, the different chapters separate Kongo history from Luba and Lunda history and also separate Kongo history from the history of the marginal peoples in the north. Even the chronological limits of our study are determined by its main theme: it is a book about states, and it starts with their origins and ends with their fall around 1900, when they ceased to be sovereign. The cut-off dates for different chapters have been provided by turning points in the history of the eastern or the western groups of states. The invasion of the Jaga in 1568 and the foundation of Luanda in 1576 are such turning points in the development of the coastal states, and so is the period between 1567 and 1710, when Kongo underwent a radical transformation and when Angola consolidated its territory and its peculiar colonial structure. The 1840's and 1850's initiate a clear change in the development of the eastern group of states. The only date which has no justification other than to facilitate synchronic comparison is the 1700 date in relation to the eastern group of states.

The Sources

The historian of Central Africa relies essentially on five different types of sources. Written records, both chronicles and archival material, are available for the kingdom of Kongo since the beginning of the sixteenth century and since 1600 for the other coastal areas. Oral traditions, of major importance as sources, are plentiful, but there is need for immediate action on the part of the historian if in many cases we are to save these traditions. Archaeological data, a third source, is in urgent need of more excavations. Linguistic evidence is also of value, but again there is need for more data and for exploitation of that data in new ways. Finally, historians rely upon ethnographic materials, but there is need here for more comprehensible ethnographic descriptions if the historian is to be adequately served.

Some of the early written sources are chronicles written by the official court historians of Lisbon. Some are archival documents: for example, instructions or *regimento* from the king of Portugal, the orders or *alvara* from the same source; correspondence between the kings of Kongo and of Portugal or between the kings of Portugal and individual Portuguese; correspondence between missionaries and either their superiors, the Vatican, or the kings of Kongo; etc. The chronicles are not contemporary whereas all the archival documents usually are; apart from the obvious normative elements in the archival documents, they reflect the actual course of events with some detail. (In later times, all the voluminous administrative correspondence in or about Angola shares the same features.) There are other archival documents, which originated for practical reasons and which have somewhat different characteristics. In this category would be accounts, "relations" by traders, such as Lopes or Barbot, or reports by missionaries, such as the "relations" of De Gallo or Lorenzo di Lucca. Here a static picture is often given, a viewpoint that is formed some time after the events. Even if the report stresses changes that have taken place, it does so to show the meaning of a present situation. The ultimate reason for all the reports is practical: to foster trade or to plan evangelization. These documents, then, although strictly speaking they are not contemporary, can practically be considered so in many cases; but they cannot be considered as an immediate participation in the actual course of events —they are interpretations. Aside from those documents, there are the histories. The two most important works are O. de Cadornega's *Historia de Angola,* and E. da Silva Correa's book with the same title. The main difference between these histories and the reports is that the histories are less contemporary, and that there is not only a practical reason for their existence but also the concern of the historian, the *laudator temporis acti,* for whom history is a *magistra vitae.*

Most of the written documents suffer from a basic defect. They record events as seen by the eyes of foreigners, who often are in conflict or in competition with the local peoples. Very often these witnesses do not know the language well.[1] They generally have only a superficial knowledge of the cultures and societies in which they live, and, of course, the concept of ethnocentrism is foreign to them. Their description must not be taken as representing the reality of the times, therefore, but of reality as seen by a European foreigner. Especially their historical interpretations are to be treated with caution, since they impute motivations to African chiefs, which are deduced from the behavior of these leaders, as foreigners who belong to another culture. Fortunately, there are a few African sources, the most outstanding of which are the letters of the kings of Kongo.

Then there are those who had axes to grind. The historians of the court at Lisbon emphasize the splendor, Christian fervor, and generosity of Portugal. The European or African rulers have to uphold official arguments in their diplomatic exchanges, missionaries have to illustrate the horrors of paganism and the value of conversion in order to raise money in Europe for their enterprise, the interest of the traders is often confined to the conditions of business, and many Europeans participated in the local power struggles. For every source, the possible bias generated by the personal position of that source should be assessed before the data are used as evidence.

Many sources have been published, especially for the sixteenth and seventeenth centuries. Barring new discoveries, the printed source collections are almost complete until 1640. After that date some collections, like the archives of the Jesuits or of the Vatican after 1650 or the Angolan archives after 1650, still remain to be published. For the eighteenth and nineteenth centuries there are thousands of documents about Kongo and Angola, and practically none have been published or have even been used by historians.[2] Yet they promise to be of great value not only for the history of Angola or for the history of the slave trade but also for the history of peoples of the interior, such as the Imbangala or the Yaka, and even for additional information about the Lunda. The documents could, especially in the case of the Yaka and the Lunda, lead to the recovery of precious chronological evidence. But the historians who have worked with these sources have been mainly interested either in the glory of Portugal or in the missionary work, and from both these points of view the eighteenth and early nineteenth centuries represent a period of deep decadence.

Oral traditions, the second main source for the history of Central Africa, are plentiful. In all the states there were recorders of the traditions at the courts. These were often persons entrusted with religious duties, as with the Bemba, Lozi, Lunda of Kazembe, Luba, Imbangala, and Ovimbundu, where the gravekeepers of the kings were the preservers of tradition; in other states, such as the Lunda or Kuba, a special titleholder was the keeper of the oral archives.[3] But apart from these political officials, traditions were kept by all corporate groups; for example, by kinship groups like clans or lineages, which have their praise names (the Kongo *ndumbululu* or the Luba *kasala* being examples), or by territorial groups like villages or subchiefdoms. Then there are traditions of a religious nature embedded in myth or ritual formulas; traditions expressed in widely known epics; family traditions which were erratically handed down for a few generations within a chain of extended families; traditions about the origin of the world and the origins of small things like crops, trade items, and the like; etc.[4] Almost everywhere, there still is a wealth of traditions of all sorts to be collected.

The biases of these sources vary with their function. Official traditions always give official points of view; they are "charters" with political or legal importance which are colored by their function. Private sources are often badly transmitted or embellished to please an audience or to teach small children. Yet the cross-comparison of all these sources in a culture can yield a very sound picture of its history. The strong point of all oral tradition, however, is that it is history as recorded by insiders; its weak point is that the chronology is always relative and often uncertain. In both these points, the oral traditions are at opposite poles from the written records.[5]

Among the oral traditions, special care must be given to the dynastic tradition, which is collected from the official historians of a kingdom. Such a tradition usually comprises a list of kings, and eventually the genealogy and a history of the origin of the state; and a description of subsequent major events in the political history of the kingdom, especially if these have led to special features in the system which are still visible today. It must be remembered, of course, that strictly speaking the migrations recalled in such traditions apply only to the ruling family[6] and that their function—that of national glorification and legitimacy of the kingship—often leads to distortion. Yet they are especially important because their lists and genealogies very often provide the only available chronological framework, but even more important is the fact that they are the only oral sources which give an over-all picture of the past history of the area. Most if not all of the other oral sources tend to be much more detailed, but they are so restricted in scope that it would be almost impossible to use them at all without a dynastic tradition.[7]

Very few traditions have been recorded, and a systematic study of the traditions of a given people has so far been carried out only for the Kuba and for the Lunda of Kazembe, although other studies are in progress.[8] Most of the dynastic traditions for all the major kingdoms have been recorded, however, in most cases since the end of the nineteenth century. But usually only one informant was used and, if more than one tradition was collected, the different variants were put together to form one history without any indications as to what the original texts were.[9] In fact, therefore, even most of the dynastic traditions will have to be collected again in all the kingdoms. The other oral traditions—and there are hundreds of them, in every culture—will also have to be gathered. This cannot be done in a short time, and there is real reason to fear that many of them will be lost before they can be recorded. Only the creation of local societies of amateur historians, advised by professional historians, can save the bulk of these data before it is too late. How catastrophic this loss would be can be gathered from the fact that the bulk of the history of all the non-coastal peoples in Central Africa is based on traditions.

Archaeology is obviously important for the early history of Africa. This is accepted by all historians without reservations. Very few excavations dealing with iron-age sites have been carried out so far, however, and it will take many more before the archaeological picture becomes even reasonably detailed. Excavations are urgently needed, not only for the new data which can be uncovered, but also to test other data derived from oral evidence or from linguistics. How much even a single dig can change the historical perspective is shown, for instance, by the excavations at Sanga in Katanga, where a fully-developed iron-age culture and trade links with the East African coast have been demonstrated for a period as early as the eighth century.[10]

In the field of linguistics much can be done for the historian. The main fact which emerges from the linguistic studies so far is that a genetic subdivision of the Bantu language family will probably be either impossible or very difficult to establish. This means that contacts between peoples and early borrowings of all sorts of linguistic features have been very great and very constant over long periods of time. None of the peoples in Central Africa, for instance, had led an isolated life, and many cultures can be suspected of being practically mixed cultures resulting from centuries of contacts with populations all around them.[11]

In view of this fact, one can expect that the contribution of linguistics to the history of Central Africa will be to trace, through different cultures, specific borrowings of separate culture items and of cultural complexes, for instance, in religion or in political structures. In all cases this will not be possible without a concomitant examination of non-linguistic anthropological data in order to determine what the significance of such borrowings has been and in which direction they have diffused.

Quite a few languages have been described in the area, and grammars, texts, and dictionaries are available for all the tongues of the more important kingdoms. But there is still a dearth of data for the marginal northwest, with the exception of the Bolia and Ntomba languages, and for most of the languages spoken in northern and central Angola. Little or no advance has been made, however, with the exploitation of the linguistic data for historical purposes. Here is a virgin field for future research.

It is theoretically clear beyond doubt that anthropological data can be of great value to the historian. For one thing, the historian must know what a given culture is like now and what it was like just before the colonial period began, and this anthropologists describe very well with the methods which are available to them. But much more could be asked from anthropological data. Knowledge about distributions of cultural items or complexes, and especially the study of cultural "fossils" or, conversely, cultural "innovations," could conceivably yield a wealth of historical information. Yet here the anthropologist lacks proper methods. The two major methodologies which have been developed to cope with these problems—the cultural history school in Austria and the American school of cultural historians—have been shown to be inefficient and to be often based on oversimplified premises. The conjectural reconstructions of past culture "stages" which are made by anthropologists of these schools do not reach high enough levels of probability to be taken seriously. In very many cases alternative hypotheses can be set up, all of which seem to share a common low degree of probability with the original reconstruction. The Austrian methodology, moreover, is based on the assumption that culture is composed of different layers of older cultures which have been superimposed one on top of the other. This is a fallacy which needs no elaborate refutation for historians, who find every day how erratic, unpredictable, and syncretistic the ways of change are. Some American studies are remarkable, but the methodologies of most monographs remain rather unrefined. It is clear, therefore, that better anthropological methods will have to be devised. It seems to me that only when linguistic and cultural data are handled together in a more cohesive way will it be possible to come to meaningful conclusions.[12]
Anthropological work has been spotty in the area covered by

this book. The social and political structures of most of the peoples of Northern Rhodesia have been well studied, and the same is true for the Kongo, Yombe, Pende, Lele, and Kuba. Information for the other cultures is either superficial or absent. The area where study has been most deficient lies in Angola, where scarcely any group has been studied at all, although in eastern Katanga the available information is almost as poor. With regard to data that go beyond the analysis of a social system, again the situation is different. Most social anthropologists have been interested in analysis of social systems to such an extent that in their publications they have suppressed the kinds of detail often most needed by the cultural historian—very often the data gathered lie for years in notebooks and are then lost. Here knowledge about Northern Rhodesia is decidedly less extensive than for the rest of the area, with the exception again of northern Angola and eastern Katanga. All in all, then, much remains to be done anthropologically. And here, too, it should be done quickly, for the societies and cultures of the peoples in this part of the world are changing rapidly. It seems to me that within this generation professional anthropologists could do the more essential research, but they should also help to create local folklore societies with the aim of preserving as much as can be recorded of the cultural heritage of the peoples involved.[13]

This study is based on all the published written and oral sources that were available. Archaeological evidence, where available, was also used. Data derived from cultural anthropology have been used to reconstruct some political systems as they existed before the colonial period. Some interesting deductions derived from such data have been discarded momentarily because of the lack of a proper methodology to cope with the documentation. Linguistics have been used very little also since, practically speaking, good studies based on linguistic diffusion have not yet been made.

Some Basic Concepts

The historical interpretation of raw data makes use of a set of basic concepts; these concepts deal both with the study unit and with the types or kinds of processes involved. For instance, such concepts would be exemplified by words such as "tribe" or "population explosion." In African history even more than in other fields, it is necessary to clarify what these concepts mean. We will be concerned with the notion of "tribe" and with the processes of "origins," "migrations," and "conquests."

The concept of "tribe," although used by many historians, is rarely defined. Usually it means—and it will be used in this sense throughout—"a community which believes that it is culturally different from all other communities around it, a belief shared by the surrounding communities." So far, so good. But the historian often implies that tribes have a history, and some will say that the history of precolonial Africa is tribal history. Here some very misleading notions prevail. In the strict sense, a tribal history should be the history of those cultural elements which differentiate it from its neighbors and, even more, the history of the beliefs held by different communities about these elements. In theory, then, a tribal history is part of a history of ideas and values, but in practice no tribal history is that. What the historians mean by the term is that the tribal history covers the history of the community or the society in question, and even here no distinction is usually made between the politically sovereign community—a political unit—and the cultural community—a cultural unit. Furthermore, many historians imagine that the cultural community, the "tribe," is perennial. It does not disappear; it does not alter throughout the ages, although it does migrate; and its migration routes can conveniently be charted. This notion of the perennial tribe is meaningless. It can easily be shown that tribes are born and die, sometimes without displacement of populations or even without changes in the objective cultures of the communities involved. The outstanding example of this is the case of the Lulua. Before 1890 there was no such tribe, there were only Luba Kasai. Yet by 1959 Lulua and Luba Kasai were so differentiated that they were engaged in bitter fighting. How did it happen? The first traders, Angolans and Europeans, who entered Kasai gave nicknames to the people they found there.[14] The one which stuck was Lulua, but the people called themselves Luba, like the groups farther south to the southeast of the Lulua River in the area of Dibaya. In the early 1890's the raids of Ngongo Leteta and Lumpungu, two slave raiders operating for Tippu Tib, chased thousands of the southeastern groups away from their homes to Luluaburg, where they sought protection at the state post. They were settled by the Europeans and thus enjoyed the first advantages of the colonial way of life: missions, schools, and hospitals. Very soon they began to feel themselves to be different from the original inhabitants and this feeling, which was shared by the latter, crystallized in the use of the terms Luba and Lulua.[15] (The case is not isolated. Another example of a newborn tribe are the Fingo fugitives of South Africa.)

The tribe is not a perennial unit, and it is also, in many instances, not the proper unit for study. Many "tribes" of upper Katanga, for instance, are so similar culturally that from the point of view of the cultural historian they should be handled as a single unit, whereas from the point of view of the political historian every chiefdom should be distinguished from every other. In this study, the unit whose history should be considered is the sovereign political community, whatever it may be—a kingdom, a village, a lineage, etc.—because this study is primarily a political history. Culturally, kingdoms can be heterogeneous, for instance, as the Lozi or Rotse kingdom; or several units can belong to the same culture, for instance, as many Lele villages belong to Lele culture. This last case happens often when one has to deal with very small units, and the historian is then justified in using the tribal name to express generalizations which hold good for similar units sharing a common culture; he is justified, for example, in talking about "the Lele" or "the Lele village," instead of repeating his statements for every single Lele village. In this case, he uses the tribal name, not as a subjective attribute, but as a label for a single objective cultural unit. This practice has been followed here, and it is hoped that in every case the reader will be able to distinguish easily between political units: sovereign communities and tribal units; culturally homogeneous communities.

With regard to processes, the first concept to examine is that of "origins," especially when the word "origins" is coupled with "tribes." Origins of the physical population, of the culture and of the languages, although obviously different things, are often confused. This is due to the unstated image that a tribe has a population which is not subject to emigration or immigration but rather remains a mass and moves as a mass, that every tribe speaks its own distinct language and often has its very own physical characteristics, etc. The a priori image is that all these things cannot evolve independently from each other. Obviously it is the other way around, and study after study shows that all of these elements do vary independently. Moreover, the process of origins is never a simple one, since all cultures are mixed, i.e., have taken elements from other cultures or invented or developed new ones *in situ:* populations are mixed in the sense that there seems to be a ceaseless, almost peristaltic, movement as a result of marriages, and of individual or familial migrations, so that webs of clans cut across "tribes" in very many instances; populations are physically mixed; and even languages, the one element in culture which is almost never mixed, still change through borrowing and through accretion by internal means.

Some historians have maintained that the quest for determining origins is useless because there never is a single origin, that to talk about origins is to oversimplify. The term origins has also been used in some cases in opposition to the notion of internal development as an alternate process of change. "Origins of," then, stands for a process of "diffusion from." However, diffusion and internal development or independent invention are not two separate and opposed processes. It takes much innovation to fit a diffused cultural element into a culture that takes it over, and there are many independent inventions that were "stimulated" by some diffusion. It is clear, however, that questions of origins can be asked provided that it is realized that the word covers an intricate and multifarious process of change and that it does not automatically mean "diffusion mechanically undergone." Finally, origins should never be confused with causes. The question, "What is the origin of?" can never substitute for the more difficult one, "Why?" The first one describes a process, the second analyzes a process.

Another process is known in the literature by the term "migrations." Some historians have a romantic attachment to the idea of "migrations," and again, in connection with tribes, the image is wrong. The image is generally that one day thousands started to move, destroying everything in their passage, or fleeing some conqueror, and that the emigrants walked in a beeline from their point of "origin" to the point where they lived at the end of the nineteenth century, that peoples forced other peoples out and threw them on the road. It would seem at times as if the whole interior of Africa was a green billiard table where the balls kicked one another eternally around and around. Again, the fallacy lies in not realizing that migrations are processes and that, because a process is always a complex affair, there can be many varieties of migrations. There are migrations of peoples, of cultural items, of languages, of genes, etc. There are a great number of different ways for peoples to migrate, ranging from the almost unconscious migrations brought about every decade or so by a move of two or three miles of a few villages—but a movement in a single over-all direction—to the rare but spectacular migration of warriors organized in military formations going on the rampage and ravaging where they go. The first case is that of the Lele migrations in the last century or two, the latter the case of the Jaga in the sixteenth century, or the Ngoni and Kololo in the nineteenth. In between there are many other processes of migration; indeed, most of them lie in between. There are also other movements of population, such as the emigration or immigration of different families going from one village to another. It is proposed for our present purpose to limit the term "migration" to movements of population on the scale of politically sovereign communities, or at least of politically-organized communities from the villages upwards. Since the term "migration" is a generalization, it will be specified whenever it is used.

A last term that crops up, especially in political histories, and that must be considered here, is "conquest." Conquest can mean all sorts of things, especially in oral traditions that have been rendered into European languages. A conquest can be a series of raids, a military occupation, an administrative but forced occupation, or the successful assimilation of one community by another. It is a process just as complicated as the process of "origins" or of "migration." The conquest of Angola is something that lasted for centuries, if one understands by it every operation from the first brawl to an administrative civilian occupation. The stereotyped image of a conquest is Caesar's *veni, vidi, vici;* but Caesar's books show well enough that this is only part of the story, and in fact was only the first chapter. The following chapters dealt with revolts. As in the case of the other concepts discussed here, the complexity of the process underlying the term and the variety of processes covered by the generalization should be kept in mind; whenever the notion is used, it should be clarified.

Only some of the basic concepts used by historians of Africa— and the stereotyped images they evoke—have been discussed here. There are many more, such as the notions "state," "village," etc., in the category of units for study, and "population explosion," "expansion," "decadence," etc., in the category of processes. It is necessary to use such concepts as analogical tools, but it is also necessary to realize the danger of misunderstanding that lurks behind the familiar notions: they often evoke the wrong images and they always oversimplify.

The Peoples and Cultures
of the Savanna

The peoples of the savanna south of the equatorial forest show a considerable degree of cultural homogeneity, and this fact has been recognized in most culture-area classifications.[1] Most scholars feel that the Lozi, Ovimbundu, and Bolia are marginal and they are often classified separately. Within the remainder of this huge area, the cultures are still different enough to be brought together in subgroups, as has been done in Chart I. References to the cultural "regions" of this chart will be made whenever necessary in the following description of the material culture and economic life, the social organization, the political structure, the religion, the language, and the origins of the different peoples of the savanna.

Material Culture and Economic Life

The material culture and economic life of all these peoples is very similar. With the exception of the Lozi, who engage in perennial cultivation on the Zambesi valley floor, all other peoples practice shifting cultivation. Although there are many variants in detail, the basic techniques are the same: every year a new area is cleared, and the grasses and tree limbs are burned

CHART I: *Cultural regions in Central Africa
and the peoples grouped in them*

Region	Peoples grouped in regions
Kongo	Vili, Yombe, Nsundi, etc. (north of the river Congo) Ambundu, Dembo, Ginga, Mahungu, Libolo, Kisama, Kipaka (central)
Kwango	Yaka Mbala, Hungaan, Tsamba, Pindi, Ngongo Shinje, Suku, Holo, Kwese, Soonde, Pende Imbangala, Songo
Lower Kasai	Tyo (Teke), Hum, Mfinu Boma, Dia, Nunu, Sakata Yans, Ding, Lwer, Ngul, Tsong, Mbuun Kuba, Lele
Bolia	Bolia, Ntomba, Sengele
Luba	Luba Kasai, Lulua, Northern Kete, Binji Songye Kaniok, Kalundwe, Luba Katanga, Luba Samba, Kikonja Luba Hemba, Buyu, Zela, Kalanga, Lomotwa, Holo
Lunda	Mbagani, Lwalwa, Mbal, Tukongo, Sala Mpasu, Southern Kete, Tabwa Nuclear Lunda Cokwe, Minungu, Western Lunda Lwena, Mbunda, Lucazi, Lwimbe Ndembu, Kaonde
Bemba	Lunda and others of the Luapula Sanga, Lamba, Lala, Aushi, Bisa, Nsenga, Ambo, etc. Bemba, Shila, Unga Tabwa, Tumbwe, Bwile [or Aanza] Lungu, Mambwe
Lozi	Lozi proper Nkoya Mashasha group
Ovimbundu	Ovimbundu, Ambuim, Ndombe

Note: The cultural regions can be compared with those of G. P. Murdock, *Africa: Its Peoples and Their Culture History* (New York, 1959), pp. 284–306, 364–74. For the purpose of this book, since Bolia and Mambwe are organized into states, they have been selected from larger groupings (the other members have not). Ndombe, included on the list, is not discussed at all because chieftainship seems not to have existed there.

and the ashes used as fertilizer. After further preparation by hoeing, which takes different forms, the main crop is then sown or planted. Rotation of different crops on the same field is practiced until the soil is exhausted, which occurs usually from two to four years after the first planting. The field then lies fallow in order to regenerate for a number of years—which may be as many as twenty. An important consequence of this method of cultivation is that the density of the population must perforce remain low and settlements must move from time to time to follow the fields.

The main crops cultivated[2] belong to what Murdock has called the American complex. Both maize or manioc are staples nearly everywhere, and groundnuts and sweet potatoes are also important in the diet. These four crops came from South America, presumably from Brazil, after 1500. Maize entered Central Africa between 1548 and 1583, possibly through the kingdom of Kongo, and from there spread along the trade routes. Manioc was introduced later, probably around 1600; it may have been first cultivated near Luanda and on the plantations of the lower Bengo, north of the city. (In a small area among the Sakata, Mfinu, and Boma Nku of the lower Kasai, another American crop, sugar cane, became a staple.) In addition to these major crops, however, older African crops are found nearly everywhere. Murdock's Sudanic complex is represented in the whole area by millets, sorghos, and even by eleusine, but they are major crops only in the Bemba and Luba regions. Beans, and where possible cowpeas, which also seem to have a purely African origin, are widely cultivated and everywhere are an important item of the local menus. Food crops of Malaysian origins, such as bananas, yams, and taro, assume great importance only with the peoples of the northern Kongo (Yombe), the Bolia, and some Luba; elsewhere they are reported as subsidiary crops. For instance, the Kuba still cultivate some isolated taro in the forest but consider them of the same order of importance as the yams: they have become cultural fossils. Before the introduction of the American complex to the area, the peoples relied heavily on plants from the Sudanic com-

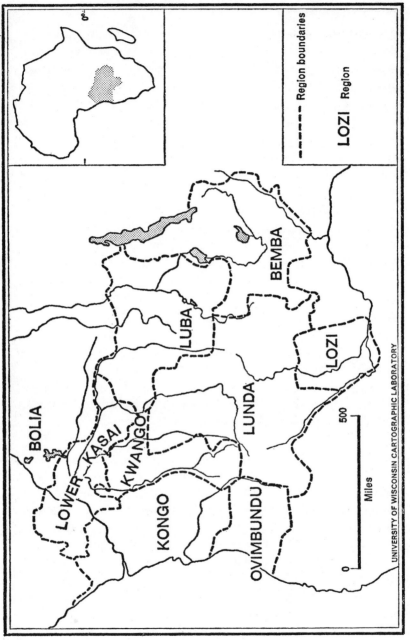

1 Cultural Regions in Central Africa

plex with the exception of the Bolia and Kwango regions, which depended mostly on root crops of Malaysian origin. Forested areas are much better suited for the latter crops, so that the distribution seems to fit with the ecological areas. Environment, not cultural traditions, was the decisive factor here, for it may be assumed that all cultures of the area knew about the cultivation of Sudanic and other African plants as well as plants belonging to the Malaysian complex. To complete the list, rice and cotton cultivation of the Bisa should be mentioned, and cotton with the Holo, but these are probably of nineteenth-century origin.[3]

Besides these basic crops, palm trees both of the different raphia and of the elais varieties are found in every suitable environment. The raphia, however, seems to have been confined to the western part of the savanna and to have been introduced east of the Lulua and the Lubudi in more recent times. It is known, for example, that the Lunda of Kazembe brought the plant to Lake Mweru. In the area where the raphia palm was well known, palm wine even now is generally the most common alcoholic drink, while in the east beer from millet or sorgho has the place of honor.[4]

Domestic animals raised throughout the whole area are chickens, goats, and dogs. Pigs and ducks are found in many places but may have been introduced during the eighteenth or nineteenth centuries. Sheep are raised by many peoples but often are the object of taboos which are sometimes especially connected with the kingship. Cattle are numerous in the Lozi and Ovimbundu regions, but they are milked only among the southern Ovimbundu[5] and the Lozi: no other animal is milked in the whole savanna. Small herds of cattle were owned by chiefs and kings as far north as Loango and by the Lunda chiefs or kings.[6] In the Lunda empire a belt of cowskin was a very special badge worn only by high titleholders.[7] None of the peoples included in our survey really exhibits what has been called the cattle complex, although some customs linked with this complex have found their way in the royal rituals of the Bemba, Lozi, and Ovimbundu.

Hunting and fishing have remained important despite the agricultural pursuits. There are communities of specialized fishermen on all major lakes and rivers. Everywhere—but especially in the Lunda and the Ovimbundu regions—hunting is valued very highly; because its significance as a source of food supply is negligible this would seem to indicate that sometimes the farmers retained the value system of their forefathers, who were hunters and gatherers a millennium and more ago.

The material culture is richer and the techniques of production are more specialized and more intricate in the western half of the savanna than in the east; the exception to this is the Lozi people who, with the Lunda region, are considered a part of the western half. The Ndembu and Kaonde, however, are joined with the Luba and Bemba clusters to make up the eastern half in this respect. This cleavage between west and east in economic matters is also important in connection with the systems of distribution. The western half knew a four-day week associated with a rotating market system and trade was brisk and well developed although there were no professional traders. In the eastern half there were usually no markets, trade was conducted by peddlers, and there was no four-day week even in places where markets existed, for example, among the Luba Kasai. With regard to weeks and to markets, the whole Lunda, Lozi, and Ovimbundu regions side with the eastern pattern. The different distributions of markets and lengths of weeks suggest that diversification of the material techniques was a concomitant of trade with the coast and that these patterns developed mainly throughout the eighteenth and the nineteenth centuries. In the Kongo region, and presumably also between Kwango and Kasai, a richer material culture and the market system have existed since much more remote times—at least since the sixteenth century.[8]

Social Organization

Most of the peoples of the savanna are matrilineal in matters of descent or social status, inheritance, and succession; and matrilinearity influences the rules for marriage and residence. However, the Bolia and Ovimbundu practice double descent, the Lozi and the northern Lunda are bilateral, and practically the whole Luba region is patrilineal, as the Kisama and Solongo also seem to be. The Tyo (Teke) are bilateral but are, moreover, organized in matrilineages. Segmentary lineage structures are completely absent. Deep lineages divided into lineages of smaller depth are noted among the Luba Kasai; this is noted also to some extent with the central Luba and the Songye among the patrilineal peoples; and with the Yombe, Kongo, and the Lwena among matrilineal groups. But the smaller lineages do not show the complementary opposition which is characteristic for segmentary systems. Over most of the area, the main corporate groups, based on ties of kinship, are small lineages of shallow depth that do not fit into any corporate clans or maximal lineages. In the Lozi and northern Lunda cases there are corporate bilateral groups which fit into similar non-corporate groups of greater genealogical depth. All the non-corporate groups mentioned, however, are exogamic and most of them are totemic as well.[9]

Marriage with cognates is prohibited almost everywhere, with the exception of certain categories of relatives who are prescribed or preferential marriage partners. Only with the northern Lunda does there seem to be a form of prescriptive marriage;[10] elsewhere, only preferential marriages are reported. Cross-cousin preferential marriage is common in many parts of the area, while in the Kongo and Kwango regions preferential marriage—or rather the right for the senior to dispose in marriage of the junior—is reported between grandfather and granddaughter or between mother's brother and sister's daughter. But the data are not adequate for assessment of the significance of this trait for the social structure. The Bolia and Kuba and probably some other neighboring peoples also have a type of marriage whereby, in return for a great amount of bride wealth, the children or some of the children are detached from the descent groups of the mother and become members of the father's lineage. Marriage is the occasion for bride service in several societies throughout the area, while bride wealth exists elsewhere. But there are different kinds of bride wealth. The typical east African *lobola* [to be paid in cattle] is found only in Lozi land; symbolic bride wealth seems the rule in the Bemba and Lunda regions as well as in part of the Kwango, Bolia, and lower Kasai regions. Some groups have a form of bride wealth which has economic value but which consists of goods that can be readily marketed—for instance, the Kongo, Kuba, and Luba Kasai—while others, like the Lele, have substantial marriage payments in goods that can be used only in a limited sphere of transactions.[11]

One of the most important effects of marriage on the social structure as such derives from rules of residence at marriage. Virilocal marriage is usually the rule even in matrilineal societies, where the husband can then live in the village of his father or in that of his mother's brother. But often there are intricate arrangements by which men and their spouses and children will shift from the village of the husband's father to that of his mother's brother, while a sizable percentage of husbands will live for shorter or longer periods in the village of the wife's father or mother's brother or mother. This leads to great mobility in residence, which reflects two fundamental but conflicting rules in matrilineal society: descent is calculated matrilineally and the corporate lineages are matrilineal; but authority rests with the men, not the women. The men of a lineage should remain together, yet if they do their matrilineal heirs are dispersed. If they do not, they will be strangers or persons with a lowered status in their wives' villages. One solution has been worked out among the Kongo or Lwena, where marriage is virilocal but where the children are sent to their mother's brother when they are still young. (It is worth noting that these two cultures are also the only matrilineal societies in the whole area with deep lineages.) The other solutions always involve moving for the whole household. They lead to the creation of small localized lineages with a limited number of usually older men. Patrilineally-linked individuals —or even groups—are attached to these lineages, while other members of the lineage are dispersed through other settlements which are often very widespread. The systems lead also to a great dispersal of clans, often across "tribal" boundaries. This is attested for the southern Kwango, the upper Katanga and the lower Kasai, and the Lwena, Mbunda, Cokwe, and Luchazi areas. Lineages usually profit from the rules of descent by making the marriages of their male members virilocal and those of their female members uxorilocal so that both maternal nephews and sons of the chiefs live at their court. Considering these rules of residence, it is not strange that villages in the whole eastern half of the area consist of a headman and of all sorts of matrilineal, patrilineal, and affinal relatives whom he has grouped around him by virtue of his personal leadership.[12]

Two special social institutions which are found mainly in the Lunda and Bemba regions deserve special mention: they are positional succession and perpetual kinship.[13] Essentially, these institutions entail that an heir or a successor acquires not only the material goods or the political office of his predecessor, but also the latter's social identity. He literally *becomes* his predecessor, taking his name and his kinship connections. Kinship, therefore, is perpetual in the sense that two men will become full brothers— for instance, even if they are only distant cousins but genealogically are descendants of ancestors who were full brothers and whose successors they are. In most cultures, positional succession and perpetual kinship are carried through most thoroughly within the political system, especially with regard to the succession of political titles and the relation between political officials. The institutions are an integrative mechanism which is social in its idiom but which is often mainly political in its purposes and effects.

Besides the descent groups, other types of social groupings are occasionally found. Age grades and sets exist in the whole lower Kasai region but are especially prominent with the Lele,[14] where they are linked to a form of polyandry. Associations entered by choice and usually accompanied by an initiation and the payment of fees are important in the whole Luba and Lunda regions but are also present to some degree in the Kongo, Kwango, lower

Kasai, and Bemba areas. Almost everywhere there are associations with religious purposes,[15] but societies of hunters, traders,
or smiths are not uncommon either. It is difficult to assess the
exact role of age sets, associations, and patterns of friendship, or
to assess a form of association in the social and political life of
these peoples, because they have been neglected in the anthropological literature.

Political Structures

The cornerstone of the political structure almost everywhere is
the village, the smallest territorial unit. Several types of villages
can readily be distinguished. In the cultures with deep lineages
(Lwena, Kongo, and the patrilineal Luba Kasai–Luba Katanga)
villages consist of localized lineages nested in one single major
lineage per village. In the Lunda and Bemba regions, and in part
of the Luba as well as the Tyo (Teke) region, villages are small
in size and usually comprise less than a hundred inhabitants.
They are created by ambitious individuals who gather a following of relatives of all sorts around them. The pivot of the village
is its headman, and when he dies the village breaks up.[16] The
Lozi, whose village structure seems to be identical to the Lunda
or Bemba types, differs from the above in that the settlement is
much more permanent and personal ambition less important at
this level. It must be remembered that the peoples are bilateral
and that the villages are located on a restricted number of
mounds in the flood plain. West of this area one generally finds
villages small in size but consisting of one localized lineage each.
The village head is also the lineage head and the villages are
much more permanent. This, with some qualification, is true for
the whole western half of the savanna. The Lele, Kuba, Ding,
and Ovimbundu have larger villages which number between one
hundred and fifty and two hundred or more inhabitants. The
Kuba, Ding, and Ovimbundu villages consist of a group of distinct localized lineages (matrilineages in the first two cases, patrilineages in the last one), while the Lele village has an organiza-

tion all its own, just as the Lele social structure is very divergent from all the others.[17] Finally, the peculiar pattern of Songye settlements in the nineteenth century must be mentioned. Most Songye "tribes" occupied but one city. Exact figures are unknown, but every town must have comprised thousands of inhabitants. City organization and over-all political organization were practically synonymous. As a matter of fact, these towns should be compared not so much with villages elsewhere but with the capitals, which had a special organization and layout of their own in all important kingdoms and chiefdoms.[18]

Beyond the village level, nearly all the societies are organized in kingdoms or chiefdoms. Some of these amount to very little. In part of the lower Kasai or the Kwango regions, chiefdoms are very small indeed and comprise only a few villages; here the different lineages have their own village headmen who recognize one lineage as the royal chiefdom and its leader as the king. The king's role is small: he is the representative or the symbol of the chiefdom and may have some religious duties, but his participation in the political decision-making process is insignificant. Then there is the case of the Lele, where every village is sovereign but where one clan is recognized by all as the "founding clan" of the Lele. The members of this clan consider themselves to be aristocrats and among them are the kings of the Lele. From the point of view of the other Lele, the founding clan is only the oldest clan in the country and it symbolizes Lelehood but has no political role beyond that. There is, then, no Lele kingdom or Lele chiefdom, but the role of king or chief exists.[19] Yet another type of political structure is provided by the Songye. Here the town was directed by a king with titleholders, as in most kingdoms, but political decisions were often made, it seems, not by this government but by a religious association, the *bukishi*. Songye towns could be tributary to other Songye towns, and it is sometimes claimed that Lumpungu, chief of the Beekalebwe [Beekaleebwe] at Kabinda, was the paramount of all Songye. Yet the *bukishi* of every town seems to have been independent of those in other cities and the structure is therefore certainly not a typical chiefdom or kingdom. Unfortunately, the data at our disposal àre too scanty for us to be able to understand how the system was built up and how it functioned.[20]

Apart from these cases, most kingdoms or chiefdoms were patterned on a general model[21] of which several variants are described in the following chapters. But it must be emphasized that among all the populations in the area a concept of chieftainship or kingship existed. This is all the more remarkable since such an institution was foreign to most of the peoples who surround this zone, such as the majority of the peoples of the equatorial forest to the north (with the exceptions of groups living to the northeast of the Mboshi in Brazzaville, Gabon, and the southern Cameroons) and most of the peoples in southern Angola and the Zambesi valley below Victoria Falls in the south.

Religion

The religion of all the peoples in the savanna is similar and this similarity is true to such an extent that even the terms used are often related; this indicates either that features of the religion of some groups have been diffused widely or that certain religious characteristics, common to most peoples, go back to remote times.[22]

In all the groups a creator, or high god, is recognized. He is far away, is not worshiped collectively, but is given private worship through prayer and sometimes by offerings of first fruits. Every individual can communicate with him directly, in contrast to many other spiritual beings who can be approached only through priests or elders. This god is not always the only god. The Kuba, for instance, used to recognize two gods: Mboom, who lived in heaven and created the "good" things, and Ngaan, who dwelt in the water and created the "bad." The populations around Lake Leopold II also seem to recognize more than one god, if the many different names to designate the several gods are an indication of this. In the Bemba, Lunda, and Ovimbundu regions it is often difficult to distinguish between the creator, a *primus inter pares,* and other gods or spirits with a more limited power over diseases, rain, etc. The theoretical distinctions one can make between a god who is effective everywhere, a nature spirit who is tied to a particular spot, and an ancestor who is a being who died very long ago are in practice often of little value.

Nature spirits are clearly prominent in only a few regions: in the Kongo, north of the Congo River, the Tyo (Teke), the Bolia, and the lower Kasai regions. But even there they are absent among some groups, such as the Sakata and the Yans, or are relatively unimportant, as among the Ding. In the Luba and Bemba regions a belief in nature spirits is present everywhere, but the distinction between them and an ancestor of long ago has definitely been obliterated. The same seems true for the southern Lunda, the Cokwe, the Lwena, and the whole Ovimbundu group, where the ancestors have even lost connection with a particular locale and thus come closer to being generalized deities. In the Kwango area and among the Kongo peoples south of the Congo, no belief in nature spirits exists at all and their functions are fulfilled by the "fetishes."

Ancestor worship is prominent among the Kongo and the patrilineal groups of Katanga. Elsewhere, worship of the shades is prominent (these are the spirits, not of remote ancestors who have founded the deep lineages, but of recently deceased persons whom the worshiper has known during his life). Such shades are prominent in the religions of the Tyo (Teke), Kwango, Lunda, and Ovimbundu, and probably also in the Bemba regions.

Belief in witchcraft or sorcery is universal, as is the belief in the magical power of some objects provided they are doctored according to known rules. These magical objects are the "fetishes" of the literature. They play an exceptionally important role among the coastal peoples and a much less important part in the religions of the interior peoples. In connection with these beliefs, there may be a general expression referring to their "force," which was derived from the accomplishment of the proper ritual. It does not exist apart from the charms, however, and is therefore only superficially comparable to the Polynesian *mana.*

Rituals, even more than beliefs, seem to be similar throughout the whole area. They include prayers, sacrifices of animals (sometimes sacrifice of humans but generally of chickens or goats), first fruit offerings of plants, divination practices of different sorts (but usually either by the use of a divinatory object or through dreams), and a ritual for the discovery and punishment of sorcerers or witches—almost everywhere in the form of a poison oracle. Nature spirits are worshiped at the place where they are supposed to dwell, but no shrines are built for them, except among the Tyo (Teke), while shrines are built for ancestors and often for shades as well, although sometimes the shades are worshiped on their tombs.

Nearly everywhere, religious specialists include medicine men and diviners. Nature spirits are approached through priests, who are their media, while ancestors can be worshiped only through the intermediary of a lineage elder. Shades and the creator are worshiped individually. Usually the worshiping groups are the village in the case of the nature spirits, a descent group in the case of the ancestors, and both groups in relation to problems of witchcraft and sorcery. There are, however, special religious associations almost everywhere which are connected with either nature spirits, special gods, or fetishes, and whose aim almost invariably is to promote fertility. The importance of the religion for the social organization is usually very clear, and religious sanctions always bolster the fundamental social values. Divine kingship is a complex of usages and reflects the belief that chiefs and kings have some supernatural power over the fertility of land and man. This power is either inherent in the kingship or derived from ancestors, even from nature spirits, or acquired by the use of special medicines kept by the ritual specialists of the court. Very often the belief is a composite one in the sense that more than one source is held responsible for the acquisition of these powers. In almost if not all of the kingdoms and chiefdoms, elements of divine kingship are present under the guise of beliefs, taboos, and rituals.

Language

All the peoples of the savanna speak Bantu languages. It is probable that it will be impossible to divide the Bantu family of languages into subgroups on a genetic basis. On a more or less practical basis this has been done, however, by different linguists. One of the most favored classifications is by Guthrie, who opposes his "practical method" to both the "historical method" and the "empirical method."[23] (It must be made clear that neither this classification nor, for that matter, any other proposed so far can be used as an argument to oppose different blocks for historical purposes.) According to Guthrie's classification, the language of the peoples of the area falls into eight groups. The Ovimbundu belong by themselves in a southwestern Bantu group, the present Lozi language is of Sotho (i.e., southwestern origin) and stands alone, as does the Bolia group, which speaks a Mongo language classified as zone C. The cultural Kongo region, with the addition of the Kwango region, makes up one whole region, zone H, while the lower Kasai group belongs to zone B which includes, in addition to what Guthrie indicates, the Kuba group. Several languages of zone B west of the Tyo (Teke) have not been included in the area of study. Zone L groups together all the peoples of the Luba region, zone K those of the Lunda region, and zone M those of the Bemba region, but the correspondence between the languages included in these zones and the peoples in the regions is not perfect. It is interesting to note that in this and other linguistic classifications the Bolia, Ovimbundu, and Lozi occupy marginal positions with regard to the rest of the area, something which significantly parallels the cultural situations.[24]

The Origins of the Population

The origins of the populations which today occupy Central Africa cannot as yet be ascertained clearly even though a small number of archaeological, traditional, and linguistic data are available. It has been demonstrated by Greenberg that the Bantu originated in the area between the Cross River and the middle Benue, and this may well account for the origin of a great part of the present populations in the area. There may have been a Negroid population in the area long before the arrival of the Bantu, but if so they must have been few in number since no trace of any language other than Bantu has been found in the area, indicating that they must have taken over the language of the newcomers. It is likely that the bulk of the present population was of Bantu ancestry.

The immigrants found that the savanna was occupied by hunters and gatherers. This is to be expected since, according to the evidence of palaeolithic sites, Central Africa has been inhabited since very early times. These people would have been rather like Pygmies or Bushmen, or at least this point is made by oral tradition all over the area from Northern Rhodesia to the Kongo.[25] These data are supported on the whole by the presence of Twa— or so-called Pygmies—in the Lake Bangweolu area, as well as their presence at the border between Kongo and Angola, near the Kwango, and deep in Angola. The incoming Bantu probably settled between dispersed groups of these hunters and gatherers without really disturbing their life, since it can be supposed that the Bantu were agriculturists. Later the aborigines would have disappeared either through intermarriage or, as seems to have happened to the Twa of Bangweolu, by being forced to go to refuge areas.

By 800 A.D. at the latest,[26] agriculturists probably lived everywhere in the area. Evidence from the Ovimbundu country and from Katanga shows that by this time iron was known in both regions, and from the presence of channeled ware in Kasai and in Lozi land it is likely that it was known at an even earlier date.[27]

By 800 at the latest, then, the peoples of the area, probably the direct ancestors of those who founded the kingdoms we will describe, had the technological means to operate societies and cultures of the type existing in 1900 since no great changes in the basic patterns of economic production occurred in the meantime (with the exception that food crops from America and from Malaysia were added to the existing plants). Also by 800, there was possibly long-distance contact between the peoples of Central Africa, since excavations at Kisale have yielded some imported glass beads from the east coast. (These same excavations in Katanga, incidentally, teach us to avoid speculation about origins and migrations.) At Kisale and Mulongo three different cultures have been recognized, probably all in succession one after another, and still a later one has been identified at Katoto. All four, moreover, are different from the channeled-ware culture which probably existed in the same area and which may have been responsible for introducing the knowledge of metallurgy there.

The other main source of information for this period before 1500—oral tradition—refers to a stream of migrants from the region of the lakes of the upper Lualaba into the northeastern Rhodesian plateau and beyond in the land bordered by Lake Nyasa, the Shire, the Zambesi, and the Lwangwa.[28] These movements took place after the initial arrival of the Bantu speakers and almost certainly before 1500. They may have lasted a very long time, and were a gradual outflow of emigrants from the lake area after it had already attained the high level of culture exemplified by the necropolis of Sanga.

The question can be asked: What were the origins of the kingdoms in Central Africa: would there be but one original center where a state structure was elaborated and then diffused or would there be many? In actual fact, at least three possible centers of origin for state structures, which were widely separated geographically, can be traced to 1400 A.D. or before. One lay around the lakes of Katanga where the Luba and the Songye place the origin of their states, which seems to be in agreement with the known archaeological facts or which at least is not in contradiction with them. Another center lay in the depths of the tropical forest from where the Bolia came. The third one lay north of the lower reaches of the Congo River—the later Kongo, Loango, and Tyo (Teke) kingdoms.[29] It is unlikely that there will ultimately prove to have been but a single center of origin for all the Central African kingdoms. A hypothesis involving multiple invention, stimulated by contact diffusions and internal evolutions, seems to be the most appropriate one. It also becomes clear that, short of a miracle, no data will be found which would document in detail the beginnings and the spread of the state systems in the area, for these beginnings may well go back to the beginning of the iron age or even beyond.

The Kingdom of Kongo
until
the Jaga Invasion

In studying the early history of Africa, there is no tale more exciting to the contemporary scholar than the history of the kingdom of Kongo during the fifteenth and sixteenth centuries. Here was a fully sovereign state which, of its own volition, attempted to incorporate Christianity and many other elements of European culture into its own fabric. Not until our own times would such an attempt at massive but free and selective acculturation be seen again.

Two circumstances made this evolution possible: the Portuguese discoveries, and the fact that by 1482 Kongo was the undisputed leader among all the coastal states of Central Africa. After 1550— and partly through Portuguese influence—Kongo's paramountcy was challenged by its Ndongo and Tyo neighbors; and in 1568 marauding bands of a people from the deep interior, the Jaga, nearly destroyed the whole area, including Kongo, the kingdom being saved only by Portuguese troops. And it was during these later years, when Kongo was helpless, that the colony of Angola was founded by the Portuguese—a colony which less than a century later would lead to the destruction of the political power of Kongo.

Acculturation and Kongolese hegemony are therefore the main

themes of this chapter, which describes in turn the origins of the
kingdom and its relations with its neighbors, the political structures of the coastal kingdoms, the reign of Affonso I, the first
Christian king, the reign of Diogo I, and finally the invasion of
the Jaga.

The Origins of Kongo

In the fourteenth century,[1] the son of a chief of the small chiefdom of Bungu—a chiefdomship which lay near the present town
of Boma—emigrated with a number of companions to the south
of the Congo River, an area then inhabited by Ambundu and
Ambwela peoples. *Ntinu* [king] Wene (or Nimi a Lukeni, as he
is named by the traditions) conquered the plateau of Kongo, a
plateau that included the present city of San Salvador. The invaders allied themselves by marriage to the main lineages of the
region. Wene himself married a daughter of the Nsaku Vunda
clan, who held spiritual rights over the land in the area. Its head,
the *mani* [titleholder] Kabunga, acted as the earth priest [*kitomi*] for the whole area. He accepted Wene as his political overlord and, with proper ritual, appointed him as such. Wene then
took the title of *mani* Kongo or *ne* Kongo. From his capital Wene
subdued the lands of what later were to be the provinces of
Mpemba, Nsundi, Mbamba, and Soyo. Two kingdoms to the
east, Mpangu and Mbata, which seem to have pre-existed, were
incorporated; this was accomplished, with Mpangu, through conquest by the governor of Nsundi, and with Mbata, through the
recognition of the new *mani* Kongo by the *mani* Mbata. As a
consequence of the voluntary recognition, in the case of Mbata,
the governorship of the province of Mbata remained hereditary—
that is, it remained in the hands of its then ruling clan, the Nsaku
Lau (a branch of the Nsaku Vunda clan), who lived on the
Kongo plateau (see Map II).

After the conquest of Mpangu, the limits of the kingdom were
to the Congo River to the north, plus a tract of territory farther
north of the river in the region of Luozi; to the east the border

reached almost to Stanley Pool and continued from there to the Nsele River and then to the watershed between the rivers Kwango and Inkisi (Nzadi); and in the south the border followed the River Loje to the Atlantic Ocean. In addition, territories

11 The Kingdom of Kongo in the Sixteenth Century

lying beyond the borders in the east, southeast, and south recognized the overlordship of Kongo and would irregularly send tribute or presents to the *mani* Kongo; this was true of the Dembo chiefdoms between Loje and Cuanza, of Matamba in the south-

east, and of Okango in the middle part of the Kwango River. But
to the north the neighbors of Kongo were independent kingdoms.
The two most powerful of these were the Tyo (Teke) or "Ansiku"
kingdom north of Stanley Pool and the Loango kingdom in the
Kwilu Nyari basin. Smaller chiefdoms were the kingdoms of
Ngoy and Kakongo, which lay on the coast between the Congo
River and Loango, and the kingdom of Bungu, to the northeast
of Kakongo.[2]

All these states were in existence by the end of the fifteenth
century and some, like Mpangu or Mbata, seem to have been in
existence even before the kingdom of Kongo was created. The
same seems to hold true in the case of Loango where, as reported
by Dapper, tradition has it that several states existed before
the kingdom was built. Loango and Tyo traditions link the
Kongo, Tyo, Woyo, and Vili by a common ancestress Nguunu.
This in part may be an etiological explanation, but it may also
convey the memory of some common origin. According to Dapper, whose statement is supported by some other indications, it
was from the area near Stanley Pool that all the other kingdoms
had derived their institutions, and as yet there is no reason to
doubt this.[3] It is likely that all the coastal states derived their political institutions from a single original state in the same area,
and that this must have happened before the fourteenth century.
It is possible that the earliest Boma states on the south side of
the lower Kasai and the Nunu political organization on the Kwa
(see Map IV), and such states as Okango and maybe others in the
lower Kwango, also derived most of their political organization
from the Pool. At the present time it is impossible to say if these
organizations were invented and elaborated near the Pool or if
some of their elements go back to areas farther away, such as the
grasslands of the Cameroons, or the region north of Lake Leopold II. However, this question cannot be profitably discussed
before much more is known about Mboshi, Hum, Mfinu, and
Boma political institutions and about their history.

The Political Institutions of Kongo

The political structures of these coastal kingdoms is exemplified by the political structure of Kongo in the sixteenth century. It has been argued by several authors that this kingdom was a creation of the Portuguese in the early sixteenth century, especially in regard to its territorial organization.[4] However, this can safely be dismissed as untrue. On the one hand, the organization of Kongo as it appears in documents of the late sixteenth century is similar to like organizations in other African states. On the other, there is absolutely no support for the contention that the Portuguese organized the whole structure, since the earliest sources stress the territorial extent and the strength of the kingdom. Indeed, it can be said with much more justice that the Portuguese in Angola copied the territorial structure of the African states. I feel justified, therefore, in using the late sixteenth-century sources to describe the state of the kingdom as it must have been in the late fifteenth century.

The basic unit of the political structure was the village,[5] and the core of every village seems to have been a localized matrilineage. In addition, the children of its head would gather there as well as the client lineages [*mbyazi*]. The headmanships of the villages seem to have been hereditary in the core lineages. At the time, it seems that already there were some slaves—criminals or persons captured in wars—as well as the free people of the village. There were no aristocrats at this level since aristocracy seems to have been tied to the holding of titles.

Above the village level there were districts headed either by officials appointed by the king or by a provincial governor, and these district officials could be removed at the king's pleasure. They carried out administrative duties and were judges[6] in the district courts. Some of the districts, like Wembo, depended directly on the king, while others were integrated into one of the six provinces: Soyo, Mpemba, Mbamba, Mpangu, Mbata, Nsundi. These provinces were ruled by governors appointed by the king and the governors were also removable at the king's pleasure. Their functions were almost identical with those of the district chiefs, although they probably were often the king's councilors as well.[7]

All the titleholders bore the title of *mani* (*ne* or *na* in the north) followed by the name of their district or province; in the case of officials at the royal court—and there were quite a number of them at the royal capital—the title *mani* was followed by the name of their function. These officials had specialized functions, such as the *mani lumbu:* governor of the king's quarters in the capital; *mani vangu vangu:* first judge and specialist in cases of adultery; etc. All these titleholders formed the aristocracy and one who could not claim to be a *mani* something or another was not an aristocrat. It is therefore clear that aristocrats would support the existing regime, if not always the reigning king, and that many freemen, since they hoped to be called to a title, would also support it.

The keystone of the whole structure was the king. In the early period every male descendant in every line of descent from Wene could make a claim for succession to the throne. After 1540, only descendants from Affonso I could do so. (The descendants were so numerous by 1700 that they formed a social class by themselves, that of the *infantes*.) There was, then, no royal clan and there was room for a genuine election. There was an electoral college of nine or twelve members in which the *mani* Kabunga held a veto and of whom the *mani* Soyo and the *mani* Mbata were the only other members we know by title. Candidates to the throne usually began to prepare for their candidacy by seeking support years in advance, and when a king died there were most often two factions at the court backing the two important challengers. The electoral council would then usually nominate the prince who seemed to have the strongest backing. The factionalism involved all the high territorial commands, since kings were in the habit of nominating their brothers, cousins, uncles, nephews, and sons as provincial governors or district heads. (For example, the two sons of Nzinga Kuwu in 1491, Mpanzu a Kitima and Affonso Mvemba Nzinga, were appointed to the provinces of Mpemba and Nsundi.) The exceptions to this rule occurred in Mbata, where the succession was hereditary in the Nsaku Lau clan, and in Soyo, where it became hereditary after 1491 in the lineage of the then ruling governor.[8]

In addition to the palace officials and the king, mention should be made of the Portuguese advisor to the king for the period after 1512.[9] At first the advisor was a secular man, like Alvare Lopes or Manuel Pacheco; however, starting with Francisco Barbudo, after 1568, he was usually the king's confessor. These men, who were devoted to the cause of Kongo, became very important in the political structure, since they informed the Kongolese kings about Portugal and the Portuguese segment of the population and since in the seventeenth century they acquired a *de facto* seat on the electoral college with a veto, just like the *mani* Kabunga. In short, it became impossible to become a king without a formal crowning by a priest or a bishop.

The military structure of the kingdom was simple.[10] The king disposed of a permanent bodyguard, made up mostly of foreign soldiers—for example, Tyo (Teke) or Hum—and therefore actually to be thought of as slaves. Other than this force, there was no standing army. In case of war, every territorial official would call upon the headmen of his villages and all able-bodied men would be directed to rendezvous in areas where the army was to be assembled. There were no military technicians, although there were titleholders with military titles, such as *tendala* or *ngolambolo*. There was no elaborate knowledge about tactics or strategy, and battle was usually carried out in a single formation, the first clash determining the issue of the battle and indeed of the war. Prolonged war was impossible because there were no logistics. The army lived off the land and if it had to remain a few weeks in the same spot the food supplies were soon exhausted; cases have been recorded where armies had to be sent home or disbanded because of famine. Later, after 1575, a new, specialized, permanent military formation equipped with arquebuses, was created

—one a royal bodyguard, and a similar unit for the governor of Mbata. There is evidence after this time of better use of tactics on the battlefield, especially among the Dembo, the southern neighbors of the kingdom.

The government derived its income from taxation and labor service. Tribute was paid in raphia cloth, ivory, hides, and slaves, and tolls and judiciary fines provided additional income. There was also the royal fishery of Luanda Island, which yielded *nzimbu* shells for the king and his treasury; these shells, used as currency and the standard of value, could not be found in any place besides the royal fishery. The king, therefore, had absolute control over his currency—a unique situation in African kingdoms—but there was no clear fiscal policy, as can be seen from the steady depreciation of the currency.[11] All government income was supervised by a set of officials called the *mfutila,* the *mani mpanza,* and the *mani samba;* the income was used to grant gifts to the titleholders at court and sometimes to territorial rulers, for only through gifts could the kings hope to retain an impressive retinue of officials, soldiers, pages, musicians, etc., at court. Presumably the provincial and district officials used their share of the taxes for the same purpose since they also kept sizable courts. The tax was paid once a year (after 1506 this was done on the feast of St. James Major[12]) at a ceremony in front of the king's palace. All territorial officials would come, hand over the produce from their territory, and renew their oath of allegiance to the king. If he was displeased with them he would dismiss them from their command; otherwise he would reappoint them for a year.

Compared to other African political structures,[13] Kongo's political structure presented one very strong point: this was its greater degree of centralization with the possibility that the king could remove inefficient officials. But there were also two great weaknesses, which in time would result in tragedy. First, the strength of the state depended on the personality of the king; second, the absence of clear rules for succession to the throne led to the constant formation of opposing factions. When one compares the political institutions of Kongo with those of Loango, the other great kingdom, the main differences between the two are that in Loango territorial officials could not be dismissed and that in the provinces there was a rotation of the governorships, positions which were automatically reserved for the sequential successors. The automatic principle of succession worked as follows: the first successor always lived in a given province, the second one in a second given province, the third one in another, etc., and when a king died, all the successors moved provinces so that at any given time the order of succession was given by the territorial positions of the different successors. The price paid for this system was apparently a much greater degree of decentralization; in the long run, however, the Loango system would outlive the Kongo kingdom.

Affonso I

In 1482 Nzinga Kuwu was king of Kongo. In that year it was reported to him that *mindele* [whales] of a special sort had been seen at the coast. They were in actual fact the first caravels and their occupants were the men of Diogo Cão. In 1485 Diogo Cão came back and left four missionaries at the court while he took four nobles from Mpinda, the harbor at the mouth of the Congo River, to Portugal. In 1487 he came back for the third time with the Kongolese envoys and took his own messengers back. At that time, then, both the king of Kongo and the king of Portugal knew the most important facts about each other's countries. Nzinga Kuwu decided that a Nsaku clansman should go as an ambassador to Portugal to ask for missionaries and for technicians—carpenters and masons. He was accompanied by a number of younger men whom the king wanted to have educated in Portuguese schools. Payment for all this was to be in gifts of ivory and raphia cloth for the king of Portugal, João II.

The Kongo embassy, after a stay in Lisbon of four years, came back with another fleet in 1491. Missionaries and artisans as well as explorers, whose mission it was to find the way to Abyssinia, came with this fleet. Its commander, Rui da Sousa,

baptized the chief of Soyo and then went with the missionaries
and the artisans to the capital. A church was built there and in
June the king was baptized as King João I, with the royal family
and most of the nobility becoming Christian as well. Rui then
joined the king in war against the Tyo (Teke) near Stanley Pool,
and in 1492 returned to Portugal.[14] Missionaries were left behind
to attend to the numerous conversions and the needs of a newly-
built school. Another fleet came from Lisbon in 1494 with some
Kongo pupils who had been educated there, but after that no
new contacts are mentioned until 1504. During the closing years
of the century, however, although no reports have survived, there
may have been visits from ships of São Thomé, whose inhabitants had received the privilege for the slave trade on the whole
coast by the *donatario* of 1486 and 1493.

Between 1494 and 1506, King Nzinga Kuwu and his son
Mpanzu a Kitima reverted to paganism, while the queen mother
and another son, Affonso, remained Catholic. The religious opposition seemed to reflect the fundamental opposition between the
two factions in the political struggle for the royal succession.
Affonso left the capital, probably in 1495, for the province of
Nsundi. From there he apparently kept in touch with Portugal,
since it is reported that in 1504 priests and religious objects were
sent to him in Nsundi.

Nzinga died in 1506. He had, it is said, told the electors to choose
Affonso. But Mpanzu a Kitima occupied the capital and had the
support of the pagan *mani* Kabunga, who stood to lose his whole
position if the Catholics were successful. Affonso was supported by
the chiefs of both Soyo and Mbata but his army seems to have been
inferior in numbers to that of Mpanzu. A battle took place on the
main square in the capital and it was won by Affonso. The victory
was attributed to St. James, who was said to have fought with a
host of heavenly knights on Affonso's side. After the battle Affonso
had his brother executed, but he spared the *mani* Kabunga, who
was converted and, rather than being the earth priest, became the
keeper of the holy water—a neat transposition of political function in a new religious idiom.

It seems clear from his correspondence that Affonso was a convinced Catholic and pro-European, and he lost no time in his attempts to convert the whole nation. Immediately after he came
to the throne,[15] he wrote to King Manuel of Portugal to ask for
priests and technicians and to the captain of São Thomé to ask
for military support to destroy "the house of the great fetishes."[16]
(The meaning of this last letter is not immediately clear—see note
16—but it seems probable that he wanted to destroy the ritual
objects of kingship and therefore the whole ideological basis for
kingship; henceforth, the right of the king to rule was to be
based on Christian values rather than on "divine" kingship.) Between 1506 and 1512 a brisk intercourse developed between
Kongo and Portugal, and from 1508 onward there were annual
expeditions from Lisbon to the African state. Affonso asked for
priests, schoolteachers, and masons, and for technicians to help
him with military matters; he also sent more young Kongolese
overseas to be trained in Lisbon, and for this sent gifts—or payments—in slaves and copper anklets. In Portugal itself, Manuel I
was obviously interested in the turn of affairs. It meant that a
large African kingdom was becoming Christian and moreover
was one which he believed to be adjacent to Abyssinia, the land
of Prester John. The Muslim world, therefore, could be surrounded by Christian forces. Also, Manuel believed that Kongo
bordered on the Portuguese settlements in Mozambique and the
empire of Mwene Mutapa which lay inland from them.

But co-operation between Kongo and Portugal soon ran into a
series of unexpected difficulties. Because São Thomé stood to lose
its monopoly on the trade of Kongo, ship captains and even the
governor of São Thomé, Fernão de Mello, as early as 1508 stole
the presents Affonso sent to Portugal and hampered as much as
they could the exchange of envoys between Portugal and Kongo.
Also, some of the technicians proved to be undesirable: by 1509
some masons refused to work and lived like nobles. The school-
teacher Rui da Rego followed this example. The ship captains
were rude to the Africans and treated them like inferior beings.
By 1510, Affonso was compelled to ask King Manuel to send a

representative who would have special jurisdiction over the Portuguese in Kongo and who would act in close co-operation with him.

This situation led to the codification by Manuel of a program for Christianization and Lusitanization of Kongo. In 1512 he sent an ambassador, Simão de Silva, with instructions codified in a *regimento*.[17] This is a document unique for its times—a blueprint for acculturation. It is not, as some authors have thought, the product of a master plan conceived solely by Manuel, but rather a systematic exposition of the demands of Affonso and the means devised to meet them. The *regimento* opened with the assertion that Catholic kings are brothers, that, therefore, Manuel will help Affonso, that Manuel hopes that the true faith will be implanted all through the kingdom—and with the reminder that Manuel's kingdom is greater than Kongo since it extends all the way to India. Then followed a number of provisions wherein the role of Manuel's representative was outlined. Simão de Silva, the representative, carried with him a copy of the new codex of Portuguese law, which Affonso might wish to copy; he would be military advisor, ambassador, and judge. But it is clear that there was no question of granting extraterritorial privileges to Portuguese subjects, for as ambassador Simão de Silva would exercise his jurisdiction only *with* the king of Kongo. The ambassador would also be a general councilor in reforming the Kongolese court, for Manuel thought that the king and the nobility of Kongo should receive European titles, carry European emblems, and follow Portuguese rules of etiquette. Simão also received the authority to expel any Portuguese subject from Kongo who was not leading an exemplary life, because, stated the document: "Our plans can be carried out only with the best people." But Manuel was not only an idealist: he realized the cost of such a program and wanted the Kongolese to pay for it. He asked his ambassador to tell Affonso that payments should be made in slaves, copper, or ivory, and these payments were especially necessary for the expenses of the king's son and the other noble children who were studying in Portugal, as well as for the missions.

There was a certain uneasiness about this part of the program, for instructions ordered the ambassador to present this part of the *regimento* as a personal suggestion, not as a demand by Manuel.

The king of Portugal was not oblivious to the economic aspects of the question. He asked his ambassador to find out what the trade of Kongo was and what it could be, how much profit could be made, and by means of which goods. He suggested that Affonso should pay an annual lump sum for the technical help and that trade should be organized on the basis of royal monopolies so that all private intermediaries would be cut out. This represented, of course, the annulment of the *donatario* which had been granted to the settlers of São Thomé. Finally, the document ends by asking the ambassador to collect all geographical and political data about the kingdom of Kongo. This, of course, was a practice which had become traditional in Europe by those times. Special mention was made about the *rio Zaire* (the Congo River), to investigate if it was possible to sail on it above the cataracts and to ascertain where it led. There is little doubt that Manuel hoped that the river would be a communication link between Kongo and Abyssinia. Other things mentioned in the *regimento* refer to the degree of help Simão should give to the Kongolese king in matters of administration and war. It was specified that if the king of Kongo went to war one "should only go with our men to places where one can go without losing troops, so that it never ends to our disadvantage"—a typical statement for many such instructions to commanders of expeditionary forces.

It has been argued, incorrectly, that this document proves that the kingdom of Kongo was really organized by the Portuguese. For example, many of its provisions were never carried out: Affonso refused to take over the Portuguese code of law, and the court was not reorganized on Portuguese lines; the feudal titulature, for instance, was adopted only toward the end of the sixteenth century. Although Affonso adhered to the general principles of the document in the fields of schooling, technical training and missionary work, these were of course the parts which had been inspired by his own demands. His argument for rejecting most of the rest was that changes had to be brought about slowly, that one could not transfer Portuguese institutions bodily to Kongo without adaptations, and that then it could be done only over a long period of time. He knew, of course, that there was resistance to change by his countrymen; the argument his political opponents in Kongo were using to discredit him was that he was abandoning the ways of the forefathers.

The plan for acculturation failed, in the long run because of the incredible difficulties that beset planned cultural change on such a scale. But more immediately it failed because of the ambiguousness of the program, because of the greed and personal ambitions of the local Portuguese, because of the very small numbers of missionaries and technicians in relation to the number of traders and their high mortality rate. The fundamental ambiguity was that Portugal was willing to help Kongo but wanted to exploit the country economically; that it recognized Kongo as an equal and arranged for its recognition as such in Rome by urging Affonso to send his son to the pope to give obedience in the name of the kingdom but wanted to limit this sovereignty—commercially by keeping monopolies, judicially by sending over special judges for the Portuguese in Kongo, and religiously by its rights over the conversion of the peoples of Africa (rights acquired by the Treaty of Tordesillas and embodied in the "patronage," the *padroado*). The local Portuguese were soon divided into two camps: there were the supporters of São Thomé, who tried to prevent the implementation of the *regimento* because it meant the end of their trade privileges; and there were the supporters of the king of Portugal, who hoped for rewards after their return to Portugal or, more commonly, hoped for rewards to be given by the king of Kongo in the management of his monpoly. The São Thomistas and their governor Ferrão de Mello acted quite independently of Portugal: it was impossible to force them to comply with rules from Lisbon—it was too far away (in fact, the De Mello family flouted royal orders for a quarter of a century before they could be dispossessed of the governorship!). The struggle between the factions was all the more bitter since the trade was slave trade and was expanding very rapidly. These two factions consisted not only of professional traders; all Europeans in Kongo were drawn into the struggle and, as could be foreseen, they tended to coalesce with whichever Kongolese political faction was in the foreground when candidates for the succession organized their support. Finally, the number of non-traders involved in the program was very small. All the missionaries were concentrated at the capital, and they numbered no more than ten at any given time and much less most of the time. In addition, some of them led dissolute lives—as did most of the traders—a state that was not conducive to the creation of a good climate for conversion.

Simão de Silva arrived in Kongo in 1512 or 1513 but was delayed at the harbor by local Portuguese informants of the São Thomé faction. Finally allowed to move to the capital, he died en route, and three of his followers claimed his succession. During their dispute, the *regimento*—with its secret provisions—was read by Affonso. It was decided that the legal successor to Simão should be Alvare Lopes, the commander of the second ship of the expedition, who had also been detained in São Thomé When he arrived with one of Affonso's ambassadors whom he had taken on board, he brought the news that the governor of São Thomé had declared that he would not recognize any trade monopoly on the Kongo coast.

At this juncture war broke out between a son of Affonso, who was in command of a border district, and a neighboring Dembo chief, Munza. Affonso left his capital in the hands of the queen and Alvare Lopes, who managed it well, and when Affonso returned, a genuine co-operation between the Portuguese envoy and himself started to develop. But the governor of São Thomé bribed a priest at the capital and sent him instructions that he should make any royal monopoly in trade impossible. Using the threat of excommunication, the priest made Affonso nominate a pro-São Thomé man as *corregidor*. After a series of bitter squabbles between the two Portuguese factions, Alvare Lopes killed

his opponent, was arrested, and early in 1516 was sent to São
Thomé. It was a victory for São Thomé, and the organization of
a royal trade monopoly by Affonso within Kongo was abandoned.
Affonso did ask Manuel of Portugal to give him the island of
São Thomé and, after this was refused, to furnish him with some
ships so that he himself could organize trade with Portugal without having to cope with ship captains who robbed him whenever they could. Manuel's answer was a general law of 1519
which stated that goods could be exported from Kongo only on
royal Portuguese ships. The Portuguese monopoly on trade between Kongo and Europe was unbroken.

During the struggle for trade monopolies, the trade itself had
developed more and more and was threatening to disrupt the internal political structure of the kingdom. The first slave caravan,
which belonged jointly to a priest of the capital and to a white
trader, is mentioned during the war of Affonso with Munza. The
slaves rebelled during the trip to the coast and the queen, with
the help of Alvare Lopes, had to restore order. Affonso brought
400 prisoners of war back from the Ambundu, 320 of whom were
shipped to Portugal. The same ship also took 109 slaves who had
been owned by masons working at the capital. In 1514 or 1515,
still another 190 slaves were sent by the king to Portugal. Everybody—tailors, shoemakers, bricklayers, tile manufacturers, clerics,
and schoolmasters—or rather everybody Portuguese, seems to
have participated in the trade, and wages in effect were paid in
slaves. Affonso complained about this as early as 1514 but nothing could be done to alleviate the situation: technicians had to be
paid and the only way to pay them was to give them slaves. To
oust technicians who participated full time in the trade would
have meant to eject all of them and to stop the program of acculturation.

By 1526 the situation had become disastrous. Affonso wrote to
Portugal: "There are many traders in all corners of the country.
They bring ruin to the country. Every day people are enslaved
and kidnapped, even nobles, even members of the king's own
family."[18] In addition, the traders in the bush encouraged the

chiefs to rebel against the king. As early as 1514, Affonso had recognized that the disrespect for the royal orders was so great that
there was immediate danger to his authority. Although the nobles
at court were influenced by Portuguese disobedience, they still
could be held in check; but what would happen if territorial rulers saw such insubordination? Affonso's fears were realized in
1526. The general situation was so bad that he decided in July to
ban trade and to expel all whites, with the exception of teachers
and missionaries. However, by October of the same year this
measure had to be revoked. It appeared that it was the Kongolese themselves, presumably territorial rulers fighting their neighbors, who engaged in kidnaping. Affonso set up a board of in-
spectors comprised of two financial officials who were Kongolese
and of one who was Portuguese. Before any slave could be
bought, the board had to be notified, and if a slave had been kid-
naped he would be freed. Traders who did not obey orders
would lose their slaves. From later documents it appears that the
board worked out well and that Affonso succeeded effectively in
constraining the traders to the capital and to Mpinda. Formerly,
traders seem to have traveled to all the established markets, including the big market of the Hum peoples at Stanley Pool; this
market was known as *pumbo* by the Kongolese and the Portuguese traders became *pombeiros*. After 1526, and probably quite
gradually, this name was transferred to the African leaders of
slave-buying caravans. These men were trusted slaves of the Portuguese traders, and they could now go into the interior and
bring the slaves to the capital. The slaves, who had become a
staple to the Europeans in the capital, from there were brought
to Mpinda and from there other Europeans shipped them to São
Thomé. Many traders of the capital were in partnership with
dealers of São Thomé and thus perpetuated the influence of the
merchants of the island in the kingdom. By 1530 the annual export figures were from four to five thousand slaves a year—and if
there were no more, this was due only to the lack of ships to
carry them. It seems that the policy of Affonso at that time was
to prevent the capture of slaves among the Kongolese them-

selves, but that persons of foreign origin like Teke, Hum, Ambundu, and others could be exported freely. It would be logical to expect that this would lead to a higher incidence of small border raids and an intensification of the general trade at Stanley Pool, and this is confirmed by the fact that wars had much increased since 1530.

As if the problem posed by the slave trade was not enough, new trade problems arose in the twenties and the thirties. In 1520 Affonso had sent a few silver rings to Portugal from the *ngola*, king of Ndongo, one of the southern Dembo states, and in 1530 he sent more rings from Matamba. These gifts plus rumors about the copper mines of Bembe led the court of Portugal to believe that there were rich mines in Kongo, and that gold, silver, and copper were plentiful. In 1536 experts—among them a German—were sent to Kongo, but Affonso prevented them from prospecting. He held that the Portuguese would try to invade his country if ores were found and that in any case there were no such ores. The Portuguese experts returned to Portugal, but a German miner stayed behind and in 1539 reported that the mineral wealth in copper, lead, and silver was greater than in Spain. From that moment on Portugal believed that this was true and would try to compel the Kongo kings to reveal the location of the mines and to hand them over. Even if the Kongo kings had wanted to, which they did not, this could not be done because there were no minerals but copper. However, Lisbon saw this as a proof of the bad faith of the Kongolese, and it was this question of minerals that would trigger off the ultimate invasion of Kongo in 1665.

There are very few data about the internal politics of Kongo in Affonso's time. There were at least two wars with Ambundu in 1514 and 1517 and by 1526 Affonso was much concerned about insubordination, not only in the capital, but in the provinces. By 1530, local wars were reported to be frequent. This evolution, of course, is connected at least in part with the activities of the slave traders. The payments made by Ndongo and Matamba in 1520 and 1530 and an intervention in Ndongo by an envoy of Affonso in or before 1526 show that the states south of the Loje recognized Kongo's superiority but that at the same time the states did enjoy a complete internal autonomy. For example, Balthasar de Castro went to the *ngola* in 1520 because the *ngola* had asked for Portuguese trade and had promised to become Christian. Castro was kept a prisoner until 1526 when Affonso succeeded in having him freed, which shows both the dependence and the autonomy of Ndongo. One vital aspect about internal politics about which nothing is known is the organization of the opposition against Affonso within the kingdom and the building up of factions in the late thirties to support possible successors. It is clear from the succession struggles, however, that there were such factions and that the Portuguese had been involved in them.

In external politics, the relations between Kongo and Portugal were of course the most important. Although Kongo's sovereignty was recognized, Portugal tried, especially after 1520, to prevent the kingdom from having contacts with other European nations. In 1525 a French ship landed at Mpinda but was captured by the local Portuguese. The king of Portugal complained to Affonso that he had employed two Frenchmen of the crew at the capital and stated that only Portuguese were to be allowed in Kongo. Affonso must have felt the restrictions on his sovereignty quite clearly at that moment: he had already been refused ships and he knew from the African students who had lived in Portugal what the general political situation was there. This determination of Portugal to keep Kongo from communicating with other powers grew stronger in time. Two embassies of Affonso to the Vatican were blocked in Lisbon in 1532 and in 1539.

Affonso accepted all the problems and iniquities attendant on an allegiance with the Portuguese only because he passionately wanted to see his kingdom converted to Catholicism and to see his people educated and literate. Yet, despite all the sacrifices, his program of conversion and his schools were not a complete success. The first schoolmaster, Rui da Rego, was a rogue, and among the first clerics were men who valued trade more than their calling. Yet by 1514 there were some literate Kongo, so that

Affonso could use one of them as his personal scribe. However, the mission station and the schools were restricted to the capital; only students went to the provincial capitals to instruct the inhabitants there in the new Christian faith. The education of Kongolese youths in Lisbon was very expensive and not always successful. Around 1515, Affonso proposed to build a school in São Thomé so that the children would not have to travel all the way to Portugal. But the plan was linked to the acquisition of the island and was rejected. One of the most successful students in Portugal was Affonso's own son, Dom Henrique, who was delegated to Rome and was consecrated a bishop. He returned to Kongo before 1520 and directed the church in Kongo until his death sometime after 1526. During those years, schools were built in the countryside, but the lack of priests was out of all proportion to the needs. In 1526 there were only four priests in the kingdom at a time when an estimated fifty were needed to carry out the program. (There was also a great dearth of objects for the Catholic cult.) Dom Henrique was sick and a new bishop was needed; in fact, a bishopric should have been erected in Kongo. But Portugal prevented this, and when a bishopric was created in 1534 its seat was in São Thomé. It is clear that under the circumstances the choice of this location was most unfortunate. We do not have any statistics about the numbers of Christians, clergy, or literate Kongolese at the end of Affonso's reign in the early forties. Their numbers must have been very small and their action was undoubtedly felt only at the capital and maybe in Soyo. Yet the general influence of Christianity on political affairs had become great enough so that one of the candidates to the throne, Dom Pedro, hoped to receive a papal bull and was convinced that he would gain the throne with this document. But the pattern which had been created during Affonso's reign would not be altered for a century. Kongo would be nominally Catholic, yet there would never be enough priests or enough schoolteachers to spread either the religion or the education beyond the walls of San Salvador (as the capital was now called).

Little is known about the last years of Affonso. In 1539 it is reported that the dissensions between the two factions of Portuguese had become so violent and their behavior so shameful that it would have been best for Kongo to have sent them all home. On Easter Sunday, 1540, eight Portuguese burst into the church and shot at the king, who escaped. This led to a general agitation against all Europeans and in the following months the Portuguese were in danger several times of being murdered in a general massacre. The dream of collaboration in equality could hardly have failed more dramatically. Affonso died sometime after 1541 (probably in 1545). Dom Pedro I, one of his relatives, succeeded and was supported, it seems, by most of the local Portuguese, but the people of the capital revolted and put Dom Diogo I, grandson of Affonso, on the throne. After his defeat, Pedro took refuge in a church where he would live for many years; his main supporter, who also was a relative, Dom Rodrigo, found his way to São Thomé where he was well received by the government of the island.

Affonso's reign set a pattern in Kongo history for more than a century to come. The slave trade, the quest for mines, the Portuguese factions, and the half-hearted efforts towards educating and converting the Kongolese would continue practically unchanged until the 1640's. Yet Kongo oral tradition sees Affonso as its greatest king. And in an odd but very important way, this was recognized even in the sixteenth century. For it became a tradition that no one could become king unless he could prove that he was a descendant of one of Affonso's two sons or his single daughter.

Modern historians (see note 15) have by and large tended to present Affonso either as a Christian saint or as a naïve savage who was completely outwitted by the Portuguese, neither of which views is true. The personal impact of this king on Kongo history has been enormous. Because he was a genuine convert he abandoned paganism and the sanctions of divine kingship for Christianity. He laid the basis for a stable Kongo mission and for a program of education which, while it remained largely theoretical, was to be the guiding principle of future policy by all his

successors. He must have been a shrewd king. Only a clever man
could have won the struggle for the succession and risked so
many dangers without disrupting the kingdom. It seems to us
that he was very well aware—and at an early date—of the nature
of Portuguese penetration in his land but that he deliberately followed a course in external politics which first of all would not
cut him off from Europe and at the same time would minimize as
much as possible the harmful effects of the actions of greedy adventurers.

Diogo I

Diogo[19] had come to the throne around 1545 with strong popular support and with the help of the Portuguese faction that
favored Portugal rather than São Thomé. It is therefore not
surprising that very shortly after his accession he sent Father
Diogo Gomes, his confessor and a Portuguese born in Kongo,
to Portugal to renew the treaty of 1517 by which a Kongo royal
monopoly over the trade had been established. The only harbor
in which trade was to be allowed was Mpinda, and measures
had to be taken by Portugal against the contraband of the settlers
of São Thomé. The embassy must not have been very successful
with regard to the trade situation, since Diogo prepared an extensive document in 1548 to prove that there was a great amount
of contraband, especially toward the coast of Angola,[20] and that
the shippers of São Thomé did not appear with enough ships at
Mpinda to export the available slaves. The document states that
about 8,000 slaves were now exported annually, but that a third
or so more were available. In January 1549, Diogo again wrote a
letter to Portugal to complain about some Portuguese, both
priests and laymen, and to ask that Portuguese commiting crimes
in Kongo be tried there. He had, in fact, already arrested some
of them in 1548 on a charge of looting the *nzimbu* fisheries in
Luanda. This move was not directed against all the Portuguese,
since he wrote another letter to recommend one of his favorite
Portuguese at San Salvador. In response, the governor of São

Thomé hastened to refute the accusations and to air his griev-
ances. The king of Kongo, he said in his letter, discriminated
against the Portuguese traders in favor of the Kongolese merchants; the king had closed all the profitable markets to the Portuguese; his taxes were too high compared with the customs pre-
vailing in Portugal; and he sequestered Portuguese goods and
allowed his guards to mistreat Portuguese citizens. The governor
also proposed an embargo on the trade to Mpinda and sought
support for Dom Pedro. Finally, he proposed to trade directly
with the area of Luanda and to by-pass the Kongo, presumably
via Loango, in trade with the Tyo (Teke). Obviously, the letter
shows how bitter the struggle between the two rival factions
still was. It also shows that Diogo I was more forceful in his
dealings with antagonistic white traders than Affonso had been.
In 1553 a political crisis had been averted and Diogo was still
able to prevent the traders from going inland. The system of
caravans led by African or half-caste *pombeiros* was unchanged
despite efforts by some traders to direct their own caravans into
the interior.

In 1556 the rivalry between the traders led to a major war.
The partisans of São Thomé had succeeded in opening a profitable trade with Ndongo and the partisans of Portugal had persuaded Diogo to go to war against the *ngola*. The war ended
with utter defeat for Diogo and from the next year on direct
relations were instituted between Ndongo and Portugal, relations
which were to lead to the establishment of the colony of Angola.

In 1557 Manuel Pacheco, who had been a councilor of Affonso
since 1520, came from Lisbon to settle matters with Diogo. But
he remained in São Thomé when he learned that Diogo had not
forgotten that he had been a partisan of Dom Pedro in the
struggle for the succession. The situation remained unchanged
until the death of Diogo in the summer or the fall of 1561.

In internal politics the reign of Diogo was not successful. In
1548 he went to war against Kiangala, the chief of Luanda Island, and subdued him. (On that occasion he captured three Portuguese who were said to have looted Kiangala's residence, but

the charge was proven to be false and they were freed.) During
the next years he still had to cope with the faction of Dom Pedro,
which very much remained an active force. In 1548 the situation
was generally insecure. When the first Jesuits arrived at Mpinda,
they had to be escorted by from ten to fifteen thousand soldiers
to protect them from an enemy of the king between Mpinda and
San Salvador. The next year Diogo demanded jurisdiction over
the whites in his capital because "it is necessary for every king
to instill terror if he wants to rule properly."[21]

In the spring of 1550 the situation with Dom Pedro came to a
head and a plot by the partisans of Dom Pedro was crushed.
I shall discuss the case at some length because it is the only one
for which the documentation shows quite clearly the pattern of
factionalism and rebellion in the Kongo state. At that moment
Diogo had only three staunch supporters among the higher
officials: the *mani lumbu,* or governor of the capital, the *mani*
Kabunga, and the *mani* Nsundi. Two others, the *mani* Mpemba
and the *mani* Mbamba, were neutral; and the position of the *mani*
Mbata and *mani* Soyo was not known. Pedro was supported by
the *mani* Wembo and felt that if he could start a revolt he would
be supported by all the lesser chiefs in Nsundi and Mbata.
Moreover, all the chiefs dependent on the *mani* Kabunga had
pledged their support to Pedro. The situation shows that the
major chiefs were hated by their followers in Mbata, in Nsundi,
and in the area ruled by Kabunga—a situation already serious
in itself. Pedro's contacts ranged all over the kingdom and his
relative in São Thomé was trying to get a papal bull recognizing
Pedro and excommunicating Diogo. The governor of São Thomé
was also on his side, trying to convince Lisbon to back Pedro.
At the heart of the plot were Pedro's own matrilineal relatives.
The rewards for his followers were to be governorships and
commands over districts. In fact, many of Pedro's followers had
been drawn from the ranks of those who had been deprived of
their revenues by Diogo. In short, Pedro thought that he could
count on at least the passive support of five out of the six provinces. The plot was discovered because the secular priests warned

their penitents that they had to confess the plot to the king. They were on Diogo's side because the Jesuits, their rivals, were pro-Pedro. Diogo arrested the major instigators of the plot— but not Dom Pedro—and the Jesuit Fathers left hurriedly for Portugal via São Thomé. In the following several years the situation remained undisturbed.

By 1556, however, the king of Ndongo was trading, and apparently had been for years, with São Thomé. The merchants in San Salvador persuaded Diogo to punish him for this breach of the royal monopoly and a campaign was organized. The *ngola* of Ndongo gave battle on the river Dande and won. From that moment on he became completely independent from Kongo. He sent an envoy to Portugal in 1557, asking for priests and promising to convert his kingdom. The embassy was well received and, after some delay (for the *ngola* died in 1558), a mission under Jesuit Fathers guided by a Paul Dias de Novaes set out for Angola in 1560 and remained there until 1568, when Dias returned to Portugal with plans to come back to Ndongo and to conquer the land. In external politics nothing changed until 1560. Portugal blocked a further Kongolese embassy to Rome in 1552 or 1553. In 1560 the decision was taken to abandon the policy of supporting the Kongo royal monopoly in Central Africa and to let São Thomé trade directly with the coasts of Angola.

The religious situation did not improve during Diogo's reign. In 1546 Father Gomes had asked for missionaries and the Portuguese Jesuits accepted, to assume charge of a mission in Kongo In the meantime, the bishop of São Thomé had arrived in Kongo with plans to build a convent to train Kongo Dominicans. But relations between the bishop and Diogo deteriorated—he came from São Thomé—and he was practically expelled in 1547. Four Jesuits arrived in 1548, enthusiastic about the possibilities for their work. A school was opened which soon numbered six hundred students and the king was to bear the cost of the program. There were many baptisms, but the process of conversion was not as smooth as was hoped at first. It was difficult to reach the women: they did not come to mass and did not receive any

religious instruction because it was felt that one could not have
any confidence in them. With the men, the problem was that
many would not admit that they had sinned and that conversion
was often a pragmatic process. A medicine man confessed, for
instance, that he had become a Christian because the white
magic seemed to work better than his own. Finally, the scribes
of the royal court were the only "civilized" Kongolese available
and the many Portuguese, over a hundred of them, led dissolute
lives. These impressions are revealing because they show all the
misunderstandings and all the problems of the acculturation
process in a way very similar to what would obtain in the late
nineteenth century.

Good relations between the king and the Jesuits turned sour
early in 1549. There had been a major crisis when one of the
Fathers had a quarrel with a princess and was scratched by her.
Diogo refused to condemn his daughter and the Father, full of
ire, denounced the king from his pulpit as "a dog of little knowledge." The result was that the Jesuits went over to the São Thomé
faction, while the secular clergy stayed with the royal faction.
In 1550 all the Jesuits had left Kongo because of the enmity of
the king—and probably also because of their part in the Pedro
plot.

In 1553, Father Gomes returned from Portugal with four new
recruits. He settled a quarrel with Diogo, who reproached
him for having misrepresented facts at the court of Lisbon, but
towards the end of the year another quarrel again broke out
between Diogo and Gomes. The mission was quarantined and
Diogo stopped the allowance in food and money which he had
granted to the Jesuits. He even refused to see the general vicar
of the bishop about the matter. Gomes was ill at the time, two of
his companions had died, and he could do little before he recovered. Once well, he managed again to rally Diogo to his side
especially by means of a proposal to open a school for the sons
of the *mani*. But Diogo did not provide financially for the school.
In the summer of 1554 Gomes asked Diogo to dismiss his concubines, and although Diogo agreed he did not carry out his

promise. Instead he married a close relative of his, and the marriage was accepted by all the other priests in the capital but Gomes. These two factors would be a source of major friction throughout the whole missionary effort. The Catholic Church could not accept polygamy or marriage with close relatives, yet these two institutions were vital in the Kongo political structure. Concubines not only were a sign of status but were a way to tie all the important kinship groups through affinal links to the king. As for the marriage with close relatives, it was the device by means of which the rulers of the provinces maintained close kinship with the king. Discouraged, Gomes left in 1555. Diogo asked now for new missionaries, preferably Franciscans. Five Franciscans and some secular priests arrived in 1557 under the leadership of the vicar general, who sent a number of priests and laymen back to Portugal, which displeased Diogo, and who repeatedly complained publicly about the king's private life. As a result, he too was obliged to leave Kongo before 1558 was out. Kongo was again left with less than a handful of secular priests.

Diogo has been described as a cruel, lascivious tyrant by the missionaries who opposed him and by some modern authors, while others see in him but a puppet of his European councilors. Although he is eclipsed by Affonso, he was an able king. He was firm with Portugal but not xenophobic or blinded with hatred against his enemies. (He even waited two years before reporting to Portugal that a Father had cruelly insulted him from the pulpit.) His political sense is shown by his handling of the succession, the plot by the opposition, and the Jesuit Fathers. He had, of course, to rule under adverse circumstances. His competitor was alive, the clergy asked for the obviously impossible, and the traders were more numerous and more boisterous than ever. Finally, some of the Portuguese were constantly stirring up trouble by supporting his rivals. It is no exaggeration on the part of Lopes, himself a trader, when he reports that Diogo had been an outstanding king, that he had been on very good terms with the white traders, that he was generous, that he supported the bishop in his quarrels with the local clergy, that he expelled

those whites who misbehaved, and that he was fond of things
European. Lopes even calls him a generous, famous, intelligent,
subtle, wise man, a protector of the Faith, a good warrior who
conquered some neighboring lands, a lover of the Portuguese.
Obviously he had his information from a trader of the Diogo
faction. But it is instructive to contrast this picture with the one
proposed by his enemies.

The Invasion of the Jaga

Diogo died in 1561.[22] As could be expected, the Portuguese
intervened during the struggle for the succession and imposed
his son Affonso on the electors. But Bernardo, Affonso's brother,
revolted and killed Affonso at a mass. During the strife, a number of Portuguese were killed, some fled, and trade came to a
standstill. No ships came to Mpinda anymore. Bernardo found
that even after his victory the shippers would not come back: the
trade with Angola was yielding much more profit. Bernardo was
rebuked by the Portuguese Queen Catharina for the murder of
his brother and seems to have been isolated for quite some time.
This might explain why in April 1566 he was said to be favor-
ably inclined toward the idea of giving permission to the Portuguese to mine whatever minerals there might be in Kongo. But
this was not followed up, for the king was killed during the
same month in a battle against the Suqua, probably the Tyo
(Teke). He was succeeded by Henrique I, who was killed in
1567 in a war against the Tyo (Teke). Henrique was followed
by Alvare I, who was twenty-five and the son of a wife of Henrique by another husband. Alvare I managed to stop the continual revolts, he regrouped the Portuguese in San Salvador, and
he received a visit from the bishop of São Thomé. But the next
year, in 1568, the Jaga fell on the kingdom. They erupted from
Mbata after crossing the Kwango, and they destroyed the army
of Mbata and destroyed San Salvador. The king fled to an island
in the lower Zaire (lower Congo) and a general famine resulted
from the looting by the Jaga. São Thomé traders bought many

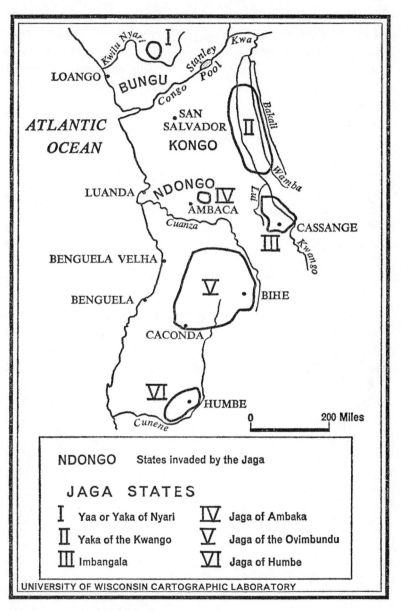

III States Founded by the Jaga

Kongolese, including nobles. In this dire extremity the king appealed to Portugal for help. The governor of São Thomé, Francisco de Gouvea, arrived in March 1571 with six hundred soldiers; after two years of strenuous war he chased the different Jaga formations out of the country, but he did not succeed in destroying them. They feared the noise of his arquebuses, but these weapons proved not to be very lethal. Gouvea remained in Kongo until 1575 or 1576 and practically occupied the country. It is said that Alvare offered to become a vassal of the Portuguese crown but that the king of Portugal refused this offer. When Gouvea left, however, the situation in Central Africa had become quite different, for Dias had founded Angola in 1575/ 1576 and Kongo had been unable to prevent it.

The history of the years 1561–1576 shows that it is not only the invasion of the Jaga which led to the disaster in Kongo but also a condition of lawlessness which seems to have started around 1561 and to have developed rapidly after 1566. Foreign enemies and revolts had racked the kingdom before the final invasion. It is possible that internal discontent, which has been seen to have existed by 1550, may have been more important in weakening the state than is generally assumed. The revolt of the subchiefs against the chiefs may have developed through the successive and bitter struggles for the kingship in 1561, 1566, and 1567 and to have exploded almost into anarchy.

Who were the Jaga who appeared as *deus ex machina* to give such a turn to the course of history? The older authors all agree that they came from the interior of Africa, probably somewhere east of the Kwango, and that their original name was Imbangola or Imbangala.[23] Our best source, the English sailor Battell,[24] who lived with the Jaga from about 1601 to 1603, tells us that they came from the mountains of the Lion and that they went from there to the capital of Kongo. (Later they retreated to the southeast—the eastern part of Ndongo—and went from there to the coast of Angola and Benguela near the Cuvo.) There are many possible mountains of the Lion and this clue is of almost no help. The origin of the Jaga has been a matter of great interest to anthropologists in Central Africa. As is usual in such cases, almost any origin has been proposed for them, including connections with the Masai or Galla, etc. The arguments are usually based on indications of cultural similarity or dissimilarity. Linguistic arguments are difficult to use since only very few Jaga words have come to us. It is clear that the Jaga were not pastoralists because they killed and ate the cattle they raided; also, they drank palm wine and preferred to direct their campaigns in areas where wine was available. In a more positive vein, it can be said that they may have had cultural connections with the Lunda-Luba peoples because every single trait of the culture described by Battell, if not already in existence in the lower Kongo area, can be found in the Lunda-Luba culture. The cultural evidence squares well with the testimony of the seventeenth-century authors and with the general appearance of Jaga names, one of which, *kalandula,* is very close to the Lunda title *kalandala.*[25]

Why did the Jaga move from the interior of Central Africa to the coast? We do not know, but it should be emphasized that this was no mass migration. When the Jaga arrived west of the Kwango, they lived permanently on a war footing in fortified camps. They would kill their babies so as not to be hindered by them in their march, but they adopted youngsters of both sexes from the areas they overran and incorporated them into their camps. Vast numbers of people could thus be aggregated quite quickly. Battell's camp numbered sixteen thousand people but only twelve men and fourteen or fifteen women were original Jaga. This was thirty-three years after the eruption in Kongo. This means that a few thousand people organized to conduct war and to assimilate some, if not many, of the defeated could upset the whole of West Central Africa. The migration may have arisen in a way similar to the Nguni build-up which led to Shaka's Zulu empire. One or two small groups may have found that by living in a war camp and by concentrating permanently on their fighting men they could take other chiefdoms by surprise even if the other chiefdoms were much more populous

than their own. From a number of very small military innovations, the huge movement could have originated. But in this
case one can point also to the fact that in the sixteenth century,
precisely in the savanna between Kasai and Lualaba, two new
empires, the Luba and the Lunda, were born. It may be or it
may not be that the original Jaga movement is connected with
the transformation there.

Jaga military superiority was to leave its mark on the history
of the coast for fifty years to come. They were irresistible because
they attacked by surprise, they knew all sorts of tricks, they practiced better discipline than the local armies, and they were divided into bands which could be dispersed or concentrated at
will. Finally, they never attacked enemies whom they believed
to be too strong. With a strong enemy, they would build a fortified camp, provoke him, and battle him from their stronghold.
Although they were cannibals, they were by no means savages.
They may have founded the states of the Yaka, of the Ovimbundu, of Humbe, and of smaller states in the Ambaca region,
and they participated in the building of the state of Kasanje.
In Battell's day there were Ambundu chieftains who were regular
subjects of the Jaga and the building of a state had already
begun.[26]

After the destruction of Kongo, some Jaga groups, like the
one to which Battell attached himself, went southeast; others
went east and founded one or more Yaka kingdoms on the
Kwango. Some went to Nsundi and founded a small but vigorous
Yaka kingdom just east of Loango and south of the Kwilu Nyari
basin. Most of them did not settle but continued to ravage parts
of Matamba, Ndongo, and the highlands of Benguela. The terror
they inspired can be recaptured from the folk legends about
them. Bastian was told in San Salvador in the 1850's that a marsh
near the capital had been created by the tears of the god Unga
when he saw the invasion and that the gods of Kasuto and
Inkisi fled to the rivers which still bear their names, and in the
market he was shown the place where, about three hundred
years earlier, the Jaga had feasted on human flesh.[27] It is this

terror, more than any other factor, which seems to explain the success of the Jaga.

The history of the kingdom of Kongo after the Jaga invasion and the history of the state of Angola is taken up in Chapter V. But before we broach this, we shall discuss first the states which were formed during the sixteenth and the seventeenth centuries in Central Africa, in that area from whence the Jaga came, and from where a Lunda group would come to Angola to found the kingdom of Kasanje. We shall also discuss the states on the northern fringe of the savanna, where the influences of Kongo and the Jaga mix with other strains. The reader will thus have a view of the history of the interior which will serve as a setting for the events relating to the foundation of Angola and to the breakdown of the kingdom of Kongo.

three

The Birth of the Luba
and Lunda Empires

Deep in the savanna of Central Africa—in the region west of the upper Lualaba and north of the Katanga lakes—a profound change in political structures took place during the sixteenth century. Invaders—the *balopwe*—occupied the area and founded a major kingdom, the Luba "empire." From there they went further west at a somewhat later date and established a kingdom in Lunda land. Groups of emigrants would leave this latter area for more than a century after 1600 and carry their political organization with them to the west, the south, and the east, so that by 1750 Luba/Lunda culture was spread from the Kwango River in the west to Lake Tanganyika in the east. This chapter describes the origins of the Luba kingdom and its further internal history and the origins and history of the Lunda empire, and the story of Lunda expansion in Angola, in northeastern Rhodesia, and in the area between the Kwango and Kasai. The history of the area is somewhat arbitrarily limited to 1700, before the expansions into the lands of the watershed between the Congo and Zambesi and into the lands later known as Kazembe (see Map A).

The Birth of the Luba Kingdom

Around 1500 the area between Lake Tanganyika and the upper Kasai was organized into a multitude of smaller chiefdoms. In the western part these were ruled by the Bungo, the ancestors of the Lunda. In the central part, between the Bushimai River and the Katanga lakes, lived the ancestors of the Luba Katanga; here there were two bigger kingdoms, that of the Kaniok and the Bena Kalundwe. East of the Bushimai the chiefdoms were very small and the people who lived in them were called the Kalanga. Between the lakes and Tanganyika lived the ancestors of the Hemba and perhaps even then some Bemba-speaking groups. The degree of political organization which obtained there is unknown, but by 1500 a great immigrant named Kongolo appeared in the Kalanga lands and was to become the founder of what has been called the first Luba empire.

There is no unified tradition with regard to the origins or the coming of Kongolo and the versions that have been collected indicate only how badly we are in need of a general study of Luba oral traditions.[1] The traditions which are extant tell that he was originally either from the northeast—from the area where the town of Kongolo stands now; or from the northwest—from the Bena Kalundwe of Mutombo Mukulu. In one version he was even said to be born near his later capital. Whatever his origin, he arrived in the country, subdued isolated villages and tiny chiefdoms en route, and built his capital at Mwibele near Lake Boya.

Some time after Kongolo had settled there, Ilunga Mbili, a hunter from somewhere east of the Lualaba, arrived with his party near the capital. He was well received by Kongolo and married the latter's two half sisters, Bulanda and Mabela, whereupon, apparently after a violent quarrel with Kongolo, he left again for his homeland. The quarrel seems to have occurred because Ilunga Mbili tried to teach the uncouth Kongolo the manners and niceties of behavior fitting for a chief; he obviously came from a well-organized chiefdom, but its location is practically unknown.²) After he had left, Bulanda bore Kalala Ilunga, and Mabela bore Kisulu Mabele.

Kalala Ilunga proved to be a marvelous warrior as a young man and helped Kongolo to subdue the whole southern part of the kingdom—which shows that the conquest of the kingdom was a process which took at least twenty years and probably more. But Kongolo, becoming suspicious of the successful Kalala, tried to kill him, and Kalala fled to his fatherland and came back with an army. Without making a stand, Kongolo fled to the caves of the river Lwembe near Kai, where he was betrayed by his own sisters and captured and killed. Kalala took the kingdom and built his capital at Munza, a few miles away from Mwibele. This was the beginning of what has been called the second Luba empire, but in fact it was the same kingdom. The story of Kongolo and Kalala Ilunga has become the national Luba epic.³

After his accession, Kalala made further wars to enlarge his domains, conquering a number of chiefdoms on the western banks of the Lualaba just north of Lake Kisale and others on the boundary of the Kalundwe. One tradition collected by van der Noot has it that when he built his capital he had to fight the Bena Munza, the inhabitants of the place. If true, it shows how weak the kingdom still was. At Kalala's death, however, the kingdom seems to have achieved its basic organization.⁴

Very little is known about its political organization and further research by a trained anthropologist is sorely needed. Only a very rough sketch of this organization can be given.⁵ The central Luba are organized in corporate patrilineages, which do not seem to fit into any segmentary system (in contrast with the Luba Kasai, where such a system obtained; however, there was no superior political organization in Kasai). Every lineage was comprised of clients linked by contract to the lineage and linked by domestic slaves. One or several lineages would make up a village, and the village was directed by a headman, undoubtedly chosen from the main lineage in the settlement but officially appointed by a superior chief, who could be the king himself. The headman was assisted by a council of all the heads of the lineages existing in the village. Several villages together formed a chiefdom (these chiefdoms may have preceded the kingdom), and the chiefdom was headed by a *kilolo,* a territorial chief. Several chiefdoms formed a province with a provincial chief, and all the provinces together made up the kingdom. The territorial hierarchy, however, was not that regular. Several chiefdoms depended directly on the king, and this was even true for some villages. A number of chiefdoms seem to have been hereditary—undoubtedly those of the "owners of the land"—while others were governed by chiefs appointed by their immediate superiors and confirmed in their appointment by the king. All the chiefs, with the exception of "owners of the land," were *balopwe* [members of the lineages of Kongolo or Kalala Ilunga]. Some chiefdoms were given out for life, others only for a period of four years. In all cases the king could depose a chief. The king ruled his capital [the *kitenta*], and every king founded a new capital. (The *kitenta* of the previous kings and an area around it was left in charge of the *mwadi,* a woman who was in contact with the spirit of the deceased king who had lived there, and a *twite,* the chief minister of the deceased king. After their death, descendants took over their functions. These areas were sacred and free from all interference by the reigning king or from the chiefs.)

The central government consisted of the king and his titleholders. Titles were ranked and various functions accrued to different titles. The most important were: the *twite,* the war leader and the head of an officer corps—the only standing police force in the kingdom; the *inabanza,* keeper of the sacred emblems and the most important provincial chief; and the third main chief, the *sungu.* Other titles varied from chiefdom to chiefdom, but important ones were the *nsikala,* or ruler during an interregnum, the *kioni,* and the *mpesi.* Many titles were expressly set aside for close relatives of the kings. Many—indeed most of the other titles —were held by his relatives, especially by members of his mother's patrilineage. Titleholders resigned at the death of the king who had appointed them and were then either replaced or reconfirmed in office. A new titleholder had to pay a heavy amount in the form of presents to the king in order to secure his nomination; thus, in many cases titles were in fact bought. Although many titles were not hereditary, close kinsmen would often succeed each other in titled positions.

Kingship was based on the concept of *bulopwe*. This was a sacred quality, vested in the blood but transmissible only through males, which gave chiefs the right and the supernatural means to rule. Without *bulopwe* nobody could have authority and all *bulopwe* stemmed from Kongolo or Kalala Ilunga. The king ruled, therefore, by divine right and was believed to have supernatural powers. This is very clear from the description of his installation rites, from the fact that he was thought of as a *vidye* [a nature spirit], from the emblems and taboos of kingship, etc. The special quality of the ideology of kingship, as compared with other African states, was its strong connection with the ancestor cult and, even more, the connection between the bloodline and divine kingship; no one could rule without the bloodline and every male who had the bloodline should rule, even if only as a subaltern chief. In theory the king exercised an absolute authority: there seems not to have been any superior council to counterbalance his power. But his power was tempered by the fact that he had half-brothers who might rise against him, supported by their mother's patrilineage, and that they would be backed by the court and the people if he were a tyrant. (Other institutional checks on the king's power may have existed but they are not reported in the literature. From Luba history and the ethnographic reports, however, it is clear that the king did not wield the power Kongo kings could have wielded and that the Luba lineage structure seems to have fulfilled important political roles.

This sketch applies to the organization of the central area of the kingdom only, to that part of it which was inhabited by the Luba. When non-Luba groups, east or far south of the Lualaba, were conquered later, the chiefdoms would be left to their original chiefs and controlled by one or two Luba villages with a supervisor chief from the central area.

The organization as described seems to be very similar in all other Luba kingdoms, such as those of Kalundwe, Kaniok, and Kikonja. (It differs in some important aspects from the Lunda organization, which will be described later.) There is no general agreement about the succession of the *balopwe* following Kalala Ilunga. Five findings, giving the source, are summarized in Chart II, and it is clear that the situation requires intensive fieldwork and, especially for the early part of the list, that no single source can be preferred over any other.

Kalala's son Ilunga waLwefu—or Liu—is known mainly as the brother of Cibinda Ilunga (who left the kingdom to found the Lunda empire around or shortly before 1600). He was succeeded by Kasongo Mwine Kibanza, a paternal grandson of Kalala, who was challenged by all of his five healthy sons. He defeated them all and conquered new lands. Ngoi Sanza, another king, is renowned because he decentralized the kingdom by creating numerous autonomous chiefdoms. Among his successors, Kasongo Bonswe had to fight his uncles, who had been by-passed in the succession and who were backed by their maternal clans. With his son, Mwine Kombe Dai, a first period in Luba history seems to come to an end. There are no reports about conquests after Kasongo Mwine Kibanza, and the references to internal struggles do not mention campaigns between brothers for the kingship. Conquests and fraternal struggles are the two foremost features of the next period, which begins with King Kadilo, Mwine Kombe's son. The scanty data for this first century and a half of Luba history point once again to the necessity of further studies in depth.[6]

Besides Kalala's state, three major Luba kingdoms were in existence during this period. In the Kikonja area, a state was founded on the lands of a previous chiefdom, that of a chieftainess, Mputu, during Kalala's reign. Its founder, a Kunda, Bombwe Mbili, would have been the brother or the son of Ilunga Mbidi Kiluwe. The new kingdom was made up of three slightly different populations: the Laba fishermen of Lake Kisale, the subjects of Mputu, and the Songo Meno on the northern bank of the Lualaba. Although this kingdom never expanded, it resisted

CHART II. *The rulers of the second Luba "empire"*

Findings of various authors on chronology of rulers

Rulers	Burton	Van der Noot	Orjo	Verhulpen	Sendwe
Ilunga waLwefu [1620] (brother of Cibinda Ilunga)		X	Ilunga Kibihile	[or Liu]	Two regents
Kasongo Mwine Kibanza	X	X	X	X	X
Ngoi Sanza	X	Kasongo Kabundulu		Kasongo Kabundulu	Kasongo Mwine Kabundulu
Kasongo Kabundulu	X	Ngoi Sanza		Ngoi Sanza	X
Kumwimba Mputu	X	X			
Kasongo Bonswe	X	X	X		
Mwine Kombe Dai	X	X	X	X	X
Kadilo [1740]	X	X	X	X	X
Kekenya	X	X	X	X	X
Kaumbo	X		Kumwimba Kaumbo		
Miketo			X		
Ilunga Sungu	X	X	X	X	X
Kumwimba 1835 Ngombe	X	X	X	X	X
Ndai a Mujinga	X	X	X	X	
Ilunga Kabale d. [1850]	X	X	X	X	X Maloba
Muloba		X	X	X	Konkola
Kitamba	X	X	X	X	X
Kasongo Kalombo*	X	X	X	X	X

* Ruled in 1875. All dates given are tentative.

Note: All the disputes are about kings who ruled for a short time, except in the case of Kasongo Bonswe. There may be telescoping in the early parts of the list before Kadilo. (See the Appendix, pp. 255-56.)

Sources:
W. F. Burton, *Luba Religion* . . . (1961), p. 16.
A. van der Noot, "Quelques éléments historique sur l'empire luba, son organisation et sa direction," *BJIDCC*, IV, No. 7 (1936), 142–45.
E. d'Orjo de Marchovelette, *Historique*, pp. 358–66.
E. Verhulpen, *Baluba et Balubaisée* (1936), pp. 98–104.
J. Sendwe, *Baluba* (1954), pp. 116–20.

all onslaughts of its neighbors in later times because the population could take refuge in the islands of Lake Kisale. In actual fact,
it seems to have been little more than a traditional chiefdom like
many others east of the Lualaba in Hemba country.[7]

In regard to the second kingdom, the Kalundwe have it that
when Kongolo arrived in their land there was a tiny chiefdom
comprising only four villages which was ruled by the Bena Basonge. After Kongolo's conquest, a Lunda family took the chieftainship and founded a new royal line, that of the Bena Kabeya.
One or more generations later, another Lunda line, the Bena
Gandu, came to the throne. After a period of civil war between
these three lineages a compromise was worked out so that the
chief was chosen in an irregular rotation between the three.
Within this period, probably before 1700, Kalundwe (also known
as the chiefdom of Mutombo Mukulu) had expanded and became strong enough to assert itself throughout the centuries.[8]

About the early history of the third kingdom, that of the Kaniok, nothing reliable is known.[9] This is also the case for all the
chiefdoms between Lualaba and Lake Tanganyika, with the exception of the Tabwa and related peoples. These people claim to
have come originally from the north and to have followed the
Luvua River, which they left to go to the area of Baudouinville
and Zongwe. They left a group at Mwenge near the Luvua, and
from Zongwe one group—the Tabwa and their ruling clan, the
Zimba—went south, while the clan Kasanga remained in the area
and fathered the Tumbwe and the Kamanya clan organized the
Hemba. The Bwile or Aanza are thought to be a later offshoot of
the Tabwa. Later on, both the Tabwa and the Tumbwe expanded to the north, the Tumbwe finally reaching the fifth parallel
south. The chronology and the details of the history of all those
peoples is so uncertain that no clear picture of their later history
emerges at all.[10]

As for the whole Kasai area, there are at present no traditions
or other documents which go back before the eighteenth century.
It may be postulated, however, that the whole area west of the
Lulua and northwest of the Kaniok was occupied by both south-

ern and northern Kete. The Luba Kasai lived in the triangle between Lubilash, Bushimai, and Kaniok country but may have already started to infiltrate the Lwalwa, Mbal, Sala Mpasu, Kongo of the lower Lweta, and Kasai valley. East of them the country was occupied mainly by Songye.

The Birth of the Lunda Empire

From the Lunda myths of origin—they tell about the creation of mankind in the valley of the Nkalaany near Sakapemb—it can be gathered that the Lunda had lived since remote times in the northern parts of their present territory.[11] From this nucleus small groups of villages would break off whenever the population increase warranted it and would settle on the plains to the west under their leaders, the "chiefs of the land"—the *mwaantaangaand* or *acubuung (tubungu)*. The relations between the villages were maintained by the notion of perpetual kinship between the leaders, and in this way Lunda land was already a loose but single political unit in the sixteenth century.

At that time—still in the mythical past—the country was governed by Mwaakw, a male twin born from a long line of twins, descendants from the first men. Mwaakw's son Nkond had two sons, Kinguri and Cinyama. They were lazy and cruel and one day beat their father almost to death. Their sister Rweej (Lueji) saved him and Nkond decided that his daughter would succeed him after his death (again a mythical theme, this time to explain the origin of matrilineal succession). According to some traditions, Nkond died from the beating, according to others he died in a war against the Cokwe whose chief, Kabamba sopa niama (or Kadiki kaDitanga), lived west of the upper Kasai. In any case, he was succeeded by Rweej. After she had become queen, Cibinda Ilunga (Cibiind Yiruung) came from Ilunga waLwefu's capital, married Rweej, and became king. This myth obviously means that Luba *balopwe* conquered the area, and this hypothesis is much strengthened by the fact that many Lunda titles are derived from Luba land[12] and that some traditions have it that a

number of Cibinda Ilunga's followers later left the country to
found the Bemba kingdom. The twin brothers of the queen, Kinguri and Cinyama, did not accept the new ruler and they emigrated, one to found ultimately the Kasanje kingdom on the Kwango (in Angola), the other to bring Lunda rule to the Lwena.
Shortly afterwards there was a general uprising which was put
down only with the help of Cokwe troops, but the Cokwe then
left Lunda land, as did the Bemba and related peoples. This,
then, is a summary of the first expansion of Lunda rule over wide
parts of Central Africa, but the traditions must be understood in
the sense that a very small body of men, maybe only a hundred
at a time or even less, would participate in the migrations.

Rweej had no children and Cibinda Ilunga married a Kamon-
ga Lwaza, whose son, *mwaant* Luseeng, succeeded to the throne.
Luseeng was a great organizer. He instituted the territorial and
court titles, and under his reign the basis of the present political
structure of the Lunda kingdom seems to have been built up. His
son and successor, *mwaant* Yaav Naweej, continued his work
and his personal name—Yaav—became a generic title for Lunda
kingship. During these first three reigns, the Lunda kingdom expanded from the valley of the Nkalaany to the whole area between that river and the Kasai in the west and to the springs of
the Lulua in the south. The local *mwaantaangaand* [hereditary
headman] would submit rapidly to the emissaries from the capital once one of them had been subdued by force, or at least this
was true if the ties of perpetual kinship which existed between
them were genuine kinship ties. In this case, the Lunda envoy
then became a *cilool (kilolo)* [or political chief] and was given a
piece of land by the *mwaantaangaand*, who recognized his authority. But if the ties of perpetual kinship were fictional, every
one of the *mwaantaangaand* would have to be conquered in
turn.[13] By the end of Naweej's life, the conquerors had arrived in
the area of Malasa and Mukulu between the rivers Luvua and
Kasileshi as well as on the river Rutembe. Here they found a new
people, the Kosa, who were culturally akin to but different from
the northern Lunda, and whose conquest was only achieved in

the reign of Muleba I in the early eighteenth century.[14]

The political structure of the Lunda as it existed around 1700 was based on the village with its *ngaand* [the surrounding land]. The villagers were ruled by a council of elders [*ciyul*] and by a matrilineally hereditary headman [the *mwaantaangaand*] who was especially responsible for the supernatural well-being of the villagers, an accomplishment that was thought to be possible because his ancestors supposedly had founded the village. Because of his ritual powers, a *mwaantaangaand* could be deposed only by the king (because the king also wielded supernatural powers). Different villages were united in groups according to the nature of the ties of perpetual kinship existing between their headmen. These headmen would be ruled by the *mbay* [elder of the headmen], and they in turn were grouped into political districts governed by a *cilool*, whose appointment was based on the proposition of a *mbay* group and who ruled after a probationary period and the payment of appropriate fees to the king and to the general council. The *cilool* had no supernatural rights or duties but mainly served as the tax collector. He would forward taxes to his superior in the capital, who in turn transmitted them to the king. The same channel served for administrative purposes as well. Every district was therefore linked to a special representative at court, and once again the link was conceived of in terms of perpetual kinship. The *cilool* himself ruled a piece of bush [*ampat*] given to him by the villages and he lived there with his own relatives. Under him there were also *mvwab* [officials who governed single villages and whose *mwaantaangaand* titles had lapsed]. This happened fairly frequently, since these titles were inherited matrilineally only (although inheritance, succession, and status in other matters were reckoned bilaterally). Over the *cilool*, and ruling the same district, was a *yikeezy*, who supervised the activities of the *cilool*. He was appointed by the king only when the honesty or efficiency of a *cilool* were in doubt, probably because it was impossible or very difficult to depose incompetent *cilool*.

At the capital, the king, the *mwaant yaav* ["the Lord of the viper"], and his titleholders comprised the centralized government. The king had sacred attributes, nominated court officials, created new titles, could depose officials of all ranks, and presided over the *citentam* [a national council and court of the highest titleholders]. He was assisted by three types of officials. Fifteen *acubuung* [headmen of the fifteen oldest villages in the land] exercised ritual duties. In the same group were included all other major religious titleholders, such as the chief war magician, the *mwadi* who was in charge of the tombs of deceased kings, etc. The second group of titleholders were residents of the capital, all closely linked to the king by ties of perpetual kinship. This included such famous officials as the *nswaan muruund* (*Swana Mulunda*) [the perpetual Mother of the Lunda], the *rukonkish* (*Lukonkesha*) [a perpetual aunt], the *nswaan mulapw* (*Swana Mulopwe*) [crown prince], the *mutiy* [war leader], etc. They were linked to different *ciloolships* by ties of perpetual kinship, the *cilool* being, in positional succession, their "sons." The third group of titleholders lived in the countryside. They were tributary chiefs represented at the capital by permanent delegates, the *ntomb*. These delegates would pay the tribute which came to them from their chiefs or from the *cilool* or *yikeezy* whom they represented. Among this type of official, for instance, was the *cibiing*, the guardian of the borders between Lunda and Luba land. He was a Luba migrant who had come later, made his allegiance to the king, and was then installed on the border. Chiefs of this third group had only a distant link of perpetual kinship with the king, or were only "children" of the king.

There was no regular standing army (although in the nineteenth century a small regiment was constantly raiding the Sala Mpasu), but there were *kakwata* or traveling chiefs who would constantly travel with a militarized retinue to collect tribute or carry out orders in distant parts of the empire. They were not used in the Lunda homeland. In addition to the *kakwata*, there was only a small police corps at the capital. The military strength of the Lunda was therefore quite small, which makes their expansion over such a large part of Africa all the more remarkable.

Tribute was paid once a year, in the dry season, by the *cilool* who were farther away whereas those who were nearer to the capital had to pay tax several times a year. Payments would be made in the form of specialized products for which an area was famous or in food. The capital, which comprised from eight to ten thousand inhabitants in 1875, relied entirely on tribute in food for its sustenance. And, as Professor Biebuyck notes, tribute paying seems to have been the outstanding characteristic of the Lunda empire.[15] The outer provinces could do as they pleased as long as tribute was paid.

The whole political structure rested on the twin mechanisms of positional succession and perpetual kinship. A successor inherited not only an office but also the personal status of the deceased, including his name and kinship relationships. Thus, ancient kinship relations were re-enacted every generation and new links were created only after all the old "positions" in the system had been filled. In practice, these mechanisms proved to be extremely useful; they divorced the political structure from the real descent structure since they were not bound to any principle of descent in particular. For example, the northern Lunda are bilateral, but matrilineal with regard to succession for the *mwaantaangaand;* elsewhere in the empire matrilineality would prevail or it might be, as in Kazembe or with the Yaka, that the people would be matrilineal but the chiefs patrilineal. All this did not matter, however, for the principles of positional succession and perpetual kinship could be applied everywhere. Therefore the mechanisms could be diffused without necessitating any changes in the existing social structures, which explains why so many Central African cultures could take over the system with little or no cultural resistance even when, as with the Lwena, there were already segmentary lineages with political functions.

Other basic aspects which enabled the system to be adapted anywhere were its "indirect rule" features. Local chieftains could be assimilated to *mwaantaangaand* and the newcomers would be *cilool.* They would settle and found a Lunda colony [*iyanga*] which would become a neutral place from the point of view of

the non-Lunda residents in an area, a place where one could go
for arbitration, a place to which one was ultimately subjected
without the use of force.[16]

When the Luba and the Lunda political systems are compared,
it can be understood why the Luba kingdom did not expand far
beyond its homeland while the Lunda did so successfully. The
Luba did not practice positional succession or perpetual kinship.
They did not exploit the division which existed between "owner
of the land" and "political chief"[17] and they never did assimilate
foreign chiefs into their own system even though they would put
Luba villages near tributary chiefs to supervise payments. From
the point of view of the tributary chief, the Lunda system was
better since he became an honored and respected "owner of the
land," while in the Luba system he was but a defeated chief who
was usually overtaxed.[18]

Apart from the regular expansion and the consolidation of the
kingdom under *mwaant* Luseeng and *mwaant* Yaav Naweej, the
most remarkable events of their reigns were their campaigns in
the north. Luseeng was attacked by the Kaniok under their chief
Sabwa. After several Kaniok invasions, the king pursued them
into their own territory but was killed in an ambush. His successor renewed the offensive and incorporated some territory on the
bank of the Mulungo River, but he could not incorporate any Kaniok territory farther north. He also attacked the Kete and the
Sala Mpasu on the Lulua and incorporated part of their territory
—in fact, the whole area between Lulua and Bushimai. The great
Sala Mpasu chief Mukoko, who lived near the present town of
Luisa, became a tributary chief. Later on, in a new set of campaigns, the king crossed the Lulua to subdue the Sala Mpasu of
the western bank, but he was defeated and killed.[19]

During the reign of Naweej, the Imbangala opened the trade
route between Kasanje and Musumba, the Lunda capital. As this
route extended in the other direction from Kasanje to Luanda, it
meant that objects and techniques of Western origin began to
infiltrate into Lunda land from this early date, which tentatively
can be set in the 1650's. It is along this route that the first cloth,

the first guns, and—more important—the cultivation of manioc and possibly of maize spread to the Lunda. It is also along this route that slaves began to move towards the coast.[20]

Lunda Expansion in Angola

When Kinguri left Lunda after the arrival of Cibinda, he emigrated towards Kahunze and the sources of the rivers "Pulo" and "Lukombo" on the high plateau between the Kwango and the Kasai. But the settlers were disturbed some time later by the arrival of a second group of emigrants from Lunda land, the ancestors of the Cokwe, Minungu, Shinje, and Songo. At that time some of Kinguri's hunters came back from what was to become Songo land and informed him that the land further west was very good and that far away at Kasanga in Ndongo there were white men who had wonderful new weapons. Kinguri crossed the Kuleulo towards Bola Cassache and arrived at the court of chief Sungwe a Mboluma. His followers plotted with Sungwe to kill Kinguri because he was too cruel; the plot was successful and Kinguri's nephew Kasanje ka Imba succeeded as leader of the group. Kasanje also migrated toward the Europeans, taking only his men and leaving the women at Sungwe's place. The road to Luanda was blocked by troops of the king of Ndongo, but some of the king's officers betrayed him and went over to Kasanje. With their help, Kasanje beat the king, joined the Portuguese, and with them drove the king of Ndongo, Nzinga, toward Pungo a Ndongo. Kasanje swore fealty to the king of Portugal and he settled at Lukamba, near Ambaca, just outside the effective control of the Portuguese. Two years later there was a famine and Kasanje trekked east through Bondo to the Lui-Kwango plains where a Pende chief, Kilamba, ruled. Kilamba made Kasanje a prisoner after a quarrel, but Kasanje's wife, whom he had married at Bola Cassache, sent for her brothers to help her. They came and, with Ngonga Mbanda, an ex-general of Nzinga, succeeded in freeing Kasanje and killing Kilamba. In the next months or the next years, the Pende were driven out of the valley and went toward the northeast, toward the southern Kwango area. It was then decided that the conquered kingdom, henceforth called Kasanje, would be ruled in turn by kings from the matrilineages of Kasanje ka Imba (the matrilineage of the brothers of Kasanje's wife), the Kalunga line, and the matrilineage of Ngonga Mbanda, the Ngonga line. All of this took place in the early seventeenth century: the act of fealty was probably passed in 1610 and the emigration from Lukamba would have occurred in 1613.[21] (The later history of the kingdom belongs to the history of Angola.) The people in the kingdom were known as Imbangala, the name for the Jaga, and the ruler's title was "Jaga." Therefore it means that some of Kinguri's or Kasanje's allies at Bola Cassache probably were Jaga. If, as we think, the Jaga were originally from an area between the Kwango and Lunda proper, such an alliance between Lunda emigrés and the Jaga would have been quite understandable.

At the time that Kinguri left, his twin brother Cinyama also left Lunda land. Cinyama traveled to the south and founded the Lwena kingdoms. From there, then, the ancestors of the Cokwe would have emigrated west. However, not all accounts accept this northern Lunda view of the matter. The Lwena have it that their ancestor was Ndalamuhitanganyi and that he had left Lunda land before Cibinda arrived. He found a primitive people who lived on water lilies and fish and did not know how to till the soil. Returning to Lunda land, he found Cibinda there, so he came south again with his son Cinyama, who became head of the Lwena. This view is certainly much simplified. The previous inhabitants seem to have been Mbwela. They were organized in large segmentary matrilineages although there was no regular complementary opposition between the lineage segments. This means that smaller segments of the same major lineage would not automatically unite if one of them happened to be at war with a foreign major lineage. This same type of organization, indeed the same clans, were found in the areas later known as Cokwe and Luvale. The incoming Lunda were first considered as being neutral arbitrators, but after a time, when they had enough local backing, the chief or *mwangana* became a judge who dealt with all feuds involving murder and who could ask a third lineage to help when he wanted to settle feuds which did not involve murder. Also, the people began to believe in the chiefs' influence on the general fertility of the land and gradually to believe in the whole concept of divine kingship. This seems to have happened at different places so that there never was a single Lwena or a single Cokwe or Mbunda kingdom. Thus, it looks as if there was not one migration under one Lunda chief but rather a set of migrations of smaller Lunda headmen who tried to become chiefs in different parts of the whole Lwena-Cokwe area. This slow growth of the chieftainship would explain why the lists of Lwena chiefs do not enable one to find a date for their arrival prior to 1750. They may have arrived much earlier, but the period of growth would have lasted until 1700 or 1750.[22]

Lunda tradition has it that the Cokwe left Lunda land some time after Kinguri and Cinyama. Imbangala tradition says that it was the Cokwe and the Songo who caused Kinguri to leave the northeastern plateau in Angola. According to other Lunda traditions, the Cokwe broke away from the Lwena, and some Cokwe traditions tell a similar story while others have it that the Cokwe left Lunda land or its vicinity after "the war of the wooden arrows." About this war, traditions collected in the Kwango have it that Kabamba sopa niama, the Cokwe chief, fought Nkond of the Lunda in the Lunda homeland. After a final Lunda victory they went to the Lunguebungu and Lwena rivers and to the headlands of the Kasai River, where they settled under different chiefs, the two most important of whom were Ndumba Tembo and Kanyika.[23] Despite these traditions, both Biebuyck and White comment that the Lunda today feel less related to the Cokwe than to the Lwena, and White remarks that the Cokwe migration consisted of a set of adventurers striking out on their own, probably at different periods in time and without much coordination.[24] The basic population of hunters and smiths which they organized was culturally similar to the Mbwela.

The Minungu and the Songo are usually associated with the

Cokwe and received their Lunda rulers at the same time as the Cokwe, although Songo tradition has it that their ancestors emigrated together with Kinguri. There was not one founder of a Lunda line in Songo land but rather there were five, not counting Kinguri. Later, their culture, like the culture and languages of the Imbangala and the Minungu, would undergo strong Ambundu influences, but their cultural links with Lunda seem to be genuine.[25]

Lunda Expansion Toward the East

The grasslands south of the Katanga lakes and the north Rhodesian plateau were occupied in 1600 by a number of peoples with very similar cultures who shared a great many clans among them. These clans had spread their settlements very widely over the area because of the virilocality in marriage associated with matrilineality and because of the pattern of settlement, according to which any man with a little following could build his own village. One might distinguish at that time between three constellations of peoples with almost identical cultures: those of the upper Katanga, those of the Luapula valley, and those of the northeastern plateau.

The oldest available traditions are those of the Luapula. According to these traditions, the lower part of the valley was occupied by clan sections led by hereditary headmen or *cikolwe*. In the upper Luapula there were small chiefdoms whose chiefs ruled over people other than their kinsmen and who received tribute from their subjects. The clans owned land and their domains [or *katongo*] were in both parts of the valley so that the political organization of these chiefdoms seems to have been fairly rudimentary.[26] Similar clan domains were found in southeastern Katanga (where they survived almost to our own day). Among other data, this is clearly attested for with the Sanga.[27] On the Rhodesian plateau the people were organized into small chiefdoms, just as in the upper part of the Luapula valley. Here the chiefs were supposedly of Luba or Hemba origin and their title was *mulopwe wa bantu* ["chief of the people"], *mulopwe*

being, of course, the Luba word for chief.[28] This fits very well
with the traditions of the Cewa and Maravi peoples further to
the southeast, who also claim to have originated in Luba land.

If this picture of the situation is correct, it implies that the
early history of this huge area can largely be recovered only by a
study of clan traditions and traditions of the descendants of the
original chieftains—sources which have as yet not been systematically tapped. Since the units of the population were clans, or
rather localized segments of clans, it is clear that the vista of
grandiose tribal migrations elaborated by authors such as
Gouldsbury and Sheane, Lane-Poole or Grévisse, are unlikely.
Population movement would occur at the level of clan section
migration. Clan sections would be very mobile, but they would
move in all sorts of directions. Over the large area, then, the
whole population could be seen as a static mass. This view is
supported by the cultural evidence, which shows that from one
point to any other in the area there is no sharp break in culture
but only a gradual change, which is exactly what could be expected under the circumstances of the hypothesis. The assumption
that the vast majority of the ancestors of the present population
were already there and formed a static mass is brought out by
every traditional history we have from the area. This means that
Lunda immigration and expansion in this area, as in Angola, did
not consist of mass movements but applied only to ruling clans,
so that the number of actual Lunda immigrants may have been
very small.

The first immigration seems to have been that of the Bemba.
The slight chronological indications we have would put their emigration from Lunda land during the reign of Cibinda Ilunga,
whose Luba followers they were,[29] which explains why students
of Bemba tradition have always quarreled over Bemba origins,
some holding that they are Lunda, others that they are Luba.
The best Bemba source known so far, the praise name of Nkole
wa Mapembwe, second king [or *citimukulu*], reads: "Nkole wa
Mapembwe . . . stretch Lunda land. You are a real Luba chief,"
which is congruent with the tradition quoted.[30]

The Bemba chiefs left Lunda because they felt neglected or humiliated and they went to the Luapula, which they crossed north of Lake Bangweolu. In their traditions the story of this migration is enlivened with a number of etiological clichés which, among others, explain the presence of the kingdom of Kazembe, whose foundation we know to be much later, and the introduction of matrilineality.[31] After their arrival north of Bangweolu they crossed the Lwena River, an affluent of the lake, then the Chambezi, and then turned south. Here, so goes the myth, a quarrel arose between two women, and as a result one party stayed behind and organized the Bisa chiefdoms while the others went further to the south in Lala country where they gave a chief, Kankomba Cibale, to the Lala. Most of them went on, however, and turned east, crossing the Luangwa and going to the small Katengoma River in the country of the Nsenga, whose chief, Mwase, lived just southeast of Lundasi in Nyasa land in a well-organized chiefdom. The leader of the Bemba, Citi Mukulu, was killed by Mwase but was avenged by his brother, Nkole wa Mapembwe, who killed Mwase. Nkole then turned to the northeast, where he had to fight against the Fipa king, Pilula. This was clearly an East African type of kingdom and the Bemba borrowed the royal burial ritual from them as well as the institutions associated with it. One of the Bemba leaders, a "white" man, Luchele Nganga, left the main group of Bemba here and turned to the east, where he disappeared. (It is said that one of his followers, Cungu wa Nkonde, founded the Nkonde kingdom, but this is apparently just an etiological explanation which is not upheld by Ngonde history.[32]) Nkole died near Fipa land and was succeeded by Cilufya, a maternal nephew, but since Cilufya was still a small boy, the regency was given to a chief named Cimba. When Cilufya came of age, he led the Bemba back to the west of the Chambezi River in the region which would become their home and gave one of the chiefdoms to Cimba. During his reign or the next one, the two major chieftainships, the *mwamba* and the *nkula*, were also created.

The Bemba set out to subdue different parts of the country.

Some of them broke away from the king and set up kingships in the neighboring groups. This happened to Mwanga, who created the Nyika chiefdom, and to Congolo, the founder of the Mambwe kingdom. Mulenga Pokiri, younger brother of Cilufya, succeeded him. He sustained and repulsed an attack by the Fipa king, Pilula, and under his reign the political organization of Bemba land took form. Little else of Bemba history is known until the 1850's. Even the king list is not firmly established as yet. The main facts which emerge from Labrecque's account for the period are the disputes over the succession, the repulsion of Mambwe invasions, and the wars against the Lungu, who lost some of their lands. From the available ethnographic data it is quite clear that a lively official tradition exists and that further work may retrieve the detailed chronicle of pre–1850 history.[33]

In Bisa land the paramount chiefs rapidly lost control over the whole country and three additional chiefdoms besides the original one arose in the seventeenth or eighteenth century under princes from the royal line. The same happened in Lala land. During the same centuries, chiefly lines of Lunda origin also established themselves over the Nsenga, the Swaka, the Ambo, and the Lamba, all of which probably broke off from the Lunda established among the Lala. The origins of the Aushi chieftainship are also linked to a Lunda group and to Lala history. Other peoples received their chiefs from the Lunda in Bemba land. Among them must be mentioned the Ngumbu, who were later conquered by the Aushi, as well as the Unga, the Mukulu, the Chishinga, the Shila, and the Bena Ngoma. The latter may have received their chiefs, not directly from the Bemba, but from the Unga—if not directly from Lunda land. It is also doubtful if the Lala chiefs really were members of the Bemba group; Lala tradition has it that they emigrated separately.[34] That the Bemba migration was not the only one is shown by the story of Lubunda of the rat clan, who left the Lunda capital during the reign of Naweej I because he was held responsible for a big fire. He fled to the Luapula and became chief in a tiny chiefdom among the others of the upper Luapula.[35]

The general picture, then, is one of several groups of Lunda adventurers who set out towards the east and founded chiefdoms all over the Rhodesian plateau and over substantial parts of southeastern Katanga. There is a possibility, however, that this picture is not correct. For example, the prestige of the Lunda could have become so great in these areas that all chiefly lines would claim a Lunda origin irrespective of their real one; but even this possible distortion shows the profound effect the Lunda have had on this vast region.

A glimpse of this process of chiefdom formation is given by the story of the Shila. It will be recalled that the lower Luapula valley was inhabited by people who did not possess any chieftainship. (They were not the first inhabitants, who seem to have been another fishing and hunting group, the Twa.) But their neighbors upstream called them the Bwilile—"those who eat their own," meaning "those who do not pay tribute"—an allusion to their lack of chiefs. A Bemba Nkuba quarreled with one of the first Bemba paramount chiefs and with a band of followers came to the Bwilile area. The incomers intermarried and showed what chieftainship was and what its advantages were. They set up a small chiefdom and, backed by their affines, they expanded slowly all around the western side of Lake Mweru. This was done in part through persuasion, in part through war; and in war the Nkuba had a decisive military superiority because even his modest manpower would overwhelm the isolated clan sections he had to fight. But persuasion was essential, since the conquered had to be convinced to accept the conquest. Here the techniques of intermarriage and the full exploitation of the prestige of chieftainship, together with the use of new titles to create a local participation in the new system, must have been used extensively. Once the whole Bwilile area was conquered, however, the chiefdom had overstretched itself and gave birth to three smaller chiefdoms, all headed by rulers whose title now was *nkuba*. Their subjects lost the name Bwilile and became Shila. The Shila were then a new "tribe," but with no mass migration having taken place. A similar evolution seems to have occurred in all other parts of the eastern area of Northern Rhodesia and in eastern Katanga. The names of the present day "tribes" may reflect not any real cultural differences but the vicissitudes of the implantation of chieftainships.[36]

Lunda Expansion in the Kwango Area

In a general sense, the area bordered to the west by the Kwango and to the north and the east by the Kasai was inhabited by two types of peoples around 1600. To the northwest, along the middle and lower Kwango, and along the lower Kasai as far east as the Kamtsha, lived populations who claimed origin in what is now Tyo (Teke) country. (Their history will be discussed in the next chapter.) They were bordered on the south by populations who spoke languages related to the Kongo, such as Mbala, Pindi, Tsamba, Suku, etc. Their settlement pattern seems to have been a very dispersed one and it may even be that they were not to be found east of the Loange, where a very sparse population of Pygmies and Kete groups roamed about.

The first reported historical event in the area was the arrival of the Jaga on the Kwango before 1568. They seem to have disrupted some peoples of the northern group but did not affect those of the southern groups to any extent. (The southern group would be uprooted by the arrival of the Lunda, for by 1880 the whole area was governed by chiefs of Lunda origin.)

The reports on the arrival of the Jaga are somewhat tangled. It seems, however, that after the Cokwe had left Lunda land Rweej sent her cousin Kandumba [or Kakilya Uhongato] to the west to build a buffer state between Lunda land and the new country of Kinguri. He bore the title of Kapenda Mukwa Ambungo and his sister's daughter, who went with him, was Mona Mavu a Kombo. The group settled first on the Luajimu, but Mavu married and her husband took her title. The other emigrants left the area, passed the Kwengo, and reached the Kwango after a slow march. The etiological myth has it that Mavu had three husbands and with each husband had one boy and one girl. The first children,

Yenge and his sister Mahango, founded the line of Kapenda ka Mulemba in Shinje land; the second set, Malundo and his sister Muzombo, organized the chiefdom of Kapenda ka Malundo to the south of the Shinje; and the third set, Masongo and Maholo, founded Kapenda Masongo to the south of Mulemba. All three ruling dynasties accepted successors one from another and all were supposed to help each other against outsiders. One lineage seems to have ruled in the three states and it may well be that the division into three chiefdoms was a subsequent development.[37]

There was rejoicing in Lunda when the news of Kapenda's settlement arrived and Cibinda Ilunga decided to send his brother Mai to the north in the country occupied by the Taba. Mai fought his way through until he reached the mouth of the Tshikapa, where he founded the state of Mai Munene. His subjects were Pygmies, Kete, and, somewhat later, Pende. A Bieng (Kuba) tradition reports a clash with the Lunda around 1650 which could then be taken as a *terminus ante quem* for this migration. This was also the date of the first arrival of Pende in the area.[38]

Further expansions brought still more Lunda in the country. Kisanda Kameshi (a cousin of Rweej) and Mukelenge Mutombo (a cousin of Ilunga) went first with Mai and then went to the Luvua. From there Kameshi built a capital on the Tshikapa River, went back for more support to the Lunda, and returned with the title *kahungula* and the permission to divide his lands among his sons. He died on the way and his eldest son, another Kameshi, partitioned the area. He left his brother Lusenge in his father's capital with the title *bungulo* and himself went to the Luajimu, while his youngest brother settled on the Luembe to contain the peoples between this river and the Kasai. *Kahungula* Kameshi II retained pre-eminence over the other centers, and his Lunda became known as the Lunda Mukundu. The chief on the Luembe also assumed the title of *kahungula* but his people were called the Taba. (All the chiefdoms named so far were matrilineal, with regard to political succession, with the exception of the two *kahungula's*, where the bilateral principle applied.) The three chiefdoms of Kameshi did not develop into satellite states of Lunda but remained provinces under closer control by the *mwaant yaav*.[39]

Mukelenge Mutombo crossed the Luvua, established himself in a region he found occupied by Pende, and took the title of *mwata kumbana*. Another tradition says that he was a son and the *mwana uta* [a favored son] of Ilunga, and that he set out after his uncle Kinguri by himself, after another emigrant, Mwene Putu Kasongo, had left the Lunda. He settled at the confluence of the Lushiku and the Loange before the Pende arrived, finding only Lele in the area. Later, around 1650, the Pende and Mbun arrived. His kingdom, about the history of which we do not know any more than about the history of the other chiefdoms mentioned so far, became of great importance in the whole Kwango. It was to be equaled only by Mai Munene and by the Yaka kingdom of Kasongo Mwene Putu.[40]

Kasongo, a nephew of Cibinda Ilunga—or a child of Rweej, which contradicts all other reports, which relate that she was sterile—wanted to find Kinguri and he emigrated due west. But near the springs of the Tungila he encountered the Holo and the Suku with whom he fought on the right bank of the Wamba. He was blocked and left his elder brother there (Lukundo Sango, the nominal leader of the expedition), returned to Lunda, and started back with reinforcements. He did not go back to his brother, however, but followed a slightly more northerly route and left colonies of Lunda everywhere west of the Kwilu. He crossed the Kwenge at the ford known since as Kasongo Lunda and finally reached the Kwango River, where he started to build the Yaka state. He quarreled, however, with some of his followers, who turned back east to the two Bwele rivers, where they settled and became the Soonde. They sent out word to the *mwaant yaav* to ask for a chief, and a *tyanza* of *koola* [*koola* is Lunda] came out and settled at Kitoto to rule over Soonde, Luwa, and some Pende. Later on, almost contemporarily, other immigrants followed. From Mwata Kumbana arrived Sha Katwala, or Mwe Nzila, who settled between Kwenge and Bwele, and four other

Lunda groups followed still later. There developed a real migra-
tory current, and one that was undertaken by isolated families or
by small groups—Lunda from Lunda land [or *koola*], from
north Angola, and from Mwata Kumbana immigrated into the
area until the 1880's. Here, then, and in northern Angola as well,
the Lunda expansion was not only a movement of small groups
but of influential ones; it was a slow drift which, over two centuries, amounted to a real mass migration.[41]

At the time of the conquests in the first half of the seventeenth
century, still another group of Lunda, led by *mukalenge* Mukan-
sansa [*mukalenge* is a Luba title] and his son *mukalenge*
Mwene Luanda, left the court and settled to the southwest on
the Kihumbwe, to the south of the Bungulo and Kahungula
chiefdoms, while a Sakambunji followed to settle on the right
bank of the upper Kasai on the lands which had been occupied
at one time by Mukwa Ambungo of the Shinje. Behind his chiefdom other *cilool* parceled out among themselves the country toward the sources of the Lulua. All of these provinces, like Bungulo and the Kahungula, remained provinces of the Lunda kingdom proper.[42]

When Kasongo Mwene Putu arrived in the Kwango valley he
found Suku organized in one or two kingdoms. These Suku spoke
pure Kongo and had been included within the kingdom of Kongo
at a much earlier date. Other people were the Tsaam (Tsamba),
who came from Kongo or Matamba, and the Jaga, who had settled there after their expulsion from Kongo in the 1570's. In the
face of organized kingdoms opposing them, the advance of the
Lunda was slow. They advanced to the upper Wamba, then to
the Kwango near the Yonso and Fufu rivers, and then a little
north to Kiamvu kia Nzadi, where the first four *kiamfu*—or Lunda
rulers—were buried. It is probable that only well into the eighteenth century did they came to grips with the Suku at the Nganga River and oust them from the valley.[43]

One more migration of a whole people occurred in the southern Kwango between 1620 and 1650.[44] The Pende, who had lived
east of the Lukala and in the plains of the Luie, had been ousted

from there by the Imbangala. In the space of thirty years they crossed the Kwango from west to east into Shinje country, and went to the headwaters of the Kwenge and then to the Kwilu near Mashita Mbanza; from here different Pende groups dispersed, generally pursuing their march to the east. They arrived near Mwata Kumbana's capital either shortly before or shortly after the Lunda, and they reached the Kasai at the mouth of the Tshikapa just after the Bieng and the Lunda. Some of their numbers were undoubtedly also incorporated in the Shinje. After their settlement, the Pende continued to live in their own chiefdoms. Mwata Kumbana and Mai placed Lunda colonies near the Pende chiefs only to exact tribute. Some chiefs in Mai's kingdom, for example, Kombo, rebelled successfully and became practically independent.

Some Pende traditions collected by Haveaux say that the people came from Ndongo and from the sea at Luanda. They retired before the Portuguese and the story identifies one Pende group with the lineage of the *ngola*. During their retreat, they found the area of the Luie, from where they were to be soon ousted. If these traditions are corroborated in many of their details, there is no doubt that the Pende brought an Ambundu culture with them, most of which survived despite two centuries or more of Lunda domination. Lunda culture did not impress itself very deeply on the Pende. Only a limited number of traits—including many traits dealing with chieftainship—were taken over. On the other hand, some Lunda colonies among the Pende became completely Pendeized. The great numbers of Pende and their relatively complex political and social structures were too much of a match for them to be assimilated by the Lunda. The Pende also influenced the culture of the Kwese very heavily—so much so, in fact, that the latter are often mistaken for Pende. A Kwese version even claims that the Kwese and the Pende were at first the same people and had moved together. The Kwese refused to accept strong chieftainship and split from the Pende. The Pende may have exercised a strong influence on the Mbuun as well,

with whom they had been in contact since their arrival at Mashita Mbanza.

The crucial event in the earlier history of Central Africa has
been not the creation of a Luba kingdom by Kongolo and Kalala
Ilunga, but the introduction of Luba principles of government
into Lunda land under Cibinda Ilunga and their transformation
by the Lunda. The new political pattern, which evolved around
1600 in the Lunda capital, could be taken over by any culture.
Its diffusion was to condition until 1850 the history and the general cultural evolution of a huge area. Even now its effects on the
peoples of Central Africa are still discernible. But curiously
enough, by 1700, when this expansion had already touched so
many peoples in the savanna, the organization of the Lunda
homeland had just been completed and the last districts between
Lulua and Lubudi had not yet been organized. The paradox between the expansion in the areas and the slow growth of the nucleus shows that it was not the military might of the Lunda
which was responsible for the upheavals: it was the superiority
and the adaptability of their pattern of government, and the adventurous spirit of the *conquistadores,* who spread it wide and
far. And this diffusion was facilitated by the simple fact that this
was an open savanna where no natural boundaries could stem
the flow.

four

The States on the Fringe
of the Savanna

In the northwestern part of the savanna and in the forests of Lake Leopold II, a number of kingdoms and chiefdoms exist which have not been created by the Lunda and which do not belong to the types represented by the coastal kingdoms. Culturally, two groups of peoples are involved. One group, the Bolia, Ntomba, and Sengele, clusters around Lake Leopold II and deep in the forests to the north and northwest of the lake. These populations belong clearly to the great Mongo culture cluster, which occupies the forests of the whole central Congolese depression. Their languages are also closely related to Mongo. The other group includes the Tyo (Teke) of the plateau north of Brazzaville, and all the populations east of Tyo along both sides of the lower Kasai, and even farther east on the southern side of the river to include at its easternmost end the Lele and Kuba cultures. Within this group there is a general cultural resemblance and all the peoples included speak languages of the same type, Guthrie's zone B.[1] But the cultural and linguistic cohesion within this group is less great than the cohesion within the Bolia group, so that four subgroups can readily be recognized: the Tyo (Teke), the Boma-Sakata, the Yans-Ding, and the Kuba.

The Bolia Group

The Bolia say that they immigrated in two separate movements from a locality called Mondombe or Bondombe, which may have been located on the right bank of the Tshuapa, southwest of Boende in the heart of the tropical forest.[2] They claim to have found the principles of their political organization, the *bokopo*, in that area. Yet the Mongo cluster does not have any political organization of a centralized nature except in the western groups, where the *bokopo* was brought in by the Bolia themselves. Therefore, the Bolia must themselves have invented and elaborated their political structure, or the group from whom they borrowed the principles of *bokopo* must have disappeared, which, since the Bolia arrived in their present habitat during the fifteenth century, is possible. The Bolia emigrated because of overpopulation or because of the pressure of the other inhabitants, and they brought the sacred objects of kingship—a lump of kaolin and a piece of ant hill—with them. They traveled to a place called Bolongo Lolendo and settled on the northeastern shores of Lake Leopold II, which is still dense tropical forest. On these shores they found the Nsese, a matrilineal people who may have been culturally akin to the Tyo (Teke). The Bolia themselves, like all the Mongo, were presumably patrilineal, but under the influence of their neighbors they shifted over to a system of dual descent. The Nsese had chiefs, the most famous among them being Lotoko, who ruled over the Bosanga. His capital was Ndongo—now Inongo. (These Bosanga may have been those mentioned by Garcia Mendes de Castello Branco around 1607.[3] If so, they must have had trade connections with Stanley Pool, because otherwise their name could not be known by the Portuguese at that time.) The Bolia did not destroy the chiefdom but borrowed some of its emblems as symbols of kingship, such as the conus shell and the *biangu* [strips of cloth embroidered with cowrie shells]. Little or nothing has been published about the later history of the Bolia other than evidence to show that they transmitted the *bokopo* to the Ntomba of Lake Tumba in the north, to the Ekonda and Iyembe in the southeast and east, to the Sengele and the Mbelo in the west, and probably to the Boma and the Sakata far south of their country.

The chief meaning of *bokopo* is "office." It is derived from the word *ekopo* [skin—in this context leopard skin, an emblem of chieftainship]. The institution of *bokopo* is tied closely to the possession of certain bits of kaolin and of ant hill. *Bokopo* can be acquired by new peoples through a mechanism, *bokapa ekopo* [the division of *ekopo*], which is in fact a partitioning of the original lump of kaolin. The whole political structure of the Bolia is associated much more closely with divine kingship and the emblems of it than is the case in other Central African kingdoms. Characteristic features of this system are: the belief that kings or chiefs must be witches and possess *iloki*—the ability to help or harm others without outward sign—and the series of tests which the candidate king must undergo at his accession. (The candidate must belong to the proper line of descent, since kingship rotates among several patrilineages.) The ancestors then appear to him in a dream, telling him that he has been chosen, and the elders, probably a royal council, must be convinced that this has happened. The candidate must then become a nature spirit and be carried by the ancestors to the first of all nature spirits, Mbombipoku, who gives him *elima* power [i.e., the power of a nature spirit]. All this again happens in a dream and is announced to the elders. During the coronation ceremonies which follow, there is a further test. The candidate is left on a specified spot and must be recognized as the chosen man by the wild animals, who must roar during the night that the man spends there. To become king, therefore, is not a matter of automatic succession or election among a limited number of candidates; it is primarily seen as a choice made by the spirits.

This is in sharp contrast to the other offices, territorial ones or court offices, which seem to be inherited automatically in the patrilineal line. The territorial structure is simple indeed. Villages comprise a core of patrilineally related persons, and the headman is the genealogically eldest male member of the community.

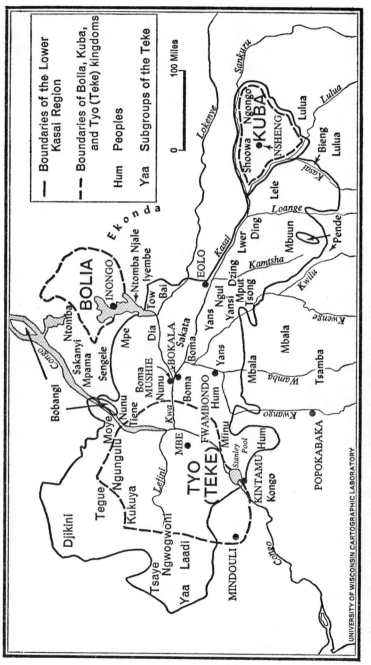

iv The Peoples of the Lower Kasai and Bolia Regions Around 1900

Villages are united in districts that are governed by chiefs stemming from a single patrilineage of which the chiefs are the oldest members. At the court there are a limited number of titled officials whose offices also seem to be hereditary in a given line. No political official can be deposed by the king.

This type of structure is rather different from the Kongo, the Luba, or the Lunda types, and it reminds one of a simple segmentary organization such as prevails among many forest groups of the Mongo cluster. This is not a segmentary lineage organization, in the British usage of the term, because district chiefs can command inhabitants who do not belong to their lineage and because there is no automatic complementary opposition. The system looks, however, to be a derivation from a patrilineal lineage organization, with the addition of the new invention of a sacralized kingship, the *bokopo*. However, details of organization may also have been taken over from the Nsese, just as some emblems had been.

The tradition of all these western Mongo groups should be assembled and studied in greater detail so that not only the internal history of the Bolia since the fifteenth century but also the developments in the other chiefdoms would be known and a firm chronology established. Here is a large area—for it included the Boma-Sakata groups and partly the Tyo (Teke) as well—where systematic painstaking work can recover five centuries or even more of history.[4]

Guthrie's Zone B Group

The Tyo (Teke) kingdom. Teke is a general name given by foreigners to all the populations who live on the plateaus north of Stanley Pool on both sides of the Congo River as far north as the mouth of the Nkeni (roughly on the second parallel Z). Even groups who are culturally related to these populations but do not live on the plateaus proper have been given the name Teke.[5] The people of the plateaus call themselves Tyo and descriptively name subgroups of their people after the name of the particular

plateau they are living on now. These names have been tran-
scribed in Kongo language and thus one finds in the literature
denominations like Boma, Wumu, Ndsiku, and others whose Tyo
names are Boõõ, Wuũũ, Jiinju, Jiju, etc., because they live on the
Boõõ, Wuũũ, Jiinju, and Jiju plateaus. But all these people are
culturally and linguistically Tyo and belonged to the Tyo kingdom. Within that kingdom, only the Ngungulu, north of the
Nkeni River, were culturally different, while the Mfunu, east of
the Congo River and south of the mouth of the Kasai, were linguistically different, and the Kukuya, west of the Mpama River,
were both culturally and linguistically distinctive. In the following discussion, the general term Tyo will be used to designate
the kingdom and its inhabitants. In the literature the name "kingdom of Makoko" is often found; the word *makoko* being the Vili
form of the Tyo word *ũũkoo* [king].

The Tyo claim that they have always lived in the areas they
now occupy and there are several indications that they have been
settled there since remote times. Similar toponyms, spread at
random throughout the area, indicate that there have been random population movements throughout the kingdom, and, since
it covers an area two hundred and fifty by three hundred miles,
it must have taken a long time to arrive at this remarkable
spread of toponyms. Traditions from neighboring peoples all
stress that the Tyo were the first inhabitants known; the Tyo are
mentioned in documents dating from 1491 as *mundequete* or *ansiku*, and there are archaeological indications that the plateau of
Mbe, where the capital was traditionally located, was occupied
at least since the fifteenth century. Moreover, the Tyo remember
several migrations of subgroups which are known to have taken
place, in one case sometime before 1620, in another around
1650.[6] If traditions of migrations are remembered in detail since
the seventeenth century and the original immigration has been
forgotten, it must have been much earlier and it is possible that
the Bantu immigrants mixed with aboriginal populations on the
plateaus.

The origins of the Tyo kingdom are also unknown. In fact, one can surmise that the kingdom is as old as the Kongo and Loango kingdoms, which were its neighbors. The original kingdom seems to have encompassed the plateau of Ntsa, north of the Lefini, and the northern part of the plateau of Mbe. By the seventeenth century at the latest, the kingdom had grown very large and its limits were approximately, to the south, to the Congo River downstream and upstream of Stanley Pool. From the mouth of the Black River the boundary ran along this stream and then along the divide between the lower Kwango and the Congo rivers to a point on the Kasai downstream of Mushie. From there it ran to Bolobo, crossed the Congo River in the direction of the mouth of the Alima River, and followed this river upstream to its junction with the Leketi River. It then followed the Leketi to its sources, ran from there to the headwaters of the Kwilu Nyari, which it followed to the region of Mindouli, and then went over Mindouli to the Congo River downstream of the mouth of the Foulakari River.

Little is known about the early history of the kingdom. In 1491 the Tyo were at war with the Kongo near Stanley Pool and by 1530 they participated in the slave trade through Mpumbu. In 1566 and 1567 they attacked Kongo and killed two of its kings. We do not know if the Jaga invasions affected the kingdom or not: there is no remembrance of such an invasion among the Tyo. By 1600 the Tyo were trading, in slaves and tobacco, with the Vili of Loango along the Kwilu Nyari basin. Probably around that time maize was introduced and replaced millet, which had been the staple crop until then. Around 1600 it also appears that trade inland with the populations of the middle Congo River and the lower Kasai was already well developed.

Probably during the eighteenth century, but perhaps even earlier, the Mboshi immigrated from the region of Lake Tumba into the basin of the Alima, fighting the Ngungulu and mixing with them as they went upstream. Finally, they pushed the boundary of the kingdom southward halfway between the Nkeni and Alima rivers. During the same century or earlier, Kongo groups—the Nsundi and the Laadi—spread slowly over the southern borders of the kingdom around the area of Mindouli and the Tyo lost the copper mines there, presumably in the 1700's. (This Laadi and Nsundi movement has been pursued right up to the present and the Kongo have thus taken over the well-watered slopes of the plateau to the south and southwest.) In the eighteenth century and through the early 1800's, Tyo culture underwent fundamental changes: manioc replaced maize as the staple crop. The crafts of melting iron, carving canoes, and making fine pottery ware were lost as was the practice of hunting with bow and arrow. The weaving industry of raffia went into decline as cloth began to replace raffia skirts and as shells or copper rings took the place of raffia squares as means of payment for trade goods and for bride wealth. Even the making of salt was abandoned. Iron and metals, guns, powder, cloth, fine European pottery, shells, and copper rings were all imported from the coast; salt also came from the lower Kasai and canoes were bought from fishermen upstream on the Congo River. The Tyo had become very dependent on the slave trade, since hunting and fishing were important means of food production and everybody needed means to pay bride wealth. This economic situation may have affected their social structure to some extent.

A major change in Tyo political structure came about between the period 1775 and 1830. A mixed Mboshi Ngungulu group around Abala invented a new political instrument, the *nkobi,* which diffused south to the plateau of Ntsa and became fully integrated into the structure of the Tyo kingdom (see below) after a war between the chiefs, said to have occurred around the 1830's.

During the nineteenth century and until the arrival of de Brazza in 1880, the most notable events were a series of skirmishes between Tyo and Bobangi on the Congo River. The Bobangi, who lived upstream, traded at Stanley Pool with the permission of the Tyo. But they began to make permanent fishermen camps all the way down to the Pool and started to raid the Tyo for slaves from these villages. The Tyo chiefs reacted independently one from another, and by 1880 the struggle had resulted in an agreement according to which the Bobangi could still trade at the Pool but could not found villages there, and they still had to pay "customs" to the Tyo chief of the river. But the agreement collapsed as soon as Brazzaville was founded.

The Tyo kingdom lost its independence when King Iloo agreed to put his country under the protection of France. The treaty, drafted at Mbe between de Brazza and Iloo and ratified by the French parliament in 1882, also gave birth to Brazzaville as a French possession. Iloo's successor tried to revolt in 1898 but the movement was subdued without difficulty.

Around 1850 the Tyo kingdom was organized as follows. The basic unit of the state was the chiefdom. A typical chiefdom consisted of a domain, a main village led by the chief, and other villages ruled by local leaders, the headmen, who were related to all their villagers. The villages were very small—from two or three inhabitants to a maximum of forty—and unstable, since every ambitious man wanted to found his own village and would secede from the village where he lived at the first opportunity. A population density of less than one person per square mile made the functioning of this system possible.

Chiefship was a hereditary position; as with the other political offices, the successor had to belong to the social class of the aristocrats, and the quality of aristocrat was acquired at birth either from having a noble father or a noble mother. All Tyo were thus divided into aristocrats and commoners. However, chiefs were succeeded most often by their sons and only exceptionally by grandchildren or sister's sons. The chief's position was essentially based on his relation to the spirit (*nkira*) of his domain. The *nkira* would care for the well-being of all who lived in the chiefdom, it would lead the chief in the settlement of quarrels, it would fight witches, and it would distribute fertility. The only formal rights of a chief were linked with the earth. Whenever a large animal was killed on his domain, the hunters had to give him a hind leg; in the case of an elephant, he was given the tusk which had struck the earth when it fell. In practice, the chief also collected tribute for the king and would keep about half of the produce for himself. He held court at his village and anybody in the chiefdom, resident or not, might bring a case to be tried. As a judge, the chief was assisted by two councilors (*aamyene*) whom he chose among the more forceful leaders who had set up villages on his domain. It should be underlined that normally he had not the right to bar access to his domain to new settlers, nor could he prevent anybody who lived elsewhere from cultivating on his land.

A hierarchy of chieftainships within the kingdom was linked to the institution of the *nkobi*. The *nkobi* was a basket, kept in a special house, which functioned as the shrine for a major *nkira* or spirit. Its "owner" bore a special title and his relation to the *nkira* was roughly the same as that which prevailed between a local *nkira* and the ordinary nontitled chief. But he could neither sacrifice nor pray to the *nkira* himself: this had to be done by two special families of priests devoted to the *nkira*, one of which would live away from the chief's village in the bush where the spirit was supposed to dwell. The *nkobi* was the justification for a titled chief's authority. If it were stolen and he could not regain it, he lost his title and his functions. Moreover, all the *nkobi* and their *nkira* were ranked in an order of importance, and consequently the titled chiefs also were ranked. Chiefs of higher rank would collect the royal tribute from the lesser chiefs, and the small titled chiefs would collect it from the nontitled chiefs living in their area. The highest titled chief would bring the tribute to the royal court.

The two most important titled chiefs were the *ngaailiino*, south of the Lefini, and the *muidzu*, north of that river. The king lived on the *ngaailiino*'s personal domain at Mbe. The *ngaailiino* would receive the royal tribute of the whole country in the name of the king, and he was also the head of one of the supreme courts of appeal in the name of the king. The *muidzu* collected tribute from all the chiefs between the Lefini and the Nkeni, including the Kukuya, and his court was also supreme; no case tried by him could be tried again at Mbe. In addition to these two chiefs, two others—the paramounts of the Ngungulu and the

Ngenge—also had their own supreme courts. With regard to the dispensation of justice, then, the kingdom was not unified.

The king (*ŭŭkoo*) was the symbol of the kingdom. He derived his authority from the possession of a hoard of sacred objects (*nkwe mbali*) connected with the spirit of Nkwe Mbali, who dwelled in the waterfalls of the Lefini. This spirit was the foremost of all *nkira* and held sway over the whole Tyo country. To rule well, the king had to undergo a secret nine-day initiation during which he was brought into contact with the spirit and was accepted by the ghosts of the kings who had ruled before him. His major duty was to keep the kingdom prosperous by performing the prescribed rituals. Guiral described him as "le pape des Bateke"[7] not only because his religious functions were so prominent but because his real political power was so limited. The king had no army, his village was scarcely bigger than those of his chiefs, there was no supreme judicial institution for the whole kingdom, and matters of life and death were not handled at all by the courts. Royal tribute came in very irregularly once every two or three years. Other administrative contacts with the chiefs were channeled through the *ngaailiino*, for the country south of the Lefini, and were practically nonexistent for the other areas.

In theory, the king could depose any titled chief: in practice he could do so only if he had the support of enough other titled chiefs to provide him with armed men so that he could forcibly remove a titled chief from his office. There was also the matter of his election. There was no royal dynasty and any aristocrat who could claim that any of his ancestors in any branch came from one of three specific domains in the country could be elected king. The electors were *ngaailiino* and *ngaandziyŏŏ* [titled chiefs who had no domain, or a *nkobi*, of their own] together with nine of the other most important chiefs, led by the *muidzu*. This meant that any king was king by the grace of the very chiefs he was later to control, and he had to make concessions before he even could be chosen. Decentralization in this kingdom was pushed so far that one can legitimately ask if this was indeed a state or not.

As far as the Tyo know, there was never any concerted military force in the field to cope with external enemies. It was up to the chiefs on the borders to fight by themselves the intruding Kongo, Mboshi, or Bobangi, and there are many instances when chiefs fought one another without intervention from above. Indeed, such wars were so frequent that rules for them had been elaborated and they had more features of a group duel than of a true war.

It is possible to surmise what the organization of the kingdom was before the *nkobi* were brought in. The titles existed,[8] the basic chiefdoms existed, and it seems likely that titled officials, with or without domains themselves, ruled over provinces. The highest officials chose the king, who could depose any of them with the active participation of the others. The titled offices like the chiefships were hereditary, but royalty was not. Nkwe Mbali certainly existed, as did the belief in *nkira* and the *nkira* shrines in the villages of all the ordinary headmen. In fact, this picture comes close to the early organization of the kingdom of Kongo except that it seems that close relatives of the king could not be appointed to the titled offices since succession there was quasi-automatic. It is still possible, however, that the Kongo, Loango, and Tyo kingdoms all grew out of one model. Maybe this is what the Tyo and Loango mean when they say that Tyo, Loango, and Kongo are all children of Nguunu.[9]

South of the Pool and between the Black River and the Kwango, a group of peoples—including the Hum, the Mfinu,[10] and the Dikidiki—have been established at least since the seventeenth century. They are organized in chiefdoms, apparently reminiscent of the Tyo chiefdoms. Culturally and linguistically they seem to be closely allied to the Tyo. They participated in the coastal trade from the sixteenth century on, and the Kongo word for slave market is derived from the name Hum. But their ethnography and historical records are almost unknown.[11] That so little is known about them is all the more regrettable since the Yans-Ding and the Kuba groups emigrated from this area and probably shared a common culture with these peoples.

North of the Tyo live the Mboshi, a large group which extends north to the middle Likouala. They too have chiefdoms, characterized by a division of the chiefly role between the chiefs of the earth and the professional judges. Nothing is known about their history and very little about their ethnography. And to the northeast of those groups there are others, extending well into the Cameroons, where chieftainship seems to exist but which are even less known. Here is a whole field for further research. It may be here that links between the political systems of the Cameroon grasslands and kingdoms of the lower Congo River may be found.

The Yans-Ding (Yanzi-Ding) group. This group is comprised of the Yans (Yanzi), the Ngul, the Lwer, the Ding, the Tsong, the Mput, and the Mbuun. The Yans, the Ding, and the Mbuun are the best-known peoples. The others seem to be mere cultural variants of one of those three. In addition, the Yans and the Ding are much closer to each other culturally than to the Mbuun. But over-all cultural differences within the group are small, even if ethnographers have generally overlooked the very great similarities which unite all these peoples.

The Yans (or Yey or Yansi) say that they originated in the area west of the lower Kwango and before that from a place, Kimput, which could have been on the coast, somewhere in the kingdom of Loango. During their migrations, they crossed the Congo River on the rapids below Leopoldville and settled at Kintamu, near Leopoldville. From there they followed the left bank of the Congo and then the left bank of the Kasai to Bokala, upstream of Mushie, which is and seems to have been the center of a Boma chiefdom. Swartenbroeckx points out (see note 12) that the Yans are called Ansiku by the Boma and that, among other names, Ding and Tsong are used for the same people. The Yans told him that before they arrived in the country north of the Pool its name was Mbuun (in Yans or Tyo) or Nguun (in Boma), which rejoins traditions collected by Laman among different groups of Mayombe. (A group of these Nguun or Mbuun still live at Fwambondo below the confluence of the Wamba and the Kwango.) They arrived east of the lower Kwango only after 1700 since they met Yaka on the right bank of that river.[12]

The Tsong (Songo) came from the middle Kwango, north of the present town of Popokabaka. First they migrated downstream and then east to the Kwenge and their present settlements on the Gobari and Luniungu. Their first migration was precipitated by quarrels with the Suku whose king, Muli Kongo, ruled on the Kwango—but farther to the south—at a time when the Yaka of Mwene Putu had not yet dislodged the Suku. The Tsong or Yans may have been the Songo who are mentioned in a *Historia do Reino do Congo*[13] around 1620 as living beyond the kingdom of Okango, toward the Wamba. Later migrations were prompted by the arrival of the Yaka in the area. It may be that the Tsong were a branch of the Yans since some clans claim to be descendants from the mythical ancestors of the Yans; neighboring people call them indifferently Yans or Tsong. The cultures and probably the languages of the two are so close that the small Tsong group can easily be conceived of as a Yans group.[14] Another Yans group with a regional name are the Mput, who live between Yans and Ding.

The political structure of the Yans and the Tsong is based on small settlements, each of which is inhabited by a matrilineal clan section. These are grouped into small chiefdoms. The chiefs inherit their position, and therefore there is a chiefly clan in every chiefdom. The different Yans chiefdoms are said to have been founded by a common ancestor, Tasat, who established several chiefdoms at the time of the migration. Every chief rules with a council of elders and has complete authority, including that of a chief justice. The Tsong have separate chief justices in every chiefdom and their courts are composed of judges who are chosen, probably by the chief. These courts apparently correspond to the council of the Yans. The authority of the chief derives from his position as head of the oldest clan in the area, a concept very close to that of the founding clan in the Kuba group. His emblems of office stress both his connection with the ancestors and the responsibility of the ancestors for the fertility

of the land and the people. This is, of course, a very simple political organization which may have grown quite naturally out of a
previous condition wherein the only head was a clan head and
where settlements were clan settlements. But virilocal marriage
and the rule that children remained with their fathers until the
latters' death—and even after that in the case of a head—may
have led to the birth of patrilaterally attached sections which
later became clan sections in their own right (but, of course, clan
sections of other clans than the founding one). The founding clan
would have continued to assert its rights, and its head would
have become a chief with a minimum of centralized political
organization.[15]

It must be kept in mind that the descriptions of migrations
apply only to certain clans—to those of the present chiefs. Movements of other parts of the population may have been quite
different. In this case, it seems that the migration tales of the
chiefly clans are more or less typical for the whole population
since chiefly clans still are often the founding clans and since linguistic criterion puts the Yans and Ding in zone B, the major
area of which clearly lies west of the Congo.

The same is not quite true for the Mbuun. Mbuun history has
been well investigated and tribal tradition has it that the Mbuun
came from the Kwango far to the south on the present border of
Angola, and therefore they would belong to the Kongo group of
peoples. From the Kwango they went to the springs of the
Kwenge, near the Pende, where they lived under one single
chief, Angung.[16] (The chief of the Pende was Hamba.) From the
sources of the Kwenge the Mbuun would have migrated north to
Mashita Mbanza, there to leave the Pende and occupy the country where they dwell at present. They found Tsong, Pindi, and
Ngongo in the area. According to what is known about their language, Pindi and Ngongo belonged to the Kongo group. For one
author the Mbuun are Ambundu, people of the *ngola* from
Ndongo and very closely related to both Pende and Shinje. The
Lunda ruler from whom they received the kaolin (see note 16)
would have been Kapenda Mukwa Ambungo, the founder of the

Shinje states.[17] The other author who studied Mbuun tradition
agrees with this interpretation, but he tries to show that, before
they arrived in Ndongo, the Mbuun ultimately derived from an
area inland of Loango.[18] Torday, who superficially studied the
traditions of all the groups in the Kwango, says that the Mbuun
originated from the upper Kwilu and before that from a neighboring area, Moshinje—which would be the Shinje. They came
first as traders and then settled on the unoccupied land in greater
numbers.[19] According to Mbala tradition, the Yans would have
arrived after the Mbuun, but the Wongo or Lele had arrived before them. A recent tradition supports Torday.[20] The Mbuun had
a main chief, Ngana Lwele, who lived at Muko Mulungu on the
Lunda plateau in Angola. He kept herds of cattle, and traded
with the Portuguese. Once he went with his cattle to the sea to
trade, but he was blocked by the white men, forced to sell his
cattle, and then migrated. The Mbuun are said to know the
ocean—both its saltiness and its ships. They also remembered the
early missionaries. But this knowledge may simply have been
diffused to them by traders who went either to Kasanje or to the
capital of the Yaka. These opinions are given in detail because
they all agree on an Angolan origin for the Mbuun.

Yet the linguistic facts do not agree. Mbuun language does not
belong to the Kongo zone of languages but to zone B, with the
Yans and the Ding. It is true, however, that there seems to be
great dialectical variation in the language and that some dialects
"look" more like the Kongo zone of languages than others. The
contradiction can be explained. A study of the traditions of
Mbuun clans shows that there is a mixture of clans stemming
from Pende, Ding, and Wongo areas and represented there by
other clan sections. Clans of Tsong or Yans origin are represented as well, and there is even one clan section from the Nkutu
who live on the Lokenye River. Data for twenty-eight clans are
available. Out of these, the origin of twelve is unknown, nine are
to be affiliated with the Ding, one with the Nkutu, three with
Kongo, and three with Tsamba (of the Kongo group in the
Kwango). Indications for most of the uncertain cases seem to

point toward a Ding or Yans origin.[21] The mixed nature of the population is also clear from the practice of the central Mbuun, who call their northern brethren Ding and their southern ones Pende. The official tribal tradition reflects the traditions of the chiefly clans and the over-all prestige of Lunda chieftainship. It may also have been true that the southern clans were the first to arrive in the area. The case has been given some attention because it is a perfect illustration of the principle that "tribal" tradition does not necessarily reflect the origin of the population, but can reflect the origins of their leading descent groups. Sometimes the tradition simply creates a link between the leading group and some prestigious place.

According to the traditions quoted, and another one which says that on arrival in the country the Mbuun had four chiefs "of the migration,"[22] chieftainship would have existed. The tradition about the kaolin (see note 16) would show that the institutional complex associated with it derived from a Lunda model, or more specifically from the Shinje. Nowadays the political system is similar to that of the Tsong or Yans. Links between headmen and chiefs are often made by the pattern of a marriage between a man of the ruling chiefly clan with a girl of the "client" clan. Their son can rule over the "client" village, or even the "client" chiefdom, and is at the same time a grandson to the political chief. The relationship between members of alternate generations is very close, and, if the persons involved occupy political positions, they are standardized in such a way that the grandson is the keeper of his grandfather's emblems and his "ideal supporter."[23] Unfortunately, the data are not good enough to make out if perpetual kinship and positional succession play a role in this organization or not. If they did, it would be a strong argument in favor of a Lunda derivation of at least part of the political system, while the over-all similarity of the system with the Tsong or Yans indicates either that parts of the organization were brought in by the northern clans or that this social organization which is almost identical in the three populations led to similar political developments or both. A last problem remains.

According to Kuba tradition, their most famous king learned from the Mbuun "how to build a capital." Some political institutions of the Kuba may have derived from the Mbuun just as some other elements of their culture did. Yet it is strange that no strong chieftainship with an elaborate political structure is reported from the Mbuun now, nor is the evidence about past chiefs really impressive. Future research may throw more light on this point, especially since the ethnographic data on the Mbuun are still scanty.[24]

The Ding tell that they, with the Ngul, Lwer, and Nzadi, came from downstream of the Kasai to a point—Eolo—near the mouth of the Kamtsha. They left the other groups there and went up the Kamtsha to Lewuma, where they dispersed. The eastern Ding became linguistically and culturally distinct enough from the Ding on the Kamtsha to be called by a slightly different name: they are the Ding Mukeen and the others the Dzing. Ding social and political organization differs on some important points from the Yans type. Villages are much larger, with probably more than one-hundred and fifty inhabitants as a mean, and they are not organized around one single matrilineage. They are, rather, conglomerates of several lineages and seem to be governed by a council in which the different lineages are doubtlessly represented, with a headman who seems to be elected for life. In this they resemble very much the Kuba. They also have given a greater role to the age grades than is the case for the Yans, and in this they resemble the Lele. The chiefdom comprises several villages which pay tribute to them—at least noble tribute, such as the skin of leopards and parts of other animals which are considered to be chief's regalia. The ethnographic report does not give any further indication as to the political organization of the Ding. From isolated remarks, one has the impression that the Ding Mukeen had a social and political organization almost identical to that of the Lele, while the Dzing were organized more like some Kuba chiefdoms. For the Ngul or Ngoli it is said that there was one paramount chief for the whole tribe. If these indications are confirmed by fieldwork, they would present us with a very revealing distribution pattern of political organization and, among other conclusions, confirm that the Lele exercised a strong influence on the Ding Mukeen, but that the Kuba type of chiefdom is older than the Lele political system.[25]

The Boma and the Sakata. No traditions of the Sakata have been recorded. The Boma—who are now divided between Boma Nku, south of the lower Kasai, and the Boma of the kingdom of the Ngeli Boma, inland from Mushie—claim to have come from the region of Bokala among the Nku, and before that from the east, from the upper Lokenye. At a given moment a clan left Bokala and founded the great Boma kingdom. This must have been before 1641 since the name *ngeli Boma*, the title of the ruler of the kingdom, has been recorded by Dapper. From the descriptions of the Boma, it is clear that their history, at least in the kingdom, has been well remembered and should be recorded. The only facts known so far are that the Boma had to deal with the Bolia and may have derived parts of their political organization from the Bolia.[26] It is also known from written sources of the nineteenth century (probably since Dapper's days) that the Boma participated in the slave trade. This is not exceptional since the Nunu of Mushie, their southern neighbors, in the late nineteenth century lived almost entirely by trading at Stanley Pool and by fishing. According to Dr. Sulzmann, two of the titles of the Nunu chief area are *nimi amaya* and *mwene Mushie*, which would correspond to the twin titles, *nimeamaya* and *monoemuji*, recorded in late sixteenth- and seventeenth-century titles. If so— and it sounds likely—the Nunu would already have been trading with the Pool in those early times.[27]

The political structure of the Boma and the Sakata, and of the smaller groups such as the Dia, Tow, Mpe, and Nunu, was more complex than that of the Yans-Ding group and seems to have undergone some Bolia influence. Among the Sakata, as among the Boma Nku, the village might count several lineages of different clans, not unlike the Ding, but they were always ruled by one of them, the one which was said to have a right over the land. The headman nominated one or two titled judges for the village and there may have been a village council and court. Some villages were independent and formed a chiefdom by themselves; others were grouped in chiefdoms, ruled by the *moju*—a chief chosen from a ruling clan. The chief had a court, with some titled officials, mostly judges or messengers *cum* policemen. The villages owed him tribute (noble tribute) and the fines of the court went to him. Several chiefdoms could be ruled by different lineages from the same royal clan, an indication either that formerly there was but one, which later split after squabbles for the succession, or that a single incoming clan succeeded in taking over command—probably more through prestige than through war—over several units. The latter seems likely because many *moju* lineages were not landowners, because chieftainship had many attributes of divine kingship and the prestige which goes with it, and because *moju* seems linguistically akin to *mojuiceu*, a chiefly title of the Dia belonging to a clan which is said to be ultimately of Bolia origin. Bolia influence here, as in all the other peoples of this group, is attested by the systems of dual descent with a slight preference for matrilineal descent.

The Dia system was slightly more complicated. The structure was similar to that of the Sakata, including the upper level, where there was but one chief [the *izule*]. But there was a third level. The Majala clan overran part of Dia land and divided the conquered territory into chiefdoms among the clan members, which were equivalent to those of the *moju* in Sakata land. But all the chiefs obeyed the *mojuiceu* [head of the clan] and paid tribute to him. He had also his own court, which was superior to the courts of the chiefs and where more titleholders were assembled than at the lower level. In the part of the country which was not conquered by the Majala, the *izule* continued to rule in a simple two-level system. It was clearly the Majala invasion that complicated the structure.

The Tow and the Mpe had a system analogous to that of the Sakata or the Dia *izule*. The Boma seem also to have had a similar system; and this is, of course, not very different from the Yans-Ding pattern. In the main kingdom of the Boma, the chiefs at the level above the village were *nkumu,* and the institution of chieftainship at this level may have been of Bolia origin, just as this can be suspected for the *moju* of the Sakata. Above the chiefs was the *ngeli Boma* [the king]. Institutions of divine kingship seem to have been numerous here. There was a royal court as well as a royal council, and there were a greater number of titleholders than elsewhere in the area, although by Luba, Lunda, Kuba, or probably even Kongo standards, the number was still low. The Boma kingdom seems to have been built on near caste lines—not an easy undertaking in a society with double descent. The *ngeli* class, including the matrilineage of the *ngeli* and patrilateral attachments five times removed, intermarried systematically and only with the *nkumu* class. Under them were the freemen, who seem not to have intermarried with the *ngeli* but could marry with the *nkumu.* It is evident from the available but sorely insufficient literature that the Boma political system was very ingenious and original. Historically it is almost certain that it represents the fusion of a Bolia type of kingship with a simple two-level political system such as is found in the Yans-Ding group.[28]

The Lele-Kuba group. The Lele and Kuba are grouped together not because they have similar political systems—for in this respect they are extremely dissimilar—but because they have a common origin, speak practically a common language, and share a common culture. Both the Lele and the Kuba traditions (at least those of the central Kuba) claim a common origin from an ancestor, Woot, who would have come from the Congo River and ascended the Kasai and then the Sankuru.

A study of the traditions shows that most of the Kuba clans claim an origin from either the lower or the middle Kwango. Some clans are found which still have branches in Lele and Ding country, and the same may be true with regard to the Mbuun. The tribal traditions, i.e., those of the chiefs among the Bushoong, the main chiefdom in Kuba land, claim that the earliest Kuba (or Pil or Mbal, as they were named) were chased away from the Kwango by the invading Jaga, probably before 1568.

Even then they had already migrated from the coast to an unknown spot north of the Congo River which they would have
crossed in the area of the cataracts. Other chiefly clans, such as,
for instance, those of the Ngongo, a Kuba subtribe, stress that
they left the Kwango area to cross the lower Kasai. They then
went east between Lockenye and lower Kasai. Some other groups,
such as some Shoowa chiefly clans, are clearly of western Mongo
origin. The political organization of the early Kuba could then
have been influenced by systems existing in the northern Kwango
before the arrival of the Lunda, and by the Bolia type of chieftainships around Lake Leopold II. The evidence is as yet tentative. Similarities such as the titles *nyim* [king, for the Lele and
Bushoong] and *nyimi* [king, for the Nunu], and the title *yeli*
[chief, for the Ngongo] and *yeli* [chief, for the Ntomba], suggest
contacts of this nature. Further study will undoubtedly clarify
the hypothesis.

Lele tradition claims that the Lele people, who would be identical with the Wongo, came first from the southern part of their
territory and then pushed slowly northwards. But they may have
had a western origin before that. The aristocratic clan, the Bashi
Tundu, would be a group issued from Woot.

When the Kuba settled in their territory around 1600, they already had a centralized political organization. Their "leaders of
the migration" had become chiefs in a two-level political organization. The villages were either built around one section of a
single matrilineage or they grouped together several sections of
several different clans, the two types which correspond to the
later Yans and Ding types being coexistent. The chiefdom encompassed one or more—sometimes many more—villages and was
led by a chief who had sacred regalia but was himself not sacred.
He was chosen from among the members of a royal clan by nine,
eighteen, or twenty-seven councilors, who were themselves elected to their posts by the other councilors among the members of
specific "founding clans," of nine or a multiple of nine clans.
(These founding clans supposedly, and probably, had accompanied the royal clan in its migration.) The chief could be deposed

and it was the council of founding clans which wielded most of the authority. Immediately after the arrival of the central Kuba, a war of long duration broke out among the Bieng and the Bushoong groups with the object of paramountcy over all other chiefdoms. The Bushoong gained the ascendancy and the Bieng migrated away, first in Lele territory, then later to the south, where they met the Lunda and the Pende around 1650. The Lunda ousted them, and they retreated to form a small but independent chiefdom near Charlesville.

The Bushoong changed the political structure of their chiefdom slightly by granting to the king rights over life and death, by proclaiming that he could not be removed, and by excluding the junior branch of the royal clan from the succession. They thus diminished the power of the council of the founding clans. By 1630 or so, the chiefdom was attacked and almost destroyed by the Pyaang, another Kuba group, which apparently was also competing for the paramountcy. The king was killed and a new king found among the Bashi Tundu in Lele land, but this king did not know the usages of kingship. (There already was some royal etiquette, and at the court the most important political titles had been created.) The king was driven out of office and killed by a certain Shyaam aMbul aNgoong who, although he came from the Ding and the Mbuun with followers, was said to be in reality the son of a Bushoong slave. He altered the culture and the political structure of the Bushoong to a considerable degree by instituting innovations said to come from the Ding, the Mbuun, and the Pende—the political innovations being of Mbuun origin. It may be that a connection will ultimately be found between Shyaam and the Lunda or the Kongo types of state as they existed in the Kwango. In any case, it would be wrong to attribute the later structure of the chiefdom and the kingdom to mere diffusion when it is clear that most of it was due to internal elaboration under Shyaam and his two immediate successors. After Shyaam the kingdom grew slowly for another hundred years until it encompassed all the chiefdoms and peoples now known as Kuba, and it then remained stationary until the nineteenth century, when some Lulua invasions and revolts from the eastern chiefdoms, together with a slow structural change, brought the country to civil war by 1900. But the kingdom survived and the kings became stronger again after 1910, when they came under effective colonial rule.

In the later political structure of the Bushoong, the two most remarkable features are the proliferation of titles, the institution of a greater number of councils, and a unique set of courts which helped to check and counterbalance excessive royal authority. The weakest feature of the kingdom as a whole was that every chiefdom enjoyed complete autonomy and that the central institutions were limited to the kingship and the presence of envoys from the chiefdoms at the royal capital. The king could arbitrate between chiefdoms only when they were at war and could extract tribute only from those chiefdoms which were close enough or small enough to fear his army. The system, therefore, was clearly different from the Luba, Lunda, and Kongo patterns. It was also very different from the Bolia pattern because, among other things, the Kuba throne was not reserved for persons directly chosen by the spirits, as was usual with the Bolia. Though institutions of divine kingship were numerous and were buttressed by a set of appropriate beliefs, there was, for instance, no ancestor worship at all and the kings derived their power not from acceptance by ancestors and nature spirits but from the creator god, who was supposed to put the right candidate on the throne.[29]

It is too soon to describe the change in Lele society in detail, but already some of the main points can be established. The Lele probably had a society very similar to the Ding and the early Kuba chiefdoms, but from 1600 onwards it evolved in a radically different manner: internal invention and local evolution changed the character of the society completely. By 1900 the Lele political unit was the village. A village comprised clan sections of different clans, and members of founding clans had a special place in village affairs and village ritual. But people were grouped not according to clan but according to age set. Younger age sets could not marry but could share a communal village wife in polyandrous marriage. Marriages were regulated by rules of preferential marriage and by a system of pawnship [*kolomo*]. (Pawns were women who were given in marriage by clan sections or villages who had received this right as a compensation for a blood debt incurred by the original clan section of the woman. The pawn status was hereditary.)

In practice, the man was backed by either his clan section or a village. Intervillage relations were usually hostile, except when villages formed alliances because they claimed to be descendants from the same original village (these matters of village descent were expressed in terms of founding clans). There was one founding clan for the whole of Lele land, the Bashi Tundu clan, and they claimed to be overlords over the whole country. They had a king [or *nyim*] and several chiefs, but neither king nor chiefs had any say in village politics or in warfare between villages. Kingship, on the Bushoong model, existed in a simplified version, but it stood alone.[30]

The changes in Lele society were concomitant with a shift in their value system, so that the two highest values, authority and old age, fused. That the Lele were the center of these inventions can be shown because some of the inventions, like the spectacular village-wife institution, for instance, is found among the neighboring Ding, Pende, and Kuba—but only among groups of these peoples bordering on the Lele. With regard to the position of the Bashi Tundu, the hypothesis must be rejected that this clan entered into the country only a short while ago and by 1900 was on its way to organizing the Lele in chiefdoms since Kuba tradition mentions the Tundu in Lele land before 1650, keeping the clan name as a name for the king, who came from the Lele to rule the Kuba. The Tundu existed, but they must have lost their control over the villages or must never have had any real control over them. The case of the Lele is of great interest to the historian because it shows how fundamental changes in the whole culture could radically change the structure of that culture in a relatively short time. To assume, therefore, that basic social structures as found in 1900 were *necessarily* identical with those in existence at much earlier dates is an error.

The past history of the populations described in this chapter is of special interest to the historian because we deal with a zone where local evolution has obviously been important. As a general hypothesis, one might say that at one moment, perhaps in the fourteenth century, the western half of this zone was occupied by peoples who shared the same social systems and the same culture—although at that time the Tyo (Teke) may already have developed a more complex political system than the simple two-level chiefdom. Then the Bolia arrived, elaborated the concept of *bokopo*, and built a centralized political structure around it, together with a mechanism of diffusion for the whole. They diffused it far and wide among the western Mongo and among the peoples of the Boma-Sakata group. The Boma obviously developed internally from there, while a later invasion changed the picture in Dia country. Later, and after some migrations, the Mbuun came under the influence of the Pende and the Lunda, the Lele developed their own system, apparently without external stimulus, and the Kuba built still another pattern of organization on their own. As for the Ding, the Yans, and the other smaller groups of that whole, it may be that they clung to old patterns or that one or more of them evolved new patterns as well. Nowhere in the whole history of Central Africa is the evidence so clear, even though it is skeletal, in showing that our traditional ideas about the immobility of African society are wrong.

five

The Rise of Angola

T hat the kingdom of Angola be subjected and captured."
Thus read a royal order written in Lisbon in September 1571.[1]
The conquest began in 1575. It led to a series of wars in Ndongo
which lasted for forty years with little or no interruption and
which ended with defeat for the *ngola* only because the Jaga
had chosen the Portuguese side. (Kongo played practically no
role in these wars both because it was recovering from the Jaga
invasion and because it was in the throes of internal strife.) By
1622 it looked as if the colony of Angola had broken African resistance, but Nzinga, the new queen of Ndongo and later of Matamba, renewed the war and the struggle went on. Although the
Dutch captured Luanda in 1641 and allied themselves with the
African powers, the Portuguese finally defeated the allies in 1648
and both Kongo and Matamba signed peace treaties in 1656. The
Angolan settlers wanted more: in 1665 they defeated Kongo,
which began to break apart, although in 1670 and again in 1674
the colonists suffered defeat in Kongo and in Matamba. By the
end of the century a new equilibrium was achieved. The colony
of Angola was the major power, but with its expansion either
kept in check or slowed down considerably by the different African states, and Kongo had disappeared as a major political
power. The conquest of Angola had brought almost nothing but

human misery—misery in war and misery in the frantic slave trade.

Ndongo and the Portuguese until 1623

Ndongo was founded as a small chiefdom, perhaps around 1500, by a wealthy smith who helped his neighbors during a famine and imposed himself as a king with the title *ngola*. By 1556 the successive *ngola* had subjected the whole area between the Dande, Lukala, and Cuanza rivers, and in that year they had become independent from Kongo. The *ngola* had desired to make contact with Portugal since 1519, probably because the trade would enrich him and heighten his prestige. Since the 1540's at least, traders had come to his capital, and contacts with São Thomé were established. After the victory of 1556 against Diogo I, the *ngola* asked, via São Thomé, for missionaries from Portugal. The *ngola* died, but his successor, Ndambi aNgola, confirmed the demand and the Portuguese court decided to send four Jesuit priests under the guidance of a young nobleman, Paul Dias de Novães.

They arrived on May 3, 1560, at the mouth of the Cuanza and proceeded to Kabasa, the capital, where negotiations about the missions and about the trade were opened. These seem to have gone well until 1561, but in the fall of that year the *ngola* reduced the only Jesuit priest left, Father Gouvea, virtually to slavery and kept Dias in forced residence as a councilor. However, in the spring of 1565 he had to face a revolt from one of his main chiefs, Kiluanji Kukakwango, and he sent Dias back to Portugal, with gifts, to ask for military help. Dias returned at the end of 1566 and immediately started an ambitious scheme to obtain a trade monopoly in Ndongo because he believed that there were huge silver mines in the interior. With the help of the Jesuits he obtained a *donatario*, or gift, in September 1571. He would colonize Angola at his own expense and in return he would receive as private property the southern part of the area while he also would remain governor of the whole during his lifetime.[2]

In February 1575 Dias appeared off the island of Luanda with four hundred men. First he settled on the island and renewed contact with the *ngola,* and then in 1576 he moved to the main-land and built Luanda. The moment for his arrival was propitious. Francisco de Gouvea, the governor of São Thomé, was still in Kongo making it impossible for the Kongo to prevent the landing of Dias. When De Gouvea left in 1576, it was believed that Alvare I, the king of Kongo, had signed an act of fealty to the crown of Portugal, which would aid Dias. Also, the *ngola* died in 1575, and his successor was fighting rebels. Although the *ngola* did not ask Dias to intervene, Dias was preparing for war because the traders complained that the routes were blocked by the civil strife. Yet, at this point it would not have taken much effort to overwhelm Dias—for example, in that same year the Portuguese underwent defeat at the hands of a small chief, Kasanze. How-ever, no war with the *ngola* erupted as yet.

In 1578 new colonists arrived under the command of a nephew of Dias and he sent them to build Benguela Velha, on his own lands, a post that was quickly abandoned. In 1579 Dias advanced along the Cuanza towards Cambambe, where there were sup-posedly huge silver mines. The *ngola* interpreted this as an act of war and retaliated by killing all the traders at Kabasa and by marching on Luanda, whereupon Dias rushed back and stopped the troops of the *ngola* at Anzele, east of Luanda. The *ngola* asked for peace but his overtures were rejected.

Dias waited for reinforcements and also induced Alvare I of Kongo to send the *mani* Mbamba with an army against Ndongo. Alvare, not realizing the Portuguese threat, agreed, but his army was beaten, north of the Bengo, in 1581. In the meantime, how-ever, Dias' reinforcements arrived at Luanda and a long cam-paign began. In 1583 Dias won a great victory and built the fort of Masangano at the confluence of Lukala and Cuanza, although further advances towards Cambambe were repulsed. Dias died in 1589 and his successor, Luis Serrão, was severely defeated by a combined army of Ndongo, Kongo, Matamba, and the Jaga, but the allies did not follow up their victory with further attacks on Masangano or Luanda

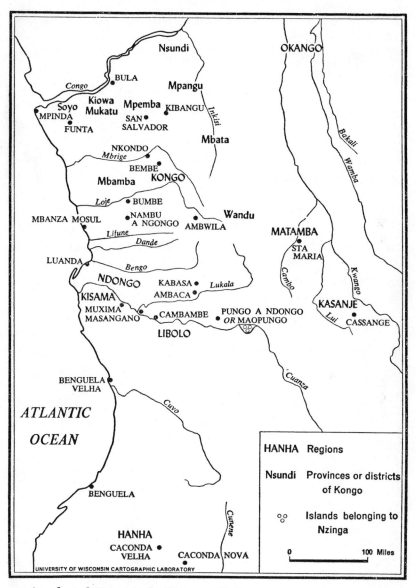

v Angola and Kongo in the Seventeenth Century

By 1592 the Portuguese had recovered enough to take the offensive again. At that moment they already had lost seventeen hundred men by illness, in combat, or as deserters, and only three hundred residents were left. They had not won a decisive advantage and had to rely more and more on African auxiliary troops, which might defect. There were no farmers but only slave traders and a few missionaries. The adventure of Angola, at least so far, was a failure. A report made up in 1591 by Domingos Abreu y Brito pointed out that Angola had possibilities and proposed a grand scheme for the occupation and settlement of the country, but there was no money, and Madrid did nothing but declare the area a colony and send a governor.[3]

The first governor revoked all grants of land made to the soldiers and to the Jesuits by Dias, at which all the settlers rebelled and he was expelled. The next governor brought reinforcements for the army and went completely over to the side of the traders. In fact, he became one himself,[4] an example that set a pattern for almost all later governors.

In the meantime the war dragged on. Raiding Jaga had appeared on the scene at least since 1600 and the war had spread to Kisama, south of the Cuanza. In 1603 Manuel Cerveira Pereira, a ruthless, greedy, but capable general, succeeded *ad interim* to the governor, occupied Cambambe, and found that there was no silver. The *raison d'être* for the conquest no longer existed, but the *ngola* was impressed and asked for a peace treaty, which Cerveira signed—against the protests both of his captains and of the slave traders, who followed the armies like vultures. The incoming governor arrested Cerveira and sent him to Lisbon on charges of double-dealing with the enemy—and this when the governor's instructions were to limit the conquest and maintain the peace!

Hostilities were re-opened on a large scale in 1608. The commander of the troops, Bento Banha Cardoso, held that every chief in Ndongo should be "given" to a Portuguese who would "rent" him for a fixed annual sum from the government and be entitled to whatever tribute—undoubtedly in slaves—he could get from his chief. This was oppression at its worst, and even some old veterans protested. They claimed that the never-ending rebellions were the fault of the captains of the *presidios* or military districts and of the field commanders because they were constantly pressuring the local chiefs for slaves; the chiefs felt that it was better to pay a tribute once a year to the *ngola* instead of so many tributes to different Portuguese officials and therefore they sided more and more with Ndongo. Moreover, they felt that the captains and commanders were starting wars without any reason and that these unofficial expeditions had to be stopped.[5]

Bento Banha Cardoso had his way, however, and the "conquest" dragged on year after year, until Cardoso conceived the idea of using the Jaga as allies. This time the balance of war swayed in his favor and he took eighty enemy chiefs in the campaign of 1614 alone. The following year, Manuel Cerveira Pereira came back from Lisbon with a mandate to conquer "the kingdom of Benguela," and also as interim governor of Angola. He defeated the *ngola* on the Lukala near the new *presidio* of Ambaca and signed a peace treaty. He then sailed for Benguela.

In the spring of 1617 the *ngola* died and his successor immediately murdered the son of his sister, Nzinga, because the child could have become a possible competitor. In August of the same year the new governor decided to break Ndongo once and for all, and he went in the field with the Jaga. Kabasa was taken, but the Portuguese army suffered heavily from illness. The governor proposed peace—but the *ngola* wanted him to evacuate Kabasa, and hostilities were renewed. Two years later the *ngola* had lost his country almost entirely and had retired on an island in the Cuanza. But the new Portuguese commander, a nineteen-year old son of the governor, had been so ruthless—he killed more than one hundred chiefs in 1619 alone—that even the slave traders protested. The markets were closed, the trade routes blocked, and there was famine everywhere. The traders were bankrupt. The Jaga went on the rampage, and moreover an attack on Kongo had been made. Lisbon finally decided, under pressure from the Vatican, to recall the governor. His successor came with definite orders to make peace.

In 1622 negotiations between Ndongo and the Portuguese were conducted at Luanda and a peace treaty was prepared. The new fort of Ambaca would have to be rebuilt farther away from Kabasa, which would be returned to the *ngola;* the Portuguese would fight the Jaga of Kasanje, a new enemy of the *ngola*—indeed a new power in the area; and all the chiefs who had become vassals of Portugal would again become tributaries of the *ngola.* In return, the *ngola* would free the prisoners he had. The treaty was a diplomatic success for Nzinga, the king's sister, who was the negotiator of Ndongo. It restored the situation of 1604. But it was not executed quickly, even when it had been ratified in Europe, for the new governor started a major campaign in Kongo, which he won by the battle of Bumbe in December 1622. However, the king of Kongo, Pedro II, mobilized his whole army and the governor withdrew. The governor also quarreled with the Jesuits, whom he expelled from Luanda. This and the Kongo invasion led to his deposition in May 1623. In the following months Angola was without a governor at what would be a critical moment.[6]

The Recovery in Kongo under Alvare I and II

After the expulsion of the Jaga from Kongo in 1572, Alvare I faced two immediate tasks: to rebuild the authority of the king and to disengage himself from the Portuguese. Nothing is known about the way in which Alvare achieved a restoration of the internal structures of the kingdom, but it is thought that he may have used the presence of Portuguese troops to bolster his position. With regard to the relations between Kongo and Portugal, the situation was serious indeed. Alvare apparently had signed an act by which he gave up Kongo's sovereignty and became a vassal of Portugal; fortunately, the act was not accepted in Lisbon, and Kongo remained independent. Yet the country was occupied by troops under the command of the governor of São Thomé, Francisco de Gouvea. He wanted to build a fort at San Salvador and to man it with a Portuguese garrison at the expense of the Kongolese treasury. The rationale was that the fort would protect Christianity and the king. De Gouvea also wished to exploit the mines, if there were any. Engineers came once again from Portugal, but Alvare prevented them from prospecting. De Gouvea finally left in 1576 and Kongo was still sovereign; there was no garrison and there were no mining commitments.[7]

Trade flourished immediately. A hundred Portuguese had remained as slave traders in the capital. The slave trade had, of course, seen a golden age during the Jaga raids; in fact, the very first embassy Alvare sent to Portugal after the wars in 1574 had to negotiate the release of all the Kongolese who had been taken during the wars. At a later period, between 1584 and 1587, Alvare II was obliged to impose new regulations on the trade because of the brutalities the slavers inflicted on their victims. Alvare I insisted on the inspection of the slaves by a royal committee so that free men would not be sold and, on a right probably acquired in 1574, to free twenty slaves a year in São Thomé. Under his reign trade routes reached the Kwango at Okango and some traders lived among the Teke of Stanley Pool. A new route led from San Salvador through Mbamba to Luanda. Alvare II also gave serious thought to the exploitation of the mines. In 1583 Alvare I had given a concession to Duarte Lopes as his ambassador to the Holy See and a concession to the pope, but the pope did not accept it, nor did he accept the concession given in 1602 by Alvare II.

Before 1607 Alvare II proposed to the king of Portugal to exploit the copper mines of Bembe. Although a number of Portuguese traders were also interested in the operation, the council for Portuguese affairs in Madrid rejected the plan. But besides the trade in slaves and the possible exploitation of minerals, since about 1600 there had also been a lively trade in ivory, redwood, and copper with the Dutch at Mpinda.[8]

In external politics the position of Kongo shifted gradually, after the departure of the governor of São Thomé, De Gouvea, from total co-operation with Portugal to increasing hostility and reliance on the Vatican. In 1581, Alvare I sent an army to help Dias in his war with Ndongo, since Ndongo was by now a traditional enemy. But by 1583 Duarte Lopes (a trader) was sent by Alvare to the Vatican to propose a mining concession in return for the support of the pope in Kongo-Lusitanian relations, and in 1590 Alvare II allied himself with Ndongo and Matamba against Portugal, although it became apparent that the Portuguese were not to be chased out of their towns. The Portuguese, of course, became more inimical to Kongo than they had ever been.

Alvare II proposed in 1604 to the Vatican to become a feudatory of the pope in return for the mining concessions so that he would then be freed from the *padroado* and all Portuguese controls. In 1595 he had already achieved a victory because a new bishopric had been created for Kongo with a seat in San Salvador; but the bishops were political supporters of the king of Spain and, in the 1602 proposal, Alvare II made it clear that he wanted from then on to have a non-Portuguese or non-Spanish bishop. The Holy See rejected the proposals but still agreed in 1611 to intercede with the king of Spain in favor of Kongo. In 1613 a permanent ambassador of Kongo in Rome was appointed, Mgr. Vivès, and from then on relations were very close. It was because of this policy that Alvare's successors were able, in 1617 and 1623, to stem invasion attempts from Angola. They appealed to the Vatican, which remonstrated with the king of Spain.

Another new element were the Dutch. In the early seventeenth century they were only traders, but their religious influence (they were Calvinists) was denounced and their general importance was such that the Portuguese began to press the king of Kongo to expel them and asked to be allowed to build a fort at Mpinda. Both demands were refused and could not be enforced.

By now the Portuguese attitude towards Kongo, as can be seen from the *consulta* of the council of Portugal, for instance, was that, if Kongo was not a vassal, it was nevertheless under Portuguese obedience. No help should be given to the king which could strengthen the power of the kingdom. He should not be allowed to have direct contacts with the Holy See or with any European power. In other words, he was not sovereign. A quarrel about the use of the title "Majesty" versus the title *Senhor*, which goes back to the time of Dias and which dragged on during the reigns of Alvare II and III, was directed toward the non-recognition of Kongo as a sovereign state. To address the king as *Altexa* (royal highness) was to see in him a king of an independent state; to call him *Senhor* was to imply that he was not independent. But Spain was not ready to go to war over Kongo and probably doubted if the kingdom could be taken in war. The policy was to restrict the kings more and more, especially by building forts, by having the bishops use excommunication threats to cow the kings into obedience, and by using other similar maneuvers. All in all, Alvare II resisted all these attempts successfully, and when he died in 1614 it seemed as if Kongo was easily holding its ground.[9]

But in internal affairs the situation had badly deteriorated. At Alvare I's death the kingdom seemed peaceful and there were no reports of rebellion. Yet there seem to have been factions, for Alvare II had to defeat in battle in 1587 a brother and a sister who apparently were supported by a number of his uncles, and it is reported that the first years of his reign were filled with wars. Even some Portuguese were involved, and around 1595 Alvare II sent one of these men to the governor of Angola, with the demand that he be punished since he had helped a competitor to try and overthrow the king. Instead, the culprit was released and received a handsome reward, for it became a policy in Portugal, or at least in Angola, to support local chiefs against their superiors. For example, in a document written by one of the *conquistadores*, Garcia Mendes de Castello Branco, it is casually mentioned that it is not necessary to have permission of the king of Kongo to mine the ore at Bembe. Also, the chief Bembe could be brought to the Portuguese side, since in any case he was not on very good terms with his overlord, the duke of Mbamba.[10] Given the political structure of Kongo, this sort of interference was very dangerous to the kingdom. Portuguese demands were responsible for the fact that, when Alvare II died in 1614, both the count of Soyo and the duke of Mbamba were in open rebellion. The succession crisis itself ushered in a new period in Kongo history—one of continual revolts and competing "palace-mayors" which would last until 1641.[11]

In all their embassies, Alvare I and Alvare II clamored for more missionaries and more technicians, yet few came. The mission was still heavily concentrated at San Salvador, seat of the bishopric after 1595, and very few priests went into the interior between 1584 and 1587, as some Spanish missionaries had begun to do. Most of them traded, because they were paid in slaves. The bishops were consistently using religious sanctions to put political pressure on the kings. Some of the clerics led dissolute lives. This, and the high death rate, prevented any serious missionary work, despite efforts by different congregations, among whom the Jesuits were the most tenacious.[12]

As for non-missionary technicians, it seems that none came. Yet this period saw some changes in Kongolese customs. Portuguese titulature came into use under Alvare II around 1590[13] and from the reading of Pigafetta it is clear that in clothing, food, and etiquette, Portuguese influence was heavy at the court. The most important outside influence on Kongo culture was undoubtedly the introduction of maize, before 1583 but after 1547, and of other American crops. By 1600, manioc was grown on the fields of the Portuguese in the Bengo area. Its spread from there was slow, and even though some Africans were cultivating manioc in 1614, it was only during the eighteenth century that it became the staple crop of Kongo.

Angola, Holland, and Nzinga

The king of Ndongo died in 1623 on an island in the Cuanza under mysterious circumstances. He seems to have been poisoned by his sister, Anna Nzinga, who succeeded to the throne and immediately sent word to Luanda that the treaty of 1622 had to be executed or that there would be war. Nothing much happened, first, because there was no governor, and also because the Portuguese in Luanda were much concerned about the Dutch —an elusive but very real power on the Central African coast. The

Dutch West Indies Company had been formed in 1621 and war with Portugal was practically declared, by 1623, when Dutch warships captured seven trading vessels and briefly occupied Benguela. In June 1624, the Dutch burned six ships in the harbor of Luanda, went from there to Mpinda, and came back in October for a second attack. It seemed as if they had an agreement with Pedro II, king of Kongo, who, it was said in Luanda, had written to Maurits van Nassau after the battle of Bumbe. Under the circumstances, then, not much attention was given to Nzinga.

In the meantime, the new queen of Ndongo had allied herself with the Jaga and was taking over Jaga customs. She also gave asylum to all fugitive slaves from Portuguese-controlled territory and induced *kimbares* [African soldiers] trained by the Portuguese to join her army by promising them land and rewards. By the end of 1624 she was thus slowly gaining the military advantage. In 1625 she finally incited one vassal chief after another to rebel against the Portuguese, and was then told that war would result if she did not return the fugitive soldiers and the slaves. Another year went by and the Portuguese did not dare to move, mainly because they feared that if the army did not protect Luanda, the Dutch would capture the city. When the governor then proclaimed that Aidi Kiluanji, a chief related to the late *ngola*, was the rightful heir to the throne of Ndongo, he was thereupon attacked by Nzinga—and this time the army in Luanda had to move. It started its march away from the capital at the very moment that news arrived that the Dutch were concentrating a fleet at Bahia to take Luanda. In July 1626 Nzinga's stronghold, an island in the Cuanza, was captured, and by October *ngola* Aidi was installed as Philip I of Ndongo in his stronghold Maopungo (Punga a Ndongo); the troops did not capture Nzinga, however, and the inhabitants of Nodongo did not recognize Aidi.

Even though defeated and chased out of the country, Nzinga carried on with the fight. Simply because she was the enemy of the barbarous Portuguese, she still had complete popular support, and in November 1627 she was back on her island and had prepared for a general revolt. The Portuguese were gone because an imminent attack on Luanda from Bahia was feared again, and Aidi lost control over his territory; after a year, Nzinga had recovered all her possessions and had again begun to attract soldiers, slaves, and rebel chiefs. Once again the Portuguese went to war and expelled her from her island, this time with orders to capture her dead or alive; but she fled through Matamba and as far away as Songo country, where she spread the news that she had been eaten by cannibals, so the pursuit was abandoned.

In late 1629 or 1630 she promised marriage to the Jaga of Kasanje and, with the help of his troops and the remnants of her own, she evicted the then-ruling queen of Matamba and thus conquered a new kingdom. Kasanje went southwest and reoccupied the islands of the Cuanza east of Maopungo. In 1630, then, the Portuguese found that their campaign had failed: Nzinga was still there and held most of her own land in addition to holding Matamba. But it was a stalemate for her too. She needed time to reorganize her kingdom and to work out a way to overcome the Portuguese the next time round. From 1630 to 1635 she settled great numbers of wandering Jaga in Matamba and began again to harry *ngola* Aidi and to attract slaves. (Her alliance with Kasanje broke off because, during a campaign she was conducting against Maopungo, he had plundered her own capital in Matamba.)

In the meantime the Dutch threat became more and more evident, and in Lisbon the council for Portugal had decided that the war against Nzinga was unjust since the provisions of the treaty had not been fulfilled by Portugal. Peace, therefore, had to be made. In 1639 embassies were received in Kasanje and Matamba: peace was promised but nothing was done, and Nzinga went on with her work of undermining the strength of the colony. By now the situation was even more serious than in 1626: in 1630 the Dutch had captured Pernambuco; in 1633 a Dutch ship, that was later captured, blockaded Benguela; in 1637 El Mina was captured; and from 1639 onward the Dutch had cut off the estuary of the Kongo, and from there sent patrols up and down the coast. Clearly the threat of a Dutch invasion became greater and greater. Yet Nzinga's action became too dangerous and in 1641, just before the Dutch invasion finally took place, the governor and the Council of Luanda decided to wage a full-scale war on her. But it was too late. The Dutch captured Luanda in August.[14]

When the Dutch finally arrived in Luanda, an army was actually being mobilized near there by the Portuguese, not against Nzinga but against a new great Kongo king, Garcia II, who was manifestly an ally of the Dutch. This change in campaign plans had become necessary, at least in the eyes of the settlers of Luanda, because ever since 1622 the Kongo had been pro-Dutch and had supported the Dembos in a campaign against the Portuguese. This war between the Dembos and the Portuguese had lasted from 1633 to well into 1635, ending with the capture of the capital of Ambwila, the most important Dembo chief. But the Portuguese army had to return to Luanda because of an invasion scare, and the Dembo had rebelled again in 1639.[15]

Benguela fell to the Dutch in December 1641. The small town was then the capital of the so-called kingdom of Benguela, a creation of Manuel Cerveira Pereira. In September or October in 1615 Pereira had arrived in Luanda with the grand order to conquer the "kingdom of Benguela," as yet nonexistent, because there were said to be "mines"—probably copper mines—in the area. After his activities in Angola, he sailed in August 1617 and landed at a place called Benguela Nova. He immediately made alliances with some chiefs and started to fight others. To survive, he was ruthless (he was once evicted by the garrison and the population, arriving in a dugout in Luanda, but he went back and fought again). He finally reached the site of the supposed copper mines near the mouth of the Cuvo in August 1620, and it was found, as at Cambambe, that there were no mines. Once again there was a conquest which had lost its *raison d'être*. But in Benguela there was no flourishing slave trade yet, so Portugal and Luanda gave the settlement little support. Even the Dutch who occupied the town in 1623 apparently did not find it useful enough to keep and left after a short stay. When Manuel Cerveira Pereira died in April 1626, only sixteen soldiers were left, there were few or no African allies, and there were many enemies, yet Benguela survived.

Pereira's successor, Lopo Soares Lasso, arrived with seventy-two veterans in May 1627 and started to hunt for mines again. He did not find any but he pacified the area around the town so that Portuguese could travel even into the interior. In 1630 an envoy was sent to a king, Mozungo a Kalunga, who lived east of the upper Cunene. The envoy married and settled there, the first *sertanejo* or "backwoodsman" we know of. Many in Benguela would follow his example from the late seventeenth century on and settle everywhere on the Benguela highlands and deep in southern Angola. This is not surprising, for the inhabitants of the town of Benguela were themselves fishermen and farmers, settlers on the land and not traders, as was the case in Luanda. In 1641 Benguela, without much support, still survived—by habit as it were and undoubtedly because of the subsistence occupations of its settlers.[16]

From Alvare III to Alvare VI: Breakdown in Kongo

When Alvare II died in 1614, the duke of Mbamba took the throne for two months and then imposed Bernardo, a half brother of Alvare II. But the new king soon displeased the kingmaker, who marched on the capital and defeated him—the first time that a provincial governor had overthrown a ruling king. The duke then imposed his son-in-law as Alvare III.

Alvare III found the kingdom in the greatest disorder. Provincial and even district chiefs rebelled against the king, district chiefs rebelled against provincial chiefs, and the whole fabric of territorial authority was rapidly breaking down. It is clear that this process of insubordination and rebellion must have started under Alvare II, but there are no documents to show how it happened. One can only surmise that gradually the support of the

Kongo population for the political regime had weakened and especially that the chiefs at all levels no longer accepted the existing patterns of authority.

Reasons for this breakdown may have been the excessive taxation by the chiefs, their inadequate protection of the population, the kidnapping of persons to be sold as slaves, the devaluation of the *nzimbu,* and the corruption of the courts. The presence of the Portuguese certainly precipitated the breakdown. The slavers tried to provoke wars and rebellions everywhere, while at the court the clergy and probably the Portuguese were still divided into two factions. The old São Thomé faction was now a pro-Angola or generally a pro-Portugal faction. Their opponents became increasingly more pro-Kongo. The bishops at San Salvador, especially bishop Manuel Baptista in Alvare III's reign, followed instructions from Madrid and exercised heavy pressure, backed by religious sanctions, to further Portugal's interests. The kings were backed by the canons and especially by their confessors. (In Alvare III's life and during the reign of his successors, one of the most able of these was Bras Correa.) Both factions did not hesitate to seek support among rebel chiefs and thus added to the unrest. Finally, the expansionist tendencies of the Angolan colonists kept Kongo under pressure until 1624 and probably compounded the general difficulties.[17]

Another factor in the development of rebellions and rifts at the higher levels must be blamed on the pattern of succession. With Bernardo I, the descendants of the first daughter of Affonso I had died out. Alvare III was a descendant of the second daughter; Pedro II a descendant of the third daughter. Since the rules were that regents could not be appointed and that all descendants from any of these children of Affonso I were eligible, the number of possible candidates increased from generation to generation. So did the number of smaller lineages within the two main blocs of the descendants of the second and third daughters. From Alvare III onward the kings showed growing concern about the pattern of succession. They tried to have the pope in Rome decree that only the eldest son of a ruling king could succeed, in order to limit the number of possible challengers, but the Holy See would not lay down any rules in this extraneous matter.[18]

Alvare III died in May 1622 having failed to restore order within the kingdom. Soyo in practice had been independent since 1600 at least, and royal demands had little effect there. The duke of Mbamba and his successor had been in perpetual rebellion, and Alvare had been able to maintain his position only by continual negotiations, which deteriorated still further the royal prestige. The duke of Nsundi, who belonged to the royalist faction, was trying to attack Mbamba. Only the diplomacy of Bras Correa kept the country from a civil war.

In external politics the situation was little better. Portugal had finally abandoned, for the time being, the idea of exploiting the copper mines at Bembe and the bishop had advised them that no fort could be built at Mpinda against the will of the Kongolese. But the colonists of Angola had been raiding in the southern parts of Kongo since 1615; the island of Luanda and the area between Dande and Bengo were gradually lost; and the Dembos rebelled against Kongo and then again appealed to Kongo against Angolan incursions. Appeals to the Vatican and representations by the Holy See to Portugal had succeeded in 1618 in lessening the tensions, at least for a year or so. However, after this event the clergy and the governors at Luanda tried to intercept all correspondence between Kongo and the Holy See. Only trade flourished in these troubled times, especially since the kings did not seem to have enough authority left to keep the Portuguese traders at San Salvador and prevent them from settling at the courts of the provincial chiefs.[19]

Under Alvare's successor, Pedro II, who ruled for only two years, there was to be little or no improvement. Thanks to Bras Correa there was no struggle for the succession, although there were four competitors for the throne instead of the usual two (the widening of the royal line was making itself felt). Soon after Pedro's inauguration, the duke of Mbata was killed by insurgents from his territory and the king of Okango was defeated by one of

his chiefs. The governor of Angola now claimed all the land between Dande and Luanda, including the island of Luanda and
the copper mines of Bembe. He went with an army against
Dembo Nambu—a Ngongo and a tributary of Kongo as well as
an ally. The duke of Mbamba and the marquis of Mpemba reinforced the Dembo but the Kongolese were defeated at Bumbe in
December 1622 and the leaders of their army killed. At that point
—when Nsundi and Soyo were the only provinces where the ruler
had not been killed within the last two years—Pedro II complained to the Vatican and mobilized an army, this being a suf-
ficient deterrent to keep the Angolans from pursuing their victory
on a large scale. The governor, who had also quarreled with the
Jesuits, allies of the Kongo king since Alvare II, was recalled.
After that the danger of an invasion from Angola was averted
until 1641. Pedro II and some of his successors seem to have
started negotiations with the Dutch so as to be able to withstand
further threats from Luanda.[20]

In 1624 Pedro II died and was succeeded by his eldest son,
Garcia I, the duke of Mbamba since 1623. But the duke of Nsundi revolted, with popular support, and drove Garcia I to Soyo,
where the latter died in June 1626. Ambrosio I succeeded, but he
died in 1631, followed by Alvare IV, legitimate son of Alvare III,
then probably eleven years old. Under his reign a revolt by the
duke of Mbamba was crushed, but Alvare IV died shortly there-
after, in 1636. His successor, Alvare V, faced rebellion by a new
duke of Mbamba and the district chief of Kiowa. They killed Alvare V, and within that year the duke of Mbamba became king
under the name of Alvare VI. He apparently belonged to a descent group, the *kimulazu,* who had never been in power before,
though the group was also a descent group of Affonso I. (This
fact would have severe repercussions after 1665, when the *kimpanzu* group from whom all kings up to 1636 had been elected
would start a civil war which was to last for forty years.) Alvare
VI went to war against Soyo in 1636 and 1637, and for a third
time toward the end of his reign. He lost the first two campaigns
and had to give up the territories of Mukatu and Kiowa. Soyo

proclaimed its independence but still retained its right to be an elector of the king of Kongo—the first irrevocable fracture in the political structure of Kongo. Even though the counts of Soyo had been practically independent since 1600, and had been the third force in the struggle between Mbamba and Nsundi for the throne, before this time they had not dared to reject the authority of the king. It was a severe blow, especially since they had control over the harbor of Mpinda and could negotiate, as indeed they did, with Holland or Portugal on their own. In fact, it is likely that military support from Holland enabled them to proclaim their independence in the first place.[21]

Alvare VI died in 1641, and his successor was Garcia II (who was to rule for twenty years and was to restore the internal cohesion of the kingdom). In that same year the Italian Capuchins arrived in Kongo and were to renovate the mission work. In 1641, also, the Dutch occupied Luanda, which would have important effects on the further history of Kongo. With the reign of Garcia II, then, a new period opened in Kongo's history.

The Dutch Period and the Restoration of Angola

The Dutch fleet took Luanda in August 1641 without a major battle, although the Portuguese army and the settlers were able to withdraw to the Bengo and regroup there. The crisis was serious, for it was only a question of time before the Dutch would ally themselves with Nzinga, Kongo, Soyo, and the chiefs of the Bengo area and those of Kisama—all enemies of Angola. A truce was signed on the Bengo, but in 1643 the Portuguese had to retreat to Masangano, where they found that only the king of Ndongo—Aidi—remained loyal to them. Most of the Africans must have felt as Garcia II of Kongo felt, who wrote that he sided with the Dutch because he wanted to be free and because he had had enough of the horrors of the slave trade. Said he:

> . . . instead of gold and silver and other goods which function else-where as money, the trade and the money here are persons, who are not in gold, nor in cloth, but who are creatures. It is our dis-

grace and that of our predecessors that we, in our simplicity, have given the opportunity to do many evils in our realm, and above all that there are people who pretend that we never were lords over Angola and Matamba. The inequality of the arms has lost the lands over there to us and our rights are being lost through violence.[22]

By 1645 Masangano and its garrison were attacked by the armies of Nzinga and the Dutch. Reinforcements from Brazil were annihilated by raiding Jaga in 1645, but a second party came through to Masangano. The outcome remained uncertain for a year and a half after that, until a string of victories by Nzinga and the Dutch led to the final defeat of the field army of Masangano in August 1648. It was now only a question of weeks or months before Masangano would fall. However, in the same month Salvador de Sa y Correa arrived with a fleet from Brazil and took Luanda. The Dutch director capitulated, despite his superior strength, both at Luanda and in the interior, and the Dutch withdrew, leaving their African allies alone.[23]

The chiefs and kings tried desperately to defend themselves without the Dutch. The chiefs of the Bengo and those around Luanda united, but were defeated and savagely massacred by the troops of Salvador de Sa. In September the governor felt enough in control of the situation to write to Garcia II, asking him to capitulate under conditions that practically included the loss of Kongo's independence. Garcia did not answer, sending instead a Capuchin to Luanda to negotiate. In the beginning of 1649, Salvador de Sa exiled the governor of the king of Kongo from the island of Luanda. Other missions were sent to Nzinga and to the Jaga of Kasanje. (The latter, who had remained neutral during the war, renewed his friendship with the Portuguese, and his capital very rapidly became the most important market place in the interior of Central Africa.) Nzinga started negotiations. In October 1650 the governor could report that all the African powers were cowed (although the treaties with Kongo and Nzinga would be negotiated for years). Neither of the two powers wanted to become a vassal of Portugal—and in fact the situation was not as desperate for the African states as it looked, for to subdue either of them would have meant a full-scale war, and the chiefs between Dande and Cuanza were not really subdued when Salvador de Sa left in 1652. Finally, Nzinga signed a treaty in October 1656 by which she lost all her rights to the lands west of the Lukala as well as to the area around Maopungo, which went to the *ngola* Aidi; but she did not become a vassal nor did she pay tribute. From then on peace was kept between her and the Portuguese until her death in 1663. She had become a Catholic again and a mission was built in her capital. As for Kongo, different drafts of the treaty were discussed and elaborated for years, but Garcia II signed only in 1657 after a further show of force by the Portuguese, who profited from a rebellion by the marquis of Mpemba to enter Mbamba. The treaty was not to lead to a long-lasting peace, since the settlers of Luanda clung to the 1649 version which foresaw, among other harsher points, the cession of sovereignty over the island of Luanda and for the Angolans to prospect and exploit all mines in Kongo. The 1657 version had deleted this point, insisting that the island of Luanda should be returned to Kongo—which was never done.[24]

In the fall of 1658, almost immediately after the signature of the treaty, Luanda mobilized again. Only a mutiny in the army prevented an invasion of Kongo in 1659–1660. In 1664 Luanda saw its chance when the duke of Wandu and the regent of Ambwila rebelled against the king of Kongo. They accepted both chiefs as vassals of Portugal and claimed the mines—which led to war in 1665. In October King Antoino I was killed at the battle of Ambwila, just as he was winning the victory, and the Kongolese gave ground, but the Angolans were not strong enough to pursue their advantage. In Kongo a civil war developed, slowly draining and destroying the country's strength. Luanda tried to intervene in it and sent an army to Soyo in 1670, which was annihilated by the count of Soyo at Citombo. As a result of this defeat, the new king of Ndongo, Aidi III, rebelled. But after the arrival of fresh troops from Brazil, he was defeated and killed in September 1671. His capital Maopungo (or Pungo a Ndongo) became a *presidio,* so that Portuguese territory now bordered directly on territories under the control of Matamba or Kasanje. Since the new ruler of Matamba had given support to Aidi, the hostility between Matamba and the Portuguese was renewed. The Angolans supported a challenger to the throne who, with their help, killed the ruler and took his place in 1674. But the new ruler, Francisco Guterres, did not remain on good terms with the Portuguese for long, for a struggle based on succession was festering in Kasanje, with Guterres backing an ousted challenger and Luanda the successful one, Jaga Pascal Machado II. Matamba defeated and occupied Kasanje and its candidate succeeded, whereupon an army was sent by Luanda against Matamba. It was defeated, however, and Angola abandoned further attempts to subdue Matamba. A peace was signed in 1684, which was to last until the 1740's. Both Matamba and Kasanje were the limits of Portuguese power.

South of the Cuanza and in the hinterland of Benguela, new advances had been made since 1648. Here campaigns in 1645 had already prepared the way. The ports of Libolo and Kisama were occupied, and by 1690 the Portuguese controlled the southern bank of the Cuanza River and the valley but did not manage to penetrate to the highlands from there. From Benguela, however, they had progressed against the Jaga of Kakonda, and a first *presidio* of Caconda Velha was created in 1680 in Hanha, which in 1685 was relocated on the southern highlands. This was to be a metropolis for generations of half-caste traders and the gate for the peaceful penetration of the *sertanejos* over the whole plateau.[25]

By the end of the century the colony of Angola was freed from its most dangerous enemies. It had expanded between the Dande and Cuanza to Matamba and Kasanje, and from Benguela it had reached the southern tip of the highlands. The slave trade was flourishing. Many slaves came from Portuguese-controlled territory but many, if not more, came from the market of Cassange in Kasanje and from the highlands of Benguela through Kakonda. Since there were no mines, slaves were Angola's wealth and before 1641 it had already been discovered that Angola's black gold was essential to Portuguese America. In the next century Angola was to become practically a colony of Brazil.

The Internal Organization of Angola Around 1700

By the end of the century, the colony—the first substantial one in Africa—had acquired an internal political organization which was not to change very much until 1900. Territorially, Angola was divided into *presidios* [captaincies], where a military commander was an absolute ruler. His despotism was mitigated only a little by the presence of a judiciary official and a chaplain. The *presidio* was divided into chiefdoms ruled by the descendants of the old chiefs tributary to the *ngola* of Ndongo, by settled Jaga chiefs, or by former independent chiefs in Kisama. The rights and duties of these chiefs were those of tributaries to their overlord and the pattern of organization was that of the old kingdom of Ndongo, except that all payments were much heavier and that justice was largely replaced by force. The commanders of the *presidio* were the great beneficiaries of the system. The cardinal principle of their policy was to take as much as possible from their subjects, and still avoid a general rebellion. Indeed, whenever Portuguese arms were unsuccessful, such a rebellion followed almost automatically in most *presidios*.

Besides the *presidios,* there were three towns, Luanda, Masangano, and Benguela, ruled by their town councils. Luanda, as the seat of government and the main port of trade, was by far the most important center in the colony. Its town council, the *camara,* carried great political weight, for it would take over government in the absence of a governor and it had to be consulted on all matters of importance by the latter. It was the *camara* who pushed most governors to war—because wars brought slaves.

General authority over the colony lay with the governor, who had to rule according to the general lines of his instructions (*regimentos*) and of further orders from Portugal. But he had to consult the *camara* of Luanda, the bishop, the *ouvidor* or chief justice, and the commander of the army. None of the officials was paid. All were traders and all supplemented their legal revenue by diverting state income. For instance, the governor would receive a large payment from a new chief after he had confirmed his installation; the military had a fixed share in the booty of war, including slaves; the *ouvidor* kept part of the fines; the commanders of the *presidios* kept part of the tribute they collected. All, therefore, including the governor and even the state, found it an advantage to further the slave trade and to oppress the local population. All were tempted—and most succumbed—to graft and to stealing property of the government, etc. The governor could not reform the system: different cases show that if he wanted to exercise any authority at all, he had to fall in line or be expelled by mobs or the military. Most of the terms of the governors in this century were very short, the governors being inexperienced and unable to cope with the entrenched officials. In effect, they were expected to make as much money as possible out of their short tenure, and many seem to have done so.[26]

The whole system, then, was clearly characterized by an unwillingness to turn to resources other than the slave trade, a steady pressure on the borders to expand the *conquista* in the process of acquiring new slaves, and a weak and corrupt central government coupled with a general unruliness of most of the Europeans. The first feature was the explanation of Angola's stagnation throughout the eighteenth and nineteenth centuries, the second made it a predatory state, and the third ensured the continuity of the whole system. From the point of view of the African subject, Angola was sheer terror.

Kongo under Garcia II and Antonio I

When Garcia II came to the throne, he inherited a difficult internal situation. Although matters seem to have improved under Alvare VI, he did not leave a completely pacified and orderly kingdom: the major internal problem was still the defiance by the counts of Soyo. When a new count was elected in Soyo in 1641, he did not ask confirmation of his appointment by Garcia. In return, Garcia appointed his eldest son, Antonio, to the district of Mukatu, which Alvare VI had given to Soyo. War followed after a maneuver by both parties to receive Dutch help. The Dutch remained neutral and the count won a victory in 1645. In a second campaign the next year, the king was again—and more severely—defeated, although the Dutch now sided with him and sent a warship to Mpinda. Finally, peace was made in 1646 and the independence of Soyo recognized by Kongo.

However, hostilities would continue on a small scale until 1650. In that year, for instance, the new duke of Mbamba, a son-in-law of Garcia II, fought against the chief of Funta—a Soyo district. This chief was a son of Alvare VI, who had sought refuge with the counts. The episode shows how different strands in internal politics—the hostility between Kongo and Soyo and the rivalry between Garcia and the sons of his predecessor, structurally a normal feature—tended to merge and form an over-all dichotomy. From now on, Soyo would be the refuge for the opposition faction at San Salvador.

Garcia II had other internal difficulties. He had to call on Dutch troops to quell a revolt by the district chief of Nsala, which shows serious weakness. When he wanted to remove another son of Alvare VI, who was governor of Nsundi, he had to appoint his man to a district within Nsundi. He did this in 1649, and in response the duke apparently fomented a revolt within the district which involved as many as 20,000 to 30,000 men in 1651, though it ended with the victory of the district head. Only then could the duke be removed and replaced, exactly ten years after Garcia's accession to the throne! The former duke was executed in 1652.

In 1654 the marquis of Mpemba, a son of Pedro II and a brother of Garcia I, who had hopes for the succession, revolted when he heard that Garcia II tried to impose his eldest son, Affonso, as his successor. But he was unsuccessful and fled to Soyo. Two years later the new marquis of Mpemba revolted and was beheaded. In 1657 the struggle for Garcia's succession began in earnest. Antonio, the second son, had been named marquis of

Mpangu and began an attack on the duke of Nsundi, a partisan of the elder son. The duke had to give ground and retreated in 1659 to the other side of the Inkisi River. In that year, or in 1660, the faction of Antonio succeeded in convincing Garcia that Affonso planned to murder him, and Garcia ordered his execution. When the king finally died in 1661, Antonio succeeded him and immediately started to prosecute and to kill all close relatives of his elder brother. In 1662, Antonio's uncle revolted, and in 1664 the duke of Wandu and the ruler of Ambwila rebelled and became vassals of Portugal, which led to the general war of Angola against Kongo.[27]

There was, then, no complete peace at any period in the reign of either Garcia II or Antonio I. Cavazzi reports on the internal situation at that time.[28] A number of natural calamities, such as invasions of locusts as well as famine, had struck the kingdom in 1642, 1643, 1654, 1658, 1662, and 1664, and an epidemic of pestilence was reported from 1655 to 1657, one so virulent that it is said to have halved the population. An earlier epidemic had already struck in 1645. Cavazzi also noted the injustices of the courts.[29] Judges could be bought and nobles would very often arrest and bind lesser persons or take their goods without any court decisions. The officers and the chiefs at all levels abetted rebellions. Every third year, when tribute had to be brought to the capital, local revolts erupted. If the king could not crush them, his prestige suffered; if he punished them, the violence bred more violence. The collection of tribute was itself often accompanied by violence. The farmers would chase the collectors away if they were not protected by soldiers; and the tribute collectors and their retinue often treated the people as enemies, and many nobles asked the king not to send the collectors, but to let them collect because there was less damage to the people. Finally, about 15,000 slaves a year were now exported to America. In practice, then, the common people were in revolt against the chiefs and the royal collectors, and the lesser chief against the more important ones of noble blood—the *infantes* who were now so numerous that they occupied all important district positions.

The *infantes* were divided between *kimulazu* and *kimpanzu* and into lesser factions within those groups. Garcia had asked the pope to rule that the succession to the throne would be regulated by primogeniture only. Once again the Vatican rejected the proposal but announced that in case of conflict the electors might be assisted by three or four clerics to watch over the legality of the election.[30] This decision left the door open for a succession crisis and, when it came, the general situation was such that the kingdom would collapse. It did not under Garcia and Antonio only by sheer force, diplomacy, and terror.

The external situation of Kongo has already been described in those years. Up to 1648 there was an alliance with the Dutch and then a desperate struggle to resist Angolan encroachment. The peace treaty was signed in 1657 and all clauses which would damage Kongo's independence were removed. This was certainly a great feat when it is realized how unstable the internal position was within the kingdom. After that date Garcia and Antonio were accused regularly of trying to send emissaries to Spain for an expeditionary force to be sent to Kongo; it was said that with these troops, and an alliance between Nzinga and the Dembo, Angola could be attacked. No proof was forthcoming of all this, but it was clear that the colonists in Angola wanted war. In 1658 an impending expedition was justified on the general grounds that Garcia did not honor the treaty, that he gave asylum to fugitive slaves, and that he levied tolls on the trade. The real reason was that Angola needed wars because they bred slaves. Finally, after 1663 the crisis came to a head when the governor of Angola was prompted by his king to find copper and gold mines, which were needed to pursue the war with Spain. The governor asked for the mines but Antonio refused to hand them over. When the duke of Wandu, on whose land the mines lay, asked to become a vassal of Portugal—just when a Portuguese force had occupied his capital—Antonio knew that there was to be a war and mobilized all his forces for it. Despite the troubled condition of the kingdom, contingents from all provinces—except Soyo—came. The battle at Ulanga was fought in October 1665. Four hundred nobles, among them ninety-eight chiefs, died when Antonio—some say treacherously—was killed toward the end of the battle at the moment when the Portuguese were being defeated. The Portuguese army took samples from the mines at Embu and then retreated to Angola.[31]

In 1645 the first Italian Capuchins landed in Soyo, the beginning of a serious missionary effort which was to last until about 1700.[32] Since the bishopric was vacant, the Capuchins arrived at a good moment. They were well received, for they were Italians and not Portuguese. Several more groups arrived, and by 1651 there were thirty priests. In sharp contrast to their predecessors, the Capuchins also undertook to missionize in the provinces. Garcia II supported them fully at first, for one reason because he wanted support from the Holy See in the matter of the succession, and later because the Capuchins were the best mediators between him and the Portuguese. It would also seem that, like Affonso, Garcia was a convinced Christian, yet very soon it became apparent that there was to be no mass conversion. First, many nobles were afraid that Christianity meant the loss of all traditional usages and of course the destruction of the kingdom. Then the Capuchins, using the full support of the king, began to burn fetishes and even to arrest "convicted fetish-doctors," who were then condemned to death—which set the pagan rural population against them. They also alienated Garcia when the prefect accused the king of leading an unchristian life in 1654. The king, probably aided by the Jesuits, who resented the intrusion of the Capuchins in their mission, retaliated by accusing the Capuchins of hiding weapons and being "pro-Spanish," but he withdrew the accusations the year after. Yet relations between the king and the missionaries slowly grew so much worse that the pope wrote a letter in 1660 to ask Garcia II to help stamp out the unchristian vice in his kingdom. When the king died, the Capuchins almost rejoiced, but Antonio also saw them as agents of Luanda, as had his father in his later years. One effect of the quarrel was to give a probably much overdone bad reputation in history to both Garcia II and Antonio I. By 1665, however, because of the missions in the provinces, the missionary effort had progressed much farther then ever before. If it had not been for the mortality of the Brothers and for the chaos which reigned after 1667 and until 1710, Kongo well may have been converted to Catholicism in half a century or so.

The Transformation of the Kingdom of Kongo, 1665–1710

After the death of Antonio I, a wave of xenophobism swept throughout Kongo. The election of a new king was not complicated by strife, although there was more than one competitor, and Alvare VII became king in 1666. He immediately tried to contact Luanda about a peace treaty, but some months later he was murdered by the count of Soyo, who put an Alvare VIII on the throne. The resulting war was savage and the nobles of Alvare VII's faction were treated with great cruelty. The wife of the marquis of Mpangu, for instance, was paraded naked through the streets of Mpinda and nearly sold as a slave. Violent acts like these bred violence, and the mounting exasperation between the enemy factions in the kingdom made a reconciliation impossible. In 1667 the negotiations with Luanda failed because there was no gold in the sample of ore their delegate had brought back from Kongo, and two new factions had elected kings—an Affonso II in Mbamba and a Pedro III in Kongo dia Lemba (or Bula) in western Mpangu. The battle would be carried on mainly between those two factions plus a third one led by candidates who in general resided in San Salvador and were backed by the count of Soyo. In 1678 San Salvador was completely destroyed and Soyo started to back the royal faction from the south—from Nkondo in Mbamba—which had now moved its seat to Kibangu. But there were splits within the Kibangu group and it was only in 1709 that a Pedro IV from Kibangu occupied San Salvador after the defeat of his last competitor, Pedro Constantino Kibenga. It was not until 1715 that João III, successor to Pedro III of Bula, submitted to the new king.

In the meantime, all the major provinces had gone to pieces as well. There was competition for the titles of Mbata, Mbamba, and Nsundi, and the provinces were divided. Even in Soyo the general revolt of everybody against everybody else with authority was felt, and several dukes were murdered in rapid succession by the people or by their opponents. When the kingship was reunified in 1710, it meant that the king had lost all power and that the kingdom of Kongo had now become a sort of Holy Roman Empire with small, even tiny, chiefdoms which recognized a far away and impotent ruler and which at the same time kept alive the dream of the wide-flung kingdom as it had once been.[33]

Why and how did this catastrophe happen? The conditions for such a breakdown have already been described when the internal situation of the kingdom under Garcia II is remembered. It is clear from the sources, which are now fairly numerous, how the disintegration of authority came about. The *kimulazu* group challenged the *kimpanzu* group, but it was not a simple cleavage between two lineages. Marriages among the royal line had been endogamous to the point that references to marriages forbidden by the Canon Law are mentioned because they united first cousins. The closely-knit royal group now fell apart in a set of smaller groups led by strong personalities surrounded by their brothers, their sisters, and their mothers and a retinue. They fought against all others and would ally themselves with any other similar group who happened to fight against a common enemy—and alliances could shift rapidly. It is because of this structure of the power groups that the civil war could not cease with a simple victory. An example of the working of this factionalism is the case of Pedro Constantino's career. In the 1690's he and his brother Alexis belonged to a faction led by their aunt, Dona Anna Leão, daughter of Garcia II. In 1691 both of them supported their cousin Manuel, of the same faction, but they turned against him in 1693 and killed him. In 1696 Dona Anna, with the support of her cousin Pedro de Valle Lagrimas and the son-in-law of the latter, attacked Alexis and killed him. Pedro Constantino offered his services at Lemba to the other great faction of nobles, who supported João III, brother of Pedro III. He was not accepted there, so he turned to Kibangu where Pedro IV, Agua Rosada, accepted him, and he became the commander of his army. Then, in 1704, when he was sent to conquer San Salvador, he proclaimed himself king and remained in the capital until the battle of 1709, when he was killed by Pedro IV.

The disintegration of authority certainly affected other aspects of Kongo society, even if those changes are not mentioned in the sources. Repercussions on the value system are preserved in missionary reports about a heresy of the so-called Antonians. Around 1700 a woman prophet began to claim that she was in contact with heaven and especially with St. Anthony and that it was her mission to find the man who would bring an end to the wars and restore the kingship. In this she was not unlike Joan of Arc. But her teaching was also pervaded with elements which are now attributed to modern movements such as the so-called African "Zionist churches." She said that Christ was black and that heaven was for the Africans, that people should not listen to the foreign missionary but to her and to her catechists. The movement was finally stopped when the prophetess was condemned and burned for heresy.[34] But the Antonian heresy shows how great the strain of all these wars was for the common people, just as it showed how deeply Christianity had penetrated into the Kongolese mentality—and thus attests to the effectiveness of the Capuchin mission.

This phase of Kongo's history may be seen as a period of decay or as a breakdown. Yet it can be examined more fruitfully as a period of transmutation when one political system with its links in the social structures was suddenly uprooted and became something else—a new system with a new dynamism and new social links. It is only thus that one can explain how the new system was to live in Kongo for another two centuries and more. The mutation process itself is one of the very few instances where such a phenomenon is documented in Africa and therefore should be fascinating to historians and anthropologists alike.

The States of
Katanga and Northern Rhodesia
from 1700 to 1850

In the eighteenth century, in the area occupied by the Luba and Lunda in Katanga and Northern Rhodesia, the main events were the founding and the development of the kingdom of Kazembe on the banks of the Luapula as well as continued expansion of the southern Lunda, and the development of the Lozi kingdom. By 1800 the main powers in this area were the Lunda kingdom of *mwaant yaav*, the main Luba kingdom, the kingdom of Kazembe, and the Lozi state. A casual observer would see the history of this period as a process of expansion by all those states and a balance of power between them, not unlike the balance of power which existed between the different European states from the sixteenth to the nineteenth centuries; but this interpretation does not stand up to the facts. There was no balance of power, there was no over-all domination of one state, there was no dichotomy between the states in a system of alliances—in other words, the area was not one supranational field for power competition. The reason lies in the structures of these states, all of which had a nucleus which was tightly controlled by the central government, and all of which had outlying provinces, where the authority and power of the central government faded away more and more the farther one went from the center toward the boundaries. Thus boundaries between the states were vague, sometimes even overlapping, and there was little conflict of power between the states, since their respective forces on the common border areas were so weak. Yet the history of these states is best grouped into one chapter because they shared common cultural and economic ties and probably influenced each other in other respects than purely political ones. This era ends in the period from 1840 to 1900, when newcomers from outside this area begin to alter the political conditions to a very great extent.

The Main Luba Kingdom[1]

Around 1700 Mwine Kadilo succeeded on the throne of Kalala Ilunga, and with his succession the first attempts at expansion of this kingdom, more than a century after its foundation, are recorded. The recorded sources do not enable us to see why it took so long before such a drive for expansion manifested itself. Kadilo fought many Songye groups, especially the Been' Ekiiye and the Beekalebwe, and defeated all of them with the exception of the Beekalebwe; but he did not incorporate any of them into his kingdom. According to V. van Bulck, this *mulopwe* would be responsible for the beginning of important migrations in the valleys of the Lulua and around Lake Mukamba; the defeated Songye would have been displaced to the west and this would have led to a displacement of the Luba Kasai, their neighbors on the west. But there is little evidence so far to substantiate this theory.[2] (See, in general, Map B.)

Kekenya, son and successor of Kadilo, had to fight two of his brothers and their maternal groups, whom he defeated and killed. When he died, his son, Ilunga Sungu, was too young to succeed, so the titleholders installed the son of one of the brothers, who had rebelled, Kumwimba Kaumbo. The new king renewed his attacks on the Songye but was defeated by the Baamilembwe, who were at that time pushing to the southeast of Songye territory. In the confusion of defeat, the king was lost and his son Miketo appointed king. The father came back, however, whereupon Miketo killed Kumwimba. The titleholders then appointed Ilunga Sungu, the son of Kekenya, who defeated Miketo and another faction led by Miketo's brother. Ilunga Sungu was a great raider. He defeated the Kalundwe of Mutombo Mukulu, although he could not integrate them into his state. He raided the area between Lualaba and Lake Tanganyika and received tribute from the founder of the Kyombo Mkubwa chiefdom, a Tumbwe foundation on the Luvua; however, he had to cope with various revolts within his kingdom, but crushed all of them.

His son Kumwimba Ngombe succeeded and is also known as a great warrior. He campaigned on the Lualaba in the northeast and conquered some chiefdoms due east of the river. He also made war in Lomotwa country, where the original chiefdoms were made tributary. Finally, he settled warriors near Kiambi on the Luvua to protect his conquests from the "Bemba"—probably the peoples from Kazembe—and all the chiefdoms between Kiambi and Mulongo just below Lake Kisale were made tributary. His razzias to the south reached Lake Bangweolu, from where he brought back a king's daughter to Mulongo, and her son became the first chief tributary to the Luba. He also organized a chiefdom of Buli in the angle between the Lukuga and the Lualaba. In the area of Kongolo, one of his war captains, with his followers, created different Luba chiefdoms, but they then broke away from the kingdom and could not be forced to pay tribute. With Kumwimba Ngombe the kingdom reached a peak in its expansion.

His immediate successor, Ndai a Mujinga, was killed by his brother, Ilunga Kabale. Ilunga Kabale had to make war in the heart of the kingdom on other pretenders and on Luba groups who revolted. Later in his reign he was constantly directing expeditions to quell revolts among the tributaries and to organize the newly acquired territories, but evidently he did not find a formula to integrate these elements effectively within the kingdom. He died, either around 1850 or somewhat earlier. In the 1860's Tippu Tib heard about him: "A long time ago we heard from our elders that the paramount chief of Urua, by name Kumanbe [Kumwimba] and afterwards Runga Karbare [Ilunga Kabale] ruled over the whole of the Urua as far as Mtoa [on Lake Tanganyika], including the Manyema [southern Maniema] country and the banks of the Rumami [Lomami river]. Over all this he had waged war and reached Utetera [southeastern Kusu]. . . ." And: "At the time Rungu Kabare had been chief, he had been the most powerful of the Warua chiefs and he was the paramount. He had waged war in all the areas of Manyema, only Lake Tanganyika halted him. . . . After his death, there were many children and there was fighting. Their power diminished and at this time [1870] the chief was Kasongo Karombo [Kalombo]."[3]

Tradition confirms Tippu Tib. Five sons of Ilunga Kabale fought for the paramountcy and eventually Kasongo Kalombo emerged as king. With him the kingdom was practically reduced to the size it had been at Kekenya's death, and also during his reign the intrusion of coastal Arab and Nyamwezi traders had changed the whole political geography of Katanga (see Chart II).

The main features of Luba history in this period, then, are two: the tendency for expansion and the increasing frequency of civil wars over the succession to the throne. The evident military superiority over all the surrounding chiefdoms was never consolidated by an organized assimilation, and there may be several reasons that explain this. First, many of these wars were nothing more but razzias; also, the technique of settling surveyors and granting titles to subdued chiefs was not often used. In the few cases when Luba warriors were settled among tributaries, they were either assimilated and finally overcome by their subjects, as in the case of Kiambi, or they proclaimed themselves independent, as in the case of the settlements around Kongolo. Finally, the recurrence all through the period of unexpected revolts of Luba groups in the center of the nuclear area of the kingdom shows that there was a serious weakness in the organization of the nucleus itself. The data do not enable us to point to what this weakness was, but it would seem that the strong, localized patrilineal lineage groups retained too many political functions and were only nominally integrated into the state pattern; it seems that practically the whole development of Luba history in this period can be explained in terms of the structural deficiencies of the kingdom. There are, however, two points which remain a mystery: Why did the kingdom, since Kekenya, start to expand, and why did the struggle for the succession since Ilunga Sungu involve only half brothers rather than fathers and sons, as in the previous period? When more is known about Luba history and political structure, answers may be found which will show that these characteristics derived from changes in the structures more than from the accident of character and demography, as the traditional interpretation has it.

The Other Luba Chiefdoms and the Songye and the Luba Kasai

Little is known about the history in this period of the other Luba chiefdoms, such as Kikonja, Kalundwe, or Kaniok. The history of the Songye chiefdoms to the north is equally obscure. They resisted Luba encroachment and seem rather to have themselves encroached on the Luba. It is said that most Songye chiefdoms have lost their traditions as a result of the dislocations caused by the Arab razzias in the 1880's, but this is difficult to believe. Songye history should be of special interest because of the unusual aspect of their political system, with its chiefs and titleholders (as are found among the Luba), but with huge towns rather than isolated villages and with the role of the secret *bukishi* society, which was of paramount political importance as well as supreme religious significance.[4]

West of the Songye, and north of the Kaniok and the Kalundwe, were the Luba Kasai. These were either organized into small chiefdoms or into independent large lineages, where the nesting of smaller lineages in a larger one was found, but not the complementary opposition of lineages at the same genealogical level. During this period in history, and perhaps earlier, these Luba had been slowly expanding, probably lineage by lineage, into the valley of the Lulua and to the southwest into the lands of the Mbagani, Mbal, Kongo, Lwalwa, and even the Sala Mpasu. They encountered Kete groups in the whole territory west of the Lulua and slowly absorbed them. The Kete themselves certainly formed two groups, which can still be recognized by the great differences in their tongue. (It is important to remember that by 1880 the emigrants were still Luba Kasai just like those who had remained in their homeland and that the tribal division between Lulua and Luba, which is so important today, is of later origin.) Reasons for the on-going migrations are found first in the traditions of great famines in the area west of the Lubilash; in addition, in the later wars with the main Luba kingdom; and finally, after 1850, in the disturbances created by the Cokwe and Arab slave raiders. The role of the Kaniok in the history of the Luba Kasai should also not be underestimated. Many groups as far north as Dibaya paid tribute to the Kaniok in the nineteenth century and the central group of the Bakwa Kalonji is said to be of Kaniok origin. The Kaniok are also held responsible by some for the emigrations which are usually linked with the wars in Katanga.

The main results of the migrations of the Luba Kasai were cultural. They introduced the Luba language in the whole of central Kasai and their patrilineal lineage system ousted the matrilineal clan section systems in the area except in the southwest, where the Mbagani and similar groups changed to a dual descent system. More intensive agricultural techniques were introduced in an area where most of the people had formerly been hunters; in addition, Luba religious practices also displaced some of the former rituals.[5]

The Lunda Homeland

After Naweej's death, a short civil war ended with the victory of Muteba, who himself fought against the Sala Mpasu to avenge the death of Naweej. Although he overcame them, he could not incorporate them. He may also have fought the Kaniok with some success, but his reign is remembered for the Lunda expansion to the south under the Lunda chiefs Musonkantanda and Kanongesha, who pushed the boundary of the kingdom so that it included the headwaters of the Zambesi; and for the campaigns of the first Kazembe, who brought the eastern boundary first to the upper Lualaba and then between Lualaba and Luapula. After his death, another Lunda chief, Shinde, founded yet another chiefdom to the far south.

Muteba was succeeded in turn by three of his brothers—Mulaji, Mbala, and Mukanza—who fought against the Kongo, the Kabeya Ilunga, and the Kaniok in the north, but without any lasting success. Mukanza made two important changes in the structure of the kingdom. He gave all the regions east of the Lualaba to Kazembe Kaniembo and made him his near equal; and in his own territory he appointed a governor, the *sanama,* for the whole southern region, who resided in the area of Dilolo. This was a consequence, of course, of the expansion since Muteba's times.

Yaav yaMbany succeeded the brothers. He made a lasting peace with the Kaniok; attacked the Kongo without much success; incorporated the Taba; and killed Kayembe Mukulu, chief of the Luba Samba, but did not succeed in incorporating his lands. It is said that under his reign the Lunda homeland achieved its greatest territorial expansion. Yaav was succeeded by Cikombe Yaav, who surrendered his throne quickly to Naweej II when he saw that he would have to fight pretenders.

Naweej II, who reigned until 1852, defeated three different pretenders and then started a long war against Kabeya Ilunga and took part of their lands. He also went to war against Kongo again and against the southern Kete, but even though his armies were victorious, he did not succeed in incorporating their territory. During this reign, a group of Minungu on the upper Lulua under chief Cimbundu were attacked by Cokwe under Mwa Cisenge, who came from Angola. In a first battle Cimbundu was killed, but his successor killed Mwa Cisenge in the second battle. This stopped the first invasion of the Cokwe in the region of Sandoa. Naweej II intervened and in effect imposed his authority on

the Mwa Cisenge. He also exchanged embassies with Ndumba
Tembwe, the *primus inter pares* of the Cokwe chiefs, making
himself acknowledged as their paramount by all other Cokwe,
and he enforced payment of tribute, against considerable resistance from all the Cokwe chiefs, in the general area of the upper
Kasai. This resistance seems to have flared up in a general revolt
of the Cokwe, but a satisfactory settlement was reached. Naweej
also saw the first European traders reach his capital, the first one
on record being Graça in 1847. From then on, mulattoes, Portuguese traders, and Ovimbundu joined the caravans of the Imbangala and the Ambaca to his capital, and some of them settled on
the lands of *mwaant yaav*. Toward the end of his long reign,
probably in 1845, Naweej repressed a plot in the capital to kill
him. When he died in 1852, the Lunda kingdom and the Lunda
empire generally were at their zenith.[6] It is worth while to re-
mark that even at the height of their power the Lunda were not
able to subject the small groups of Kongo or Sala Mpasu to the
north. It shows to what a great extent conquest depends on the
acquiescence of the conquered.

The Southern Lunda

Around 1700, matrilineal peoples of the Mbwela Nkoya stock,
probably not unlike the Lwimbe, Luchazi, or many Lwena
today, lived on the watershed between Zambesi and Lualaba.
They were overrun by three Lunda chiefs—Musonkantanda,
Shinde, and Kanongesha. Ndembu tradition has it that these
three chiefs separated on a large plain west of Mwinilunga town.
Musonkantanda returned north and settled around Musonoi, and
Kanongesha turned east and Shinde south, each to found a chiefdom.

According to the tradition of the Kanongesha, the first Kanongesha, Nkuba, came with twelve Lunda nobles and their retinue,
and the Lunda overcame the Mbwela, though it probably took a
generation of raiding to achieve this. The gradual expansion of
the area of the new chiefdom ended only when it abutted on the

west on the Zambesi, which was the boundary of the Lwena of Nyakatolo and Cinyama. Once the conquest was achieved, Kanongesha divided the land among the nobles, his own sons, and his matrilineal relatives, setting a large share apart for himself. The twelve subchiefs and the relatives who had received subchiefdoms had to send an annual tribute to Kanongesha, who in turn sent tribute for his chiefdom to the *mwaant yaav*. As for unrelated headmen in the area, they had to send *ntombo* [tributary wives] from their own matrilineage to the court, and the children of these wives later succeeded them and would be Mbwela and Lunda at the same time. After the division of the land had taken place and it was organized, a long period of peace followed. But the local headmen and chiefs became increasingly autonomous from Kanongesha. The tradition reports feuds between local chiefs and between vicinages and villages without intervention from central authority.

Factors responsible for this loss of centralization, according to Turner, were the isolation from the Lunda capital, with its relatively high level of culture; the small density of the population, scattered over a large area; and the low and rudimentary level of economic production associated with small shifting settlements. The spatial mobility of the village contributed considerably to village autonomy. But Turner may have overestimated centralization elsewhere in the Lunda empire and underrated it in Kanongesha's chiefdom, for the factors cited are operative in many parts of the Lunda empire, including the homeland.[7]

The first Shinde, or Ishindi, was Mwenifundi Kasongu, who left after Muteba's death and settled near the Mukulweji River in Katanga, then the frontier area of Lunda. His son Mukandakunda moved to the Lufwiji River in the present area of Ishindi. The next successor, Kazanda, lived for a long time and adopted the title *ishindi*. After his death there was a struggle between three pretenders, who all succeeded for short periods, after which Kazanda's son Kawumbu Sakapepala became a chief and built on the Lufwiji, where Livingstone met him as an old man in 1854.[8]

Musonkantanda I Kiwanakene found Kaonde groups around

Musonoi. The Kaonde tell that they originally were Luba from the north—and they do speak Luba. Three groups came south and crossed the middle Kafue into Ila land, and from there one group, headed by chief Nyoka of the Longa clan, came back north. Another group had gone northwest under Mulima Nzovu and his titleholders. Mulima died on the way and his titleholder, Kainde, settled on the Lwenge, while Mulima's daughter settled near Kansanshi and her son at the salt pans of the Lualaba at Kecila near Kolwezi. Three titleholders—Mushima, Kikando and Musompo—settled in the basin of the upper Lualaba. Mushima traveled to Musumba to ask for a Lunda investiture, with the prestige it entailed, from the *mwaant yaav,* and received the title *ilunga.* But shortly after, Musonkantanda attacked the *ilunga's* settlement on the Lubudi, killed him, and took the title for himself; thus, Mushima's Kaonde became his tributary. Later Musonkantanda went farther east and subdued the Kaonde who lived at the headwaters of the Lualaba and those living in Northern Rhodesia. Melland even feels, probably correctly, that the unity of the Kaonde tribe stems only from their common dependence on Musonkantanda.[9]

These short accounts of the traditions concerning the history of the three southern Lunda chiefdoms show that the conquest in every case seems to have been a rather long process, that the conquerors were adventurers who arrived at different times, settled on the sparsely populated plains, and recognized a paramount chief of their own—probably either the *conquistador* with the biggest following or the man with the prestige derived from a title received at Musumba. It was the continual arrival of new immigrants with their families and retinues together with the very low population density that explains the conquest of the Ndembu of Kanongesha and Shinde. In the case of the Kaonde, who seem to have known a chieftainship on the Luba model, the prestige of the Lunda name attracted one of them to become a Lunda chief, which is a good example of the powerful attraction the Lunda political system exercised on surrounding peoples. Musonkantanda, an adventurer, killed the man, took the title, and was obeyed by his group. In this instance, his successors would have had to overcome one chiefdom after another, whenever the circumstances were favorable.

The Formation of the Kingdom of Kazembe[10]

Just after his accession around 1690, Muteba sent chief Mutanda Yembeyembe—probably his father's brother—to fight a clan head or a chief, Mwin Tibaraka, and his nephew Cinyanta of the centipede (Ciyongoli) clan; they were a fraction of the Kosa who lived west of the Lubudi and would not submit to Lunda rule. It is possible that this war had been going on since the latter days of *mwaant* Yaav Naweej I's rein; in any case, after many years of fighting, Cinyanta capitulated and was then well received by the *mwaant yaav*, at whose capital he remained. During his stay a fire broke out, and the blacksmith Lubunda was accused of having caused it. Lubunda fled to the Luapula where he was taken into the Mbeba [rat] clan and founded a small chiefdom. Some time later a couple arrived at the capital with conus shells (ultimately determined as being from the Indian Ocean) and copper bracelets. The man mentioned the names of chiefs Katanga, Mpande of the Sanga, and many others—including Lubunda—when he explained where he had come from. The Lunda wanted to go to Lubunda and fitted out an expedition, although the real motive may have been to occupy the copper mines and the salt pans. Mutanda Yembeyembe was commanding the expedition and Cinyanta was his *ntikala* [second in command]. The Lunda reached the Lualaba and found there Mwine Mpanda and his nephews, all of them of the Kosa na Ndembu clan. The Lunda army was overwhelmingly superior in numbers and Mwine Mpanda surrendered. He became a Lunda ally and led the Lunda to the Kecila, where there were big salt pans on the Lualaba, and where they defeated chief Cibwidi, who had command over the salt pans. After that the whole population west of the upper Lualaba accepted Lunda's rule. Cinyanta, who had spearheaded the Lunda advance, arrived at the salt pans first and tried to send a sample of the salt to the *mwaant yaav*, but Mutanda intercepted all his couriers. Finally, a messenger of Cinyanta smuggled some salt through and denounced Mutanda at the capital. Mutanda was recalled but was able to justify his conduct and returned to the Lualaba. Cinyanta also arrived at the capital and received the special insignia of Lundahood together with Mwine Mpanda, Cibwidi, and a man named Mpande wa Mwombe. When Cinyanta also returned to the Lualaba, Mutanda arrested him and then drowned him in the Mukuleshi, after two tentative evasions. (This happened probably around 1710.)

The children of Cinyanta complained to Muteba, and the council of Lunda decided to invest Cinyanta's son, Nganda Bilonda, with the title of "Kazembe" and gave him orders to kill Mutanda Yembeyembe. Mutanda heard about this decision, however, and fled somewhere to the south. (It was in these years and the next that Musonkantanda, Kanongesha, and Shinde made their conquests, while to the north of the Kecila, Mafunga and others organized smaller chiefdoms to stop a southward advance of the Luba Samba.)

Nganda Bilonda organized the administration of the conquered territory between Lubudi and the Kecila until his sons were grown. He crossed the Lualaba, then, and went through the lands of the Sanga, Lomotwa, and Lamba after having left chief Cisenge on the Lualaba near Kecila with the title of "Kazembe of the Lualaba." When the Lunda, after having crossed Sanga and Lembwe territory, arrived in Lomotwa land, they were stopped by chief Mufunga, who received support from Luba troops. The Lunda were put on the defensive and dug fortifications, but after two days of fighting the Lomotwa were defeated and Mufunga was killed. Very soon afterward, Kazembe Nganda Bilonda died also (Lunda tradition attributes his death to a vengeance by the ghost of Mufunga).

Immediately after his death, a succession crisis broke out between Naweej, the brother of Nganda Bilonda, and Kaindu, the officer who had killed Mufunga. The contestants withdrew to the Lualaba, where they buried Nganda Bilonda, and went from there to Musumba to settle the matter. The *mwaant yaav,* Mukanza, invested Kaniembo, Nganda Bilonda's son, elevating him to a rank equal to his own, and the Lunda territories were divided between the *mwaant yaav* and Kazembe II.

According to the Kazembe version, it is only at this time that the southern Lunda chiefs were sent out together with Mushidi, a member of Cinyanta's family, who was to organize a chiefdom near Solwezi. Ndole, also a member of Cinyanta's family, received a chieftainship, as did Mukonkoto, a follower of Cinyanta. Musonkantanda, Mushidi, Ndole, and Mukonkoto also received titles of "Kazembe," but they were never the equal of the *mwaant yaav.*

Kazembe Kaniembo set out for the Lualaba, where he married Mwonga, the daughter of Cibwidi, the Luba head of the salt pans at Kecila, and there he organized his army for a whole year. He then crossed the Lualaba and took the field against the Sanga chief, Mutombo Kola, whom he defeated, but he spared his life since Mutombo said that he also came from Lunda. Kaniembo then went into Lamba land and Lemba land and defeated chiefs Katanga, Mutondo, Mpoyo, Cembe, and Kaponda, all local clan heads of some importance, and the other headmen in the area began to surrender and to send tribute. The last one to be defeated was Kapwasa of the snake (Nsoka) clan, who lived on the banks of the Luapula.

But when Kazembe was in that chiefdom, he learned that the Luba had sent an army to stop his progress. This army was reinforced with Lunda deserters who were followers of Kasombola (the younger brother of Cinyanta, who had also been killed by Mutanda Yembeyembe along with Cinyanta). Kapwasa helped the Lunda, the Luba were driven off, and the captured deserters and their commanders were formally deprived of their Lundahood. After this battle, the chiefs of Lomotwa in the area of Mpweto and all the smaller chiefs of the west bank of the Luapula sent tribute. The whole country between Lualaba and Luapula as far north as the Lomotwa and as far south as the Lamba was subjected.

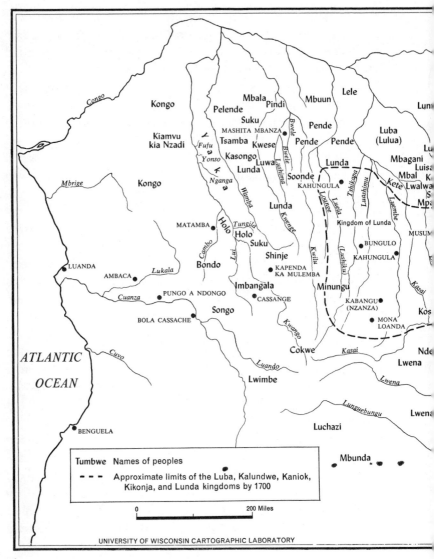

A The Luba-Lunda States by 1700

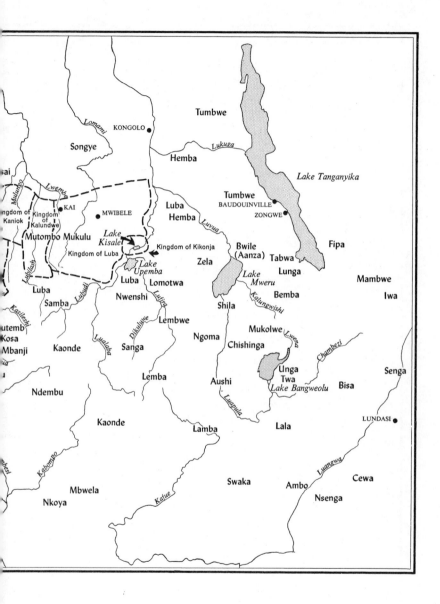

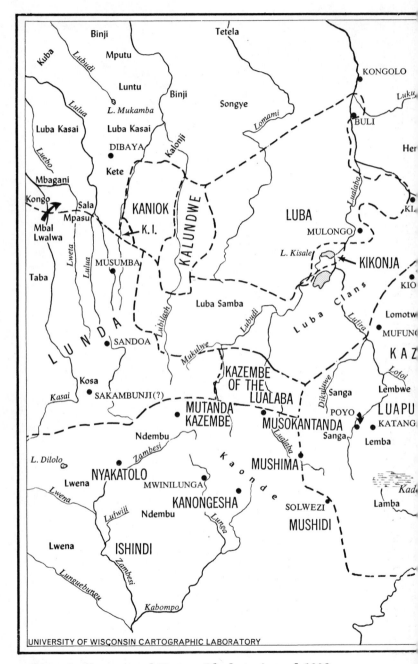

B States in Katanga and Eastern Rhodesia Around 1800
Note: The names of places are often identical with the names of the chi...

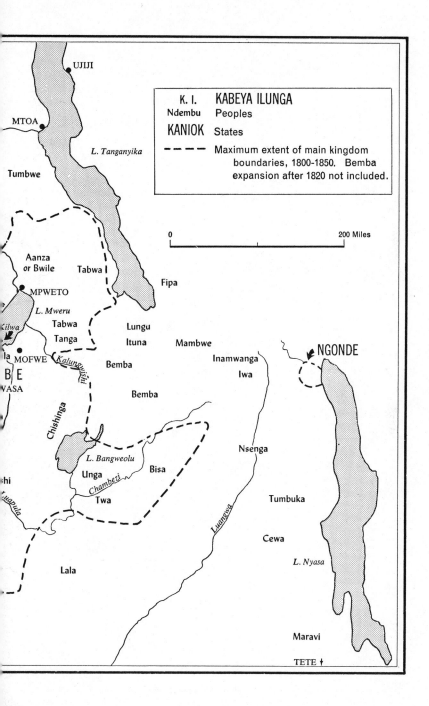

UJIJI

MTOA

L. Tanganyika

Tumbwe

K. I.   **KABEYA ILUNGA**
Ndembu Peoples
KANIOK States
– – – – Maximum extent of main kingdom
         boundaries, 1800-1850. Bemba
         expansion after 1820 not included.

0   200 Miles

Aanza
or Bwile   Tabwa
                    Fipa
MPWETO
L. Mweru
        Tabwa   Lungu
ilwa Tanga   Ituna   Mambwe
la MOFWE *Kalun...*   Inamwanga   NGONDE
B E   Bemba   Iwa
VASA
                 Bemba
Chishinga
            L. Bangweolu   Nsenga
hi   Unga   Bisa
        Chambezi   Tumbuka
            Twa
uanula   *Luangwa*   Cewa
                                                    L. Nyasa
        Lala

                                           Maravi

                                           TETE †

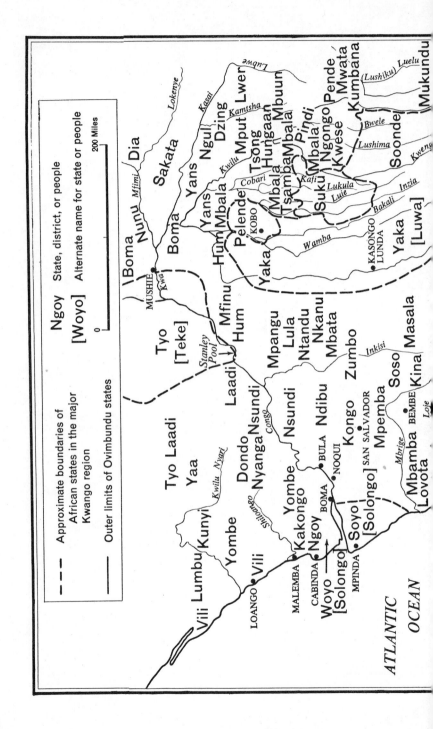

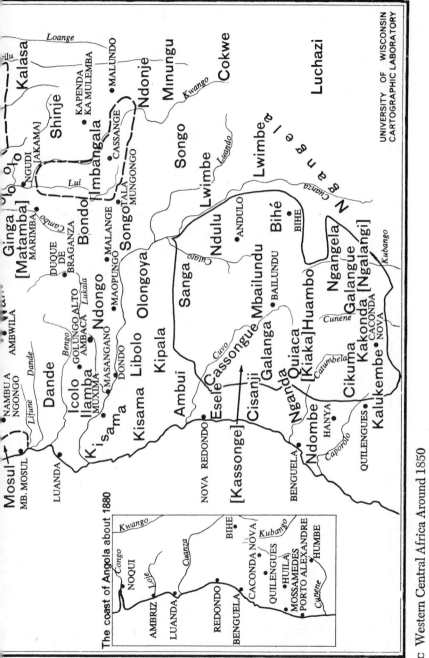

The coast of Angola about 1880

Kwango
Congo
NOQUI
Loie
AMBRIZ
LUANDA
Cuanza
REDONDO
BENGUELA
CACONDA NOVA
QUILENGUES
HUILA
MOSSAMEDES
PORTO ALEXANDRE
BIHE
Kubango
Cunene
HUMBE

Mosul
MB. MOSUL
NAMBU A NGONGO
AMBWILA
LUANDA
Dande
Lifune
Dande
Bengo
Icolo
Ilamba
GOLUNGO ALTO
AMBACA
Lukala
MUXIMA
MASANGANO
DONDO
Kisama
Libolo
Kipala
Olongoya
Ambui
NOVA REDONDO
Esele
Cassongue
[Kassonge]
Cisanji
Sanga
Ndulu
Cuvo
Galanga
Nganda
Ndombe
BENGUELA
Quiaca
HANYA
Caporolo
[Kiaka]
Huambo
QUILENGUES
Cunene
Catumbela
Cikuma
Kalukembe
Galangue
CACONDA NOVA
Kakonda [Ngalangi]
Ngangela
BIHE
Bihé
BAILUNDU
Mbailundu
ANDULO
Songo
Lwimbe
Lwimbe
Lwimbe
Ngangela
Kubango

Mosul
Ginga [Matamba]
Oto [AKAMA]
NGUDI
Shinje
KAPENDA KA MULEMBA
MALUNDO
Kalasa
Loange
Lui
Cambo
MARIMBA
Imbangala
CASSANGE
Bondo
DUQUE DE BRAGANZA
Ndongo
MAOPUNGO
MALANGE
Songo
Tala
MUNGONGO
Ndonje
Minungu
Kwango
Cokwe
Luando
Cuanza
Luchazi

Maopungo
Cuito
Cunene

UNIVERSITY OF WISCONSIN
CARTOGRAPHIC LABORATORY

c Western Central Africa Around 1850

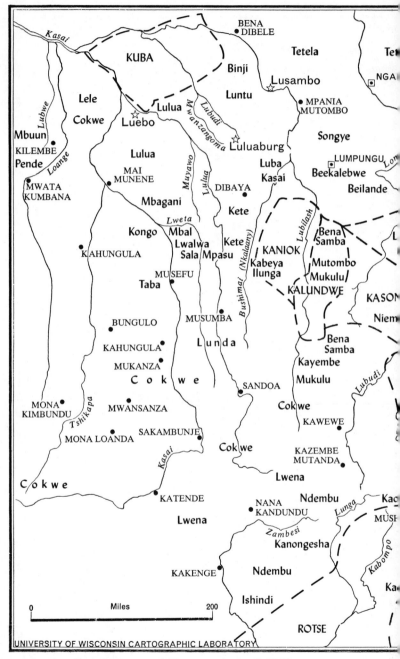

D The Peoples of Kasai and Katanga Around 1890

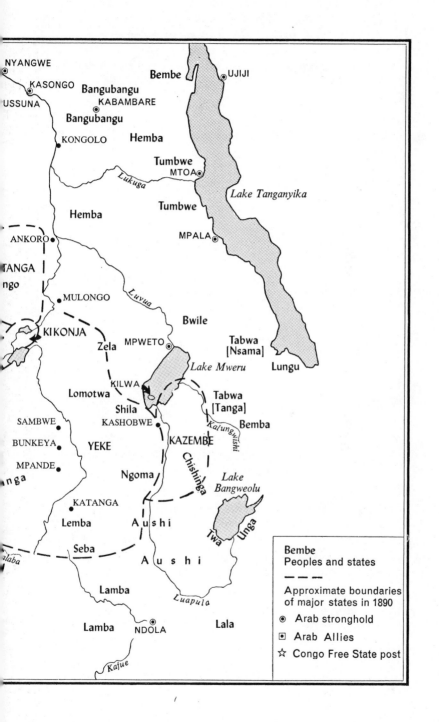

NYANGWE

KASONGO

USSUNA

Bembe

UJIJI

Bangubangu

KABAMBARE

Bangubangu

KONGOLO

Hemba

Tumbwe

MTOA

Lukuga

Hemba

Tumbwe

Lake Tanganyika

ANKORO

TANGA

ngo

MPALA

MULONGO

Luvua

Bwile

KIKONJA

Zela

MPWETO

Lake Mweru

Tabwa
[Nsama]

Lungu

KILWA

Lomotwa

Shila

KASHOBWE

Tabwa
[Tanga]

Kalungwishi

Bemba

SAMBWE

KAZEMBE

BUNKEYA

YEKE

MPANDE

Chishinga

*Lake
Bangweolu*

nga

Ngoma

KATANGA

Lemba

A u s h i

Twa

Unga

Seba

A u s h i

laba

Lamba

Luapula

Lamba

NDOLA

Lala

Kafue

Bembe
Peoples and states

— — —

Approximate boundaries
of major states in 1890

◉ Arab stronghold

▣ Arab Allies

☆ Congo Free State post

After a year, the army of Kaniembo crossed the Luapula just north of Johnston Falls and went on to fight the Aushi, who were under their chiefs Kalaba and Myelemyele (or Cawala Makumba). Kashiba I, the first titleholder of Kazembe, went with the first army and killed Kalaba but was defeated and killed by Myelemyele. His deputy commander Mulanda carried on with the fight until Kaniembo came to the rescue with the rest of the army. Myelemyele was killed, and *makumba*—the fetish of the Aushi—was "neutralized" after an epidemic had broken out in the Lunda army and after Kaniembo had "married" *makumba* to placate it. After the Aushi war, Kashiba II was placed on the Luapula to rule the Aushi, and Kaniembo went further east, where he defeated the Bisa and Chishinga. Mwine Mpanda, one of the chiefs conquered by Mutanda, was left to rule the Chishinga area but was killed in a battle with Cungu, the ruler of the Mukulu. Kaniembo counterattacked with the main army, Cungu was killed, and the Mukulu surrendered.

Kazembe then went downstream to fight the Shila, whose chief bore the title *nkuba*. First he attacked Katele, nephew of the paramount *nkuba*, and took the area of Lunde where Katele ruled. During the attack, Kaniembo's brother—and possible successor—Cinaweej (or Naweej), was killed on purpose by Kaniembo's own men because the Kazembe suspected him of plotting his death. Katele escaped in the swamps, where the Lunda could not follow him. Kaniembo now decided to build a capital at Lunde and he proceeded with the ritual ceremonies of the installation. Many Lunda were homesick and realized the Kazembe was determined to stay in this faraway country; some tried to desert, but Kaniembo had guarded the ferries of the Luapula so that, willing or not, they had to stay. Soon after this Kaniembo died and was buried near the Lunde River.

Toward the end of Kaniembo's life, one of his sons tried to take his father's throne, but failed, and he then fled back to the Kecila with the intention of cutting communication between his father and the *mwaant yaav*. However, he was killed by a small headman. As an indirect consequence of this affair, troops were sent by both the *mwaant yaav* and the Kazembe to this area, and another of the Kazembe's sons, Mukenji, leader of the army, revolted, becoming "Kazembe of the Lualaba." He ruled between Lualaba and Lubudi, north of Musonkantanda, and subjugated even the southernmost Luba Samba clans. In the east he bordered on the Kazembe of the Luapula, whose westernmost districts did not go farther than the valley of the Kikulwe. Kazembe of the Lualaba remained an enemy of Kazembe of the Luapula and also of the *mwaant yaav*. When the later conqueror of Katanga attacked Kazembe of the Luapula in the late nineteenth century, the *mwaant yaav* refused to help him. The different Kazembe's of the Lualaba tried continually to get control over the salt pans of the Kecila but never quite succeeded, although the salt makers did pay them a heavy tribute. Their relations with Cisenge, the chief Nganda Bilonda had appointed near the Kecila, are as yet not clarified.

How was it possible for the Lunda of Kazembe to conquer such a large area without ever losing the final battle? The answer, to begin with, is that the Lunda army was larger than that of their opponents, which were headed generally by small chiefs. Also, the further they went the more contingents of auxiliary troops were given to them by their former adversaries. Mwine Mpanda, a former independent Kosa chief, had become a Lunda—and indeed, Kazembe himself was a descendant of Cinyanta, a non-Lunda. When, during this long campaign, Kazembe had arrived at the Luapula and fought the battle near Kapwasa, the Sanga chief Mutombo Kola was there with Sanga troops to help the Lunda. Their former adversaries were so quick in changing sides because the Lunda did not reject them but rather impressed them with their prestige and their hierarchy and then invested them with the belt of cowskin, the sign of Lundahood. Finally, the Lunda had guns, which had come all the way from Luanda to Cassange and then to Musumba. These frightened their opponents, although actually they inflicted little harm. Their net effect, however, was to dishearten the adversary so much that he often capitulated without further ado. In addition, the Lunda

used techniques of entrenchment and maneuvering which were
probably unknown in this area. The fortifications in Lomotwa
country or the counterattacks by Kaniembo against the Aushi
and the Mukulu are cases to the point.

Kazembe's Kingdom at Its Height (1760–1850)

Kazembe III Ilunga (or Lukwesa) succeeded around 1760. Immediately after his coronation, he crossed the Kalungwishi, east
of Lake Mweru, and went to Tabwa and Lungu land, where all
the chiefs surrendered without battle. He then decided to attack
the Mambwe in order to take their cattle but first sent his mother's brother, Cibamba Kasonkoto, back to the capital with orders
to pursue the war against the Shila, and to capture Katele but
not to kill him. He himself went southeast and defeated a series
of Mambwe chiefs. While on the march, he met emissaries of the
Bemba chief, Mwamba, who greeted him as Mwamba's "uncle,"
reminding him that Mwamba was also a "Lunda," and asked him
not to invade Bemba land—which he promised not to do. From
the Mambwe, Lukwesa went on to the Nsenga and the Inamwanga kingdoms, and to the Ngonde kingdom near Lake Nyasa.
There, says the Lunda tradition, the Kazembe was forced to
build fortifications, but he finally overcame the Ngonde. (The
Ngonde have not recorded anything of this sort in their traditions.) From there Lukwesa came back to Tabwa country where
his son, the future Kazembe IV, Keleka, was born in the area of
the Tabwa chief Nsama. It is not clear from the accounts wheth-
er or not Lukwesa tried to organize all the Tabwa chiefdoms as
part of his kingdom, but later the Tanga fraction of the Tabwa
was certainly tributary to Kazembe. From Tabwa land Lukwesa
returned to his capital.

When he arrived, he found that Cibamba had killed Katele,
against his orders, and thus usurped a royal prerogative, for
which he was punished. Katele died in Lukwesa's capital, and
according to custom it was then necessary to move the capital.
Lukwesa settled his new headquarters near Mofwe lagoon.

Shortly afterward the sister of Nkuba, the paramount of the Shila, came to complain that Nkuba had killed her son. Nkuba Kawama, who had been conducting a successful guerilla warfare until then, was finally killed, with her help, and his land was formally given by his sister to the Lunda. (This episode of their history is, for the Lunda of Kazembe, the charter or their legal ownership of land.) The conquest of the southern Shila kingdom was followed by the conquest of all Shila territory around Lake Mweru.

After that Lukwesa started to organize the conquered territories. The *kalandala* was to rule the former Shila lands and some of the chiefs of the upper Luapula, among whom the Lubunda became *kilolo* and were put under three *kalulua*. The Kashinge ruled Kilwa Island. The Shila chiefdom west of Lake Mweru went to the Musanda, but in these areas no colonies were established because the tribute was paid regularly. A *kalulua* was sent to Mpweto to rule over the Aanza, the northern Shila of Mpweto, and some smaller Luba Hemba groups. The Kasumpa settled on the Kalungwishi in order to control one of the three major Tabwa groups, while the Mwilu was put in command of the area northeast of Lake Bangweolu. The whole region west of Luapula came under the Kashiba, who built a capital, "Kalundwe," on the Lofoi in Lembwe country and ruled mainly over Lembwe and Lomotwa. Far in the west, Cisenge, "Kazembe of the Lualaba," kept in touch with Kashiba. The Mulanda ruled the Aushi; the Mwine Mpanda the Chishinga, Mukulu, and the Bisa north of the Chambezi. The Lungu paid tribute of their own accord and no colonies were made. The same was true for the two remaining major Tabwa groups. All the Lunda chiefs organized the sending of tribute to the capital and Kazembe regularly sent gifts to the *mwaant yaav*. (This somewhat tedious description shows the thoroughness of this whole organization and the time it must have taken to set it up and have it function properly.)

Around 1790, when the Bisa were conquered, Lukwesa heard about the Portuguese at Tete and tried to come into contact with them. Trade relations with the settlers around Tete were established, and in 1798–1799 a major Portuguese expedition visited the country. The Kazembe refused to let it go through to Musumba and then to Cassange but kept the Portuguese in his capital. Despite this setback, trade developed rapidly, and soon Kazembe's capital was a regular terminus of a route to Lake Nyasa and then to Kilwa as well as of the route to Tete.

Kazembe Lukwesa died in October 1805. His son Kibangu Keleka, or Kazembe IV, took the name Kaniembo on his accession. The first year of his reign he toured around the eastern and northern parts of his country in order to subdue recalcitrant tributaries. At the end of 1806 two *pombeiros* from Angola, Pedro Baptista and Anastasio José, arrived at his capital and remained there until 1810. During their stay, the Kazembe had to fight the Tanga Tabwa and could not open the route to Tete, which was blocked by a rebellion of some Bisa chiefs. In 1807 he also had difficulties with his brother Kapaka, who coveted the throne. Later, at an unknown date sometime before 1830, a great Luba army came to the Luapula under the command of Nkumbula Mwine Kabende and Bitentu, but they were ambushed in the Luapula swamps and exterminated. (This was the third and last Luba army to attack the Kazembe's.) In 1830–1831 the Kazembe was visited by another Portuguese expedition led by Monteiro and Gamitto, and Gamitto (see note 10) has left a very full description of the kingdom at the time. After their departure and around 1840, Mwamba, the Bemba chief of Tuna province and the first titleholder of the Bemba, came with the *citimukulu* to ask the Kazembe for help against their enemies and were given war magic and kaolin. (The *citimukulu* was Cileshye Cepela, the founder of the present line of Bemba kings and chiefs, who was then fighting to establish his supremacy.) At this moment the Bemba had been expanding to the south in Bisa country since 1825. After this episode Keleka had to fight his heir apparent, who wanted to take the throne. He killed him and then he himself died somewhat later, around 1850.

During his reign it is reported that the *mwaant yaav* sent a great caravan with all sorts of goods which had been unknown in the Luapula valley before. Slit drums, xylophones, and statuettes are specifically mentioned. One may add that such important culture traits as the cultivation of manioc and raphia palms had already been introduced earlier by the Lunda in this area. The kingdom of Kazembe certainly introduced many other new customs in the valley directly from Lunda and indirectly by opening routes to the east African coast.

The same tradition about the caravan sent by the *mwaant yaav* goes on to tell that a caravan with countergifts was sent to the *mwaant yaav*, but that its commander was killed by the *mwaant yaav*, who was displeased with the gifts. However, a second caravan was more successful. This story and the report of the *pombeiros* seem to indicate, contrary to Luapula tradition, that the *mwaant yaav* still looked upon the Kazembe as one of his tributaries and not as an equal.

Keleka's successor, Mwonga Mfwama, an older man, evicted a challenger, Cinyanta Munona, who fled to Musumba (the capital) of the *mwaant yaav*. Mwonga took the name of Kazembe V Kapumb. He made war on the Shila in the area of Mpweto—who had killed Kasumpa, the surveyor of the Kalungwishi area. Kashinge, the governor of Kilwa Island, had been sent against the Shila but had been killed. The Kazembe mobilized all his troops and beat Mpweto and the Aanza (Bwile) decisively. He then went into the Marungu and defeated Manda Cilonda (a recent Tabwa immigrant in Tumbwe country) at the Mrumbi mountain. He turned west again and subdued the Bwile chiefs of the upper Luvua, after which he went due west into Zela country and defeated their chiefs, Kiona and Mulenge. He appointed a special governor for the Tabwa who was to supervise the Tabwa, second to chief Nsama. During his absence Aushi chiefs had tried to storm the capital but had been beaten off. Later in Kapumb's reign, Kashiba left the Lomotwa and settled again in his first post on the Luapula. On the Lualaba, chief Cisenge (or Cisanda) —or rather his successor, Cilundu—was replaced by a new chief Mpukumbele.

Soon after all these events the Kazembe died accidentally. His successor was to be his former rival, Cinyanta Munona, who came all the way from the capital of the *mwaant yaav*. Meanwhile, Kasau, sister of Cinyanta, took the regency and warded off other rivals for the throne, among them the Kashiba. Cinyanta arrived a year after Kapumb's death and became Kazembe VI, and with him begins the decadence of the kingdom. It would be brought about by a Nyamwezi stranger, Msiri, who arrived in the capital in 1856, and by the recurring struggles for the throne after Cinyanta's death.

The kingdom of Kazembe was probably the greatest in size and the strongest kingdom of all the Luba and Lunda states. From 1750 to 1850 it was paramount in southern Katanga and parts of the northeastern Rhodesian plateau. It brought security to the local populations, who suffered from raids by the Luba clans established further north, and it brought change and novelties to the area. But if the kingdom meant some security for its inhabitants, it also implied the payment of heavy taxes, some unwarranted cruelty by Lunda governors, and a restriction on the liberty of action of many clans which had formerly been completely independent. The kingdom was built on the prestige and the attraction of the Lunda political system. It would be destroyed by a withdrawal of support and by the flaws in the succession practices of the same system.

The Lozi Kingdom[11]

The Lozi myth of origin tells that the woman Mbuyambwamba was the wife of the creator Nyambe. She lived in Lozi land but left it to go toward the Lunda to Kaumbu, who was then the king of the Lunda. Mbuyambwamba was the daughter of Mwamba—the first woman, and also a wife of Nyambe. From this women all Lozi are descendants. From Mbuyambwamba the royal dynasty has sprung, and also all the cattle, for this woman brought forth at one time a cow and at another a human being. The myth is typical for many Lozi traditions in that more than elsewhere it is a mixture of the etiological and the historically

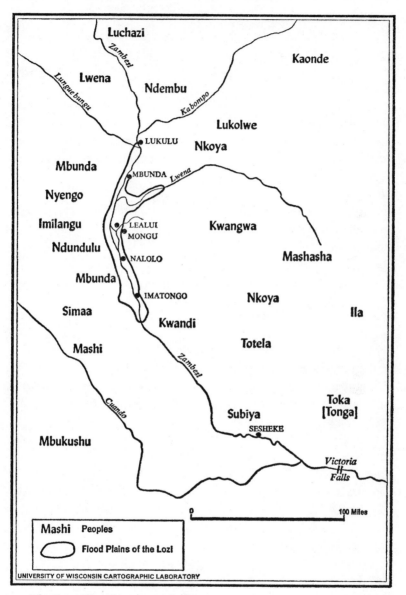

VI The Lozi Kingdom Around 1830

possible.[12] It seems to imply that the Lozi royal dynasty was aboriginal to the flood plain of the Zambesi, but it also establishes a connection with the Lunda. The proverb "The Luyi are of Mbuyambwamba, the Lunda are of Mbuyambwamba" does the same, and so does the fact that artificial mounds, such as those existing on the flood plain, are found on the northwestern tributaries of the Zambesi. The Lozi are the only group in the area who build them, so the mounds to the northwest can be attributed to them.[13] It is possible, then, that the Lozi kingdom was created either by the Lunda patterns or, roughly, after the image of Lunda patterns to the north. If this is true, it must be added immediately that the Lozi have shown considerable ingenuity in working out their institutions, for the political structure of the nucleus of the kingdom, the Lozi flood plain, is very different from the Lunda pattern.[14]

Mbuyambwamba's son Mboo, the first king, may have flourished in the seventeenth century and founded the kingdom before the southern Lunda states were established. When Mboo was living on the flood plain, he once went hunting far in the west and met Isimwa, a king who ruled over a fishing people, the Imilangu and the Ndundulu. He showed Mboo how to ask for tribute in fish and how to organize councils and the tribute system. When Mboo came back with this knowledge, he started to build a state on the pattern Isimwa had shown him. He began the practice of building artificial mounds in the valley to house his capital and other villages, and he fought different peoples in the valley and started a policy of southward expansion. He also quarreled with his younger brother, Mwanambinji. Although the dispute is told in terms of a series of magical contests, its conclusion seems to be that Mwanambinji carved out a small kingdom for himself, first on the eastern side of the flood plain and later in the southern half of the plain, where he subdued peoples like the Subiya and the Mbukushu. He is said to have lived to the time of the fourth Lozi king, Ngalama.

Inyambo, successor and brother of Mboo, is known to have further added to the political institutions and also to have extended the state by defeating the Simaa. His successor, Yeta I, brother of Mbuyambwamba, lived for only a very short time and was followed by Ngalama, the son of Mboo's sister. He was a great warrior and overcame the Kwangwa and the Totela in the east and the Imilangu of Isimwa in the west. He also sent armies against Mwanambinji, who vanished after a series of wars at Imatongo—or in other words who was defeated. Mwanambinji's son Mulia would have fled to Mushidi, one of the chiefs of the southern Lunda.

Ngalama's son, Yeta II, did not even have time to organize a royal herd of cattle or to name his drum capital before he died. His younger brother Ngombela, who succeeded him, divided the country into a northern and a southern half, each with its capital and with a vice royalty at Nalolo, the southern one. Since this happened only a short time after Mwanambinji's disappearance, it may be that the southern half was a transformation of this former kingdom. Ngombela also created a further set of new titles, appointed special chiefs to settlements on the western and southern borders of the kingdom, and organized a system for the recovery of an annual tribute. These reorganizations were in all likelihood the consequences of a further expansion of the kingdom, for Ngombela conquered the Zambesi valley to a point close to Victoria Falls and the Cuando valley, even raiding the cattle of the Tonga far to the southeast. Ngombela died a very old man—and the most important king since Mboo in regard both to the organization of new administrative institutions and to his conquests. His name became the title of the most important official of the state, after that of the king.

Ngombela's three following successors were not very distinguished kings who ruled for rather short periods. Then another great warrior came to the throne. At his accession, Mulambwa faced a great revolt by his tributaries, which he crushed. He then transplanted some Nkoya peoples who had participated in the revolt and placed them in the flood plain, giving their king, Katusi, a seat in the main Lozi council. Near Sesheke in the south he defeated a group led by Mwana Mukasa, probably a Tawana, and pushed the invaders back to the Kalahari. He also fought a protracted war against Cinyama of the Lwena. Although the Lozi sources stress either that the Lwena were rebels or that they were brought into the kingdom at this occasion, it is clear from the general ethnographic situation and from Lwena accounts that this is not correct, although the Lozi probably won a victory over their enemy. Under Mulambwa's reign, two Mbunda chiefs, Mwene Kandala and later Mwene Ciyengele, fled into Lozi land to other Mbunda chiefs and asked asylum. Mulambwa settled Kandala, who had arrived with a small following, and when Ciyengele arrived later, with a large following, Mulambwa at first thought that they came to attack him; but he then settled the newcomers on the woodlands to the east of the plain, where they made themselves useful by driving off isolated Lwena raids. The influence of these Mbunda on the Lozi was very great, at least culturally. Lozi art, for instance, is largely of Mbunda and Lwena inspiration.

Under Mulambwa, some *pombeiros* reached Lozi land. This was not surprising, because trade with the Lwena had been reported since 1795 and the existence of the Lozi kingdom had been known since then in Angola. But Mulambwa, according to Livingstone (see note 11), refused to trade in slaves, and the *pombeiros* did not come back. It is also reported, however, that shortly after Mulambwa's death traders from both the west and east coast visited the kingdom and so did Griqua from the south. If so, it was a prefiguration of the role Rotse land would play after the 1850's.

Mulambwa died around 1835 and was succeeded by his son Silumelume—but his elder brother, Mubukwanu, did not recognize him. Mwene Ciyengele sided with Mubukwanu and eventually killed Silumelume. Mubukwanu had just been enthroned when the Kololo crossed the Zambesi and overran the kingdom around 1840.[15] With them something entirely new came to the Zambesi valley.

It is sometimes believed that in 1840 the kingdom was of the same extent as it had been after the Kololo conquest. This seems to be quite incorrect. In actual fact, it was much smaller, limited in the west by the Cuando (Linyanti); in the north by the confluence of Lunguebungu and the Zambesi near Lukulu; and in the east by the Kaonde and Ila, who were definitely not tributary, and by the Nkoya, most of whom were also free from tribute. To the south the borders were blurred, since most of the lands between the Zambesi and Cuando are unsuited for settlement. In the Zambesi valley, the Tonga, east of Victoria Falls, were also definitely not tributary. It was, then, still a sizable kingdom but not much bigger than some other states in the north. This may explain why the first written mention about it in 1795 does not extoll it as an especially powerful kingdom, or of great interest for traders.[16]

seven

Traders
on the Central African Coast
1700–1900

Any history of Angola, then, that makes sense, must be an economic history," says the historian of the Ovimbundu.[1] This is literally true in regard to the whole Central African coast and its hinterland, especially since 1700. Politics, or social or cultural changes—nothing makes sense if trade is not seen as the major motive for it all. On the coast there was the competition between the Portuguese traders in Angola and their British or French counterparts north of the Dande. In the colony of Angola itself the whole political structure, the whole foreign policy, was dictated by the necessities, first, of the slave trade, and of other kinds of trade later. In the Kongo area and north of the Congo River, the social and political organizations of the peoples underwent far-reaching changes as a result of the trade. Behind the coast, the middlemen, the Ovimbundu, the Imbangala of Kasanje, and the Ginga of Matamba, adapted their societies to suit the demands of the trade. Farther away, over the Kwango, populations were raided and displaced by the Imbangala and by the Yaka. The latter, however, seem to have been motivated less by commercial motives than by their aim to build a Lundalike state in this area.

180

The Colony of Angola in the Eighteenth Century

During the eighteenth century, Angola changed very little from what it had become in the last decades of the seventeenth century. Indeed, its stagnation politically and culturally is the main historical fact for this century.[2] The slave trade was still the mainstay of its economy, and the political institutions, which were adapted to it, remained unchanged: a military regime in the interior, a government led by governor–traders and occasionally by a junta of traders, and ever-decreasing missionary action. Until 1764, no major reforms were attempted or even proposed. Foreign policy showed a remarkable continuity. The military fought regularly against the Dembos in the north and Matamba in the northeast, but they maintained a policy of co-operation with the Jaga of Kasanje, where the main market place for slaves from the interior was located—the *feira* of Cassange. Farther south there was a slow expansion around Kakonda and a deep infiltration of bush traders within the Ovimbundu states all over the plateau. None of the African states was any longer a serious threat for the colony; the only real threat lay on the sea, which was not symbolized by warships but by the merchant men of England and France. Their commercial domination north of the Dande could be a very serious threat and dictated need for expansion. (See, in general, Map C.)

The calendar of the main events for the period can be summed up quickly.[3] In the southern interior, the chief of the Hanha or Kakonda, as well as other Ovimbundu chiefs, attacked and were attacked by the Portuguese in 1698 and from 1716 to 1722. In the last campaign they proved to be such formidable foes that, apart from smaller clashes between Ovimbundu raiders and Portuguese traders, no further expansion occurred until the 1770's. Matamba was attacked in 1704 and in 1744, and at that time it lost some of its lands to the *presidio* of Maopungo. (The war in 1744 occurred because a white trader and some *pombeiros* were said to have been killed in the country.) On the coast, the French burned Benguela in 1704, but this did not elicit a very strong response. However, British and French trade north of the Dande did. From 1733 on plans were made to stop this trade by an occupation of the whole coast as far north as Soyo and by the building of a *presidio* there. In 1758 the *camara* of Luanda complained that the foreign merchants were so successful that they sold their goods through middlemen in the Lunda market itself and that the goods were of better quality and cheaper than the Portuguese products. In 1759, therefore, a major campaign led to construction of the *presidio* of St. José d'Encoge (Encoje) to stop trade in the Loje valley. But the situation did not improve much; by 1760 there was talk of occupying Ambriz, Cabinda, Malemba, and Loango. A decision of 1720, effective in 1725, forbidding governors and other high officials to participate in the trade, was the only major attempt at change in the internal structure of the colony, and the measure was never taken seriously. Another change, the expulsion of the Jesuits in 1760, deprived the colony of its most intellectual elements and accelerated the missionary decline.

In 1764 Innocencia de Souza Coutinho arrived—a protégé of the marquis of Pombal.[4] He recognized how much Angola was dependent on the slave trade and how little had been done to exploit her other resources, and he tried to alter this situation by creating a foundry, by making the citizens of Luanda cultivate their food on plantations near the Bengo, and by studying the possibilities for exploitation of the sulphur in Benguela and the asphalt on the Dande. He also recognized that the whole structure of the colony needed to be improved. He overhauled the financial, military, commercial, and administrative organizations by instituting controls everywhere to fight against corruption, graft, and bad faith. He also realized that many Portuguese were escaping completely from any control by the government: those were the *sertanejos* who lived in the Ovimbundu states on the highlands of Benguela. He created "bush jurisdictions" for them and appointed one of them as captain major in every major area of concentration. He also repealed a law of 1620 which forbade settlers to leave Portuguese-held territory. It had never been obeyed and its only result had been to lead to the complete autonomy of the *sertanejos*. Finally, the dynamic governor undertook a series of ventures that were in line with what other governors had done: he built a new *presidio* at Nova Redondo, repaired most of the fortifications of all the *presidio's*, and crushed rebellions. His program was not taken up by the white inhabitants of the colony and none of his projects was a smashing success. Yet his example was important, for his plans were to be the blueprint of reform policy in the nineteenth century.

Under Coutinho's successors, life in Angola reverted to its sluggish ways, although lip service was given to the need for the development of new resources, for the immigration of decent settlers to the highlands, and for new explorations, some of which were actually undertaken.[5] Under Souza Coutinho's immediate successor, a major war was fought against the Ovimbundu. The main result was to make the kings of Bihé and Mbailundu allies of the colony, which encouraged further immigration from *sertanejos* and led to an intensification of the trade inland east of Bihé. Two other major military adventures took place in 1783: the occupation of Cabinda, where a fort was built but was destroyed by a French squadron in alliance with the kings of Mgoy and Kakongo in 1784; and a series of operations against the Dembos. In 1788 a war was conducted against the marquis of Mosul, who controlled the harbour of Ambriz. In 1790 the marquis invaded the colony with the intention of capturing Luanda, but failed. Finally, reinforcements had to be brought from Brazil and the Azores before he was defeated in 1792 and became a nominal vassal of Portugal. His defeat led to renewed Portuguese expeditions against the Dembos around Encoje in 1793 and 1794. All these campaigns were unsuccessful because they did not result in the establishment of a Portuguese trade monopoly north of the Dande. French and British goods flowed in in ever greater quantities.

Economic development was extremely slow. A naturalist visited the country in 1783, and southern Angola was explored in

1785 by Pinheiro Furtado along the coast and by a *sertanejo* inland. Pinheiro de Lacerda explored and mapped the Benguela highlands in 1790. From 1800 on, efforts were made to find an overland route to Mozambique and resulted in the transcontinental travels of the two *pombeiros,* Pedro Baptista and Anastasio José, between 1805 and 1815 (see note 5, Lopes de Lima reference). The iron industry created by Souza Coutinho periclitated, but a small foundry was put in operation again in 1800 at Trombeta (Ilamba). Typically enough for the evolution in Angola, the project of Coutinho resulted in 1809 in a regulation according to which the local chiefs in Golungo were each supposed to pay a tribute of one-hundred bars of iron a year. From 1800 to 1810, other developments included regulations for the advancement of agriculture, the study of economic possibilities with regard to the exploitation of sulphur, the establishment of a few tile factories, the dispatch of samples of iron, copper, gum copal, and asphalt to Rio de Janeiro—but all this was done in a desultory fashion. The agricultural production around Luanda was so insignificant that food was imported from Brazil and major famines occurred in 1783, 1799, and 1816.

A sensitive description of Angola around 1789 is given by the Brazilian Da Silva Correa, the eighteenth-century historian and critic of the country.[6] The territorial and administrative structures had changed very little. In 1779 Benguela was restored as a governorship but remained dependent on Luanda. The new *presidio* of Nova Redondo and those of Muxima, Masangano, and Galangue had no troops in residence. Golungo, Icolo, and Dande were administrative districts dependent on Luanda, but the administration was carried out by a single person, the regent. At the capital a few changes had come about in accounting procedures. The laws which forbade high officials to trade were not observed, corruption was not checked, and—even more important —the increasing autonomy of the army and of the *presidio's* captains had not been curtailed. The settlers and *sertanejos* led a life of opulence and almost complete independence, especially in the Ovimbundu kingdoms. Trade statistics show that the export of slaves accounted for 88.1 per cent of the income of the colony as against 4.09 per cent revenues from tithes, 4.81 per cent from ivory, 0.9 per cent from salt, etc. Angola was still completely dependent on the slave trade for its existence. The need for more slaves led the traders to lobby constantly for more military expeditions, and the colony was constantly raiding its African neighbors. Contraband in slaves, ivory, and even wax was flourishing and went unchecked. Since ivory was still a royal monopoly, the contraband in this product was especially active. The reason for the disinterest in the development of other resources is summarized by governor Miguel Antonio de Mello in a comment that it was rare that one lost money in the slave trade. Why abandon such a certain source of revenue for other business where risks, at least in the initial stages, were greater?[7]

De Mello's report of 1802 completes Da Silva Correa's picture. Even by this date the colonial government was still so afraid of the Africans it exploited that it forbade the import of mares, for fear that the Africans would build up a cavalry. De Mello also stresses, even more than Da Silva Correa, how bad the discipline of the troops was. This was not surprising since most soldiers were either convicts or adventurers.

The Colony of Angola in the Nineteenth Century

In the nineteenth century, Angola changed slowly from a slave-trading establishment, with a basic administration not unlike that of its African neighbors, into a colony, surrounded by other colonies and ruled from the metropolis.[8] Tovar de Albuquerque, governor from 1819 to 1821, introduced the cultivation of cotton and promised that the state would buy the crop if no other buyer could be found. He organized a transportation service by canoe on the Dande and the Bengo, a mail service to the *presidios,* and a few small factories of tile, brick, and limestone around Ambaca and Masangano, and he restructured the state budget. But he was ousted in 1821 after a dispute with the bishop, and no stable government existed from 1821 to 1840. Governors came and went, troops revolted, junta's were appointed, there was even a movement in Benguela in 1823 to join newly independent Brazil. However, these years of near anarchy were very important. Brazil was now sovereign and Angolan trade had to be reoriented toward Portugal, where slaves were not wanted; the royal monopoly on ivory was abolished in 1834, and on December 10 a bill to outlaw the slave trade was passed in Lisbon. The trade in ivory surged upward, but the prohibition of the slave trade was not carried out. In 1838 a governor had to be recalled, on representations of the British government, because he himself was still engaged in the slave trade. His successor was forced out by the local population at the end of 1839 and it was only from 1840 on that order in the government was restored.

In 1836 Portuguese territory to the east had expanded to include the *presidio* Duque de Braganza on land taken from Matamba or Ginga; and between 1839 and 1845 a complete survey and mapping of all Portuguese territory was held, explorations were made in the area south of Huila, and prospecting for mineral wealth was conducted.[9] In the 1840's Mossamedes and Huila became *presidios* and coffee plantations began to be organized in the north. From 1845 on a prize court was organized in Luanda under English pressure, and the export of slaves rapidly became impossible, although the internal slave trade and export to São Thomé went on as before. In 1848 a group of Pernambucanos, joined in the 1850's by Portuguese emigrants, settled at Mossamedes, the first groups of settlers for at least a century who were not convicts. In 1853 some Algarve fishermen moved to Porto Alexandre south of Mossamedes and a few other families to Huila. But the hardships the new settlers encountered were so great that further immigration was delayed until the 1880's.[10] Lopes de Lima gives statistical information for 1845.[11] At that time about 400,000 people were living in the colony, only 1,832 of whom were white, and most of these lived in Luanda. Benguela, now the most important port of trade, counted only thirty-eight white men and one woman. Exports were declining: in 1844 their value was only a fifth of what it had been in 1823 to

1825. No wonder that the colony went almost bankrupt in the 1830's and the 1840's. Around 1845 the main products exported were ivory, urzella, wax, and gum copal, with small quantities of palm oil, hides, coffee, skins, and horns—in that order of importance. Angolan harbors had been opened to foreign trade in June 1844, but the effects were not yet visible. And by 1845 no item of trade had yet replaced the export of slaves.

In the 1850's and the 1860's the trend of the 1840's was reinforced. There was more order in the colony, the plantations were beginning to prosper, and those settlers who did not want to turn to another business after the suppression of the slave trade had left for Brazil. But no effective substitute for the slave trade had yet been found by 1870 and Angola was still on the verge of bankruptcy.

In 1858 a new decree about slavery stated that no one could be enslaved from then on and that by 1869 the status of all slaves would be altered to that of *libertos*—a less harsh term for the same state—but that by 1878 slavery would be abolished altogether. Since the slave trade was still flourishing in the interior of Angola and provided the plantations with labor, resistance against the decree was strong (but it was carried out, and in 1875 the slaves were declared free and a labor code proclaimed). A temporary substitute for the slave trade was found in cotton, at least during the Civil War in the United States, but when the war ended the Angolan cotton dropped out of the market. Even during the cotton boom, however, deficits were great and the metropolis did not help out. After the collapse of the cotton market, a financial crisis broke out, which was met by curtailing all expenses, especially the military ones.

From 1848 to 1852, military operations had been conducted in Bondo, and at Cassange to ensure total freedom of trade at the market there. Although the expedition met with military success, it again failed in its economic aims. The market place was moved back from Cassange to Malange and the Imbangala kept the monopoly of the interior trade even more rigorously than before. Further campaigns in 1861 and 1862 led to Portuguese defeat in the field, and by 1863 Kasanje was completely independent again and in control of the trade route to the interior. To the north the Portuguese had occupied Ambriz in 1855, and from there they went to the copper mines of Bembe, a century-old aim. The mines were exploited by an English company, which unfortunately found them to be marginal at best and abandoned the exploitation by the 1860's. In 1860 Portuguese troops even entered San Salvador and manned a fort there. They also exercised some control over Soyo and the mouth of the Congo River. The whole area south of the Congo was organized, at least on paper, into administrative districts, but by 1866, probably as a direct result of the financial crisis and the disillusion about the Bembe mines, the posts of Mpinda, San Salvador, Bembe, and even the old *presidio* of Encoje were abandoned. Only eleven years later Stanley would reach Boma, but by then Portugal no longer could claim occupation of the lower reaches of the river.

After 1870 the financial situation, and with it the general development of the colony, improved magically.[12] Rubber, first exported in 1869, was beginning to take the place of the slave trade. In 1882 it reached second place among the exports; in 1886 grass rubber began to be exploited and a boom started which reached its peak in 1899, to decline sharply afterward. But rubber tided Angola over its most difficult years—those of the scramble for Africa.

In 1875 a labor code was promulgated which included clauses against vagrancy but which abolished slavery and forced labor. Local resistance was strong enough to sabotage its application; finally, in 1899, a new labor code was promulgated which was a step backward, since it instituted forced labor, probably as a result of the development of coffee and other plantations between 1875 and 1899.

From the 1870's to 1920 Angola also turned into a colony along the general pattern that was emerging around her in Africa. The boundaries of the country were fixed by international agreement between 1870 and 1900. Explorations by Serpa Pinto, Ivens, Capello, and Dias de Carvalho were organized in the 1870's and the 1880's to give substance to territorial claims. And from 1885 on the real occupation of the areas that theoretically had been claimed began with the campaigns in the south of Artur de Paiva, which were concluded in 1888. The Ovimbundu kingdoms were subjected from 1890 to 1902. In Kasanje and Mahungo, military operations led to occupation by 1910 and 1911 while what was later the Lunda province was occupied peacefully during the same period. The bitterest enemies of the colony, the Dembos and the Kongo, were overcome in the Dembo campaigns of 1907 –1910 and the Kongo wars of 1913–1918. In the far south the Humbe campaign of 1915 concluded the major operations of "pacification." By 1918 Angola's territory was under effective control. The internal territorial and administrative structures did not undergo major changes until the 1890's, when Paiva Couceiro proposed new territorial administrative structures which would no longer be military. Civilian circumscriptions were created and replaced the *presidio* system after 1913. Another typical feature of the transformation to a colony in the twentieth-century style was the renewal of the missionary efforts. From 1875 on, Catholic and Protestant missions were founded and started with their triple work of conversion, education, and healing. But here, as in most other fields, it was only after 1900 that their efforts began to make an impact on the traditional way of life in Angola.

Kongo, Ngoy, Kakongo, and Loango

The major change in this whole region in the eighteenth century was the transformation of Kongo from a unitary kingdom into a series of chiefdoms which still recognized a single king—but somewhat in the manner of the Holy Roman Empire. For all practical purposes, every petty state was independent.[13] This change had largely been induced by economic conditions and its most important effects were commercial as well. The new states

in Kongo and in the area north of the Congo River were organized for trade, but they inherited the ideal of divine kingship
from the splendor of what Kongo had been.

By 1710 the kingdom of Kongo again had a single king, but
Pedro IV never recovered the authority and the control over the
provinces that his ancestors had enjoyed. Soyo was independent;
Mbamba, Mbata, and Mpemba had been torn by struggles over
the succession to the chieftainships there and were divided between the competitors; and parts of Mpangu and Nsundi had
been incorporated into the domain of the chiefs of Bula. By 1720
there was no longer even a single Kongo nation but rather at
least three peoples or tribes: the Solongo in Soyo, the mushi
Kongo in the central areas, and the Soso in eastern Mbata and in
parts of Nsundi. By 1900 the Ntandu and Zombo [Zumbo, Map C]
emerged as distinct cultural groups separated from the Soso, the
Ndibu had split off from the mushi Kongo, and in northern Nsundi several separate tribes had sprung up. This cultural disintegration followed the weakening of the political ties. It is clear that
by 1720 Kongo had broken up into a set of chiefdoms, which
themselves kept dividing and subdividing until, by 1780 or before, a chiefdom consisted only of a capital town, the *mbanza* of
two hundred huts or more, and a few villages or *libata* of fifty
huts each—or less. No chiefdoms were bigger in size than twelve
miles or so across.[14]

Another major change which occurred in the eighteenth century was a spectacular decrease in the total population. This was a
consequence of the political disruption, the perpetual wars, and
the concomitant slave trade. The population also seems to have
been reduced by famine and smallpox. In addition, there were
many years during which millet or maize could not be harvested
because of the never-ending attacks on the villagers. After 1750
the population decline was stopped, however, when manioc
began to be cultivated on a large scale; after six months of growing, this crop could be harvested at any moment during a year
and a half. It meant that the manioc crops were not lost if the

villagers had to flee during the harvest season, and thus famine was averted.[15]

The connection between trade and disintegration can be followed in a few cases. It is clearly because the princes of Soyo possessed Mpinda, and because of the ammunition and cannon sold to them by the Dutch, that they were able to break away from Kongo between 1636 and 1645. And there is direct evidence of Dutch help of this kind during the war between Soyo and Angola in 1670. A similar case is that of Mosul,[16] which was an insignificant district of Mbamba before 1640. During the 1640's, the Dutch established a trading post at Ambriz in the territory of Mosul. By the end of the century Mosul had broken off from Mbamba and had been able to do so because the duke of Mbamba was fighting the chief of Mbamba Lovota, who had tried to oust him—but probably it was also possible because the marquis of Mosul now had easy access to guns and gunpowder, for Ambriz had become one of the smaller harbors on the coast. During the eighteenth century, Ambriz became more and more important because the major trade route in Kongo lay along the Loje River in its hinterland. Moreover, it was via Ambriz and through Mosul toward the south that French and British goods were sold within Angola. By 1720, then, Mosul controlled the coast between the mouths of the Loje and the Lifune where it bordered on Angola. In the interior, to the east, its neighbors were Bumbe, which became an insignificant chiefdom, and Ambwila and Wandu, which reverted to powerful independent Dembo chiefdoms. In the north along the Loje valley, Mbamba disintegrated during the eighteenth century to such an extent that by the 1790's every major village had become independent and had erected its own custom posts on the trade route of the valley. There is little doubt that this breakdown in the valley was also an effect of the trade. It is interesting to note, however, that all the independent petty states in that area shared a common religious oracle, located on a small affluent of the Lui, which may have prevented major cultural estrangement.

We may find, when we have a reasonably clear picture of the situation, that the social and political structure in Kongo around 1720 may have already been what it was in 1780. The kingdom then comprised a great number of petty chiefdoms all ruled by *infantes* [i.e., descendants of one of Affonso's three children], who had become very numerous. The villages around a *mbanza* were also governed by *infantes*, but ones who had not received a title—such as prince, duke, or marquis—and therefore could not succeed as the head of a chiefdom. (Titles could be given only by kings.) Other villages were governed by *fidalgos* (or free men), probably descendants of the man who had founded the core of the village in the past. Most of the inhabitants in the *mbanza* or in the village seem to have been domestic slaves who were carefully distinguished from "slaves for export." In 1793 San Salvador, the capital, was a village of twenty-two huts among imposing ruins, and the king lived there in an ordinary hut like any of his subjects. Kingship was still elective and there were still—indeed, there would be at the end of the nineteenth century—wars of succession. There were now six electors, councilors of the town, led by the marquis of Vunda (*mani* Kabunga), who had to be an *infante*, whereas the others were not *infantes*. The electors ordinarily chose the *infante* who bore the title of prince or king of the exterior—that is, ruler of the capital outside of the king's compound—and one who was not a child of the deceased king. The elected king could not reign unless he had been crowned by a missionary and, since missionaries appeared only sporadically between 1725 and 1780, it meant that for long periods at a time the king could not rule. When elected, the king left his *mbanza* of origin to his immediate successor—his maternal nephew—who would be the only chief to send him tribute. Other royal revenues came from the handing out of habits of the order of Christ, for which the new knights paid either a hog, a goat, or the equivalent; the payments made by the *infantes* when they came to ask for a title of prince, duke, or marquis; and payment made by nobles from all over the country when they brought their dead to be buried in the ruins of the churches. In administrative matters the king had a say only in his own compound and over his own slaves and wives; even the town of San Salvador was not under his command. His army were his own slaves, and Henrique, a king of the period, had only twenty or thirty guns. The king still played a role as mediator between different chiefs, but he was not even the highest judiciary instance. In addition to the king, there was a prince called the king of the exterior who was the presumed successor to the crown, and commanded San Salvador. If he were absent, the *nelumbu*—one of the oldest titles in Kongo—took charge of the "capital." There also was the *mani* Kabunga or *mani* Vunda; in matters of administration he made the final decisions, hidden behind a curtain because the king could not see him after the coronation ceremonies—in which the *mani* Vunda still played an important role. In military affairs, both the prince and the *mani* Vunda had to give their assent, and in that case they had to back the king with their own "armies." Justice was given in every settlement not by its head but by an elected elder, the *mani* Pemba. When two settlements were involved, a third *mani* Pemba arbitrated. Appeal was then possible to the six councilors at San Salvador, from them to the king, and from the king to the *mani* Vunda.[17] This was true for the immediate surroundings of San Salvador, although in the 1870's or 1880's a case from Dembo country was once brought to Pedro V Elelo.

The kingdom was reduced to nothing and kingship to a mere symbol, yet tremendous prestige was apparently placed on the possession of knighthood and titles, and the *infantes,* who had broken it up, still acted as if the kingdom were the imposing state it had been in the 1500's. The prestige of the kingship still led to struggles at almost every succession and would do so until 1911. San Salvador and the kingship was not a mere memorial but a living myth for which the *infantes,* trapped in their own dream, would still shed their blood.

The kingdom was there even when, in practice, the small chiefdoms kept dividing and splitting. By the 1850's they were smaller than in the eighteenth century and by 1900 almost every village was now independent. A village in 1900 consisted of a set of tiny hamlets, the most important of which now had become the *mbanza*. All of the hamlets were localized branches of the same matrilineage and the lineage head was head of the village. Political chieftainship, as distinct from leadership in the clan, had almost disappeared. By 1910 there were only two "crowned chiefs" left in the valley of the lower Inkisi and their authority was restricted to their own village.[18]

Clearly the dynamics of fragmentation, which by 1900 formed a pattern two centuries old, are not simply "decay" but have to be approached as a way of life, a sociopolitical structural system. The greatest fact of Kongo history, then, is that between 1667 and 1710 an extraordinary mutation took place. The old political structure did not simply collapse and leave the smaller political units, such as the chiefdoms or the villages, to take over its functions. It became a new structure with a king, with *infantes* and *fidalgos,* and with a huge domestic slave population. It would also be wrong, presumably, to imagine the dynamics of fission as a purely social phenomenon of lineage fission. It is clear that personal initiative and wealth came to play a tremendous role.

In other words, the dynamics of this new society were linked very closely to the trade. In Kongo, as in Mayombe, Kakongo, or Loango, the power of a man in the eighteenth century was in direct relation to the number of slaves he had. If he had none, he was not noble, not a *fidalgo.* If he had many, he had his village and would try to break off from his *infante,* or he would become an *infante* himself. This system implied a permanent state of unrest and of war, and of prisoners of war who ended up at the coast to be sold or to join the parties of their captors.[19] The perpetual turmoil in the interior brought a flood of slaves to harbors which had been trading in slaves probably since the sixteenth century but which had not developed much before 1700—the harbors of Cabinda in Ngoy and Malemba in Kakongo. Even Loango,[20] where the Vili had brought slaves, ivory, and other products from the interior as far away as Stanley Pool since 1600 or earlier, must have felt the increase in the supply of slaves after 1700. The demand also increased sharply at this time because of the appearance of the French and the English in these harbors. The Vili began to organize routes to San Salvador and to the whole of central Kongo. (They were first reported in 1704 and were still trading when Bastian[21] visited San Salvador in 1857.) There they would meet the Hum, who organized the trade from the Pool to this area. The other major trade route from the old kingdom Okango or Kwango—which had been destroyed, also around 1700, and replaced by the kingdom of the Yaka—had been taken over by the Zombo, who exported either to the harbors of the north or via the Loje valley to Ambriz. Finally, the Solongo from Mpinda also visited central Kongo to buy slaves.[22]

The great flood of slaves also soon started to alter the social and political structures of the kingdoms north of the Congo River.[23] A distinction between domestic slaves and slaves for export was soon made and retinues of domestic slaves became politically important. Special political offices in relation to the trade were created: there was a governor of the harbor in both Ngoy and Kakongo and a minister of trade and Europeans. This position became so important that these men, the *mafuk* or *mambuk*, soon could challenge their kings with impunity. By the latter part of the eighteenth century in Kakongo and Ngoy, the nobles would recognize the kings only as long as they did not have to pay tribute or have their autonomy interfered with. Otherwise they would threaten the use of arms and force the kings to make concessions. The kings nominated titleholders by awarding the offices to the highest bidders in what became almost a public auction. Kings, princes, and officials constantly exacted tribute in the name of the king from the villagers and, according to the wealth of the village, in slaves, in cattle, and in agricultural products. But slaves could not be pressed too hard for they would flee to another lord and thus strengthen his armed force and reduce that of their former master. Tribute had to be exacted from the freemen because slaves were the real source of power and slaves could be bought with wealth. Slaves also could not be pressed into hard work, so the freemen were squeezed, with the result that fewer and fewer ordinary freemen survived; they either became slaves or amassed enough wealth to become nobles. Another tendency in the political structure was to lengthen the interregnum after the death of a king, for then the princes were completely free. This led almost to the disappearance of kingship in Loango around 1786 when a long interregnum set in. Kingship survived, however, albeit the royal authority was reduced to nothing.

In the twentieth century the states' structures collapsed. The nobles, who in the century before had profited most from the power derived by trade, now found that they could not maintain their rights as lords of the land against commoner village headmen. Some of these headmen, with their lineages, had amassed a great number of domestic slaves and had become as powerful as their lords. By the 1880's, Loango was reduced to a multitude of small districts, all independent one from another. Ngoy and Kakongo withstood better, and it was probably only after the 1830's that disintegration set in, in a manner similar to Loango, because of the refusal of the nobles to elect a new king. When the slave trade ended in the 1860's and 1870's, no change occurred at all in the process, for the slaves were still carried to the coast and sold there as domestic slaves in return for European products. When the colonial regimes came in the late 1870's and the 1880's, they froze an essentially fluid system of competition for power. This was by now not restricted to the three traditional kingdoms on the coast but had spread all along the Congo River at least as far as Noqui, for, after 1800, different traders established centers in many places along the lower Congo.[24] The local rulers and the local population seem to have undergone the same process that was destroying the kingdoms of the coast. In Boma, for instance, there was one fairly strong king in 1816, but by 1860 there were nine different chiefs, none of whom was powerful.

It is clear that the original causes which led to the breaking up of Kongo and of Loango are different. There was no Portuguese pressure on Loango, nor was there the rule of succession which triggered the civil wars of 1667–1710. Yet in both cases the influence of the slave trade was great—even very great. It may be

that the evolution which took place in Kongo and led to a fragmentation of power down to the village level was different from
the process which led to the same result in Loango. Yet what evidence is available today would indicate that in both cases the
process, once started, was similar if not identical. The whole culture of the Kongo, Woyo, and Vili in the eighteenth and nineteenth centuries was re-structured by the slave trade. The new
unit of the sociopolitical structure had become the band of followers and slaves. Anybody could lead such a band, but it could
only be built up by wealth from this trade. Political leadership
was therefore closely linked and conditioned by the slave trade.

The Middlemen: The Ovimbundu

Most of the Benguela highlands were occupied in the seventeenth century by peoples who spoke a language close to southwestern Bantu, who were pastoralists, and who may have practiced double descent, as do the southwestern Bantu today.[25] From
the oral traditions, the reference to the name Imbangala in 1797,
the cultural evidence, especially with regard to details of the political structure, and from the knowledge that Jaga roamed at
least one part of the highlands about 1600, it seems that during
that century a set of kingdoms were created by the Jaga on the
highlands. The earliest certain reference in the literature to one
of these Jaga states, at that time in Hanha, deals with Kakonda
and dates from 1641. By 1680 several of them existed, but there
is still no mention of Mbailundu[26] and Bihé, which appear in
written documents only from the time of Souza Coutinho. It may
well be, therefore, that some of the kingdoms were still in the
process of formation during the earlier part of the eighteenth
century. By 1799, however, all of the kingdoms known in the
nineteenth and early twentieth centuries existed. The most important ones among them were Ndulu, Mbailundu, Bihé, Wambu,
Ciyaka, Ngalangi, and Kakonda.

The political structure of these states can be seen as belonging
essentially to the general Kongo type with a few Lunda innova-

tions which may have been acquired from the Imbangala of Kasanje. A typical kingdom such as Mbailundu was territorially divided into districts. The smaller districts were made up of villages, while the larger ones were divided into subdistricts and were in fact very often tributary chiefdoms rather than mere districts. Mbailundu had a population around 1850 of about 450,000 and counted two hundred districts, with from three to three hundred villages per district. Some districts were ruled by princes of royal blood who could themselves establish dynasties there, while other rulers were appointed and were either promoted or demoted from time to time by the central government. Other districts belonged to separate dynasties, some of which were natives of the region, at least more so than the ruling royal family. Still other districts were ruled over by court officials. In Mbailundu about twenty districts were ruled around 1850 by members of the royal family, including heirs and the queen, and it can be surmised that revenues from these districts were used by the chiefs for their needs and not sent as tribute to the king. The revenue from about twenty other districts went to court officials, and here, too, parts of the tribute may well have been kept by them. One fifth of the districts, therefore, were in this case immediately dependent on the royal court. Villages were ruled by headmen who succeeded almost automatically one after another through the eldest line of the patrilineage, which formed the core of the settlement.

The central government at the royal court consisted of the king, the queen, and a number of titleholders who often met in council [*olusenje*] for administrative and judicial matters. This council had great political authority since it elected kings from among the members of the royal patrilineage and could depose unpopular rulers. Some of the titleholders had predominantly ritual duties, others were administrators or warriors. Some were traditionally nobles related to the royal patrilineages or matrilineages, others were free men, and others—and among them the war leader—were royal slaves. Some of the most important titles, such as *ngolambolo* or *tendala,* were also found in Ndongo and in Kasanje and are a clear indication of northern influences on the structure. The kings played a most important religious role since their ancestors were responsible for the general fertility of the country. In political matters, however, they seem to have been comparatively less important than their counterparts in Kongo or in the Lunda states, which of course meant that the strength of the states was not so dependent here as elsewhere on the personal qualities of the rulers. Finally, it must be emphasized that raiding of cattle or of people was much more prominent among the Ovimbundu than among the other Central African kingdoms and that from an early date on, maybe even since the eighteenth century, royal caravans participated in the long-distance trade between the coast and the interior. Both these features remind us that the marauding Jaga had founded the kingdoms and that Portuguese influence was present there almost from the onset of their history.[27]

The Jaga had been in contact with Portuguese traders at least since 1600 and had sold some of their captives to them in return for European goods, among which were fire weapons.[28] They subdued the older inhabitants of the plateaus not only because of their superior military organization but also probably because of their use of fire weapons. Once the kingdoms started to organize themselves, traders from Ndongo would travel to them to buy slaves, which the Ovimbundu obtained by their razzias against their southern neighbors or among themselves. After the foundation of Kakonda, some *sertanejos* began to marry and to settle among the people of the highlands. They had no special privileges, but it is probably from them that the Ovimbundu acquired the taste for the pursuit of wealth and for their entrepreneurship, which characterizes them in the nineteenth century. The organization of caravans and the adventurous spirit of the Ovimbundu may have derived from the nomadic military organization and the ways of life of the Jaga. In any case, by the 1770's the major Ovimbundu kingdoms had become political powers of the first rank and their capitals were staples for the slave trade. A great war against Mbailundu, Ndulu, and Bihé was waged by the Portuguese between 1774 and 1776. The net result was that these states refrained from raiding Portuguese-held areas later on and became allies of Angola against other Ovimbundu territories. The campaigns, however, taught the Portuguese that these kingdoms were so powerful that the military superiority might not lie with the Portuguese troops, and thus that an alliance with them was the wisest policy. Moreover, as the years went by, it was also clear that especially Mbailundu and Bihé had to be treated with great consideration since around 1800 they became the greatest purveyors of slaves, ivory, and wax for the harbors on the coast.

It is not known when the long-distance trade started on the highlands, but it is certain that by 1795 Ovimbundu traders and resident *sertanejos* had already reached Lwena territory in eastern Angola.[29] By the 1840's the trade into the interior, now clearly concentrated at Bihé, had reached the capital of the *mwaant yaav*, and the Imbangala and Ovimbundu caravans were fighting each other on the roads, to maintain or to break the trade monopoly which Kasanje had enjoyed on this route since the 1650's. Eventually, in the 1850's, the Ovimbundu succeeded in their objectives here. In the east they had certainly reached the Lozi kingdom before 1840—and by 1854 some of them—in the service of Da Silva Porto, a Portuguese trader of Bihé, had crossed the continent and reached Mozambique. By the early 1850's they regularly reached as far as the southern Lunda and they apparently appeared occasionally in Katanga. A decade or two later they also appeared in the Kasai valley in competition with the Imbangala and also with the Cokwe, who seem to have entered the trade only by the mid-century. Details about caravan organization among the Ovimbundu are not known, but it seems that, apart from the royal caravans, others were rarely fitted out by a single man. More often they were conglomerates of several entrepreneurs who were accompanied by a few members of their close king groups, and perhaps with matrilineal relatives being preferred over patrilineal kin and slaves. The caravans marched into the general area where slaves were to be bought, and on the way to and from these markets members of the group would also hunt for elephants. Trade went on uninterrupted throughout the century, slaves being brought from the interior until at least the 1880's. In the 1880's more and more rubber was collected until after 1886—when the boom in red rubber began (which had been discovered by Ovimbundu east of the Cuanza). Then hardly a man or an unmarried teenage girl remained in the country, and countless caravans participated in the rush. This came to an end in the 1890's because of the war between Ndunduma of Bihé and the Portuguese in 1890 and the wars against the Mbailundu in 1896 and 1902. When the wars were over, the price of rubber had dropped, the colonial governments began to bar access in their territories to traders from Angola, and a great famine in 1911 killed many traders in eastern Angola. In Ovimbundu tradition, this date marked the end of the long-distance trade. For more than a century their caravans had drawn slaves, ivory, wax, and rubber from the interior of Central Africa. In return, the traders had brought many cultural innovations, such as the cultivation of cassava to Northern Rhodesia. But they had also initiated the Cokwe and the Lwena to the attractions of the trade—and when the latter followed the Ovimbundu example, the consequences were to be disastrous for huge areas in Central Africa.

The Middlemen: The Kasanje and the Matamba

The state of Kasanje, which had been founded around 1620 by emigrants from Lunda, had never lost contact with the *mwaant yaav*.[30] By the 1650's a regular trade had developed between the Lunda and Cassange, where Portuguese traders had settled near the capital of the Jaga. The official caravan of the Lunda king in Cassange was mentioned in written sources by 1680. By that time this kingdom was the strongest African state near the coast and the oldest ally of the Portuguese—the only one that had not risen against them during the Dutch occupation. The Portuguese could not afford to attack the kingdom because of its power, and also because it apparently yielded more slaves than any other part of Angola and a war would break the lines of supply. On the other hand, the Jaga wanted to maintain the trade monopoly but also not to antagonize the Portuguese too much, for in that case the profits from the trade would be lost.

This general political and economical situation seems to have remained practically unchanged during the eighteenth century. In 1802 De Mello again testified that the Cassange fair was of primary economic importance.[31] At the same time, however, the Portuguese were still anxious to by-pass the Imbangala and to break their monopoly, and the expeditions of the *pombeiros* from 1802 to 1815 were such an attempt. The relations between traders and Imbangala at Cassange seem to have worsened; when an acute quarrel arose between them, the Angolan governor sent troops—with a cannon—to support the traders and the Jaga accepted the government proposals, which no doubt included an indemnity. A similar dispute, apparently in the 1830's or the 1840's, ended in a similar fashion.

Meanwhile, the Imbangala were losing their monopoly as the Ovimbundu began to by-pass them in the 1840's. By the 1850's the Imbangala were pushed north of their former route and they opened a new road to the Pende of Kasai with the help of the Shinje, their eastern neighbors. But here too they had to reckon with competition from the traders of Ambaca and their caravans of Ginga. In 1847 Jaga Mbumba imposed a duty on spirits and tobacco on the traders of the fair. When a Portuguese expedition was operating in Bondo in 1848, the traders appealed to the military, and the Jaga was ousted and replaced. In 1850 the new king decided to track the fugitive Mbumba down with the help of the Portuguese traders, but they were ambushed and defeated and the Jaga and the Portuguese director of the fair were killed.

A new military expedition was undertaken against the Imbangala from 1850 to 1852, but Mbumba fled again. As a result of the tense situation, the market place of Cassange was abandoned and Malange was founded, further west. In 1853 or 1854 Mbumba came back and resumed his throne. In 1857 he signed an agreement with the Portuguese, but in 1861 he found himself backing a candidate to the chieftainship in a Minungu chiefdom who was a Portuguese enemy. This led to a new war, which the Portuguese lost in 1862. From that time on, the Jaga resumed his independence completely and blocked all further Portuguese progress through his territory. He now sent his Imbangala caravans to trade in Malange and barred the Portuguese from entering his lands. The trade monopoly was saved, even though by now it had lost much of its value because of the Ovimbundu and Cokwe activities.

The effects of these events in Imbangala country were serious for Angola. The shortest route to Lunda was blocked by Kasanje so that Portuguese expansion had to take the roundabout way and was able to affirm itself only by 1884. By then it was too late, and many parts of the Lunda empire in the Kwango and Katanga went to the Congo Independent State instead of Angola.

Very little is known about the history of Matamba during the period covered in this chapter apart from losses of territory in 1744 and 1838 when the *presidio* of Duque de Braganza was founded. (This foundation resulted from a military expedition sent out to avenge the murder of a white trader and some *pombeiros* in Matamba.) For Matamba also played middleman in the slave trade. Here the entrepreneurs were the inhabitants of Ambaca—Portuguese, mulatto or African, the Ambaquistas or Baptistas, descendants of settled Jaga, and *sertanejos*. The Ginga of Matamba furnished only the carriers for the caravan. The caravans of Ambaca would go to the Kwango, probably to the capital of the Yaka, and east from there all the way to the Kasai. It is not known when this trade originated or how important it was.[32]

The Peoples on the Kwango and on the Middle Kwilu[33]

By 1700 the Lunda of Kasongo Mwene Putu were settled upstream of a kingdom ruled by Minikongo, chief of the Suku, whose capital lay on the Nganga. The Suku culturally were Kongo and had even been listed in the early sixteenth century as tributaries to the king of San Salvador. But in the first half of the eighteenth century they were gradually pushed downstream by the Yaka and their Lunda chiefs until they had to abandon the Nganga, and from there they fled to the east. The Yaka then overran the lower Kwango valley until they reached, near Kingushi, different Mfinu chiefdoms.

Still during the eighteenth century, a dispute broke out between the *kiamfu* [the Yaka king] and one of his main chiefs, Pelende, who was settled between Wamba and Inzia, east of Kasongo Lunda, the new Yaka capital. During a quarrel, Pelende's wife had either been insulted or been killed by the *kiamfu* or one of his men and Pelende claimed a slave in compensation. The *kiamfu* refused to give him one and Pelende, determined to break away from the Yaka, gathered his followers and went north, driving the Tsamba and their chief Mwene Mafu from the lower Bakali over the Inzia. The *kiamfu* sent an official after him to collect tribute, but Pelende refused to pay. In the ensuing war, the Yaka army was plagued by famine and they fled, abandoning the *kiamfu* and his first wife, who were killed by the Pelende at Tsumba Milembe. But the Pelende then started to pay tribute—out of fear for the spirit of the deceased *kiamfu,* as tradition has it, or more simply because they were defeated in a second campaign. From then on, however, they formed a separate kingdom, with a capital at Kobo, and were tributary to the Yaka. A few partisans of Pelende had not followed him and still live on the Wamba east of Kasongo Lunda.

After the Pelende war the Lunda did not expand much more, but they did begin to raid wide and far, apparently for slaves but probably to conquer new territory as well. The expression "then we fled for the Luwa [Yaka]" is a commonplace in the history of most of the peoples of the middle Kwango-Kasai. The *kiamfu's* state was extensive by that time. It went all the way from Pelende and Kobo in the north to Ngudi [Akama] in the south and it included all Lunda chieftaincies to the Lushiku, Mwata Kumbana not included, and the Pende chiefdoms of the Kwilu. It had become the counterpart of Kazembe's kingdom in the western part of the Lunda empire. Later conquests in the nineteenth century seem to have been directed toward the north against Mfinu, Yansi, and Tsamba of the lower Kwango and the lower Kwilu area. But all the peoples under Yaka control did not accept their rule willingly. The process of assimilation obliged the *kiamfu* to use his military strength to crush revolts and his diplomacy to convince the old conquered chiefs that it was best to accept Yaka overlordship. When the Europeans arrived in the 1880's this process of razzia–conquest–assimilation was still in progress at many points in the Kwango valley.

When the Suku left the Kwango, they first fled to the Lukula and then to the Pesi, an affluent of the Kafi, pursued all the time by the Yaka (or Luwa) raiders. On the Pesi they met the Mbala and Suku chief, Tona di Lukeni, who had led the emigration from the Nganga and had convinced the Mbala to fight the Yaka. The Mbala dug themselves in at Kazuwa near Pay Kongila and killed a *kiamfu*. This stopped the Yaka advance, and the Suku could settle down and reorganize their kingdom. Some Suku had not followed their chief but had settled first between Luie and Lukula and Kingombe. These Suku later came back to the Inzia and settled there, where they were gradually absorbed completely in the Yaka state. Later on, the Minikongo himself seems to have paid tribute to the Yaka as an autonomous tributary more or less like the Pelende at Kobo.[34] Variants of Suku history tell that the Yaka could oust the Suku because they had guns, and that the pursuit of the Yaka was only stopped on the Kwenge River, where the Lunda commanders were killed. The availability of guns to the Yaka—here, as in Kazembe—may have helped them considerably in their conquests.[35]

The territory occupied by the Suku after their migration was not empty. The river valleys were occupied by Hungaan, Ngongo, and Pindi, who either were assimilated or fled to the Kwilu valley near the present town of Kikwit. All these migrations were not mass migrations but movements of chiefly lineages or clans, for today clans cut across tribes, and tribal denomination is not based on descent but on political allegiance and common territory. For instance, there are clans which can be found among the

Lunda of Kwango, the Tsamba, the Suku, the Hungaan and the Pindi. Still, the creation and expansion of the Yaka state must have upset a relatively great number of people: the raids lasted for two centuries, and even if people migrated by small groups and a few miles at a time, such a prolonged pressure must have resulted in considerable displacement over time. This would be the main explanation for the high belt of population density found in the middle Kwango today.[36]

When the Lunda first arrived on the Kwango, they cut a considerable group of Suku off from the main kingdom. Those are the Suku of the kingdom of Ngudi [Akama], whose chief in the 1880's bore the title *kambongo*. This chiefdom then had resisted the Lunda of Kapenda ka Mulemba, the Lunda of the Yaka kingdom, and Imbangala invasions. Its link with the ancient kingdom of Kongo was still remembered by one of the royal insignia—a church bell from San Salvador.[37]

The ethnic complexity of the population on the middle Kwilu today is bewildering. In this small area, pockets of Hungaan, Pindi, and Ngongo are mixed with each other and enclaved in greater groups of Mbala and Kwese. The original inhabitants are said to be Pindi. After them the Kwese, closely related culturally to the Pende, seem to have settled where they now are. As for the Hungaan, they could be a composite population, one half of which would be of Yans or Tsong origin and the other half linked with the Ngongo, who themselves are closely allied to the Mbala culturally and historically. The Mbala claim to have lived in the valley of the upper Kwango and to have been chased away by the Lunda or *miluwa*. Their original home would have been south of the Wamba, and they too could not resist the invaders because the latter were armed with guns. When they arrived in their present territory—apparently only in the nineteenth century —they pushed some Yans back and infiltrated between the different Tsong settlements. Other Mbala traditions speak of men, probably Imbangala, who came to their original homes to buy slaves. Later they started to raid the Mbala villages for slaves, so the Mbala moved—but then they arrived in Yaka territory. The Yaka claimed tribute, the Mbala refused, a war followed, and the Mbala were again pushed out. Up to that time, there had been but one Mbala chiefdom. But during the war with the Yaka, the royal lineage was exterminated with the exception of one child, and the chiefdom broke up into several smaller chiefdoms. This particular tradition conflicts with the Suku version, according to which the Mbala were already near the Kafi when the Suku were pushed out by the Yaka. Therefore, they could not enter Yaka territory from the south after the major Yaka-Suku war, as this Mbala tradition implies. To complicate matters even further, another Mbala tradition has it that the Mbala lived near the ocean from where they moved to the upper Kwango when the white men arrived with their guns. This tradition would link them more with the Ambundu and maybe even the Pende. The confusion in Mbala traditions may be caused by contamination of one set of traditions with traditions from other groups, or by intermixture of different groups in one Mbala people which would have evolved culturally only in the nineteenth century, or simply by faulty collecting. Their migrations were prompted, however, by the activities of the Lunda and the Imbangala, and they seem to be the last major group to have settled down in the middle Kwilu valley. It seems probable that their history will become more meaningful when it is postulated that they were the victims of the slave trade, but this can be only a hypothesis until new data throw more light on the problem.

eight

The Fall of the Kings
1840–1900

After the middle of the nineteenth century the patterns of history in Central Africa change suddenly. Instead of the uniform succession of more or less able rulers at the head of a set of stable kingdoms semi-isolated in or around the huge Lunda empire, there now appears a pattern of violent struggle. A crowd of newcomers, of conquerors, attack the old kingdoms with new and superior military techniques or with more and better fire weapons. The old states—ill prepared, with weaknesses such as their mode of succession and their burden of overtaxation or official cruelty which had alienated their subjects—collapse. Some disappear forever, while others, toward the end of the century, recover. The isolation is broken down; wars and revolts rage everywhere; and in the end all the states find themselves under colonial rule. The genius of Shaka and Dingiswayo in South Africa are the causes for these upheavals, as well as the ever-expanding tentacles of the slave trade and the structural weakness of the Central African states. The process is repeated over and over: invaders come, rule, and are finally overthrown. The actors are mainly the Kololo from South Africa, the Cokwe traders from the west, and the Yeke and Arab traders from the east.

Fugitives from the South: The Ngoni and Kololo

In 1816, Zwide of the Ndwandwe killed Dingiswayo of the Mtetwa, but in 1818 he was ousted from his home territory by Shaka, successor to Dingiswayo. The wars were fought with new techniques elaborated by Dingiswayo and Shaka. After the Ndwandwe army was defeated, it trekked north under the leadership of Zwandengaba and crossed the Zambesi in November 1835. From there it went to Nsenga land and later to Fipa country, where the leader died around 1845. The Ngoni, as they were now called, then split into three groups. A group under Ntabeni settled west of Lake Tanganyika but was quickly destroyed by Tabwa, Bwile, Lungu, and Arabs. Ntuta and his men went east of Lake Tanganyika to become the scourge of East Africa for the next fifty years. Mgai led the third group, but he soon died and, after some dispute, was replaced by Mombera. In 1850 new groups split off and began raiding on both sides of Lake Nyasa. Mombera pursued these split-off groups without success and then settled in Tumbuka country. Here Mpezeni and Mperembe left his group and invaded Bemba land, where they were defeated in 1856 by the Bemba, assisted by Arabs (for Ngoni tactics and military organization could not stand up against fire weapons). After the battle, Mperembe rejoined Mombera while Mpezeni went on the rampage in Bisa and Lala country, as far as Lake Bangweolu, but then turned back for fear of the Bemba and of Kazembe. In about 1865 he arrived in Nsenga country, and between 1870 and 1880 he moved to the Fort Jameson area (where the Ngoni of his group are still). They raided all the surrounding peoples: the Cewa, Bisa, Kunda, Senga, Lala, Lenje, and Soli. Either Mpezeni's or Mombera's group attacked the Bemba again in 1868 but were again defeated. The Bemba proved to be a bulwark against the Ngoni, which saved the peoples north and west of them from the Ngoni ravages, but there was a price to be paid—Bemba raids and those of their Arab allies.[1]

In 1822, a group of seven or eight Sotho villages ruled by Mangwane was forced over the Vaal River by the Tlokwa, who

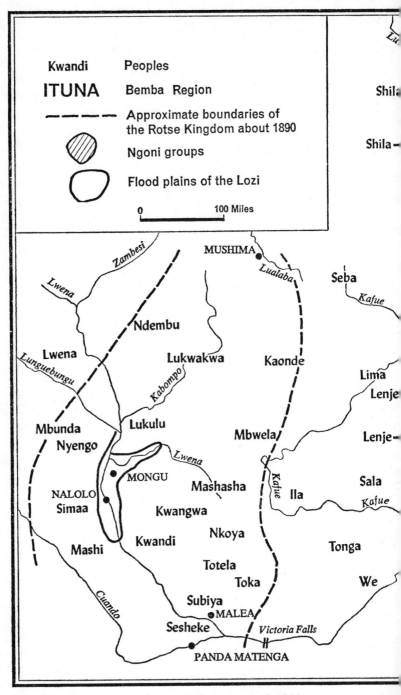

VII The Peoples of Northern Rhodesia Around 1890

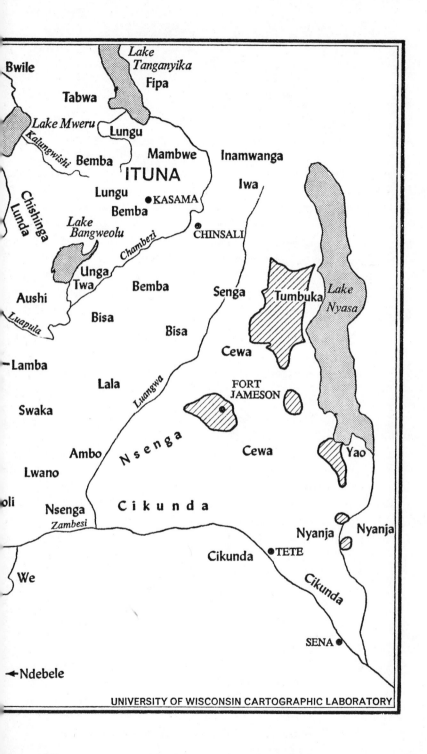

Bwile

Lake Tanganyika

Tabwa

Fipa

Lake Mweru

Lungu

Kalungwishi

Bemba

Mambwe

Inamwanga

Chishinga

Lunda

ITUNA

Iwa

Lungu

●KASAMA

Bemba

Lake Bangweolu

Chambezi

●CHINSALI

Unga

Twa

Bemba

Senga

Tumbuka

Lake Nyasa

Aushi

Luapula

Bisa

Bisa

Cewa

Lamba

Lala

Luangwa

Swaka

FORT JAMESON
●

Ambo

N s e n g a

Cewa

Yao

Lwano

oli

Nsenga

C i k u n d a

Nsenga

Zambesi

Nyanja

Nyanja

Cikunda

●TETE

We

Cikunda

SENA ●

←Ndebele

UNIVERSITY OF WISCONSIN CARTOGRAPHIC LABORATORY

were themselves being pressed by the Zulu. These villages organized themselves in Zulu fashion in 1823 under a new chief Sebitwane and took the name Kololo. He first tried to resist the Tlokwa but they were too strong. He then turned on other Sotho groups and moved northwest among the Mangwato, a Tswana group. In the 1830's Sebitwane went from there slowly north to Lake Ngami, where he defeated the Tawana and settled for a time. He heard about Europeans on the west coast and decided to trade with them. Moving again, he settled at the Cuando (Linyanti) between 1838–1840. With the help of the Subiya and a Tonga group, he later crossed the Zambesi near Victoria Falls and trekked to the Kafue, where he was attacked by the Ila from the north and the Ndebele in the south. Sebitwane defeated the latter and then suddenly went west into Lozi land, where a struggle for the succession of the kingship was still in progress. Two battles opened the Lozi flood plain to the conqueror, and the Lozi chiefs fled, leaving Sebitwane to found the Rotse kingdom.

The Lozi princes settled at Nyengo to the northwest and at Lukulu in the north, where Imasiku rallied the old Lozi court around him. Sebitwane attacked Imasiku at Lukulu in 1845, but without success. A second attack in 1848 or 1849 dislodged Imasiku, who fled up the Kabompo valley in the Lukwakwa area. After his success against Imasiku, Sebitwane had to ward off a major attack by the Ndebele, who were allied with the Subiya and the Malea. Despite initial reverses, he won the war and remained on the Zambesi to raid the Tonga and the Ila. In 1850 he moved again to the Cuando, where he fought the Tawana and also fought in an area where Portuguese traders had opened a small trading center, leaving his nephew, his brother, and his daughter in charge of the old Lozi capitals. When he died shortly afterwards, probably in 1851, Mamocesane, his oldest daughter, took over; she could not maintain her position, however, and had to hand the crown to her brother Sekeletu.[2]

Sekeletu first crushed a rebellion led by a relative of Mamocesane, who seems to have been helped by Angolan traders who operated in Ila and Tonga country. He then went on, raiding the Tawana and the Damara from his capital on the Cuando, leaving Rotse land proper to be administered by councilors from his own lineage—who ignored the traditional chiefs and subchiefs Sebitwane had appointed, because he knew and trusted them. Moreover, the Kololo conquest was not complete and Imasiku still survived and had his court in the Lukwakwa area. Sekeletu's complete neglect of the kingdom, with the exception of its southern border, led to several rebellions by different populations, but it did not grow into an over-all opposition. In 1860 the first missionaries arrived, but the king did not help them and they died. Shortly afterward Sekeletu developed either leprosy or yaws and spent the last years of his life in almost complete isolation. He died in 1864.

A struggle for the succession broke out and divided the Kololo so that Sepopa, a Lozi prince from the Lukwakwa, overcame the Kololo army in 1865. All the Kololo men were killed or fled to the Tawana, where they disappeared, whereas their women were married by the victors.[3]

Sepopa had come to prominence in exile only because the powerful Mbunda chiefs there had finally killed Imasiku around 1859 and had fetched the young Sepopa from the plain to lead the Lozi royal family. Now, in 1865, Rotse land was Lozi again, but peace did not return immediately. Another Lozi prince, Imbuwa, who had led the group that fled in 1840 to Nyengo and had later returned to the plain, kept rebelling, and he finally entrenched himself in the Lukwakwa. Sepopa first fought the Subiya and the Tonga, then in 1870 faced a major Kwangwa rebellion, and finally turned against the Lukwakwa rebels in 1872.

Imbuwa was killed but his son Sikufele took the leadership of his faction and managed gradually to force Sepopa south. The latter left the Lozi flood plain and built his capital at Sesheke, partly because of Sikufele's pressure but also because an important center of trade was developing at Panda Matenga, where South African and Angolan traders met each other. Sepopa gradually lost all support of his people and when his first minister, the *ngambela* Mamiri, revolted in 1874, Sepopa was almost power-less. He fled to the Subiya and tried to rouse them; meanwhile, he planned to get help from the traders, but he was killed before he could accomplish this. Mamiri appointed Sepopa's sister's son —and Sepopa's enemy—Mwanawina, brother of Imasiku, to the throne. But supporters of Sepopa rallied behind Lobosi or Lewanika, son of Sepopa's brother Litia. Mwanawina killed Mamiri and tried to subjugate the different Lozi chiefs, which alienated many powerful persons from Mwanawina's faction; by 1878 Lewanika was able to stage an open rebellion, and Mwanawina fled to the Mashi and then to Tonga land, where he died in 1879. However, his faction did not disappear with him.[4]

Lewanika settled in the capital and invited the traders there, and in 1883 he received Coillard of the Paris Evangelical mission and helped him to open a station. But suddenly, in 1884, revolt flared up again. Imbuwa's son, Akufuna (or Tatira), and his *ngambela* Mataa, who was the real leader now, led the Mwanawina faction and attacked the capital by surprise. Lewanika had to flee to the Lukwakwa, but with the help of the traders, and after several months of fighting, he killed Mataa, ousted all the pretenders, and succeeded finally in rallying the support of prac-tically the whole nation behind him.

Between 1885 and 1900 the Rotse kingdom expanded consider-ably. Even during Sepopa's reign, some territories, mainly Nkoya and Mashasha, had been added to the kingdom, in addition to Mbunda territory, which Sepopa's daughter had inherited from her aunt; and in 1880 the Subiya had also been incorporated. But now, with peace in the kingdom—and with the friendship of his councilors, the European missionaries, and the traders who pro-vided him with guns—Lewanika embarked on a career of con-quest. He raided the Ila and from 1884 on fought constantly against the Kaonde.

In the earlier phases of the Kaonde wars, Lewanika had placed tribute collectors among the Kaonde, and in 1891 one of the col-lectors was killed in the chiefdom of Jipumpu. Lewanika did not react, not even when Jipumpu was attacked the next year by other Kaonde chiefs supported by Musonkantanda, their theoretical Lunda overlord, and by the Yeke. But around 1895 Mushima, Jipumpu's main opponent, asked for help from the Lozi, and although he was given an army by Lewanika, was defeated by Jipumpu. After the battle, Jipumpu came to terms with the Lozi and formally became a tributary, as Mushima already had done by marrying a woman provided by Lewanika and accepting a tribute collector. From then on, the southern Kaonde chiefdoms were detached from Musonkantanda. In the north, the Lunda chief Ishindi asked for Lozi help against the Lwena. An army was sent out in 1892 but did not achieve any results because it was decimated by smallpox. Still, Lewanika became overlord over Ishindi and over some Lwena chiefdoms.

After 1890 the British missionaries and traders helped Lewanika in his expansionist policy. In 1890 Lewanika had accepted the protection of the British South Africa Company and from then on his interests, especially in the west, were the interests of the British, who feared that the Portuguese would claim the whole area as far as the Zambesi. Claims were put forward on Lewanika's behalf for the whole Lwena area and for large tracts of land west of the Cuando in Ganguella territory. Only a small part of these excessive claims was recognized by the king of Italy when he arbitrated what had become the Anglo-Lusitanian boundary dispute of 1905, and by then Lewanika was no longer a sovereign ruler. Since 1897, an administrative post had been built at his capital and the Rotse kingdom had slipped into the grip of indirect administration.[5]

The most striking and unusual event in this whole section of Lozi history is not the longevity of the factions which first arose at Mulambwa's death in the thirties and survived until at least 1884, nor is it the fact that the revolt against the Kololo was not merely a play for princes, as the other revolts were, but a national upheaval; these factors are paralleled so often elsewhere that they almost become a stereotype. The unique feature of Rotse history in this period is the exceptional degree to which the Kololo left their imprint on the culture of the valley. Today, the Lozi speak a Sotho language and whole parts of their customary legal system are Sotho, to mention one well-studied aspect of their culture.[6] Here the victor was not assimilated by the conquered—or at least not up to now—even though all Kololo men were killed in 1865 and only the women survived. In fact, it is quite possible that it was because the Kololo heritage was treasured by the women that it spread among the Lozi and could maintain itself until our own day.

The Cokwe, Lwena, and Ndembu

The Cokwe are responsible for the overthrow of the traditional patterns of life in the western half of Katanga, in Kasai, and in the southern parts of the Kwango-Kasai area. Yet, by 1850, they were still almost unheard of. They were originally a small group of seminomadic peoples who lived near the headwaters of the Kasai and the Kwango, living more from hunting than from agriculture—but able smiths—who were politically organized by their Lunda chiefs. First mentioned in 1795, they were by then on the trade route from Bihé to Lwena land. In 1846 they were reputed to be traders in wax—a good article for hunters—and were acquiring a reputation for attacking caravans. Graça's report[7] does not mention if they were tributary to the *mwaant yaav* or not, but probably they were taxed only from time to time because they lived so far away from Lunda land. The Lwena, closer to the Lunda, were complaining bitterly about the cruelty of *mwaant yaav* Naweej II and his tribute collectors, the *kakwata*, with their armed bands of soldiers, but no such complaints were heard among the Cokwe. From Lunda history we know that Naweej II sent an embassy to Ndumba Tembo, the most senior of the Cokwe chiefs, and that the Cokwe showed a tendency to expand, as is shown by the war of Mwa Cisenge and Cimbundu. In any case, Naweej II told Graça that the Cokwe were his tributaries but did not list them among those tributaries for whom the amounts of annual tribute were specified. It is clear from all the accounts—up to and including Livingstone's observations[8]—that

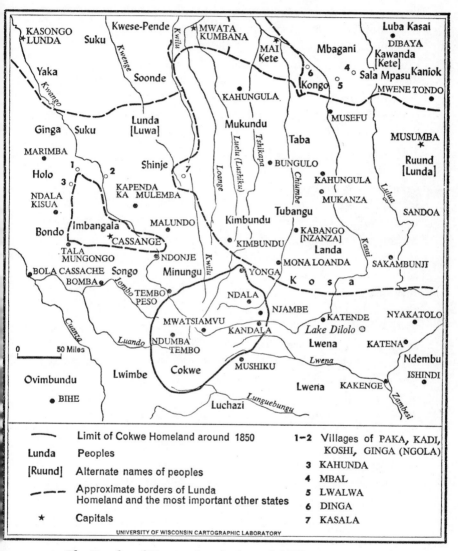

Limit of Cokwe Homeland around 1850

Lunda — Peoples

[Ruund] — Alternate names of peoples

Approximate borders of Lunda Homeland and the most important other states

★ — Capitals

1–2 Villages of PAKA, KADI, KOSHI, GINGA (NGOLA)
3 KAHUNDA
4 MBAL
5 LWALWA
6 DINGA
7 KASALA

UNIVERSITY OF WISCONSIN CARTOGRAPHIC LABORATORY

VIII The Peoples of Eastern Angola Around 1850

the Cokwe were limited within an area bounded in the northeast by a point on the upper Luajima and in the east at the sources of the Chiumbe. From there the boundary ran across the Kasai to the sources of the Lwena and the northern headwaters of the Lunguebungu—which were included in Cokwe territory—and then westwards to a point on the upper Luando, from which it ran to the springs of the Kwilu and along the upper reaches of the Tshikapa to the Luajima. A comparison with Cokwe territory today shows the tremendous expansion which took place after 1850 (see map IX). They now are found in the southern Kwango, and some pockets even reach the lower Kasai near Basongo; they occupy tracts of territory deep into Katanga as far north as Kamina and as far east as Kolwezi, and the whole of northern Angola is culturally dominated by them. All this is the result of Cokwe trading and raiding since 1850.[9]

The Cokwe lived a walking distance of only two weeks from the Ovimbundu, and by 1850 they had had at least a half a century of experience with the long-distance trade in wax, ivory, and slaves. Their own society was very well suited for participation in this trade. As hunters, the collection of wax and ivory posed no problems, and their seminomadic life well-inclined them to be traders. They developed their own methods of trading: they did not come out in large caravans; rather, they sallied forth in numerous small parties which would camp in suitable areas for extended periods and would then finally consider these areas to be their regular hunting territories. They would first settle their tiny villages on the unused bush, and eventually recognize the paramountcy of whomever the local chief was. Then, later, they would choose a chief of their own—a man of chiefly descent who had hunted with the others. Thus there would be two chiefs in the area. When the Cokwe finally had a superiority, not in men but in guns, they would fight and subjugate the original inhabitants. These tactics presupposed an organization which could unite the scattered small lineages, and the Cokwe had this quality within their traditional political structure, which was of Lunda origin. The process of expansion also required that the first

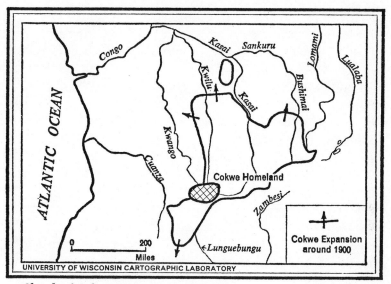

I X Sketch of Cokwe Expansion to 1900

infiltration would not hinder the original inhabitants, and the Cokwe were in this regard not unlike the Fulani in West Africa: as hunters, they filled an ecological niche which was not occupied, or was occupied imperfectly, by others. (They never infiltrated into the areas of the Lwena, Luchazi, and Mbunda, because there the inhabitants were also hunters.[10])

Finally, the Cokwe expansion required a great population, yet in their original domain there were not many peoples. (It is obvious that there was no population pressure of any sort, which would have led to expansion.) But Cokwe society provided for a rapid assimilation of foreigners. It seems that they kept women slaves and granted them equal status with other women, except that the children belonged to the matrilineage of their fathers and therefore became full-fledged Cokwe. (The population increase which such a measure can bring about can be appreciated when it is known that eighty per cent of the Pende population before 1930 was of slave descent.) The Cokwe also assimilated whole foreign populations by settling around them. Gradually the enclosed groups began to be considered as Cokwe by outsiders and they were assimilated culturally, so that they themselves began to see themselves as Cokwe.[11] Among others, this was the case with Lunda Mukundu of northeastern Angola. Cokwe expansion was caused by the trade. The lines of expansion followed the pre-existing trade routes: to the north, mainly to Mai Munene on the Kasai; to the northeast, to the capital of the Lunda; and, somewhat more southward, into Katanga. The major effects of the Cokwe expansion in Central Africa were felt in two regions: the Luba region of Kasai and the Lunda kingdom. (See Map D.)

The Cokwe, first among all the traders, crossed the Kasai to hunt elephants between the Kasai and the Lulua, east of Mai Munene. They reached the Muyawo and the Lulua around 1865, arriving at a crucial moment. A few years earlier a certain Mwamba Mputu, a traditional chief of the Bena Mushilu, had invented a new religious cult, the *lubuku*. Adepts smoked hemp— a trait which had probably infiltrated from Angola earlier—and then dreamed. During their dreams, they saw their *bajangi* or ancestors, who promised them peace and plenty and gave them spiritual direction. The cult was supposed to unite the small Luba Kasai groups into a brotherhood, and, once this was done, the ancestors would come back and take over the leadership of the renovated society. The Bakwa Mushilu, who at that time lived just east of the central Lulua, rallied some other groups on the west bank of the Mwanzangoma to this cult. Among these groups was a small fraction of the Bena Katau, another tiny group; the other fraction of the Katau was led by Mukenge Kalamba, a relative newcomer to the area who started a *lubuku* on his own. At this point he met a Cokwe hunter, Mukwadianga, in the Muyawo valley and traded with him, receiving a red gun and some cotton cloth, and introduced the Cokwe to his covillagers as an ancestor who had already come back. Kalamba understood that this stunt by itself would not be enough to win all the Katau to his *lubuku*—that firearms were needed for that—so he set up his own trade and in 1875 went with a large following to

Mona Kimbundu, a trade center in northeastern Angola, where he met the explorer Pogge as well as Saturnino Machado,[12] a Portuguese trader with whom he established permanent contact. In this fashion the way to the Lulua was opened to Portuguese and Bihean traders. When Pogge and von Wissmann came back in 1881,[13] they were guided by one of Saturnino's men and arrived at Kalamba's village on the Lulua. Kalamba managed gradually to obtain full support from von Wissmann, so that from 1885 on he had the backing of the German explorer in his effort to unify all the Luba of the Lulua Valley. In this fashion he overcame many Luba groups around the present Luluaburg—but not Mwamba Mputu's people. Kalamba also sought support from the caravans who came to trade and tried to prevent his rivals, such as Mwamba Mputu or Katende, from getting guns. Cokwe, Ambaquistas, Imbangala, and even Biheans became his councilors. (The import of firearms was so great that in 1878 some Cokwe were already worried about its effects, and they tried to block further caravans to Kalamba but without success.) Nevertheless, Kalamba did not succeed in his aim. After 1887 he gradually lost favor with the Belgian officers of the station at Luluaburg, who relied more on a group of Songye, the Zappo Zap, who had fled from the east to the fort to avoid Arab slave raiding. In the 1880's, also, Cokwe slave raiders in the southern Kasai around Dibaya started to loot and burn villages, and ten years later they met slave raiders there from the Songye chief Lumpungu, who worked for the Arabs. The Luba populations of the south Kasai were decimated, and after 1885 they fled to Luluaburg in great numbers, where Belgians protected them and then settled them. These people retained the name Luba, while Mukenge Kalamba's group and his neighbors acquired the name Lulua—which the Cokwe had first given them. The distinction between the two new "tribes" was based mainly on the fact that the Luba had fled their homeland and lived on the lands of the others; the Lulua had not suffered in a similar way, which was largely Kalamba's work. He was too powerful to be attacked, and if Luluaburg and European protection came when it came, it was also his doing.

The conditions resulting from the slave trade in 1895 and just afterwards led to the creation of a new tribe, the Lulua—and eventually to the tragic Lulua-Luba wars of 1959–1962.[14]

On their way to the north, the Cokwe gradually settled farther and farther away, among groups just north of their original domains, that were part of the Lunda kingdom. Trade brought them increasing numbers of guns and they were becoming a menace in Lunda internal politics.

Naweej II, who died in 1852, had been abhorred because of his cruelty,[15] and popular resentment against the *mwaant yaav* ran high. He himself had traded with the Portuguese at least since Graça's visit in 1843–1846, and the fact that he sent an embassy to the commander of the Angolan army in Imbangala land in 1852 shows that he wanted to expand the trade.[16] But his methods of trading did not gain for him sympathy from his people; when a caravan arrived, Naweej II would take all the produce and then designate to the caravan a village which they could raid, taking the population into slavery. Moreover, the caravans were composed of strangers, since the Lunda themselves do not seem to have gone out much. His first successor, Mulaji II a Mbala (1852–1857), who was old and sick, appointed Muteba Mbumba as his *sanama*. His successor, Cakasekene, was ousted by Muteba ya Cikombe, a son of Cikombe who had fled in his time with one of the wives of Mulaji a Mbala. Muteba ya Cikombe had been called in by the *citentam* council because of the murders and cruelties which Cakasekene had committed since his accession. Muteba II ruled until 1873. Militarily, his reign was not very different from those of his predecessors; he raided the Kabeya Ilunga, made eight Kanoik villages tributary, defeated Kete, Taba, and Tukongo groups. After the Taba campaign, the revenue from the tribute paid by the Taba was given to the *mwaant yaav*'s favorite general, Mukaza. *Sanama* Mbumba had formerly enjoyed these revenues, and it upset him so much that he went to war and captured Mukaza and the Taba chief in question. Thereupon the king went to war against Mbumba, who backed down and sent the prisoners back to the king, who did not pursue the campaign. This happened in 1872. In 1874 the king died, probably having been poisoned, and was succeeded by Mbala II. Mbumba rebelled, made an alliance with the Cokwe chief Mwa Cisenge, now already in Mukundu land west of the Kasai, and took the capital. Mbala fled with his son to Kayembe Mukulu, where they were killed on orders of the new king Mbumba.

This was the first time that the Cokwe had intervened in a succession crisis in Lunda land. The success of the Cokwe troops armed with rifles was too great for the safety of the Lunda, but they did not realize this. Another ominous fact for the Lunda was that Mbala had not been supported by the Lunda because of his great cruelties, yet Mbumba started his reign with equal savagery. He first fought against the Taba and the Mbagani. Then, in 1876, after he had met Pogge in his capital,[17] he campaigned against Kayembe Mukulu where a challenger, Cimbindu, a son of Naweej II, had fled. Mbumba succeeded in making the Samba tributary. Then he attacked the Kaniok, but was severely defeated by them. Around 1880 Mkaza, the general who lived among the Taba, allied himself with the Cokwe of Mwa Kandala and Cikidila to fight the Kete of Musangu. The Cokwe took the Kete by surprise and captured a rich booty in slaves. But they had also crossed the Kasai into the nucleus of the Lunda kingdom. Mbumba realized the danger and prepared to march against them, but he was prevented from doing so by Cimbindu, who had come back from the Luba kingdom where he had fled after the campaign against the Samba. Mbumba was abandoned by his own army and killed in 1883.[18]

It was during Mbumba's reign that the great Cokwe expansion west of the Kasai began. In 1875 the Cokwe were reported to have villages in the vicinity of Mona Kimbundu (the village of the Lwena chief) on Lunda land of Mona Loanda, which had been founded at least twenty-five years before where the road to Musumba and the roads to Mai Munene and the Kasai bifurcated. In 1878 these Cokwe of Mona Kimbundu had inundated the country, but they still paid tribute to Mona Kimbundu.

But now there were Cokwe villages in the whole area between this point and Mai Munene's capital on the Kasai. In 1879 the emigration movement was so strong that a traveler[19] reports that Cokwe were trekking in great numbers along the rivers Kwilu and Luajimu, thus cutting the Lunda domains in portions. In 1880 two travelers[20] confirmed that the whole area from Mona Kimbundu to Mai was now filled with a mixed Cokwe and Lunda population and that Mwa Cisenge was practically in rebellion against the *mwaant yaav* and remained unpunished. Farther south the population around Kimbundu was by this time described as solidly Cokwe. Between 1878 and 1883 or so, the Cokwe took control of this huge area without great resistance. Mwa Cisenge had first backed one of the two challengers for the title of *bungulo*. The other candidate went to Mbumba and came back with twenty-five *kakwata,* who ousted Mwa Cisenge's man—who had to let the matter rest. But Mwa Cisenge intervened in other successions also. Here he found that his main opponent was the Lunda Musefu (Mwasefo or Musemvo). Both supported rival candidates for the chieftainships of Mai, Kahungula, and Mwata Kumbana. In 1880 Musefu was killed during one of these campaigns and the field was open for the Cokwe, who were also strengthened by their alliance with Mukaza. They destroyed all the Lunda chieftainships east of the Kwilu and west of the Kasai —Mai and Mwata Kumbana included—between 1885 and 1887.[21]

Meanwhile, in Lunda land Cimbindu was overthrown after five months by a rival Kangapu, while the Cokwe were still crossing the Kasai unchecked. Kangapu ruled less than a year and was then killed in 1885 by Mudiba. By now the Cokwe who had tried to progress northwards had been stopped by the warlike Sala Mpasu, and they turned southeast against the Lunda capital. Mudiba gave battle and, after a first victory, was defeated and killed in a second battle, partly through betrayal by some Lunda chiefs who were backing still another pretender. The Cokwe took the capital and sold its inhabitants into slavery. The new king, Mukanza, fled to Kayembe Mukulu but rejoined the capital after the Cokwe had left. When new bands of Cokwe were announced in January 1887, he fled again and was deposed by the *citentam* council and replaced by Mbala III in May 1887, who in turn was ousted and killed by a competitor, his cousin Mushiri, before the end of the year. (To do this, Mushiri allied himself with Cokwe troops!) But toward the end of 1887, the most important Cokwe chief, Mawoka, who had settled near Sandoa, came north and stormed Musumba. Mushiri and his brother Kawele fled and the Cokwe now remained in the country for ten years. They took one fortified village after another, killed or chased the inhabitants away, and went on from Lunda land to attack the Kalundwe and the Kaniok. After several years of campaigning there, it seemed in 1895 that they were overrunning the Kaniok who had been attacked and badly defeated by Ngongo Leteta, an ally of the Arab slave-raider Tippu Tib. It looked for a moment as if the Cokwe, Ngongo Leteta, and Lumpungu, another Arab ally, were overrunning the whole Lulua basin and nearly all the Luba states. In these years—from 1888 to 1898—only a small fraction of Lunda land, the country of the Ine Cibingu, was not occupied. However, Mushiri and Kawele did not despair. They built fortified villages, assembled troops in different hideouts, and suddenly attacked in 1898. All the Lunda now supported the movement and the Cokwe villages which were not fortified were easily destroyed. Mawoka concentrated a huge army near Sandoa in order to battle Mwene Mpanda on the Lulua. After three days of fighting the Cokwe were completely defeated. The Lunda, however, could not follow up their victory, for at this moment Congolese troops began to arrive in the country. Mushiri and Kawele attacked the detachment, but they were defeated and replaced by a new king, Muteba III. However, the two heroes kept up a guerilla war against the Congo Independent State until Muteba finally captured and killed them in 1909.[22]

The Cokwe advance in the Kwango was stopped at about the same time, also by a popular movement against them. The Pende, the Mbuun, and the Wongo, who had been infiltrated deeply after the collapse of Mai Munene, united their efforts and counterattacked at Mbanda, near Kilembe on the Lubwe. Mwata

Kumbana and the other Lunda chiefs of the Kwango, east of the Kwilu, who had survived but were almost powerless, then united themselves with the Mukundu and the victors of Mbanda and tried to oust the Cokwe out of the country completely, but they were not successful; after these wars of the 1890's, when the Congo Independent State occupied the area, the Cokwe had given up very little territory. They maintained a huge enclave in Lele land and were still immigrating west of the Kwilu into Yaka areas around Panzi.[23]

The Lwena seemed to have followed the Cokwe pattern but on a smaller scale, with some territorial expansion eastwards against the southern Lunda. By 1885 the Luvale chiefdoms of Nyakatolo (Nana Kandundu) and Kangombe were raiding and looting the settlements of the Ndembu of Kanongesha. Much Lunda country had already been captured, and the movement went on in the following years. In 1891 Nyakatolo even succeeded in appointing her nephew as *kakenge,* the senior chiefly position among the Lwena. Lunda resistance in the chiefdoms of Ishindi and Kanongesha was relatively slight. There was little political control by the chiefs to begin with; the people did not feel that the whole nation was in danger or that the looting and burning of a neighboring village was important to them, while the aristocracy was thoroughly discredited because it had favored the slave traders in earlier days and had even sold off villages to the raiders, just as Naweej II had done. Kanongesha himself was raided by one of his own chiefs, and the citizens of his capital were sold as slaves. And through it all there was the perennial fight between the members of the aristocratic families for the chieftainships with its sequel of short reigns, assassinations, and lack of chiefly authority. In 1887 some southern Lunda even joined the Cokwe in their campaign against Lunda. But here too a reversal came about in the 1890's. Chief Ishindi asked the protection of Lewanika and was incorporated with a small tract of Lwena territory in Rotse land in 1892. In Kanongesha's chiefdom the rescue came from a simple village headman, Cipenge. He defeated a big raiding party of the Lwena chief, Kangombe, and after that

the attacks subsided. Kanongesha incorporated him into the political system by giving him his sister in marriage and the old system was re-established. To the north of Kanongesha, a Ndembu
warrior, Suwola, defeated the Cokwe around the sources of the
Lulua and then he defeated the Luba Samba near Mutshatsha.
Kazembe of the Luapula, hard pressed by the Yeke in the east,
asked for his help, and Suwola was again victorious and settled
on Samba lands near the upper Lubudi, under the name of Kaw-
ewe. After 1895 another Ndembu commoner, Fwelu, defended
this area successfully against a band of Tetela mutineers of the
Force Publique. But somewhat later a famine obliged these
Ndembu to retreat to their homeland. By 1908 they were back
and have been expanding ever since in the direction of the upper
Lualaba.[24]

The Yeke Kingdom in Katanga and Its Rival, Kazembe

Around 1800,[25] some Nyamwezi had already found their way
to Kazembe's capital, presumably to buy ivory to carry to the
east coast, but the copper from Katanga must very soon have become a major attraction to them.[26] In the first half of the century,
one of the visitors was a certain Kalasa, a subchief from à Sumbwa kingdom, whose mother was a Hinda, the royal family of
many of the interlacustrine chiefdoms. The chiefs of the Sumbwa
knew the political techniques used in the interlacustrine area and
may have adapted some of its features to their own organizations. Kalasa himself had been a leader of caravans from Nyamwezi country to the coast since his youth. During his trip to Kazembe, he reached the western part of the kingdom and made
blood covenants—an east African custom—with the most important
local chiefs, such as Mpande of the Sanga, Kinyama of the Aushi,
and Katanga and Sambwe of the Bena Mitumba. He bought copper and left there some of his men, now known as Yeke. On his
next trip he came with his second son, Ngelengwa (or Mwenda
or Msiri). Msiri decided to return once more, possibly because

his father had succeeded as chief at home. He traveled over Fipa land to the capital of Kazembe, from where one branch of his caravan went to the Aushi while he himself, with others crossed the Luapula. The Kazembe (then Cinyanta Munona) gave him permission to go to Katanga because Msiri had given him the secret to the vaccination against smallpox. All this happened around 1856.[27]

Cinyanta Munona had been elected in 1854 and was then residing at the court of the *mwaant yaav*. While he traveled to the Luapula, his sister Makao governed as a regent. When he arrived back at his kingdom, he found that his sister did not want to be relegated to a secondary position, and she even tried to murder him, so he was finally obliged to exile her to the capital of the *mwaant yaav*. (But Makao remained near the ford on the Lualaba and began to rob caravans; finally she was burned there in her hut, probably by the order of the Kazembe.)

Shortly after the passage through of Msiri, an Arab, Mohammed ibn Saleh, arrived at the capital with a retinue of riflemen, or *rugaruga*, and set up his headquarters there.

Cinyanta Munona died in 1862 and was to be succeeded by a Lukwesa Mpanga, who was not circumcised yet and was isolated in a camp in the bush for this purpose. During his absence, the people of the capital, fearing his forceful personality, elected and crowned Mwonga Nsemba, alias Sunkutu—a fateful decision which was to bring civil war to the country during the next thirty years. When Lukwesa heard the news, he went to his father-in-law, chief Kwalama, in Tabwa country and attacked the local Lunda commanders there. The Kazembe set out for Tabwa country and defeated Nsama, the most important Tabwa chief. But Lukwesa and an Arab slave trader Mpembamoto, whom he had met in Tabwa land, fled to the area of Mpweto, where they settled, and the Kazembe did not pursue them there.[28]

In the meantime, Msiri had settled near chief Katanga and was joined there by Yeke who were already resident in the area. He married Katanga's daughter and also contacted Mpande of the Sanga. Some time later Katanga asked him to fight a rebel village headman, which Msiri did brilliantly, and no doubt the slaves taken during this expedition were given to the Yeke. A short time later Msiri also helped Mpande against two rebellious clan chiefs. Around 1862, six years after his arrival, he refused tribute to Katanga and chased him out. From there he went to Mpande and made him a tributary. After this he spent the next years repelling Luba invaders from the north. It had been the habit of the Luba clans, who lived south and in the area of the lakes, to attack the Sanga and the other populations around them, and the troops of Kazembe had never been able to stop these raids. Msiri now tried to stop this practice. His main enemy there was Kayumba's chiefdom, a small Luba state of the lower Lufira.[29]

Around 1865 two nephews of the Kazembe, Lubalila and Shakadyata, direct descendents of Cinyanta, went to the region of the Lualaba with the intention of rebelling against the Kazembe and of founding a state in Katanga. Kashiba, the Lunda governor of the area, allied himself with Msiri. Msiri's army defeated the rebels and about sixty Lunda were killed. Msiri from then on became an independent power. When news of the defeat reached the Lunda capital, the Kazembe was infuriated and retaliated by killing all easterners—Arabs and Swahili—he could find. Only Mohammed ibn Saleh was spared, but his son was killed. This angered the Swahili and the Arabs, who fled from the Luapula kingdom to flock around Mpembamoto and Lukwesa at Mpweto. In 1868–1870 the groups there felt strong enough to advance against the Kazembe, whom they defeated on the Kalungwishi, but they did not follow up their advantage and returned to Mpweto. The Kazembe hurried to his capital, to find his prestige was gone and that his orders were no longer obeyed. He then fled to the Chishinga, who had always been his allies, but very soon after his arrival there he was killed.[30] (Among the Arabs who had joined Lukwesa was probably a young man, Tippu Tib, who was to become the most famous Arab of them all.)

Kazembe VIII Cinkonkole Kafuti succeeded, but very soon after his election Lukwesa and Mpembamoto came back from

Mpweto and he had to flee to Msiri. Mpembamoto installed Lukwesa as Kazembe. Soon after their arrival, the Arabs wanted to
attack the Chishinga. Lukwesa sent word to the Chishinga that
Mpembamoto was coming and should be attacked. The Chishinga
ambushed the Arab party and killed Mpembamoto. In the meantime, Cikonkole came back with an army composed of Yeke
officers and Lamba soldiers. Lukwesa defeated the Yeke and
Cinkonkole was killed. (This happened in 1872.) Lukwesa Mpanga now came officially to the throne and the first civil war was
over. The new Kazembe even named his capital "the civil war is
over; there is peace in the kingdom." Gradually, however, he became suspicious of his brother, Kaniembo Ntemena, who fled in
1883 to the Chishinga. Kaniembo also ralled the Tabwa of
Nsama, and attacked and routed Lukwesa, who fled to Msiri and
asked him to intervene, even promising his country to Msiri after
his death. He married a daughter of the Yeke king and received
the Yeke insignia of chieftainship.[31]

By now Msiri had become a political power of the first rank.
Between 1865 and 1871 he had incorporated all the possessions
of Kazembe west of the Luapula in his state. His prestige then
was so great that the Sumbwa princes in Tanganyika asked him
for his advice in their war against Mirambo, but Msiri was not
yet omnipotent: in 1872 he lost the campaign against Kazembe
Cikonkole and about the same time he sent a bribe in ivory to
Tippu Tib, who had settled in Kayumba's chiefdom, to fend off a
war with him. Less than a year later he entered into a trade relationship with Tippu Tib, who sent Said ibn Ali as his agent to re-
side in Msiri's headquarters. By 1875 Msiri was reported to be in
alliance with the Swahili and the Arabs. He traded both with the
east and the west coasts and the volume of his trade with the latter was increasing. He was now powerful enough to oblige the
western border villages of the great Luba kingdom to fortify
themselves against possible attacks. He knew that his military
strength depended on the acquisition of ever-increasing numbers
of rifles, which were bought with slaves, copper, and ivory. Therefore, it became a constant part of his policy to remain allied

with at least some of the traders and with those who could close the trade routes. He apparently even sent presents from time to time to the *mwaant yaav*, who could have cut the road to the west coast, and for the same reason he never waged war in western Katanga, with the exception of attacks on Kazembe of the Lualaba. In the late seventies or early eighties, Msiri's father died and Msiri took the title of *mwami* or king. In this move he was backed by the Yeke who arrived with him or after him, while the older Yeke backed the faction of a Mutimbi, the older son of Kalasa; the Wanamutimbi, the Mutimbi party, overcame Msiri in a first battle, but in a second fight Msiri was victorious and the rebels fled to the Luvua near Mpweto and settled there. After this, Msiri fought a revolt by the Bena Mitumba in the Lufira valley, discovered the site of Bunkeya, and built his capital there. Then, from about 1880 to 1884, he conducted campaigns against the Luba chiefdoms on the right bank of the Lualaba. This major set of wars had been sparked off by a Luba chief, Ntambwe, who had killed the younger brother of Said ibn Ali. Said invaded his chiefdom with a Yeke army, took many slaves, and left for Zanzibar with them, entrusting his Swahili soldiers to Msiri. Msiri broke the power of all these chiefdoms with the exception of Kikonja. Yeke residents were placed to watch over the Luba chiefs. But then Kayumba rebelled and it took until the spring of 1884 before Msiri regained control, although he had not won a clear victory. His campaign was cut short by warnings about impending rebellions in the area of Bunkeya, probably by the Bena Mitumba, and, farther away, by the southern Lamba.[32]

Msiri backed Lukwesa and sent a Yeke army with him against Kaniembo in 1885. Kaniembo was defeated and fled and Kazembe Lukwesa entered his capital again. But now he found that the Yeke could be convinced to return to Bunkeya only with great difficulty. Kaniembo, who had fled to the Chishinga, returned from there with their help, and maybe with some Bemba troops, so that Lukwesa thought it wiser not to fight. He crossed the Luapula and settled on the western bank at Cibondo (now Kashobwe) and then at Mwambo, where he was surprised by Kaniembo's troops and killed. (It was now 1886.) But the Yeke who had settled at Cibondo and Mwambo had not been chased away and Kaindu Kakasa, a cousin of Lukwesa, now headed the faction supported by the Yeke. Moreover, Msiri wanted to avenge Lukwesa's defeat because it was also a setback for the Yeke and the insignia given by Msiri to Lukwesa had been burnt. Three Yeke armies, one after another, were sent out against Kaniembo, who first fled to Kilwa Island and then to chief Mwamba of the Bemba, who was just then engaged in a war with the Mambwe. The Yeke sent a force into Bemba country but retreated without giving battle. For several years there was a stalemate which was broken when Kaniembo came back to build his capital at Mwansabombwe in 1890, while the Yeke remained in their strongholds at Cibondo and Mwambo. The war flared up again with varying successes for more than a year, until the death of Msiri became known on the Luapula. This brought a lull in the fighting and Kaniembo sent his Bemba and Chishinga allies back home in 1892. A year later skirmishes broke out again, and Bemba troops were called in once more. The Yeke chiefs Kashobwe and Kaindu realized that they were now quite isolated, since the heartland of the Yeke kingdom was occupied by the Europeans, and they made peace with Kaniembo. For a few years the Luapula valley remained a small haven of peace for a great number of displaced persons from all around who fled the great slave raids. Among them were Nsama and many Tabwa, the Chishinga chiefs, many of the smaller Lunda and Lamba chiefs of the Luapula, and chiefs east and northeast of Lake Mweru. The Arabs—or rather the coastal Swahili-speaking *rugaruga*—were overrunning the whole northern Rhodesian plateau, except for the valley. They were gradually defeated and pacified by the British South Africa Company, which also obliged Kazembe in 1899 to accept colonial rule.[33]

From 1884 to 1887 Msiri was at the height of his power. His interventions in Kazembe's country had almost made him master of the entire kingdom on the Luapula. To the north, Kasongo Kalombo had died around 1885 in the Luba kingdom, and probably Msiri intervened during the succession wars there so that he was able to place tribute collectors next to all major Luba kings and chiefs with the exception of Kikonja. Yeke residents were placed especially in the smaller chiefdoms on the right side of the Lualaba, from Ankoro to the Lomotwa. This, of course, was one of the main trade routes to Msiri's country. In the west, the Yeke stopped at the Lualaba and entertained good relations with most of the *mwaant yaav's* small tributaries there. To the south, they raided deep into Kaonde and Lala territory, some raids even going deep into Ila land. Msiri's prestige was great. He had married Matayu, an Arab girl related to Nsimba, a most important Arab trader near Mpweto, and a Portuguese girl of the Coimbra family, which had been trading in Katanga since the 1850's. Foreign caravans came from everywhere to Bunkeya, and Msiri's own caravans went to the east coast and as far west as Bihé and even Benguela. In 1886, however, Msiri's power began to crumble. Kaniembo Ntemena had killed Lukwesa, but this was soon avenged. Worse was a revolt by the Sanga in the heart of the country. The revolt was occasioned because Msiri had taken the wife of a Sanga man into his harem, but the real reasons were that the Sanga rebelled against the slave raiding of their villages and against overtaxation, for Msiri was in this respect even harsher than the old Lunda masters had been. Despite his superiority in fire weapons, Msiri simply could not crush the revolt, which turned into a guerilla war so successful that it severely hampered trade with the west coast from the end of 1886 onwards. Then, in December 1887, Matayu was killed and Nsimba swore to avenge her. The Yeke first defeated Nsimba but were later driven back by him. However, peace was concluded rapidly with Nsimba on his terms, to prevent a total closure of the route to the east coast.[34]

Missionaries had been at Bunkeya since 1886, and it was known in Europe that there might be great mineral wealth in Katanga. An agent tried to negotiate a treaty by which Msiri would recognize the suzerainty of the British South Africa Company, but Msiri refused. Three Congo Independent State expeditions, especially fitted out to take over in Katanga, arrived in 1891. The second expedition, which arrived in October, found that Msiri would not sign a treaty, so its head, Delcommune, tried to contact the rebel Sanga and also now the Lamba rebel chiefs, notably Katanga and Ntenke, whereupon Msiri called for the agent. But his message was intercepted by the third expedition, which arrived in December. While his dealings with this expedition were going on, Msiri was shot during an interview on December 20. Immediately after his death, the general revolt against the Yeke spread even more, and it seemed as if the Yeke would not even hold a single chiefdom. But the Sanga turned against the Congo Independent State too; they wanted no more conquerors, so that after a year Mukundabantu, Msiri's son and successor, was allied with the Congo Independent State, and campaigned with the Force Publique against the Sanga, the Arabs, and the Swahili until 1900, when a regular administration was built up.[35]

Msiri and his Yeke organized their state on the lines of the pre-existing Lunda patterns, but they added some things and altered some other cultural aspects in upper Katanga. They introduced the sweet potato to the Lamba, new techniques of divination, vaccination against smallpox, blood-brotherhood, a technique to make copper wire, new insignia, new titles, new political ceremonies—to name only some of these changes. Customary law was changed on a number of points by edict, mainly in matrimonial cases, where Sanga law had been very harsh for relatively minor offenses, and to adapt a traditional law, which was not suited to the kind of kingdom Msiri ruled. All in all, however, the Yeke lost their culture and became so incorporated into the local populations that most of them have forgotten their Sumbwa language by now.[36]

The reasons for the great weakness of Kazembe's kingdom and later of Msiri's state have been clearly formulated by Grevisse.[37] It is not only a matter of disruption brought about by civil war over a succession, or of the arrival of larger and larger groups of east Africans and Arabs armed with rifles. A combination of these two trends explains much, but a basic element is the general dissatisfaction of the peoples who were ruled by the Kazembes. They were often cruel and greedy and their lieutenants did not offer protection against the Luba raids to the populations of upper Katanga. The chiefdoms there passed easily to Msiri's side because he stopped these raids and because they fancied they would have a better life under him than under the Lunda. Once the disillusion came, it led to guerilla warfare which no amount of weapons then available could suppress. The importance of the popular dissatisfaction can be measured by the fact that the Sanga fought more than five years against Msiri, and then another nine against the Force Publique, before they surrendered. These general causes are very similar to those which have been invoked earlier to explain the collapse of the Lunda state of *mwaant yaav.*

The Arabs

Arab trade came early to Central Africa. From the 1750's on, the hinterland of Kilwa reached as far as Lake Nyasa, and not much later the Bisa were selling to Arabs—or to Yao who sold to Arabs. Before 1800 Zanzibar was already one of the destination points of this trade. In 1831 there were Arabs at Kazembe's capital and there was now a new route to Zanzibar: from Tabora around the southern tip of Lake Tanganyika or from Tabora to Ujiji, across the lake to Mtoa, and then through Tumbwe and Tabwa land to Kazembe. Ibn Habib and two companions followed the latter road when they crossed the continent between 1850 and 1852 with a party of forty, having left a stock of ivory at Kazembe. Soon afterward, Arab traders like Mohammed ibn Saleh began to settle in Central Africa, first at the Kazembe and later at courts of other chiefs. These settlers would remain in contact one with another and ally themselves with powerful local chiefs to fight other chiefs and to carry the slaves away.

Tippu Tib illustrates the process. One of his first trips, probably in the late fifties or early sixties, led him to Luba land, east from the Lualaba. With a modest retinue of twenty men, he visited Mulongo Tambwe's settlement probably just north of Lake Kabamba. The trading was moderate, and the party returned over Mtoa. Around 1865, after some other trips in East Africa, Tippu Tib went to Bemba and Lungu land. In 1867 he made a second voyage to that region but left his brother in Bemba country while he himself reached the Lungu, where he found an Arab who told him that a long time ago Mohammed ibn Saleh and Habib ibn Hamed had resided in Tabwa land and had been defeated by Nsama, the Tabwa chief. Both were kin of Tippu Tib, which may explain the early interest the latter had in the country west of Lake Tanganyika. From the Lungu, Tippu Tib went to the Tabwa and battled with the defeated Nsamu in alliance with Cungu, the main Lungu chief and an old enemy of the Tabwa. He then went to the Bwile and to Mpweto, where he helped Livingstone.[38]

But the pattern of Arab traders coming out with smaller groups and allying themselves with local chiefs, buying slaves and ivory or copper, relying on the help of kinfolk or relatives by marriage, was already changing. The parties were bigger, raids were made on their own, and Arab merchants influenced local politics to a very great extent. Also, some able personalities emerged among the traders who became leaders and organized territories for a systematic commercial exploitation. Tippu Tip himself was the most able and successful of the new leaders. In his next trip, around 1869 or 1870, he had four thousand men in his caravan. He re-established contact with kinfolk in Bemba and Lungu country, went over to Kazembe, participated in some raiding in Lomotwa land, and then stayed for more than a year in Kayumba's chiefdom and traded with Kayumba, Mulongo Ntambwe, and Msiri. He then went on through Beilande (Songye) to a Kusu or Tetela chief, Kasongo Rushie, who lived on the Lomami, where he succeeded in being invested as chief on the strength of a dubious genealogy. He built up a local army, attacked different neighbors of Kasongo, and stocked slaves and ivory. In the meantime, Mwine Dugumbi had established the

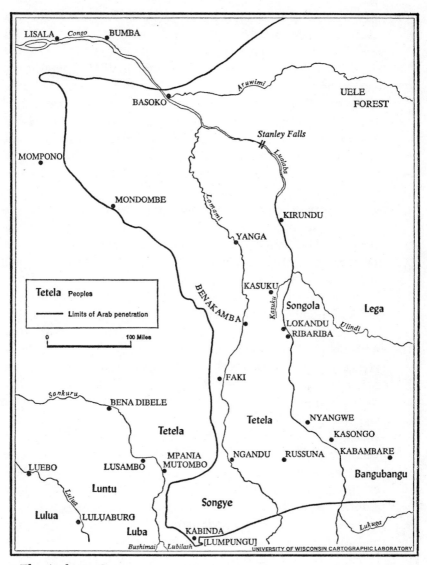

x The Arabs in Congo

post of Nyangwe on the Lualaba since 1869, and a number of Arabs connected with the latter were raiding in Maniema on the road between Nyangwe and Lake Tanganyika, while a few had even reached Lega and Songola country. In 1871 Nyangwe was one of the biggest slave markets in Central Africa. In 1874 these Arabs got involved with a chief who was an ally or a tributary of Tippu Tib. Tippu Tib notified the Nyangwe leaders, Mwine Dugumbi and Munie Mohara (or Mtagamoyo, a relative newcomer), that he would back his ally Russuna against the Nyangwe traders. The leaders capitulated and the settlement came under the loose control of Tippu Tib.

From then on Tippu Tib was no longer a simple trader: he was organizing a state. From Nyangwe he went to Kasongo, upstream on the Lualaba, where he had kinfolk, and here he was given full authority. Everywhere in the region between Lomami and Lualaba, north of the Luba kingdom of Kasongo Kalombo, he replaced chiefs or confirmed them in office, as a paramount would. He imposed a monopoly on the hunting of elephants, he built roads and he organized plantations around the main Arab settlements of Nyangwe and Kasongo, and Islam began to be preached. Tippu Tib himself settled at Kasongo in 1875. In addition to the territory under his direct control, his caravans now went as far as the Sankuru and the capitals of Kasongo Kalombo and Msiri, and shuttled back and forth between Lake Tanganyika and the Lualaba. In 1876 Stanley arrived and Tippu Tib went down the Congo River with him to the mouth of the Kasuku, just below the confluence of the Ulindi, which had been reached some years before by Mtagamoyo. From there he made a fruitful trip to the Lomami and came back to Nyangwe. He and others followed Stanley's trail, and in 1882 Kirundu was founded and expeditions were sent down the Congo River and the Lomami, so that by the summer of 1883 the most advanced groups had reached the confluence of the Congo and the Aruwimi. Stanley came back and founded a European post at Stanley Falls on November 1883. In July 1884 a treaty was signed between the commander of the post and the local Arabs which stated that no more raids were to be undertaken downstream from the cataracts.

During this time, Tippu Tib was putting down a revolt with Russuna in the Lomami-Lualaba area. His representative on the Lomami had died and was replaced by an African, Ngongo Leteta, a Tetela or a Songye, who was given full backing and a great number of rifles, handed out for the first time on such a grand scale. Tippu Tib also went to Kabinda, seat of Lumpungu, chief of the western Beekalebwe and theoretically the paramount of all the Songye. Years before Tippu Tib had helped Kalamba Kangoi, Lumpungu's father, and in 1882 Lumpungu himself had been to the Arabs for help against the eastern Beekalebwe. (Lumpungu too would raid and conquer large areas in the eastern Kasai.) From Kabinda, Tippu Tib went to the Falls, where he arrived in November, and he refused to sign the treaty of July. Instead, he sent twenty caravans downstream. He also received a request by the Sultan of Zanzibar to occupy the eastern half of Congo and replied that he would do so if given the necessary weapons. He remained at the Falls until 1886, when he had come to an agreement with the post commander which was satisfactory for both parties. He left in 1886 for Zanzibar, where the Sultan had called him for consultations.

In the following months a disagreement between a new post commander and the Arabs at the Falls led to the storming of the state post by Bwana Nzinge, Tippu Tib's lieutenant. A state of undeclared war resulted and the Arabs raided with impunity down the rivers and up in the Aruwimi basin and the Uele forests. The Congo Independent State was not able to stop them, but in Zanzibar the Sultan told Tippu Tib that there was a great danger that the Europeans would take over the Sultanate itself. When he was approached by Stanley and the British Consul to come to an agreement with the Congo State, he signed a contract in February 1887 which made him governor of the district of the Falls in the name of the Congo Independent State. He rejoined the Falls in August 1887, where he remained until April 1890— when he left Congo for good. In the meantime he was in a most difficult position. The Europeans believed that he had control over all Arab traders, which was not true, and held him responsible for everything, including the disaster of the rear column of Stanley's Emin Pacha relief expedition. But they were not willing to let him buy or to give him weapons, which were necessary in order to bring all the Arabs under his control. As for the different Arab factions, they blamed him for having sold them out to the Europeans. His departure for Zanzibar in 1890 was motivated by a law suit filed by Stanley, who made him responsible for the rear-column tragedy. On his way to Zanzibar, he fell dangerously ill, but he recovered and arrived at Zanzibar in July 1891.

In the meantime, his old rival Mtagamoyo was making the most of his leave. He had swayed Rumaliza, Tippu Tip's representative at Ujiji, into joining his faction, which was not hard for Rumaliza was already practically at war with the Congo Independent State's posts on Tanganyika. Kibonge and other independent chiefs also joined Mtagamoyo. In May 1892, this faction killed an expedition led by Hodister at Ribariba, a commercial venture destined to break the Arab monopoly. No immediate action followed the murder, but a general war was sparked off in Kasai when Dhanis—still in 1892—maneuvered Sefu, Tippu Tib's son and representative, into the arms of his old enemy Mtagamoyo.

Ngongo Leteta had raided here so much that Tippu Tib had found thirty-two tons of ivory in Kasongo when he came through in 1886. At that time he appointed Sefu as supervisor over the area, a fact which Ngongo Leteta, who had built his camp at Ngandu on the Lomami, did not appreciate. Lumpungu, in alliance with a slave of his father, Mpania Mutombo, had devastated the Been' Ekiiye so thoroughly that remnants of that group under their chief Zappo Zap had fled to Luluaburg in 1887. In 1888 Lumpungu poisoned the chief of the Sanga, a Songye group on the Lubilash, and appointed Mpania Mutombo in his place. In the whole eastern Kasai, slaves and ivory were now no longer traded but were captured in war. By 1889 Ngongo Leteta was overlord over Lumpungu and Mpania Mutombo, as well as over several Tetela settlements, and he raided from Bena Dibele on the Sankuru to the upper Lubilash. But in 1890 the Free State founded the post of Lusambo to stop his advance, and state troops defeated Ngongo. By this time he did not want to be dependent exclusively on the Arabs for his supplies in ammunition, and in 1891 he advanced far west with the intention of making a deal with the Cokwe or with Mukenge Kalamba and receiving weapons from them. Kalamba's military potentialities impressed him so much that he did not attack him, even though Ngongo was refused an open trade route to the west. In 1892 Ngongo returned, attacked Luba Kasai groups near the confluence of Bushimai and Lubilash, and was coming back when a state column under Dhanis surprised and defeated him, whereupon both Ngongo Leteta and Lumpungu went over to the European side. Sefu could not accept the defection of his best ally and was forced to join Mtagamoyo. Dhanis was camping in Ngandu and Sefu tried first to negotiate about the matter, but to no avail. He then attacked in November 1892. Both of the commanders in the field, Sefu and Dhanis, were disobeying orders in fighting. Despite some difficulties, the troops of Dhanis defeated the Arabs in a campaign which lasted until January 1894. The war was inevitable since both the Arabs and the Congo Independent State were competing for a monopoly in ivory and also since the State had to put an end to the slave trade if it wanted to justify its very existence in the eyes of the humanitarians.[39]

South of the Lukuga, Arab penetration was completely different. Here there was absolutely nothing constructive about their presence. Bands of *rugaruga* and of Arabs operated without co-ordination. There was a camp at Mpala on Lake Tanganyika, another near Mpweto, a third one on Kilwa Island, and still another major one near Ndola. Nsimba, who commanded at Mpweto, was forced by the Yeke after 1892 to go to Kilwa and was there ousted by Congo Independent State troops in 1893. Shiwala, the commander of the camp of Ndola, fought for years against the Aushi chief, Kinyama, who succeeded in preventing him from completely ruining the upper Luapula valley. He was finally defeated—but barely—by the Congolese in 1897, and in

1900 by the troops of the British South Africa Company. In this area there never had been a Tippu Tib to co-ordinate and organize Arab power, which shows, by contrast with the events farther north, how much the personality of a single man has been instrumental in the Arab penetration of Maniema.[40]

The Luba and Bemba Kingdoms, Allies of the Arabs

Kasongo Kalombo came to the throne of the Luba in the 1860's after wars of succession which had eliminated three of his brothers. He himself killed one more brother and defeated his paternal uncle as well. During the struggle, all the conquered provinces of the kingdom were lost. Kasongo, however, restored the royal authority by showing great severity and cruelty, but he never did eliminate another brother and contender, Dai, who had taken refuge with Kikonja—whom Kasongo could not overcome, just as Msiri had failed, because he had no fleet. Toward the beginning of Kasongo's reign, Juma Merikani, an Arab trader, entered the country. He was well received by the king, and so were the Angolan traders. Kasongo let these caravans raid and burn the villages that he indicated had refused to pay tribute or had otherwise revolted. He would accompany the raiders himself, and when no faulty village was found he would attack any village, or start a campaign against a foreign enemy—such as, for instance, the Kaniok in 1874.[41] His people must have been outraged and a revolt led by a commoner broke out. A smith named Dela rose up and had so great a following that first he defeated his *mulopwe*. But Kasongo received help from the Angolan traders, and in the second battle the rifles were more powerful than the enthusiasm of Dela's followers. During one of those expeditions of raiding for slaves, Kasongo's gun exploded in his hand and he died shortly afterwards. (This was around 1885.)

Dai Mande, probably the contending brother, followed him in succession and fought against several other brothers who claimed the throne. He killed many of them but lost out against Kasongo Niembo, who killed him. Kasongo Niembo was then challenged by

Kabongo Kumwimba Shimbu. Unfortunately, neither succeeded in ousting his rival and in 1891 both were still at war with each other, but in the meantime they had to accept tribute collectors from Msiri and had become his tributaries. When the Congo Independent State expeditions arrived, Kasongo Niembo took their side, while Kabongo attacked them. In 1895, some of the mutinous Tetela soldiers of the Force Publique arrived in the region and took Kabongo's side, and he was also joined by a number of Angolan *pombeiros*. The State finally won in 1905, however, and divided the kingdom equally between Kabongo and Kasongo Niembo.[42]

By 1850, when the Arabs started to arrive in the territory, the Bemba had just undergone a territorial expansion which subjected most Bisa groups to them. The ivory trade of the Bisa had not been stopped by these wars, and the Bemba were now participating in the trade. Around 1840 a certain Cileshye, chief of a Kasama district, had thus become a wealthy man because the Bisa of Cinsalu traded for him. The *citimukulu* (either Cimbola or Citinta) was not much liked by the people of his district, who told Cileshye that, if he revolted, they would not back their king. This happened, and Cileshye became king, his younger brother became *mwamba*, the next younger one became *nkula*, and so forth. All the chieftainships were reassigned to close members of the king's lineage, a major transformation in the Bemba political organization. The main effect was that the chieftainships which had been autonomous in their relation to the kingship were now again united.[43] Cileshye learned a lesson from his own revolt and proclaimed the ivory trade to be from now on a royal monopoly, which concentrated all wealth and power in his hands, for ivory was often exchanged for guns. When the Ngoni attacked in 1856, the Bemba guns stopped them; it is quite possible that some Arabs were there to help the Bemba—but the guns did it.

After the Ngoni battle the Arabs began to have influence on the different chiefs and on the king. The Bemba, who had always been warlike, soon turned into raiders who were just as predatory as the Ngoni, the Cikunda, the *rugaruga*, and the Yeke, to name only those who raided on the plateau. Around 1870 slaves were very cheap in Bemba land which meant that the Bemba had been highly successful in their raids against the Mambwe, Lungu, Iwa, and Bisa. Another indication was that by now the whole of Bisa land was under Bemba domination. By this time Cileshye had died and had been succeeded by the simple-minded Bwembia, who in turn was ousted by Citapankwa, the younger brother of the *mwamba*. He was a warrior of renown and remained on the throne from 1866 to 1887, but his successor was weak and the *mwamba*, traditionally the second strongest chiefdom and now a chiefdom occupied by an older and more experienced man, began to take the lead in Bemba affairs until his death in 1898. Before his death, Bishop Dupont of the White Fathers took over the direction of the chiefdom—and practically of all the Bemba for a while—and brought them peacefully under British control in 1899. The Bemba came out of the years of turmoil much stronger than before, in large part because of the reorganization of Cileshye, and because of the determined personalities of rulers since Cileshye, their alliance with the Arabs, and the raiding of other peoples and their refusal to allow east coast traders to attack other Bemba settlements. They used their alliance with the slave traders to their advantage—unlike the Luba, who suffered under them.[44]

Conclusion

Change unfolds itself in unpredictable ways. Yet an account of the history of the states of Central Africa often gives the impression of a *déjà vu:* there are leitmotivs which occur over and over again. Even a superficial analysis shows that these regularities in history are related to the structural features of the political systems involved, and over and above this there is the great event in Central African history from 1500 to 1900—trade, and especially the slave trade.

All the major kingdoms in Central Africa shared three structural features which led to similar developments, or "consequences," in their history. Everywhere, even among the Ovimbundu to some degree, not only was the ruler at the apex of the political structure but he was its prime mover. Therefore, the varying personalities of kings have left a deep imprint on the history of their realms. States undergo "expansions," "ages of splendor," and "periods of decadence" in rapid succession and in no logical order of development because of the happenstance of the changing personalities of their rulers. The best-documented case can be seen in Kongo history; the most celebrated one is the epic of Nzinga, queen of Matamba.

Everywhere, too, the system of succession to the throne allowed for the possibility of civil strife, of armed conflict between challengers to the throne, and inevitably the power of a state was at its weakest during an interregnum. There are numerous examples of outside powers who allied themselves with one faction or another, thus entering into the internal politics with the resulting possibility of breaking up that kingdom. The Portuguese tried it in Kongo during the sixteenth century, the Cokwe succeeded in Lunda, Msiri against Kazembe, the Kololo in Lozi land. And in all cases where a state ceased to exist, the breakdown was the immediate result of a civil war during an interregnum.

Another common feature of the major kingdoms was a system of territorial rule whereby the outer provinces were considered as tributaries, often enjoying an internal autonomy and even sometimes being ruled by the very houses of chiefs who had been their rulers before their incorporation into the kingdom. This was least true of the kingdom of Kongo—but even there the province of Mbata was a case in point. And in all the states that were not on the coast, this autonomy was a prominent feature. The practice of "indirect rule" and the concomitant ubiquitous fading away of the power and authority of the central government in the outlying provinces explains why a balance of power never existed between the major states, and why there never was a struggle for hegemony over large parts of the savanna. For instance, the power of the Luba and the Lunda over their peripheral provinces was too weak to lead to a conflict between them; there are many cases similar to that of the province of Kayembe Mukulu, which lay between Luba and Lunda and which paid tribute now to the Lunda, now to the Luba, and was left in peace by both. The Luba, Lunda, Kazembe of the Luapula, Bemba, and Lozi never fought each other for long and never participated in a system of alliances, of building up a balance of power over the whole interior. The same is true of the coastal states, with the partial exception of the colony of Angola, which was striving for hegemony; but even here the fringes of Portuguese-controlled land were ruled by "vassal" chiefs who essentially were in charge of tributaries.

One of the first consequences of this feature was that provinces could break off from the kingdom whenever circumstances were favorable. This happened in Kongo, in the Kuba kingdom, and in the Lunda empire, where every ruler who was far enough away from the *mwaant yaav* became independent. The most classic instance of this is revealed by the story of Kazembe of the Lualaba, who set himself up as an independent power at the border between the lands of the Kazembe of the Luapula and the country of the *mwaant yaav*, the point where the power of both was weakest.

A second consequence of autonomy was that the existing system of territorial control often reduced itself to sheer exploitation: outer provinces paid protection money against possible raids from the center, and the center tried to obtain maximal tribute from these regions but felt no obligation to protect them against enemies from the exterior. The populations of these provinces resented this and could not be expected to remain loyal followers of the kingdom. When they saw an opportunity to free themselves from the exactions of the center, they took it. A good example of this is provided by the developments in the Luapula kingdom, where the chiefdoms of what is now southern Katanga defected to Msiri.

The regularities outlined are evident and the link with structural features of the political system are obvious. It is the task of anthropologists to work them out in greater detail.

Trade, mainly the slave trade, began in 1500 and increased in volume and intensity throughout the centuries. It was the one great continuing event in Central African history until 1900. The slave trade fostered raids and wars, since most slaves were prisoners of war, and it brought guns, first to the traders themselves, then to rulers in the interior, who exercised a monopoly on the markets which were growing at or near their capitals. With these guns came power. The Lunda used them to found the Luapula and the Yaka kingdoms. The traders used them in Kongo and, later, in the interior in the nineteenth century, to overrun the established states and to raid their populations. The whole history of the colony of Angola is motivated by economics, by the desire for mines to exploit and people to use in the slave trade. Although raids and wars cannot always be attributed to the desire to capture slaves, it seems that the perennial raids of the Lunda on the Sala Mpasu, of the Yaka and the Imbangala on the populations of the Kwango, of the Angolan troops on the fringes of the colony—and of course of the expeditions by the Arabs and their Bemba, Songye, Tetela, and Swahili allies—are to be explained mainly as wars for slaves. The slave trade has conditioned the developments in inland Central Africa since the 1840's, and it has conditioned the history of the coastal states almost since its inception around 1500. But it has also exercised a deep influence on the interior, especially in the Lunda realm, since the second half of the seventeenth century.

The history of Central Africa is the story of a number of kingdoms that underwent a regular and fairly predictable development. It is possible that, despite the succession problem, the development of the African states would have gone on had there been no influence from outside. But as it actually happened, the political structures could not cope with the new stresses fostered by the slave trade and tended to collapse during an interregnum, when their power was weakest. The interaction between the growing slave trade and the normal evolution of the political systems explains most of the history of the kingdoms in Central Africa from 1500 to 1900.

*Reference
Matter*

A Note on the Chronology of Central African History

The chronology of the African kingdoms on the coast, at least since 1485, has in general been derived from written contemporary or near contemporary documents. Earlier dates, such as placing the foundation of the kingdom of Kongo in the fourteenth century, have been derived from written data of a later period. For instance, this date for Kongo was based on two reports dated around 1620.[1] The approximate dates for the foundation of Loango, Kakongo, and Ngoy, although they seem to be earlier than 1485, are unknown. With regard to the kingdom of Ndongo, it has been argued that it took form only around 1500, although it was certainly well established by 1519.[2]

The chronology of the African states in the interior has usually been derived either from a calculation by generations, one generation being thought, more or less arbitrarily, to cover a span of thirty years, or by lengths of reigns, which are often arbitrarily calculated as covering spans of twenty years. A few other dates, derived from written sources, are available, and it is thought that once the written documentation about Angola in the eighteenth and nineteenth centuries has been sifted through additional specific dates will become available. The earliest of these dates are the foundation of the Lunda state in 1600 (certainly not later and possibly twenty to thirty years earlier),[3] the foundation of the state of Kazembe around 1740,[4] the existence of the Boma state by 1641,[5] and the existence of the Yaka state of Kasongo Mwene Putu by 1700.[6] (This state may have been founded after 1657, although the evidence here is not conclusive.) Finally, the Kuba kingdom must have been established after 1668, because the Imbangala, at a time when they had not yet overrun the Kongo state, are mentioned in the tradition. Another date from Kuba history, derived from a sun eclipse, is 1680 for the reign of King Mbakam.[7]

These early dates give us the general framework of the whole chronology for the interior. Lunda expansion took place between 1600 and 1740; the foundation of the Luba kingdoms before 1600; and so forth. The method used has been to take all known data—oral, written, or astronomical—and then to calculate, by length of reign or by generation, so as to get fairly reliable dates. Results are given here for the Luba and Lunda kingdoms only, since those for Kazembe history and for the Kuba are accessible elsewhere. So far, detailed chronology of the Yaka kingdom is impossible to obtain because of the lack of data, and the same is true for the Bemba and to a lesser degree for the Lozi or Rotse kingdoms. In the last two cases, dates are available since 1840 or 1850, while for the Yaka nothing definite can be said between plus or minus 1700 and 1870![8]

There is a great gap in Lunda chronology between 1600 and 1846, the date of Graça's arrival at the court of Naweej II. However, after the death of Naweej II in 1852, the chronology is well established by written contemporary testimonies. The only known date between 1600 and 1846 is 1740, when Kazembe II left the court to conquer his kingdom on the Luapula. At that time the *mwaant yaav* was Mukanza. At the time of Kazembe I (Nganda Bilonda—the father of Kazembe II), Muteba, elder brother of Mukanza, was *mwaant yaav*. In fact, Kazembe I was the son of Cinyanta, and was born in Muteba's capital. Muteba's reign must therefore have been at least twenty years (childhood of Kazembe I plus part of his reign). On the Kazembe side one must equate two generations (active lives of Cinyanta and Kazembe I) with one in Lunda (the reigns of Muteba and Mukanza). This would seem excessive if it were not that a variant on Lunda tradition tells us that two more brothers ruled between Muteba and Mukanza. It can be shown theoretically that the combined reigns of half brothers from the same father are equivalent to the life span of the youngest *at the most,* i.e., in the extreme case, to seventy years or so.[9] Taking thirty years per generation, it could then be estimated that Kazembe II started to rule in plus or minus 1740, Kazembe I in plus or minus 1710, Cinyanta in plus or minus 1680, Mwin Tibaraka in plus or minus 1650. Muteba ruled from 1690 at least, and perhaps even from 1680. His predecessor, *mwaant* Yaav Taweej I, came to the throne in 1650; *mwaant* Luseeng, predecessor of Naweej I, in 1620; and Cibinda Ilunga in 1590, which fits the plus or minus 1600 date for the foundation of the Lunda empire, with a ten-year difference.

The next item to consider is the ascendancy of Mutanda Yembeyembe. If he was a younger brother of Naweej I and a coeval of Cinyanta, the dating would correspond closely to the one proposed above for Muteba. We know that Mutanda did not die at the accession of Muteba and indeed was alive when Kazembe I came to power. He disappeared about 1710, which we assume to be the date of his death. If Naweej started to rule in 1650 or 1660, we have then a sixty- or seventy-year span for a set of half brothers. Seventy years comes very close to a maximum, sixty years seems more reasonable. If this is so, Naweej I's accession would be in 1660 and Muteba's in 1690, and it also leaves a shorter time span for the half-brother reigns of Muteba and Mukanza.

This conclusion is supported by data from Lunda history after 1740. Between Mukanza and the death of Naweej II, three rulers and three generations are given by Verhulpen and Duysters[10] with a mean of thirty-seven years per reign and per generation, which seems excessive. Dias de Carvalho gives three rulers and three generations, with two of the four brothers of the Mukanza-Muteba set, which also agrees better with tradition as preserved in Kazembe.[11] Van den Byvang gives only two reigns covering two generations plus two of the four brothers, which seems even more unlikely than the Verhulpen date.[12]

On the face of it, the Carvalho version would seem to tally best with the other chronological data. The main problem now is that the reigns of the four brothers cover not only the period 1690–1740, i.e., fifty years, but a longer one. The maximum to which this period can reasonably be lengthened is twenty years, to 1760; in that case the lifespan of the youngest brother would cover seventy years, and his father Naweej I would have died almost immediately after his birth. If so, the three generations of later rulers from 1760 to 1852 would have a mean length of generation and of reign of about thirty-one years, which seems reasonable.[13]

Lunda chronology from 1600 to 1852 as proposed would then be as given in the list below.

Lunda dates		*Kazembe of the Luapula*	
Cibinda Ilunga	1600–1630		
Mwaant Luseeng	1630–1660	Mwin Tibaraka	1650–1680
Mwaant Yaav Naweej			
I	1660–1690	Cinyanta	1680–1710
Muteba	1690–1720	Kazembe I	1710–*1740*
[Two brothers ruled?]		Nganda Bilonda	
Mukanza	1720–*1740*	Kazembe II	*1740*–1760
Mulaji	1740–1750	Kaniembo	
Mbala	1750–1760		
Yaav yaMbany	1760–1810		
Cikombe Yaav	1810–1810[a]		
Naweej II	1810–*1852*		

[a] Ruled only two months.

This chronology is of course not definitive. New dates could be ascertained. If, for instance, it could be known who the *mwaant yaav* was who ruled when the *pombeiros* passed, data would be available for the period 1806–1815. Eighteenth-century documents from Angola may yield more information as well; and the sun eclipse of 1680, if still remembered in the oral tradition, could then be ascribed to a particular king.

Additional rulers for Kazembe and for Lunda, as given in the text, are as follows:

Lunda rulers	*Kazembe of the Luapula rulers*
Mulaji II a Mbala	Ilunga or Lukwesa: Kazembe III
Cakasekene	Kibangu Keleka: Kazembe IV
Muteba II ya Cikombe	Mwongo Mfwama: Kazembe V
Mbala II	Kapumb
Mbumba	Cinyanta Munona: Kazembe VI
Cimbindu	Lukwesa Mpanga (1)
Kangapu	Mwonga Nsemba or Sunkutu:
Mudiba	Kazembe VII
Mukanza II	Cinkonkole Kafuti: Kazembe VIII
Mbala III	Lukwesa Mpanga (2): Kazembe IX
Mushiri	Kaniembo Ntemena: Kazembe X
Muteba III	

In Luba dates, the earliest one is Ilunga Liu's [Ilunga wa-Lwefu], who lived around 1600 when his younger relative, Cibinda Ilunga, founded Lunda. Between that date and 1874, when Cameron visited Kasongo Kalombo, no certain date is known. In addition, as has been seen, there is quite some controversy over the number and order of succession of the kings (see Chart II).

Kalala Ilunga was a generation older than Liu, and Kongolo a generation older than Kalala Ilunga. Roughly speaking, one could place Kongolo's arrival during the sixteenth century. To calculate the dating more closely is not very useful now. In Luba's later history, better information can be given, for example, about Kasongo Kalombo's immediate predecessors. Ilunga Kabale fought against Msiri, which means that he must have died after 1865.[14] Kumwimba Ngombe, Ilunga's father, was remembered by old Arabs in Tippu Tib's time.[15] If we count generations by thirty years, he may have died about 1835. His father, Ilunga Sungu, would also have ruled for thirty years, or from about

1805; in other words, the reigns of Ilunga Sungu and his successors belong to the nineteenth century. Because oral tradition specifies that all these kings had long reigns, a full reckoning of thirty years per reign would not be too excessive. Kadilo, two long generations before Ilunga Sungu, could then be said to have come to power around 1740. There would, thus, be six generations of rulers between Liu and Kadilo according to the longest possible count, or four according to the shortest. If one reckons that Liu died in 1620 or thereabouts, even the shortest count by generation gives an acceptable estimate: four generations at thirty years equals one hundred twenty years from the year 1740 equals the year 1620. And of course, with the longer number of generations, which seems to us the more likely possibility, a mean between 1600 and 1740 per reign/per generation would be a mean of twenty-three years and four months.[16]

In short, it is clear that Luba chronology could be considerably improved. It is more than likely that a correct order of reigns can be elicited from the traditions and a few more dates (such as the arrival of the first Arab, contacts with Lunda or Kazembe, and astronomical data) can be ascertained. It would then be possible to date other events in this whole area with reference to the histories of Lunda, Luba, Kazembe, Kuba, and Yaka. And hypothetical data for one chronology could be checked by comparison with another one. For instance, it seems that Mai Munene founded his kingdom around 1650—certainly between 1600 and 1700 (Lunda data). He arrived at the same time as the Pende, who had been ousted from the Luie valley around 1620. The Bieng, a Kuba group, encountered the Lunda, and somewhat later around 1650, the Pende. Mai met the Pende after—but just barely after—he had settled. Finally, there are some dates to be deduced from the number of age groups which succeeded each other in Pende land in relation to the first arrival of the Cokwe traders, i.e., plus or minus 1850. This calculation also gives plus or minus 1650 as a date for the arrival of the Pende. All the estimates then concur to fix the foundation of Mai Munene's state and the final settlement of the Pende at about 1650.

The list of Kongo and Lozi (Rotse) rulers, as mentioned in the text, are given below. In some cases with the Kongo chronology the dates should be regarded as tentative.

Kongo kings	*Lozi rulers*
Wene	Mboo
. . .	Inyambo
Nzinga Kuwu [1491]	Yeta I
[contender, Mpanzu a Kitima]	Ngalama
Pedro I	Yeta II
Diogo I d. 1561	Ngombela
Affonso II d. 1561	Yubia [regent]
Bernardo I d. 1566	Musanawina
Henrique I d. 1567	Musananyanda
Alvare I d. 1576	Mulambwa
Alvare II d. 1614	Silumelume
Alvare III d. 1622	Mubukwanu
Pedro II d. 1624	Sebitwane (Rotse)
Garcia I d. 1626	Imasiku (Lozi)
Ambrosio I d. 1631	Mamocesane (Rotse)
Alvare IV d. 1636	Sekeletu (end Rotse)
Alvare V d. 1636	Sepopa (Lozi)
Alvare VI d. 1641	**Mwanawina II**
Garcia II d. 1661	Lobosi or **Lewanika**
Antonio I d. 1665	
Alvare VII d. 1666	
Alvare VIII d. 1666	
Affonso II	

. . .

(approximately thirty rulers between Affonso II and Pedro IV)
[contender, Pedro III]
[contender, João III] **[1715]**
Pedro IV Agua Rosada (1709–reunifies country)
Pedro V Elelo

List of
Abbreviations

Amer. Anth.	American Anthropologist
Amer. J. Phys. Anthr.	American Journal of Physical Anthropology
ARSC	Académie royale des sciences coloniales. Classe des sciences morales et politiques. Mémoires in 8°. Nouvelle série (succeeds IRCB).
ARSOM, *Bull. des séances*	Académie royale des sciences d'Outre-Mer. Classe des sciences morales et politiques. Mémoires in 8°. Nouvelle serie (succeeds ARSC).
BJIDCC	*Bulletin des jurisdictions indigènes et du droit coutumier congolais*
Bol. cult. museu Angola	*Boletim cultural do museu de Angola*
Boll. soc. geog. ital.	*Bollettino de la società geografica italiana*
BSGL	*Boletim da sociedade de geografia e de história de Lisboa*
Bull. amis art ind. au Katanga	*Bulletin des amis de l'art indigène au Katanga*
Bull. géog. hist. et desc.	*Bulletin de géographie historique et descriptive*
Bull. inst. d'etud. centrafr.	*Bulletin de l'institut d'études centrafricaines*
Bull. inst. hist. belge	*Bulletin de l'institut historique belge de Rome*

Bull. soc. anth.	*Bulletin de la société d'anthropologie de Paris*
Bull. soc. rech. congo.	*Bulletin de la société des recherches congolaises*
Bull. soc. roy. belge d'anth. et préhist.	*Bulletin de la société royale belge d'anthropologie et de préhistoire*
Bull. soc. roy. belge de géog.	*Bulletin de la société royale belge de géographie*
Cahiers d'étude afr.	*Cahiers d'études africaines*
CEPSI	*Bulletin du centre d'etude des problèmes sociaux indigènes*
Deutsche geog. Blät.	*Deutsche geographische Blätter*
Geog. J.	*Geographical Journal*
IRCB	Institut royal colonial belge. Classe des sciences morales et politiques. Mémoires in 8°
J. Afr. Admin.	*Journal of African Administration*
JAH	*Journal of African History*
JRAI	*Journal of the Royal Anthropological Institute of Great Britain and Ireland*
J. Roy. Geog. Soc.	*Journal of the Royal Geographical Society*
J. soc. African.	*Journal de la société des Africanistes*
La géog.	*La géographie*
Mens. admin.	*Mensario administrativo* [Angola]
MRAC	Musée royal de l'Afrique Centrale: Annales. Série *in 8°. Sciences humaines* (succeeds MRCB)
MRCB	Musée royal du Congo Belge: Annales. Série *in 8°. Sciences humaines linguistique, anthropologie, ethnologie*
NADA	*The Southern Rhodesia Native Affairs Department Annual*
N. Rhod. J.	*Northern Rhodesia Journal*
Précis hist.	*Précis historiques*
Prob. Afr. Cent.	*Problèmes d'Afrique Centrale*
Proc. Roy. Col. Inst.	*Proceedings of the Royal Colonial Institute*
Rev. belge géog.	*Revue belge de géographie*
Rev. congo.	*La Revue congolaise*
Rev. ethnog.	*Revue d'ethnographie*
Rev. géog.	*Revue de géographie*

Rhodes-Livingstone J.	*Rhodes-Livingstone Journal*
Roy. Col. Inst. Proc.	*Royal Colonial Institute Proceedings*
S. Afr. Arch. Bull.	*South African Archaeological Bulletin*
Verhand. Gesell. für Erd.	*Verhandlungen der Gesellschaft für Erdkunde*
Zeits. Erd.	*Zeitschrift für Erdkunde*
Zeits. Ethnol.	*Zeitschrift für Ethnologie*

Notes

Introduction

1 Very few missionaries in Kongo, for instance, knew the language, and interpreters played a prominent role at the mission stations (see M. l'Abbé L. Jadin, "Le Congo et la secte des Antoniens . . . ," *Bull. inst. hist. belge*, XXXIII [1961], 442, 446, 451–53, 456–57, 487). For example, see pp. 534–35: "Not to know the language is indeed a great evil and prevents great good"; and see pp. 581, 586, for the importance of the interpreters. De Gallo was an expert among the missionaries at the beginning of the eighteenth century because he spoke the local language. For the 1750's, see *La pratique missionaire des PP. Capucins Italiens . . .* (1931), pp. 83–113, in which the role of the interpreters is made clear.

2 Many of these documents have been used, however, by Jadin, especially in the archives of Luanda, Lisbon, and the Vatican, and of the Capuchin Fathers of different Italian provinces. Jadin has an article ("Relation sur le royaume du Congo du P. Raimondo da Dicomano, missionaire de 1791 à 1795," ARSC, *Bull. des Seances*, III [1957]) about the missions in the eighteenth century.

3 For Bemba, see A. I. Richards, "Social Mechanisms for the Transfer of Political Rights . . . ," *JRAI*, XC, No. 2 (1960), 175–90; and A. E. Jensen, "Die staatliche Organisation und die historischen Ueberlieferungen der Barotse am oberen Zambesi," *Jahresb. Würt. Ver. Handelsgeog.*, L (1932), 79. For Lozi, see

M. Gluckman, "The Lozi of Barotseland . . . ," in E. Colson and
M. Gluckman, eds., *Seven Tribes of British Central Africa* (1951),
pp. 30–31; and M. Gluckman, *The Judicial Process among the
Barotse of Northern Rhodesia* (1955), *passim*. For Luapula
[Lunda of Kazembe], see two works of I. Cunnison: *The Luapula
Peoples of Northern Rhodesia* (1959), p. 149; and *History on the
Luapula* (1951), *passim*. For Ovimbundu, see A. C. Edwards, *The
Ovimbundu under Two Sovereignties* (1962), p. 13. For northern
Lunda, see L. Duysters, "Histoire des Aluunda," *Prob. Afr.
Cent.*, XII (1958), 76; for Luba, see V. L. Cameron, *Across
Africa* (1877), pp. 305, 308; and use fieldnotes for Kuba in
A. Neves, *Memorias do expedição ao Cassange* (1854), pp. 113–
15.

4   For matters relating to Kuba, see J. Vansina, *Geschiedenis
van de Kuba . . .* (1963), chapter I. For examples of praise song
in Luba Katanga, see S. Peeraer, "Gouwzang der Bene-Lupulu,"
Congo, I (1938). Praise poetry is to be found in three works by
R. van Caeneghem: "De kasalazang der Baluba," *Congo*, I, No. 5
(1936), 680–705 [Kasai]; "De kasala-zang van den Bakwanga-
stam," *Congo*, II, No. 5 (1936), 677–715 [Luba Kasai]; "De
kasala-zang der Bakwa-Tshimini," *Congo*, I, Nos. 1–2 (1937),
103–33 [Luba Kasai]; and praise poetry of the Kongo in J. van
Wing, *Etudes Bakongo: I. Histoire et Sociologie* (1960), 37–38,
46–66, 71–72, 76–77. For praise names, see E. Labrecque, "La
tribu des Babemba," *Anthropos*, XXVIII (1933), 634, 636, 638,
640–42, 646. For examples of history embedded in ritual, see
M. Bastin, *Art décoratif Cokwe* (1961), pp. 42–45, and J. de
Decker, *Les clans Ambuun (Bambunda) d'après leur littérature
orale* (1950), p. 27; the latter also gives instances of many other
oral genres which can be useful to historians.

5   Cunnison, *History on the Luapula;* and J. Vansina, *De la tradition orale. Essai de Methode historique* (1961).

6   To apply to a whole people what applies only to a ruling family
is the standard error often made in the appreciation of oral
sources.

7   See Cunnison, *History on the Luapula.*

8   See Cunnison, *History on the Luapula;* and Vansina, *Geschiedenis
van de Kuba. . . .*

9   A typical case of this way of proceeding is exemplified by E.
Verhulpen, *Baluba et Balubaisés* (1936), where oral traditions
from all over northern Katanga, written down by different mem-

bers of the administration, are merged together. However, many other authors have proceeded in the same fashion.

10 For archaeological reports on the iron age, see B. Fagan, "Pre-European Ironworking in Central Africa . . . ," *JAH,* II, No. 2 (1961), 199–210; J. Nenquin, all references (see Bibliography); and J. Hiernaux and J. de Buyst, "Note sur une campagne de fouilles à Katoto . . . ," *Zaïre,* XIV, Nos. 2–3 (1960), 251–53. G. M. Childs conducted an important excavation at Feti (Ovimbundu) which is not yet published.

11 See V. [G.] van Bulck, *Les recherches linguistiques au Congo Belge* (1948); M. A. Bryan, *The Bantu Languages of Africa* (1959); and R. J. Jones, *Africa Bibliography Series: South-east Central Africa and Madagascar* (1961), the section on linguistics, for available materials.

12 Vansina, *Geschiedenis van de Kuba* . . . , is a case where it can be shown that population immigration and emigration has gone on from about 1600 until now; this means that the Kuba were exposed to new culture elements continuously rather than discontinuously, as is postulated by the American (Kroeber) and Austrian schools. Moreover, immigration from a single foreign culture over a period of time does not mean exposure to the same culture elements during the whole of that period, because the foreign culture also changes constantly. (See, in this same volume, map 14, showing the distribution of Mongo and Luba Kasai [Lulua] elements in Kuba country. The map represents in actual fact the impact of at least a century and a half of immigration. During that period, Luba [Lulua] culture underwent foreign influences and great changes as well.) See also P. Denolf, *Aan de rand van de Dibese* (1954), vol. I.

13 See G. P. Murdock, *Africa: Its Peoples and their Culture History* (1959), pp. 284–306, 364–74; see also C. D. Forde, ed., *Ethnographic Survey of Africa: East Central Africa* (1950).

14 See H. von Wissmann, *Unter Deutscher Flagge: Quer durch Afrika* (1890), pp. 82–106, 371; von Wissmann, *Meine Zweite Durchquerung Aequatorial Afrikas vom Congo zum Zanzibar* (1890), annex; and A. van Zandijcke, *Pages de l'histoire du Kasaï* (1953), pp. 7–14.

15 Van Zandijcke, *Pages de l'histoire du Kasaï,* pp. 116–54. The events which led to the distinction between Luba Kasai and Lulua would lead in the long run to the hostilities between them in 1959–1961. See P. Rauq, "Les relations entre tribus au Kasai.

Leurs incidences géopolitiques et économiques," *Africa-Ter-vuren*, VII, No. 2 (1961), 47–58.

Chapter One

1 See H. Baumann and D. Westermann, *Les peuples et les civil-isations de l'Afrique* (1948), pp. 146–70, for his "cercle Zam-bèze-Angola"; and pp. 170–91 for "cercle congolais du sud." The Bolia are part of his "cercle congolais du nord" (see map after p. 203). The Boma and Sakata are also included in this group. The "cercle Zambèze-Angola" includes many groups which are not included here: the matrilineal Bantu east of the Lwangwa and the Ambo group of southern Angola. See M. J. Herskovits, *The Human Factor in Changing Africa* (1962), p. 57 (map), pp. 62–94 (text). Ovimbundu and Lozi are part of the "East African Cattle Area," the rest of the "Congo area," which encompasses many more groups to the north. G. Mur-dock, *Africa . . .* (1959), pp. 284–306, has a Mongo province, to which the Bolia group belongs, a Luba province, and a cen-tral Bantu province, which again includes the matrilineal peo-ples east of the Lwangwa. The Ovimbundu belong to his "South-western Bantu," pp. 369–74, and the Lozi to his "Middle Zam-besi Bantu," pp. 364–69.

2 Murdock, *Africa . . .*, on pp. 234–35 describes the American complex: on pp. 206–7 the Malaysian complex, and on pp. 68–70 the Sudanic complex. V. Baesten, "Les Jésuites au Congo (1548–1659)," *Précis hist.* (1892), p. 532, mentions the crops cultivated in Congo in 1548. Maize is not mentioned. F. Pigafetta, *Rela-tione del Reame di Congo e delle circonvicine contrade . . .* (1591), mentions maize as *Masa maMputo*, "grain of the Portu-guese," and since Lopes, his informant, left Kongo in 1583, it must have been cultivated by then. Evidence on the introduction of manioc is less clear. It is not mentioned by Pigafetta but G. A. Cavazzi, *Istorica descrizione de'tre'regni Congo* (1687), writes that by 1667 it was widespread. See M. de Morais Martins, *Con-tacto de Culturas no Congo Portugues* (1958), pp. 84–85. The Jesuits and residents of Luanda had established farms on the Bengo River by about 1600. They may have introduced manioc there. See R. Delgado, *História de Angola*, II (1948), 82, about donations of land to soldiers in the Bengo area in 1622, which had been occupied almost from the beginning of the *conquista*.

3 On agricultural techniques, see A. I. Richards, *Land, Labour and Diet in Northern Rhodesia* (1939), as an example. Almost every

group has peculiarities of its own in its method of agriculture. For the main crops cultivated, see Murdock, *Africa* . . . , pp. 284–306, 364–74. In 1798, the Bisa did not cultivate any crop of the American complex, or cotton or rice; see F. J. M. de Lacerda e Almeida, *Diarios de Viagem* (1944), pp. 239–40, 247. Both cotton and rice are mentioned by the *pombeiros* of Silva Porto in 1854; see A. da Silva Porto, *Silva Porto e a travessia do continente africano* (1938), pp. 129–30. But manioc, which was spreading from the Atlantic coast, had not yet reached the Bisa. It was not known to the east of the Lozi.

4   P. Denolf, *Aan de rand van de Dibese*, I (1954), 823, discusses for the Kasai the distribution of palm-wine drinkers and palm-oil users. To the east of Kasai, the raphia palm was unknown. For the introduction of palm wine on the Luapula, see R. F. Burton, *The Lands of Cazembe* (1873), pp. 42–43. It has nowadays gone completely out of use and is not listed in recent surveys when alcoholic drinks are mentioned.

5   See L. Magyar, *Reisen in Süd-Afrika* . . . (1859), pp. 320–21n28.

6   For the Lunda of Luapula, see Burton, *The Lands of Cazembe*, p. 42. For the northern and southern Lunda, see D. Livingstone, *Missionary Travels and Researches in South Africa* (1857), p. 321. For the Yaka, see H. Capello and R. Ivens, *From Benguella to the Territory of Yacca* (1882), II, 124. In Kongo in 1595, only the king and the nobles could own cattle: see J. Cuvelier and L. Jadin, *L'ancien Congo d'après les archives romaines (1518–1640)* (1954), p. 97. Also for Kongo, see A. de Sousa Barroso, *O Congo* . . . (1889), pp. 36–37. For Loango, see L. de Grandpré, *Voyage à la côte occidentale d'Afrique 1786 et 1787* (1801), I, 18; and O. Dapper, *Naukeurige beschrijvinge der Afrikaensche gewesten* (1676), p. 149. In Kongo and Loango the possession of cattle was not restricted to royalty, but milking was unknown before the nineteenth century.

7   For the Luapula Lunda, I. Cunnison, *The Luapula Peoples* . . . (1959), pp. 152, 174; and for the northern Lunda, a personal communication of F. Crine.

8   On the markets, see W. Froehlich, "Das afrikanische Marktwesen," *Zeits. Ethnol.*, LXXII, Nos. 4–6 (1940), 234–328; P. Bohannan and G. Dalton, eds., *Markets in Africa* (1962); and J. Vansina, "Long Distance Trade Routes in Central Africa," *JAH*, III (1962), 375–90.

9   For Kongo, Yombe, and Bemba, see A. I. Richards, "Some Types of Family Structure Amongst the Central Bantu," in A. R. Rad-

cliffe-Brown and C. D. Forde, eds., *African Systems of Kinship and Marriage* (1950), pp. 207–51. Cunnison, in *Luapula Peoples* . . . , p. 62 *nl*, adds most of the upper Katanga peoples to the Bemba type of family structure. See V. W. Turner, *The Lozi Peoples of North-Western Rhodesia* (1952), pp. 41–42, for an example of a bilateral system. Information on the northern Lunda derives from personal communication of F. Crine. For the dual-descent systems of the Bolia and Ovimbundu, see N. van Everbroeck, *Mbomb'ipoku: Le Seigneur à l'abime* (1961), pp. 125–60. Also for the Bolia, see M. McCulloch, *The Ovimbundu of Angola* (1952), pp. 17–20. (The Ovimbundu practice simple double descent, and not a more complicated system, as implied by McCulloch.) See A. C. Edwards, *The Ovimbundu under Two Sovereignties* (1962), pp. 14–15; Von Mattenklodt, "Die Kisama," in H. Baumann, ed., *Koloniale Völkerkunde* (1944), pp. 71–108; H. Bogaerts, "Iets over stamboomen," *Congo*, II, No. 4 (1939), 410–25; H. Bogaerts, "Un aspect de la structure sociale les Bakwa Luntu," *Zaïre*, V, No. 6 (1951), 563–609; G. Brausch, "La justice coutumière chez les Bakwa Luntu," *African Studies*, I, No. 4 (1942), 235–42; Denolf, *Aan de rand van de Dibese*, vol. I; L. Liétard, "Etude sommaire sur la tribu des Lulua," *Rev. belge géog.*, LIII (1929), 40–43; A. Samain, "Les Basonge," *Congo*, I (1924), 48–52; R. P. Vervaecke, "Les Bena Lulua," *Rev. congo.*, I (1910), No. 1, 69–86, No. 3, 325–45; C. Wauters, *L'ésotérie des Noirs dévoilée* (1949); C. van Overbergh, *Les Basonge* (1908); W. F. P. Burton, "L'Organisation sociale des Baluba," *BJIDCC*, IV, No. 7 (1936), 150–53; and E. Verhulpen, *Baluba et Balubaisés* (1936), who describes the different patri-lineal systems in the area. G. Vancoillie, in "Grepen uit de Mbagani traditie," *Aequatoria*, X, No. 4 (1947), 123–27, holds that the Mbagani (or southern Binji) practice double descent.

10　Information on northern Lunda from personal communication by F. Crine.

11　For cross-cousin marriage, see J. Delaere, "A propos de cousins croisés," *BJIDCC*, XVIII, No. 7 (1950), 197–215; and L. de Sousberghe, *Structures de parenté et d'alliance d'après les formules Pende* (1955). For the Bolia, see van Everbroeck, *Mbomb 'ipoku* . . . , pp. 167–218; for Kuba, my fieldnotes; for the Lele, M. Douglas, *The Lele of Kasai* (1963), pp. 85–185; for the Kongo, J. van Wing, *Etudes Bakongo: I. Histoire et Sociologie* (1960), 83–104, 154–204. For the Lulua and the general dis-tributions in the western Kasai, see Denolf, *Aan de rand van de*

Dibese, vol. I. Richards, in "Some Types of Family Structure . . . ," has a survey of variants among the matrilineal peoples.

12 M. Gluckman, "The Village Headman in British Africa," *Africa,* XIX, No. 2 (1949), 89–106.

13 I. Cunnison, "Perpetual Kinship: A Political Institution of the Luapula Peoples," *Rhodes-Livingstone J.,* No. 20 (1956), pp. 31–36, and "History and Genealogies in a Conquest State," *Amer. Anth.,* LIX, No. 1 (1957), 20–31.

14 See Douglas, *The Lele* . . . .

15 For instance, among the Kongo, see van Wing, *Etudes Bakongo,* I, 426–508, as an example of a religious association.

16 Gluckman, "The Village Headman . . . ."

17 The Lele village is described by Douglas, *The Lele* . . . , pp. 68–84, 128–40, 168–219; see also p. 28, where comparative figures for size of the village with other Central African peoples are given. Kuba data are from personal notes. For the Ding, see J. Mertens, *Les Ba Dzing de la Kamtsha* . . . (1935), pp. 43–58, 331–43. Data for the Ovimbundu are in G. M. Childs, *Umbundu Kinship & Character* (1949), pp. 25–39, 63–74, and in Edwards, *The Ovimbundu* . . . , pp. 49–75 and *passim.*

18 See P. Timmermans, "Les SapoSapo près de Luluabourg," *Africa-Tervuren,* VIII, No. 2 (1962), 29–53; see especially H. von Wissmann, *Unter Deutscher Flagge* . . . (1890), pp. 147–50; and see also L. Stappers, *Zuid Kisongye bloemlezing* . . . (1953), pp. 3–29.

19 See Douglas, *The Lele* . . . , pp. 186–203; R. de Beaucorps, *Les Bayansi du Bas-Kwilu* (1933), pp. 29–38, 67–102; De Beaucorps, *Les Basongo de la Luniungu et de la Gobari* (1941), pp. 62–101; and Mertens, *Les Ba Dzing* . . . , pp. 331–56.

20 Wauters, *L'ésotérie* . . . ; Timmermans, "Les SapoSapo . . . "; Stappers, *Zuid Kisongye bloemlezing* . . . , pp. 29–37.

21 See J. Vansina, "A Comparison of African Kingdoms," *Africa,* XXXII, No. 4 (1962), 324–35; M. Fortes and E. E. Evans-Pritchard, eds., *African Political Systems* (1940).

22 On African religion generally, see C. D. Forde, ed., *African Worlds* . . . (1954), and P. Tempels, *Bantu philosophie* (1946). Examples of religions are van Wing, *Etudes Bakongo,* I, 281–508; W. F. Burton, *Luba Religion and Magic* . . . (1961); T. Theuws, *De mens Luba* (1962). For the Luba Kasai, R. van Caeneghem, *Over het Godsbegrip der Baluba van Kasai* (1952), and van Caeneghem, *Hekserij bij de Baluba van Kasai* (1955). For the Sakata, see N. van Everbroeck, *Religie en magie onder de*

Basakata (1952). Speaking generally, beliefs are described better than rituals.

23 M. Guthrie, *The Classification of the Bantu Languages* (1948), pp. 20–28.

24 See Guthrie, *Classification of the Bantu Languages;* Guthrie, *The Bantu Languages of Western Equatorial Africa* (1953); M. A. Bryan, *The Bantu Languages of Africa* (1959); J. Greenberg, *The Languages of Africa* (1963); V. van Bulck, *Les recherches linguistiques au Congo Belge* (1948); and van Bulck, "Carte linguistique . . ." in *Atlas Général du Congo* (1954).

25 For *Akafula* of northern Rhodesia, see J. D. Clark, "Early Man in Northern Rhodesia," *N. Rhod. J.*, II, No. 4 (1954), 49–59. For *Tumandwa, Tutwamani* of Katanga, see A. van Malderen, "Contribution à l'histoire et à l'ethnologie des indigènes du Katanga," *BJIDCC*, VIII (1940), No. 7, 193–206; No. 8, 227–39. For *Mazumbudi, Tukokolo, Mbaka*, etc., of the lower Tshikapa, see L. de Sousberghe, "Noms donnés aux Pygmées . . . ," *Congo-Tervuren*, VI, No. 3 (1960), 84–86. For *Tupokolo* of same area, see G. L. Haveaux, *La tradition historique des Bapende orientaux* (1954). For *Akwa Pinji* or *Mbaka* of the Kahemba area, see I. Struyf, "Kahemba: envahisseurs Badjok et conquerants Balunda," *Zaïre*, II, No. 4 (1948), 351–90. For *Mbaka-mbaka* of the lower Inkisi, see van Wing, *Etudes Bakongo*, I, 25. W. Whiteley, in *Bemba and Related Peoples* . . . (1951), p. 9, mentions the Twa of Lake Bangweolu; Murdock, in *Africa* . . . , p. 49, mentions those living among the Nyanyeka of southern Angola, Lake Bangweolu, and the Kafwe River. The presence of Bushmen in Kongo country would explain the survival of a click in an isolated Kongo word. See W. de Mahieu, "Un cas isolé de click en langue Kongo," *Aequatoria*, XXV, No. 1 (1962), 19–20.

26 And maybe as early as the first century A.D., according to R. R. Inskeep, "Some Iron Age Sites in Northern Rhodesia," *S. Afr. Arch. Bull.*, XVII (1962), 172–73. The conservative estimate of 800 A.D. is put forward because most of the sites so far excavated throughout the area have been dated from the eighth to the nineteenth centuries, with the exception of the Northern Rhodesian sites of Kalundu and of Barotse land.

27 J. Nenquin, all references (see Bibliography). For Katanga, see J. Hiernaux and J. de Buyst, "Note sur une campagne de fouilles à Katoto . . . ," *Zaïre*, XIV, Nos. 2–3 (1960), 251–53. For Northern Rhodesia (Lozi land), see B. Fagan, "Pre-European Iron-

working . . . ," *JAH*, II, No. 2 (1961), 199–210. For Ovimbundu
(Feti), communication of M. Herskovits, from an excavation conducted by G. M. Childs.

28 See E. H. Lane-Poole, *The Native Tribes of the East Luangwa
Province* . . . (1949); E. Labrecque, "La tribu des Babemba,"
Anthropos, XXVIII (1933), 644. (Bemba land was occupied by
groups originally from Luba country before the arrival of the
Bemba, as is evidenced, among other facts, by the use of the title
mulopwe for kings.) Immigrations on the northeastern Rhodesian
plateau and across the Lwangwa from Luba land are earlier
than indicated by Fagan, "Pre-European Ironworking . . . ."

29 More ethnographic information about the peoples of the area is
available in the relevant volumes of the *Ethnographic Survey of
Africa*: Whiteley, *Bemba and Related Peoples* . . . ; J. Slaski,
Peoples of the Lower Luapula Valley (1951); McCulloch, *Ovimbundu of Angola*; McCulloch, *The Southern Lunda and Related
Peoples* (1951); Turner, *The Lozi Peoples* . . . ; M. Tew, *Peoples
of the Lake Nyasa Region* (1950); J. Vansina, *Les tribus Ba-Kuba
et les peuplades apparentées* (1954); M. Soret, *Les Kongo nord-
occidentaux* (1959).

Chapter Two

1 See J. Cuvelier, *L'ancien royaume de Congo* (1941), p. 253 *n*4.
Recorded traditions about the origin of the kingdom do not agree
on the number of kings who ruled before Nzinga Nkuwu. The
number varies from four to seven.

2 See J. Vansina, "Notes sur l'origine du royaume de Kongo,"
JAH, IV, No. 1 (1963), 33–38. The southern boundary of the
kingdom is sometimes said to have been on the Bengo, the
Dande, or the Lifune. In that case, the Dembo chiefdoms are
included in the state.

3 O. Dapper, *Naukeurige beschrijvinge der Afrikaensche gewesten*
(1676), pp. 144, 184; Vansina, "Notes sur l'origine du royaume
de Kongo," pp. 37–38. But R. Lethur, *Etude sur le royaume de
Loango et le peuple Vili* (1960), p. 21, throws a new light on
Nguunu.

4 M. de Morais Martins, *Contacto de Culturas* . . . (1958), p. 108;
H. Felgas, *História do Congo Português* (1958), *passim*; R. Delgado, *História de Angola* (1948), I, 66.

5 This description of the structure at the village level is extrapo-
lated from the situation around 1900. See J. van Wing, *Etudes*

Bakongo: I. Histoire et Sociologie (1960); Mpangu history as recorded in their traditions stresses the role of the clans very much (see pp. 44–66).

6 One doubtful point is the presence of judges, separate from the governors or district heads, at the lower tiers of the structure. Dapper, *Naukeurige beschrijvinge* . . . , p. 203, mentions these. But on the other hand it seems that, as elsewhere in Central African states, the territorial heads were judges. See R. L. Wannyn, *L'art ancien du Métal au Bas-Congo* (1961), p. 38, who relates a Kongo tradition that Affonso I gave crosses to the chiefs who were entitled to judge either at the capital or in the provinces.

7 The whole territorial and central structure is described in Cuvelier, pp. 297–306, 312–15, and in A. Ihle, *Das Alte Königreich Kongo* (1929), pp. 141–93. See also F. Pigafetta, *Beschrijvinghe,* trans. Martyn Everart, ed. A. Burssens, *Kongo-Overzee,* VII–VIII (1941–42), 23–86, 113–16. L. da Paiva Manso. *História do Congo. Documentos* (1877), pp. 101–10, copies an act of 1550 dealing with a conspiracy against King Diogo I, and in this act many of the important territorial and central titles are already mentioned.

8 See Cuvelier, *L'ancien royaume* . . . , p. 298.

9 Portuguese advisers are mentioned by contemporary sources after 1512 (the embassy of Simão da Silva). It is, however, dangerous to overestimate their influence, as Delgado does constantly, for example, when when he writes *(História de Angola,* I, 85) that King Affonso had become a puppet in the hands of his advisors.

10 On military matters, see Cuvelier, *L'ancien royaume* . . . , pp. 306–12, and Dapper, *Naukeurige beschrijvinge* . . . , pp. 279–80.

11 On financial matters, see Cuvelier, *L'ancien royaume* . . . , pp. 306–12, and Dapper, *Naukeurige beschrijvinge* . . . , pp. 202–3, 203–5. Dapper also states (p. 207) that certain titleholders received yearly salaries from the king. A still later source, G. A. Cavazzi, gives many details on all aspects of the organization of the kingdom in his *Istorica descrizione dé'tre'regni Congo* (1687), Books I–V, *passim.*

12 J. Merolla, *Relatione del viaggio nel regno di Congo* (1692), in J. Pinkerton, ed., *A General Collection of . . . Voyages* . . . , XVI (1814), 241, describes a ceremony of tribute offerings on St. James Major in Soyo.

13 See Merolla, *Relatione del viaggio nel regno di Congo,* pp. 239–46,

for an account of the political structure in Soyo; although it is taken from testimony of the late seventeenth century, it can be compared usefully with earlier accounts about the political organization of Kongo.

14 Cuvelier, *L'ancien royaume* . . . , pp. 277–79, gives the relevant texts. He thinks that the war was directed against rebel subjects in the area of Luozi. But the texts seem definitely to indicate that it was fought against the Tyo (Teke) and in the region of Stanley Pool.

15 The reign of Affonso has been best described by Cuvelier, *L'ancien royaume* . . . , *passim,* for whom the king is the Apostle of the Kongo. This attitude should be contrasted with Delgado, *História de Angola,* I, 55–176; A. L. Farinha, *Dom Afonso, Rei do Congo* (1941), *passim;* J. E. Duffy, *Portuguese Africa* (1959), pp. 12–19. Most of the published documents about the period are available in de Paiva Manso, *História do Congo* . . . , pp. 6–80, and in A. Felner, *Angola* (1933), docs. 7–9.

16 See de Paiva Manso, *História do Congo* . . . , pp. 15–16, for the demand of Affonso to Fernão de Mello (the governor of São Thomé)—in connection with the intended burning of the "house of the great fetish," and his fear of a subsequent rebellion—for weapons, including cannon. Such fetish houses are known to have existed because of the Kwango area and are there used to keep the emblems of the divine kingship. It is unlikely that Kongo would have been the only Central African state which did not have a divine kingship. An interpretation of the letter brings these two elements together to explain what has been an obscure passage.

17 On the *regimento,* see Felner, *Angola,* doc. 5, pp. 383–90; A. da Silva Rego, *Portuguese Colonization in the XVIth Century* . . . (1959), pp. 42–53; Delgado, *História de Angola,* I, 99–103; Duffy, *Portuguese Africa,* pp. 13–16.

18 See de Paiva Manso, *História do Congo* . . . , p. 54.

19 For Diogo's reign, see Delgado, *História de Angola,* I, 177–219; V. Baesten, "Les Jésuites au Congo (1548–1659)," *Précis hist.* (1892–93, 1895–96); Pigafetta, *Beschrijvinghe,* pp. 150–52; and de Paiva Manso, *História do Congo* . . . , 80–114; J. Cuvelier, *Biographie coloniale belge* (1951), pp. 293–94.

20 De Paiva Manso, *História do Congo* . . . , pp. 83–91. See also Delgado, *História de Angola,* I, 197; L. Cordeiro, *Escravos e minas da Africa* (1881), pp. 13–18.

21 De Paiva Manso, *História do Congo* . . . , p. 92.

22 For the period 1561–1569, see Delgado, *História de Angola,* I, 241–47; J. Cuvelier and L. Jadin, *L'ancien Congo d'après les archives romaines (1518–1640)* (1954), pp. 125–26; Felner, *Angola,* pp. 59–85; Pigafetta, *Beschrijvinghe,* pp. 152–58; Cuvelier, *Biographie coloniale belge,* pp. 4, 6, 55.

23 Pigafetta, *Beschrijvinghe,* pp. 42, 84, 155; O. de Cadornega, *História Geral das Guerras Angolanas,* III (1940), 222; Cavazzi, *Istorica descrizione . . . ,* book II, sect. 1; B. Rebello de Aragão, *Terras e Minas Africanas* (1881), pp. 16–17.

24 E. Ravenstein, *The Strange Adventures of Andrew Battell of Leigh . . .* (1901), pp. 19–20, 83–84, 84 *n*2, 19 *n*4, gives the account of Battell.

25 R. Avelot, "Les grands mouvements de peuples en Afrique: Jaga et Zimba," *Bull. géog. hist. et desc.,* XXVII (1912), 75–216, summarizes the opinions until his own time. H. C. Decker, "Die Jagazüge und das Königtum im mittlerem Bantugebiet," *Zeits. Ethnol.,* LXXI, Nos. 4–6 (1939), 229–93, brings the literature up to 1939. "Kalandala" as a Lunda title is mentioned in I. Cunnison, *The Luapula Peoples of Northern Rhodesia* (1959), pp. 170 ff.

26 Ravenstein, *. . . Adventures of Andrew Battell . . . ,* pp. 19–35, 83–87, especially p. 27, for building a state. See also Cavazzi, *Istorica descrizione . . . ,* book II, sect. 2, pp. 35–36, 41, 70.

27 A. Bastian, *San Salvador* (1859), pp. 188, 150.

Chapter Three

1 E. d'Orjo de Marchovelette, "Notes sur les funérailles des chefs Ilunga, Kabale et Kabongo Kumwimba . . . ," *BJIDCC,* XVIII (1950), 354–55. A. van der Noot, "Quelques éléments historiques sur l'empire luba, son organisation et sa direction," *BJIDCC,* IV, No. 7 (1936), 141. P. Colle, *Les Baluba (Congo Belge),* I (1913), 353; Colle, "Origine et explication du pouvoir des chefs dans l'Uruwa," *Rev. congo.,* I, No. 1 (1910), 58–59; W. F. Burton, *Luba Religion . . .* (1961), pp. 3–4; E. Verhulpen, *Baluba et Balubaisés* (1936), pp. 86–96, 233–35. All the versions differ from each other.

2 See Colle, *Les Baluba . . . ,* I, 45, 353; Colle, "Origine et explication . . . ," p. 59; Burton, *Luba Religion . . . ,* pp. 4–6; Verhulpen, *Baluba et Balubaisés,* p. 97; D'Orjo, "Notes sur les funérailles . . . ," pp. 355–56; van der Noot, "Quelques éléments historiques . . . ," pp. 141–42. For Colle, Ilunga Mbili came from Kibawa not far from Albertville; for Burton, from Moba or even

east of Lake Tanganyika; for van der Noot, from Lake Upemba; for Verhulpen, from beyond the Kibara Mountains beyond Lake Upemba and maybe from as far as the western shores of Lake Tanganyika; for d'Orjo, from Kiombo on the Lovua. D'Orjo gives a long route from there to Mutombo Mukulu and back, which other authors attributed to Kongolo.

3 See Colle, *Les Baluba* . . . , I, 353; Colle, "Origine et explication . . . ," pp. 59–64; Burton, *Luba Religion* . . . , pp. 6–9; Verhulpen, *Baluba et Balubaisés*, pp. 97–98; D'Orjo, "Notes sur les funérailles . . . ," pp. 356–58; van der Noot, "Quelques éléments historiques . . . ," p. 142; A. C. L. Donohugh and P. Berry, "A Luba Tribe in Katanga . . . ," *Africa*, V, No. 2 (1932), 181–83; B. Makonga, "Samba kya Buta," *BJIDCC*, XVI (1948), 308 ff. This part of the epic is more similar in the different versions. Kongolo's death is placed at Kai for most authors. Verhulpen is an exception and says that he was killed in the Mita Mountains.

4 See van der Noot, "Quelques éléments historiques . . . ," p. 142; Verhulpen, *Baluba et Balubaisés*, pp. 98–99; D'Orjo, "Notes sur les funérailles . . . ," pp. 358–59.

5 See W. F. P. Burton, "The Country of the Baluba . . . ," *Geog. J.* LXX (1927), 321–42; Burton, "L'Organisation sociale des Baluba," *BJIDCC*, IV, No. 7 (1936), 150–53; Burton, *Luba Religion* . . . , pp. 19–29, 155–59; D'Orjo, "Notes sur les funérailles . . . ," 350–54, 359–64 (for examples of the importance of the matrilateral patrilineage, see pp. 9–12 and see p. 12 for a list of signataries); van der Noot, "Quelques éléments historiques . . . ," pp. 145–49; T. Theuws, "Naitre et mourir dans le rituel luba," *Zaïre*, XIV, Nos. 2–3 (1960), 115–74; Verhulpen (for the Kalundwe), *Baluba et Balubaisés*, pp. 177–95, 277–300, 251–52; A. van Malderen, "Organisation judiciaire des Bakunda," *BJIDCC*, III (1935), 58–60; van Malderen, "Organisation politique et judiciaire coutumières des Bazela de Kiona Zini," *BJIDCC*, IV (1936), 278–83; van Malderen, "Organisation politique et judiciaire coutumières de la chefferie de Mufunga," *BJIDCC*, IV (1936), 174–78; M. Brohez, "Ethnographie katangaise . . . ," *Rev. belge géog.*, XXIX (1905), 463–69; V. L. Cameron, *Across Africa* (1877), pp. 294–334, 340–41.

6 See van der Noot, "Quelques éléments historiques . . . ," p. 142; Verhulpen, *Baluba et Balubaisés*, pp. 98–100; d'Orjo, "Notes sur les funérailles . . . ," pp. 358–61.

7 See Burton, *Luba Religion* . . . , pp. 10–15 (he also discusses the Mwanza area); Verhulpen, *Baluba et Balubaisés*, pp. 89–90,

105, 345–46; and van der Noot, "Quelques éléments historiques
. . . , pp. 341–42.

8 Verhulpen, *Baluba et Balubaisés,* pp. 89, 233–36, 287–91.

9 *Ibid.,* pp. 331–32.

10 See Colle, *Les Baluba* . . . , I, 49–67, II, 737; R. P. Colle, "Généalogie et migrations de quelques grands chefs du Haut-Congo,"
Rev. congo., I, No. 2 (1910), 193–207; Colle, "Origine et explication . . . ," pp. 65–68; J. Weghsteen (for Katanga), "De
toren van Babel in de overleveringen van de Watabwa," *Kongo-
Overzee,* XXI, No. 2 (1955), 157–59; and Weghsteen, "Origine
et histoire des Watabwa (Haut-Congo)," *Annali Lateranensi,*
XXIV (1960), 364–71; Verhulpen, *Baluba et Balubaisés,* pp. 374–
86; R. Schmitz, *Les Baholoholo* (1912), pp. 1, 29–33, 549.

11 F. Crine, personal communication; D. Biebuyck, "Fondements
de l'organisation politique des Lunda . . . ," *Zaïre,* XI, No. 8
(1957), 798–801; M. Plancquaert, *Les Jaga et les Bayaka du
Kwango* (1932), pp. 74–75; P. Denolf, *Aan de rand van de Dibese,* I (1954), 365–67; H. Dias de Carvalho, *Expedição ao Muatiamvu* . . . (1890), pp. 57–64; L. Duysters, "Histoire des Aluunda," *Prob. Afr. Cent.,* XII (1958), 81–82; M. van den Byvang,
"Notice historique sur les Balunda," *Congo,* I (1937), No. 4, 426–
30; I. Struyf, "Kahemba . . . ," *Zaïre,* II, No. 4 (1948), 358, 365,
369–70, 373; P. Pogge "Das Reich und der Hof des Mwata
Jamvo," *Globus* (1877), pp. 224–26; P. Ambrosius, "Inleiding
tot de Chichoksche spraakleer," *Congo,* I, No. 3 (1935), 366–67;
E. Labrecque, "Histoire des Mwata Kazembe . . . ," *Lovania,*
XVI (1949), 10–12; Mwata Kazembe XIV, *My Ancestors and
My People* (1951), pp. 1–6.

12 F. Crine, personal communications, and "Aspects politico-sociaux
du système de tenure des terres des Luunda septentrionaux," in
D. Biebuyck, ed., *African Agrarian Systems* (1963), pp. 157–
63; Dias de Carvalho, *Expedição ao Muatiamvu* . . . , pp. 64–75;
Duysters, "Histoire des Aluunda," pp. 82–83; van den Byvang,
"Notice historique sur les Balunda," p. 431.

13 Crine, personal communication.

14 Dias de Carvalho, *Expedição ao Muatiamvu* . . . , pp. 524–35;
Duysters, "Histoire des Aluunda," pp. 85–86; van den Byvang,
"Notice historique sur les Balunda," 437–38; 548–52, 554–55.

15 Biebuyck, "Fondements de l'organisation politique des
Lunda . . . ," p. 813.

16 Crine, "Aspects politico-sociaux du système de tenure des terres
des Luunda septentrionaux"; Biebuyck, "Fondements de l'organisation politique des Lunda . . ."; Pogge, "Das Reich und der Hof

des Mwata Jamvo," pp. 133, 166, 173, 196, 226–34; F. Valdez, *Six Years of a Traveller's Life* . . . , II (1861), 203 (information from Graça), 207; Dias de Carvalho, *Expedição ao Muatiamvu* . . . , pp. 529, 536, 540, 553; Duysters, "Histoire des Aluunda," pp. 76–79.

17 Verhulpen, *Baluba et Balubaisés*, pp. 194–95, where he opposes the idea of the *kadilu* [landowning chief] to the *kilolo* [the political chief].

18 See, for example, Cameron, *Across Africa*, pp. 296–352.

19 See Dias de Carvalho, *Expedição ao Muatiamvu* . . . , pp. 524–35; Duysters, "Histoire des Aluunda," pp. 85–86; van den Byvang, "Notice historique sur les Balunda," pp. 437–38, 548–52, 554–55. It is worth noting that for the Lunda of the Luapula *cikawand* denotes the Lunda language. The word has the same root as *Akawand*, the Lunda name for the southern Kete. Carvalho and van den Byvang make a major error in placing the exodus of the Lunda of Kazembe under Luseeng. See Kazembe, *My Ancestors* . . . , p. 9.

20 See Duysters, "Histoire des Aluunda," p. 84. In the 1680's the Lunda were in trade contact with the Imbangala and via them with the Portuguese. See G. M. Childs, "The Peoples of Angola . . . ," *JAH*, I, No. 2 (1960), 275, 277.

21 J. Vansina, "La fondation du royaume de Kasanje," *Aequatoria*, XXV, No. 2 (1962), 45–62.

22 See C. M. N. White, "The Balovale Peoples and Their Historical Background," *Rhodes-Livingstone J.*, No. 8 (1949), pp. 33–36; White, *An Outline of Luvale Social and Political Organization* (1960), pp. 43–48; White, "The Ethno-history of the Upper Zambezi," *African Studies*, XXI (1962), 15–18.

23 For the Lunda versions of the Cokwe dispersion, see Dias de Carvalho, *Expedição ao Muatiamvu* . . . , pp. 99–101; Duysters, "Histoire des Aluunda," pp. 78–79, 84–85; van den Byvang, "Notice historique sur les Balunda," pp. 433–37. For the Cokwe versions, see M. Bastin, *Art décoratif Cokwe*, I (1961), pp. 21–23; H. Baumann, *Lunda* . . . (1935), pp. 139–41, 233; E. Torday and T. Joyce, "On the Ethnology of the South-West Congo Free State," *JRAI*, XXXVII (1907), 151–52; H. Capello and R. Ivens, *From Benguella to the Territory of Yacca*, I (1882), 187–90; Ambrosius, "Inleiding tot de Chichoksche spraakleer," pp. 367–68; Struyf, "Kahemba . . . ," pp. 365–66, 369–70, 372–73. Kazembe, *My Ancestors* . . . , pp. 7–8, does not agree with the other Lunda versions.

24 White, "The Ethno-history of the Upper Zambezi," pp. 17–18;

Biebuyck, "Fondements de l'organisation politique des Lunda . . . ," p. 789.

25 Capello and Ivens, *From Benguella to the Territory of Yacca,* pp. 157–62. A. A. de Magalhães,, "Origem dos Basongos," *Mens. admin.,* XV (1948), 33–38.

26 See I. Cunnison, *The Luapula Peoples of Northern Rhodesia* (1959), pp. 35–37. The most important chiefly lineages were Mbeba [rat], Ngoma [drum], Shimba [leopard], Nsoka [snake], and Kunda [frog]. See also Cunnison, pp. 81–82 and 234.

27 See Cunnison, *Luapula Peoples* . . . , p. 74, to show the pervasiveness of some of these clans. For evidence in Katanga about the chiefdoms they organized, see F. Grevisse, "Notes ethnographiques relatives à quelques populations autochtones du Haut-Katanga industriel," *CEPSI,* No. 40 (1958), p. 58; No. 35 (1956), p. 97. In fact, the chiefdoms were apparently clan domains and, since the clans were diffused over the whole of upper Katanga, domains with similar clan names are found frequently. The chiefly lineages mentioned in Note 26 are to be found also among the Sanga, Lamba, and Kaonde (Grevisse, all references; see Bibliography).

28 E. Labrecque, "La tribu des Babemba," *Anthropos,* XXVIII (1933), 644; Verhulpen, *Baluba et Balubaisés,* p. 91.

29 Struyf, "Kahemba . . . ," p. 359, may be the only tradition relating to the departure from Lunda land of the Bemba which is not of Bemba origin. Others are Labrecque, "La tribu des Babemba," pp. 633–37; A. I. Richards, "The Bemba of North-Eastern Rhodesia," in E. Colson and M. Gluckman, eds., *Seven Tribes* . . . (1951), p. 164; Richards, "Social Mechanisms for the Transfer of Political Rights . . . ," *JRAI,* XC, No. 2 (1960), 181; C. Gouldsbury and H. Sheane, *The Great Plateau* . . . (1911), p. 30. The last two authors favor a Luba origin, in opposition to Labrecque, Struyf, and Cunnison (*Luapula Peoples* . . . , pp. 37 *n*1, 40 *n*1), where a chronological indication is given as to the earliest possible date of their arrival (the Nkuba peoples whom Kazembe met at his arrival were the fourth holders of the name, the first being the ones who had immigrated from Bemba country). F. Tanguy's writings were unfortunately not available. Kazembe, *My Ancestors* . . . , pp. 6–8, reports a tradition about followers of Cibinda who fled east over the Luapula. These may be the Bemba. Colle, *Les Baluba* . . . , records a very different version from all the others (I, 46–48).

30 See Labrecque, "La tribu des Babemba," p. 642.

31 *Ibid.,* pp. 633–38.

32   See Labrecque, "La tribu des Babemba," pp. 637–40. G. Wilson, *The Constitution of Ngonde* (1930), relates Ngonde traditions.

33   Labrecque, "La tribu des Babemba," pp. 640–48. Father Labrecque never published a promised continuation of this Bemba history.

34   F. M. Thomas, *Historical Notes on the Bisa Tribe* . . . (1958), is the standard Bisa history. It does not take written evidence from Lacerda and Gamito into account, however, and appears to be erroneous in many particulars. See also J. T. Munday, all references (see Bibliography); L. Lambo, all references; R. Philpott, "Makumba: The Baushi Tribal God," *JRAI*, LXVI (1936), 189–208; W. V. Brelsford, "History and Customs of the Basala," *JRAI*, LXV (1935), 205–15; L. Stienon, "Note concernant la tribu Baushi," *Congo*, VII, No. 2 (1926), 59–61; R. Marchal, "Histoire des Balamba . . . ," *Artes Africanae* (1936), p. 13; Marchal, "Le tribunal des Balamba," *CEPSI*, No. 2 (1946–47), pp. 85–93; Marchal, "Comment le clan des cheveux prit le pouvoir au clan des chèvres," *Bull. amis art ind. au Katanga*, XIX (1938), 12–17; G. Cuvelier, "La vie sociale des Balamba orientaux," *Congo*, II, No. 1 (1932), 5. The Lamba claim a vague connection with the Lunda, but not through the Bemba; F. Grevisse, "Les traditions historiques des Basanga . . . ," *CEPSI*, No. 2 (1946–47), pp. 65–66, 68–70, gives traditions of several peoples. His interpretation seems sometimes unconvincing and his migration maps are obviously not supported by the data. W. Watson, *Tribal Cohesion in a Money Economy* (1958), pp. 12–14, has it that the first Mambwe chief was a Mulua (Lunda) from Kola (Lunda homeland). He might be of Bemba origin. M. Wilson, *Peoples of the Nyasa-Tanganyika Corridor* (1958), pp. 21–22, has it that the Namwanga and Iwa chiefs are of Bisa origin and thus ultimately linked to the Bemba too.

35   See Cunnison, *Luapula Peoples* . . . , pp. 37–39, 152.

36   *Ibid.*, pp. 34–41.

37   The Shinje, who were found in the area where they now live, were closely related to the Pende, who had just been expelled by Kasanje ka Imba. Kapenda Masongo bordered the Songo, in the south. This tradition was collected by Carvalho and is the only one which has been published. (See Dias de Carvalho, *Expedição ao Muatiamvu* . . . , pp. 91–98. Compare with De Magalhães, "Origem dos Basongos.") Some of its details conflict with Songo tradition. Here too more data are available and should be collected.

38   On Mai, see A. F. da Silva Porto, *Novas jornadas* (1885–86), pp.

631–33; O. Schuett, *Reisen im Südwestlichen Becken des Congo* (1881), p. 136; Dias de Carvalho, *Expedição ao Muatiamvu . . .* , p. 98. J. Vansina, "De handelingen der voorouders," *Kongo-Overzee*, XXII, Nos. 4–5 (1956), 292–93, provides a link with Kuba chronology. Mai would have arrived around 1650.

39 Dias de Carvalho, *Expedição ao Muatiamvu . . .* , pp. 99–100; Plancquaert, *Les Jaga et les Bayaka . . .* , pp. 84–85.

40 Schuett, *Reisen im Südwestlichen Becken . . .* , p. 136; and Dias de Carvalho, *Expedição ao Muatiamvu . . .* , pp. 99, 112. Mwata Kumbana seems to have arrived later than Mai according to Pende traditions recorded in G. Haveaux, *La tradition historique des Bapende orientaux* (1954). See also Struyf, "Kahemba . . . ," pp. 362–63.

41 H. van Roy, "L'Origine des Balunda du Kwango," *Aequatoria*, XXIV, No. 4 (1961), 136–41; Planquaert, *Les Jaga et les Bayaka . . .* , pp. 70–74, 85–99; Struyf, "Kahemba . . . ," pp. 356–80.

42 See Dias de Carvalho, *Expedição ao Muatiamvu . . .* , p. 101.

43 See Plancquaert, *Les Jaga et les Bayaka . . .* , pp. 86–97.

44 The main source on early Pende history is Haveaux, *La tradition historique des Bapende orientaux*. See also L. Bittremieux, "De inwijking der Baphende's," *Congo*, I, No. 2 (1938), 154–67; R. P. Struyf, "Migrations des Bapende et des Bambunda," *Congo*, I, No. 5 (1931), 677–70; J. Maes, "Le camp de Mashita Mbansa et les migrations des Bapende," *Congo*, II, No. 5 (1935), 713–24; Plancquaert, *Les Jaga et les Bayaka . . .* , pp. 79–80; L. de Sousberghe, all references (see Bibliography); E. Torday and T. Joyce, *Notes ethnographiques sur des populations habitant les bassins du Kasai et du Kwango oriental* (1922), pp. 232–35, 249–50 (but he confuses Pende and Kwese and Pende and Pindi). See De Sousberghe, "Etuis péniens ou gaînes de chasteté chez les Bapende," *Africa*, XXIV, No. 3 (1954), 214–15. Torday and Joyce, ". . . South-West Congo Free State," make the same errors; H. von Wissmann *et al.*, *Im Innern Afrikas* (1888), pp. 48–50, 66. All Imbangala sources agree that the Pende lived in Imbangala country before their arrival. See Vansina, "La fondation du royaume de Kasanje," for these data. The Kwese version was from Dr. I. Kopytof.

Chapter Four

1 See M. Guthrie, *The Bantu Languages of Western Equatorial Africa* (1953).

2 Data on the Bolia are very scanty. I am very grateful to Miss E.

Sulzmann for giving me so much of her unpublished information. Without it this section could not have been written.

3   G. M. de Castello Branco, *Da Mina ao Cabo Negro* (1881), p. 8.

4   For this section, see E. Sulzmann, "Die Bokopo-Herrschaft der Bolia," *Archiv für Rechts- und Sozial philosophie,* XLV, No. 3 (1959), 389–417; N. van Everbroeck, *Mbomb'ipoku: Le Seigneur à l'abime* (1961), especially pp. 1–50, 125–60; L. Gilliard, "Au Lac Léopold II: Les Bolia . . . ," *Congo,* II, No. 2 (1925), 223–38; J. Lazariste, "Les Nkumu chez les Ntomba de Bikoro," *Aequatoria,* II (1939), 10–11, 109–23; G. Vanderkerken, *L'ethnie Mongo* (1944), especially I, 328–37, 365–73, 437–45, and II, 561–76, 630–49.

5   Nearly all the data on the Tyo were gathered during a stay in the field from October 1963 through April 1964. M. Soret, *Carte ethnique de l'Afrique équatoriale française* (1955), gives the Kongo forms of the Tyo names for their subgroups. He places the Ndziku near Djambala, who in Tyo are the Jiinju. Obviously, the seventeenth-century name of Ansiku is derived from Ndziku. The name probably came to the European authors via the Loango, who gave it the form Njiku and Ndziku. The ethnographic literature about the Teke is still scanty. Data were obtained from Badier, "Monographie de la tribu des Batékés," *Bull. soc. rech. congo.,* X (1929), 37–43; E. Decazes, "Chez les Batékés," *Rev. ethnog.,* IV (1885), 160–68; A. Dolisie, "Notice sur les chefs Bateke," *Bull. soc. rech. congo.,* VIII (1927), 44–50; E. Dusselje, *Les Tegues de l'Alima* (1910); E. Trezenem, "Les Bateke Balali," *J. soc. African.,* X (1940), 1–63; Miletto, "Notes sur les ethnies de la région du Haut-Ogooué," *Bull. inst. d'etud. centrafr.,* NS, II (1951), 19–48; G. Bruel, *L'Afrique Equatoriale Française* (1918); M. P. Delafosse and D. Poutrin, *Enquête coloniale dans l'Afrique Française . . .* (1930); L. Guiral, "Les Batékés," *Rev. ethnog.,* V (1886), 135–66; L. Papy, "Les populations Bateke (A.E.F.)," *Cahiers d'Outre-Mer,* II, No. 6 (1949), 112–34; L. Guiral, *Le Congo Français . . .* (1889). None of these is outstanding.

6   The Teke recall the crossing of the Congo River from west to east by Ngenge and Mfunu (Mfununga). These are mentioned around 1641 by O. Dapper. It is also told that in the 1620's a group of Portuguese traders going to Okango were captured by the inhabitants of the area, probably the Mfunu, who carried them to their king, the Tyo king. They were sent back to Stanley Pool after a stay of a few days. Another migration deals with a

village that was settled first on Mbamu Island, then on the southern part of the Pool at Kitamo. This migration is authenticated by the accounts from Montesarchio in 1667 and Da Caltanisetta and D'Atri in 1698. Ngombela—or Concobella, or Ngobela—as the settlement and its leader are called in the documents, is obviously *ngobila,* a current Tyo title.

7 Guiral, *Le Congo Français* . . . , p. 293.

8 See Note 6, in relation to the title *ngobila.* Dapper mentions Mfununga, which is the title *mfununga,* the paramount of the Mfunu.

9 R. Lethur, *Etude sur le royaume de Loango et le peuple Vili* (1960), p. 21, where Ngunu is a woman who had four sons: the Woyo, the Vili, the Kongo, and the Tyo. The Tyo proverb runs: "The Tyo come from Ngwuunu, the Kongo come from Ngwuunu." In addition to my own notes, ethnographic data used for the Tyo were Badier, ". . . la tribu des Batékés"; Decazes, "Chez les Batékés"; Dolisie, ". . . les chefs Bateke"; Dusselje, *Les Tegues* . . . ; Trezenem, "Les Bateke Balali"; Miletto, "Notes sur les ethnies de la région du Haut-Ogooué"; Bruel, *L'Afrique* . . . ; Delafosse and Poutrin, *Enquête coloniale dans l'Afrique Française* . . . ; Guiral, "Les Batékés"; Papy, "Les populations Bateke . . ."; Guiral, *Le Congo Français* . . . ; and G. Sautter, "Le plateau Congolais de Mbé," *Cahiers d'études afr.,* II (1960), 123–66.

10 The Mfinu live south of the Black River and are different from the Mfunu who live between that river and the mouth of the Kasai. The Mfunu were part of the Tyo kingdom, the Mfinu were not.

11 See R. Tonnoir, "Contribution à l'enquête de constitution du secteur des Bawumbu," *BJIDCC,* III (1935), 25–27, 47–50, IV (1936), 71–77, 95–96; S. de Vos, "Les Bamfunuka," *Rev. congo.,* I (1910), 87–91; H. Bentley, *Pioneering on the Congo* (1900), p. 459; and R. Buettner, *Reise im Kongolande* (1890), pp. 187–237.

12 J. Swartenbroeckx, "Quand l'Ubangi vint au Kwango," *Zaïre,* II, No. 7 (1948), 721–55. See also R. de Beaucorps, *Les Bayansi du Bas-Kwilu* (1933); L. van Naemen, "Migration des Bayanzi (Bayeye)," *Congo,* I, No. 2 (1934), 189–96; E. Descampe, "Note sur les Bayanzi," *Congo,* I, No. 5 (1935), 685–88; P. de Quirini, "Les fiançailles de droit chez les Bayansi," *Zaïre,* VI, No. 5 (1952), 499–504.

13 See A. Felner, *Angola* (1933), doc. I, p. 375 (*os masongos* are the

Tsong). See also J. Cuvelier, *L'ancien royaume de Congo* (1941), p. 9a, for date of *Historia*.

14 See R. de Beaucorps, *Les Basongo de la Luniungu et de la Gobari* (1941). On their affinities with the Yans, see De Beaucorps, pp. 21, 87–88, 167–69: the clans mentioned there and the clans mentioned in his "Le pouvoir politique et social dans la société indigène," *BJIDCC*, XIII, No. 1 (1945), 27, seem to be the same as some Yans clans and maybe even the Mbuun and Ding.

15 See De Beaucorps, all references (see Bibliography); De Quirini, "Les fiançailles de droit chez les Bayansi"; H. Nicolai, "Le Bas Kwilu . . . ," *Bull. soc. roy. belge de géog.*, CLXXXI (1957), 21–66; Kund, "Bericht über die Kongo-Expedition," *Verhand. Gesell. für Erd.*, XIII (1886), 318–28.

16 It seems that even in 1930 there was but one "chief" for the Mbuun. He kept the *pio* or kaolin, the emblem of chieftainship, for all the Mbuun. This kaolin was believed to be of Lunda origin and tradition had it that formerly one bloc of kaolin was used for both Pende and Mbuun, and that there was but one "chief" for both peoples. But in 1930 Kambace, the "chief" who kept it, had no over-all political authority. He is described as a "religious" figure, who ruled only over a small chiefdom, one of many in Mbuun country. See G. Weekx, "La peuplade des Ambundu," *Congo*, II (1937), No. 1, 24.

17 See Weekx, *ibid.*, No. 2, 150–65; No. 1, 24–25.

18 See J. de Decker, *Les clans Ambuun* . . . (1950).

19 See E. Torday, "The Northern Babunda," *Man*, XIX, No. 26 (1919), 49–55; E. Torday and T. Joyce, *Notes ethnographiques sur des populations habitant les bassins du Kasai et du Kwango oriental* (1922), pp. 231–33. See also R. P. Struyf, "Migrations des Bapende et des Bambunda," *Congo*, I, No. 5 (1931), 667–70.

20 See De Decker, *Les clans Ambuun* . . . , pp. 16–17, quoting a manuscript by L. van Naemen.

21 For the data on clans, see De Decker, *Les clans Ambuun* . . . (tabulation of clan origins by me). Note also p. 93 for the central Mbuun (the northern Mbuun are Ding, the southern, Pende), and p. 96, for linguistic and cultural ties between Ding and Mbuun.

22 See Weekx, "La peuplade des Ambundu," pp. 25–28, 165.

23 *Ibid.*, pp. 13–35, 150–66; De Decker, "Contribution à l'étude du mariage chez les Bambunda," *BJIDCC*, X, No. 7 (1942), 125–46; J. Delaere, "A propos de cousins croisés," *BJIDCC*, XVIII, No. 7 (1950), 197–215.

24 See De Decker, "Contribution à l'étude du mariage chez les Bambunda," pp. 229–30, on the possibility of a single great Mbuun chief in the past. For Kuba tradition, see J. Vansina, *Geschiedenis van de Kuba* . . . (1963), chapter V, "Shyaam."

25 For history, J. Mertens, *Les Ba Dzing de la Kamtsha* . . . (1935), pp. 9–18; for ethnography see pp. 19 ff. See also I. Struyf, "De verhuizingen bij de Kamtsha," *Congo*, II, No. 3 (1936), 343–50; and Nicolai, "Le Bas Kwilu." See also L. Frobenius, "Forschungsreise in das Kasaigebiet," *Zeits. Erd.*, NF, IV (1905), 469–70 (where it is stated that Ding are Yans, Lwer and Ngul are Ding); and Swartenbroeckx, "Quand l'Ubangi vint au Kwango," pp. 724–25 (where it is stated that Ding and Yans are the same name).

26 See O. Dapper, *Naukeurige beschrijvinge der Afrikaensche gewesten* (1676), pp. 218–19.

27 Dr. E. Sulzmann, personal communication.

28 R. Tonnoir, *La pierre de feu* (1939), gives the only bits of Boma history known, after Boma migrations. See other historical data for the Nunu in M. Storme, *Ngankabe, la prétendue reine des Baboma d'après H. M. Stanley* (1956); A. Verdcourt, *Notes sur la population Badia* . . . (1935); E. Focquet and G. Vanderkerken, "Les populations indigènes des Territoires de Kutu et de Nseontin," *Congo*, II, No. 2 (1924), 129–71. For details on social and political structures, see also N. van Everbroeck, *Religie en magie onder de Basakata* (1952), pp. 12–19; P. J. Denis, "L'organisation d'un peuple primitif," *Congo*, I, No. 4 (1935), 481–502; M. Baeyens, "Les Lesa," *Rev. congo.*, IV (1913–14), No. 3, 129–43, No. 4., 193–206, No. 5, 257–70, No. 6, 321–36.

29 See Vansina, *De geschiedenis van de Kuba* . . . ; Vansina, *Les tribus Ba-Kuba et les peuplades apparentées* (1954), pp. 36–37; M. Douglas, *The Lele of Kasai* (1963), pp. 23–27, and map.

30 Douglas, *The Lele of Kasai*.

Chapter Five

1 This quotation is taken from part of the first sentence of the donation of Angola to Paul Dias; see G. Sousa Dias, *Relações de Angola* (1934), p. 213, no. 1.

2 See Sousa Dias, *Relações* . . . , pp. 10–66, 213–29 (for text donation), 231–45; A. da Silva Rego, *Portuguese Colonization in the XVIth Century* . . . (1959), pp. 50–53, 97–116; L. da Paiva Manso, *História do Congo* . . . (1877), doc. lx; L. Cordeiro, *Escravos e minas da Africa* (1881), pp. 9–11; Cordeiro, *Esta-*

belecimentos e resgates portugueses na costa occidental de l'Africa por um anonymo (1881), pp. 21–24; A. Felner, *Angola* (1933), pp. 93–122, docs. 13 and 14, pp. 397–404; J. J. Lopes de Lima, *Ensaios sobre a statistica das possessões Portuguezas* (1844–62), II, part 2, 8–9; R. Delgado, *História de Angola*, I (1948), 131–40, 187–90, 225–39. G. A. Cavazzi, *Istorica descrizione de'tre'regni Congo* . . . (1687), II, no. 1 ff., E. Ravenstein, *The Strange Adventures of Andrew Battell* . . . (1901), pp. 140–42.

3 See Delgado, *História de Angola*, I, 253–342; Felner, *Angola*, pp. 123–79; Sousa Dias, *Relações* . . . , pp. 51–212; Abreu e Brito, *Um inquerito a vida administrativa e economica de Angola e do Brasil* (1931); J. E. Duffy, *Portuguese Africa* (1959), pp. 49–57.

4 Ravenstein, . . . *Adventures of Andrew Battell* . . . , pp. 7–9. Battell traded for the governor.

5 B. Rebello de Aragão, *Terras e Minas Africanas* (1881), doc. 1, pp. 10–18; G. M. de Castello Branco, *Da Mina ao Cabo Negro* (1881), pp. 13–17, 17–25; Delgado, *História de Angola*, II (1948), 24–29.

6 For the preceding discussion of the period from 1592–1623, see Delgado, *História de Angola*, I, 343–82, II, 1–101; Felner, *Angola*, pp. 183–217; Cordeiro, *Estabelecimentos e resgates portugueses* . . . ; Rebello de Aragão, *Terras e Minas Africanas;* De Castello Branco, *Da Mina ao Cabo Negro.*

7 See F. Pigafetta, *Beschrijvinghe*, trans. Martyn Everart, ed. A. Burssens, *Kongo-Overzee*, VII–VIII (1941–42), 155–60; J. Cuvelier and L. Jadin, *L'ancien Congo* . . . (1954), pp. 22–23, 126–27; Sousa Dias, *Relações* . . . , pp. 73–77; De Castello Branco, *Da Mina ao Cabo Negro*, pp. 8–10; H. Felgas, *História do Congo Português* (1958), pp. 68–70.

8 F. del Nino Jesus, *La Misión del Congo* (1929), pp. 57–64; Cuvelier and Jadin, *L'ancien Congo* . . . , pp. 160–63, 169, 264–65, 402 n10, 520–39; T. H. Simar, *Le Congo au XVIe siècle* . . . (1929), pp. 240–44; J. Cuvelier, *Biographie coloniale belge* (1951), 111–13.

9 See Felner, *Angola*, doc. 46, pp. 473–76, doc. 48, pp. 476–79; De Castello Branco, *Da Mina ao Cabo Negro*, pp. 7–13, 16–17, 26–32; Cuvelier and Jadin, *L'ancien Congo* . . . , all documents for the reigns of Alvare I and II, and pp. 520–39; Cuvelier (for Alvare I and II), *Biographie coloniale belge*, pp. 6–8; Delgado, *História de Angola*, II, 13–20, 28–29, 35–38.

10 De Castello Branco, *Da Mina ao Cabo Negro,* p. 11.
11 De Paiva Manso, *História do Congo* . . . , pp. 132–33, 162–65; Cuvelier and Jadin, *L'ancien Congo* . . . , pp. 165 n4, 262, 538, 402; Felner, *Angola,* p. 475.
12 See Del Nino Jesus, *La Misión del Congo;* Cuvelier and Jadin (for the bishopric), *L'ancien Congo* . . . , pp. 184–216; Felner (for intervention bishop), *Angola,* 473–79; Da Paiva Manso, *História do Congo* . . . , pp. 132–33.
13 The titulature is first mentioned in 1595, while in existing documents before that date (for instance in 1583 or 1587) it is not used. See Cuvelier and Jadin, *L'ancien Congo* . . . , pp. 195, 186.
14 See Delgado, *História de Angola,* II, 102–236; J. Cuvelier, *Koningin Nzinga van Matamba* (1957), pp. 51–100; Felner, *Angola,* pp. 212–45.
15 See Delgado, *História de Angola,* II, 167–69, 232–33; G. Sousa Dias, *A Batalha de Ambuila* (1942), p. 29.
16 See Felner, *Angola,* pp. 331–71, 578; L. Cordeiro, *Benguella e seu sertão por um anonymo* (1881); Delgado, *História de Angola,* II, 132–43.
17 Felner, *Angola,* pp. 469–70.
18 Delgado, *História de Angola,* II, 135–43.
19 Da Paiva Manso, *História do Congo* . . . , pp. 162–79; Felner, *Angola,* pp. 561, 475–79; Cuvelier and Jadin, *L'ancien Congo* . . . , pp. 345–76, 402–3, 408–9, 412, 422–23, 468 n2; Felgas *História do Congo Português,* pp. 71–73; Delgado, *História de Angola,* II, 38–45; Cuvelier (for Alvare III), *Biographie coloniale belge,* pp. 8–9.
20 Da Paiva Manso, *História do Congo* . . . , pp. 174–79; Cuvelier and Jadin, *L'ancien Congo* . . . , pp. 436, 450–71; Felgas, *História do Congo Português,* pp. 73–74; Delgado, *História de Angola,* II, 79–93; Cuvelier, *Biographie coloniale belge,* pp. 759–60; V. Baesten, "Les Jésuites au Congo (1548–1659)," *Précis hist.* (1893–96), pp. 129–36.
21 Delgado, *História de Angola,* II, 93–101, 107–8, 124–31, 153, 161–69, 233, 236–37; Cuvelier (for Garcia I), *Biographie coloniale belge,* p. 398; for Ambrosio I, pp. 14–15; for Alvare IV, p. 9; for Alvare V and VI, p. 10; see also Baesten, "Les Jésuites au Congo . . . ," pp. 136–43; Felgas, *História do Congo Português,* pp. 74–77; Cuvelier and Jadin, *L'ancien Congo* . . . , pp. 478–79, 484–86, 492–96, 502 n2, 506–16.
22 See Delgado, *História de Angola,* II, 281 n62.
23 For the Dutch period, see C. Boxer, *Salvador de Sá and the*

Struggle for Brasil and Angola (1952), pp. 169–96, 240–74; A. da Silva Rego, *A dupla restauraçao de Angola (1641–1648)* (1948); Delgado, *História de Angola*, II, 243–429; Cuvelier, *Koningin Nzinga van Matamba*, pp. 101–19.

24 See Delgado, *História de Angola*, II, 436–61, III (1953), 45–214; Boxer, *Salvador de Sá* . . . , pp. 274–87; P. Salmon, ". . . voyage de M. Massiac à Angola et à Buenos Aires," ARSOM, *Bull. des séances*, NS, VI, No. 4 (1960), 585–604; Cuvelier, *Koningin Nzinga van Matamba*, pp. 120–87; Sousa Dias, *A Batalha de Ambuila*, pp. 28–40, annex II; Da Paiva Manso, *História do Congo* . . . , pp. 200–208, 230–31, Nos. 123, 128, 132.

25 See Delgado, *História de Angola*, III, 45–56, 189–204, 214–439; Cuvelier, *Koningin Nzinga van Matamba*, pp. 188–232. For the history of Angola generally until 1680, see O. de Cadornega, *História Geral das Guerras Angolanas* (1940), vols. IIa and I.

26 General descriptions of Angola in De Cadornega, *História Geral das Guerras Angolanas*, vol. III; Cavazzi, *Istorica descrizione* . . . , who gives much historical information about Nzinga in books V–VII and Congo at the time of Garcia, books I and II, No. 25, Nos. 35–39; O. Dapper, *Naukeurige beschrijvinge der Afrikaensche gewesten* (1676), pp. 232–49. On the territorial organization, see Ravenstein, . . . *Adventures of Andrew Battell* . . . , pp. 168–69, 185–87; Felner, *Angola*, 471–72, 469–70; Cordeiro (for the situation around 1610), *Estabelecimentos e resgates portugueses* . . . , pp. 21–24. See also Duffy, *Portuguese Africa*, pp. 62–71.

27 See A. Ihle, *Das Alte Königreich Kongo* (1929), pp. 90–97; Dapper, *Naukeurige beschrijvinge* . . . , pp. 209–15, 187; O. de Bouveignes and J. Cuvelier, *Jérôme de Montesarchio* (1951), pp. 25, 123–35; Cuvelier, *Biographie coloniale belge*, pp. 398–99 (Garcia II); p. 13 (Alvare Affonso). For the events leading to the battle of Ulanga, see Sousa Dias, *A Batalha de Ambuila*. See also Cavazzi, *Istorica descrizione* . . . , I, II, No. 25, Nos. 35–39, III, No. 24, No. 32, No. 79, No. 84, No. 117, IV, No. 22, No. 45, No. 59, No. 60, No. 68.

28 See Cavazzi, *Istorica Descrizione* . . . , I, No. 245, II, No. 110, IV, No. 114, No. 145, V, No. 23; and De Bouveignes and Cuvelier, *Jérôme de Montesarchio*, pp. 35–36, 119–22, for the calamities.

29 For the general discontent, see Cavazzi, *Istorica Descrizione* . . . , I, No. 321, II, Nos. 73–75, I, No. 154; Cuvelier and Jadin, *L'ancien Congo* . . . , p. 166 n2.

30 Cuvelier and Jadin, *L'ancien Congo* . . . , p. 31; G. Hildebrand, *Le martyr Georges de Geel et la mission du Congo* . . . (1940), pp. 98, 107 *n*3; Ihle, *Das Alte Königreich Kongo,* pp. 95–96; Dapper, *Naukeurige beschrijvinge* . . . , p. 209.

31 Sousa Dias, *A Batalha de Ambuila,* pp. 38–159.

32 The official historian of the Capuchins is Cavazzi, *Istorica descrizione* . . . . Hildebrand, *Le martyr Georges de Geel* . . . , describes missionary work in this period and De Bouveignes and Cuvelier, *Jérôme de Montesarchio,* have published the travels and the adventures of one of the Capuchins. See also Da Paiva Manso, *História do Congo* . . . , docs. 119–20, 125, 153–54; Cuvelier and Jadin, *L'ancien Congo* . . . , p. 53; L. Jadin, "Le Congo et la secte des Antoniens . . . ," *Bull. inst. hist. belge,* XXXIII (1961), 432–40.

33 Jadin, "Le Congo et la secte des Antoniens . . ."; J. Cuvelier, *Relations sur le Congo du Père Laurent de Lucques (1700-1717)* (1953); De Bouveignes and Cuvelier, *Jérôme de Montesarchio;* A. da Paiva, "Relation," ms. 3165; Da Paiva Manso, *História do Congo* . . . , docs. 161–211, pp. 254–369; J. Merolla, *Relatione del viaggio nel regno di Congo* (1692); A. Zuchelli, *Relazioni del viaggio e missione di Congo* (1712); Felgas, *História do Congo Português,* pp. 86–94; Cuvelier, *Biographie coloniale belge,* at the names of the different kings, gives the relevant information for the period.

34 See Jadin, "Le Congo et la secte des Antoniens . . . ," pp. 411–17 and texts.

Chapter Six

1 For the following material in this section, see E. Verhulpen, *Baluba et Balubaisés* (1936), pp. 100–103; E. d'Orjo de Marchovelette, "Notes sur les funérailles des chefs Ilunga Kabale et Kabongo Kumwimba . . . ," *BJIDCC,* XVIII (1950), 361–64; A. van der Noot, "Quelques éléments historiques sur l'empire luba . . . ," *BJIDCC,* IV, No. 7 (1936), 142–43; W. F. Burton, *Luba Religion and Magic* . . . (1961), pp. 16–17; A. van Malderen, "Organisation politique et judiciaire coutumières des Bazela de Kiona Zini," *BJIDCC,* IV (1936), 278–83. R. P. Colle, "Généalogie et migrations de quelques grands chefs du Haut-Congo," *Rev. congo,* I, No. 2 (1910), 200–202; P. Colle, *Les Baluba (Congo Belge),* I (1913), 56–61.

2 P. Denolf, *Aan de rand van de Dibese,* II (ed. V. [G.] van Bulck) (1954), see index: *Kadila.*

3 Tippu Tib, *Maisha ya Hamed bin Muhammed el Murjebi yaani Tippu Tib* (1958–59), parag. nos. 89, 104.

4 See C. Wauters, *L'ésotérie des Noirs dévoilée* (1949); H. von Wissmann, *Unter Deutscher Flagge: Quer durch Afrika* (1890), pp. 147–50; A. Samain, "Les Basonge," *Congo*, I (1924), 48–52; C. van Overbergh, *Les Basonge* (1908), pp. i–iv, 187, 37–43, 457–60, 387.

5 See Denolf, *Aan de rand van de Dibese*, vol. I; Verhulpen, *Baluba et Balubaisés*, chapter on Kaniok ("Les Bena Kanioka"); R. P. Vervaecke, "Les Bena Lulua," *Rev. congo.*, I (1910), No. 1, 69–86, No. 3, 325–45; L. Liétard, "Etude sommaire sur la tribu des Lulua," *Bull. soc. roy. belge de géog.*, LIII (1929), 40–43. G. Brausch, "La justice coutumière chez les Bakwa Luntu," *African Studies*, I, No. 4 (1942), 235–42; A. Verbeken, "Institutions politiques indigènes: accession au pouvoir . . . ," *BJIDCC*, III, No. 1 (1935), 1–3 (this includes remarks on the Songye).

6 See L. Duysters, "Histoire des Aluunda," *Prob. Afr. Cent.*, XII (1958), 87–90; H. Dias de Carvalho, *Expedição ao Muatiamvu . . .* (1890), pp. 536–80; M. van den Byvang, "Notice historique sur les Balunda," *Congo*, I, No. 5 (1937), 555–59. Graça's trip is recorded in F. Valdez, *Six Years of a Traveller's Life in Western Africa*, II (1861), 174–211; and in M. Ferreira Ribeiro, *Homenagem dos heróes . . .* (1885), p. 14 (only his recommendations as published in *Annaes do Conselho Ultra Marino*, vol. for 1854–1858, p. 142); and A. C. Pedroso Gamitto, *O Muata Cazembe* (1854), pp. 487–95 (for the earliest publication of the text). For Naweej, see also D. Livingstone, *Missionary Travels and Researches in South Africa* (1857), pp. 317–18.

7 V. W. Turner, *Schism and Continuity in an African Society* (1957), pp. xx–xxi, 1–7, 318–27. See also C. M. N. White, "The Balovale Peoples and Their Historical Background," *Rhodes-Livingstone J.*, No. 8 (1949), 35–36; F. Grevisse, "Notes ethnographiques relatives à quelques populations autochtones du Haut-Katanga industriel," *CEPSI*, No. 32 (1956), pp. 110–12.

8 See C. M. N. White, "The Ethno-history of the Upper Zambezi," *African Studies*, XXI (1962), 14–15; Livingstone, *Missionary Travels . . .*, pp. 268–332.

9 See F. M. Melland, *In Witch-bound Africa . . .* (1923), pp. 28–46. See also F. Grevisse, "Salines et salniers indigènes du Haut-Katanga," *CEPSI*, No. 11 (1950), pp. 18–19, 22–25; Grevisse, "Notes ethnographiques . . . ," 89–91, 100–103; W. Watson, "The Kaonde Village," *Rhodes-Livingstone J.*, No. 15 (1954), pp. 3, 29;

S. J. Chibanza, *Kaonde History* (1961), pp. 43–114.

10 For the next two sections, see I. Cunnison, "Kazembe's Charter," *N. Rhod. J.*, III, No. 3 (1957), 220–32; Mwata Kazembe XIV, *My Ancestors and My People* (1951), pp. 1–80; E. Labrecque, "Histoire des Mwata Kazembe . . . ," *Lovania*, XVI (1949), 9–33, XVII (1950), 21–48, XVIII (1951), 18–31; R. F. Burton, *The Lands of Cazembe* (1873); Pedroso Gamitto, *O Muata Cazembe;* I. Cunnison, "The Reigns of the Kazembes," *N. Rhod. J.*, III, No. 2 (1956), 131–36.

11 For Lozi history, the best text is probably A. Jalla, *Litaba za sicaba sa Malozi* (1939). It was not available to me but I used Jalla, *Pionniers parmi les Ma-Rotse* (1903), pp. 322–25; Gluckman, "The Lozi of Barotseland . . . ," pp. 1–5, 26; A. E. Jensen, "Die staatliche Organisation und die historischen Ueberlieferungen der Barotse am oberen Zambesi," *Jahresbericht des Würtemberger Vereins für Handelsgeographie*, L (1932), 71–106; M. Richter, *Kultur und Reich der Marotse* (1908), pp. 10–15 (see the bibliography mentioned there); Livingstone, *Missionary Travels* . . . , pp. 115, 214–17. Remarks all through Gluckman, *The Judicial Process* . . . , make it clear that there are still many traditions to be recorded. Further research will probably also clarify the situation indicated by White, "Ethno-history . . . ," p. 11. White holds (p. 12) that it is chronologically impossible for Mulia, grandson of Mbuyamwamba, to have emigrated to Mushili. In fact, the Mushili referred to may be not a Yeke but one of the Lunda Kazembe in Katanga, which makes the story quite possible. For the limits of the kingdom by 1840, see G. C. R. Clay, *History of the Mankoya District* (1945), pp. 1–21; and White, "Ethno-history . . . ," pp. 11–12, 16.

12 B. J. W. Lisulo, "The History of the Barotse Nation," *NADA*, V (1927), 81–84. See also White, "Ethno-history . . . ," p. 121, on Lozi myth.

13 See White, "The Balovale Peoples . . . ," p. 36; M. Gluckman, "The Lozi of Barotseland in North-Western Rhodesia," in E. Colson and M. Gluckman, eds., *Seven Tribes* . . . (1951), p. 4. From the Lunda side it is proposed to connect the Lozi royal house with Mutanda Yembeyembe or Kakoma Mangandi (by Kazembe of Luapula tradition and Ndembu tradition, respectively). See White, "Ethno-history . . . ," p. 11.

14 For the social and political institutions of the Lozi, see Gluckman, "The Lozi of Barotseland . . ."; M. Gluckman, *The Judicial*

Process among the Barotse . . . (1955); Turner, *The Lozi Peoples of North-Western Rhodesia*, pp. 32–43.

15 See White, "Ethno-history . . . ," pp. 26–27, for a discussion of the date.

16 See Ferreira Ribeiro, *Homenagem dos heróes* . . . , pp. 30–31, for the 1795 reference.

Chapter Seven

1 See G. M. Childs, *Umbundu Kinship & Character* (1949), p. 191.

2 This seems to be the main reason why historians have neglected the history of Angola in the eighteenth century to such an extent. There is nothing spectacular, nothing glorious about it. Many documents about this period are extant and very few of them have been used by authors, so that this summary will be out of date with the first original work on the sources.

3 See H. Felgas, *História do Congo Português* (1958), pp. 98–102; J. J. Lopes de Lima, *Ensaios sobre a statistica das possessões Portuguezas*, III (1845), xxxiii–xxxiv, parte I, *catalogo dos governadores*, pp. 111–19; E. da Silva Correa, *História de Angola* (1937), I, 327–67, II, 7–28.

4 For the following material, see Da Silva Correa, *História de Angola*, II, 29–43; Lopes de Lima, *Ensaios sobre a statistica das possessões Portuguezas*, III, xxxiv–xxxv, *catalogo* . . . *1765–1772* (*I. de Souza Coutinho*), pp. 119–21; J. E. Duffy, *Portuguese Africa* (1959), pp. 71–73, 119–20; F. Egerton, *Angola in Perspective* (1957), pp. 50–53; Childs, *Umbundu Kinship* . . . , pp. 195–97. Childs and Duffy probably somewhat overrate Coutinho. Under his predecessor, Antonio de Vasconcellos, an attempt had been made to diversify Angola's economy with the exploitation of limestone (Lopes de Lima, III, *catalogo* . . . , p. 119) and concern had been expressed for the amelioration of agricultural resources (Da Silva Correa, II, 13).

5 See Da Silva Correa, *História de Angola*, II, 43-end; M. A. de Mello, *Angola no começo do seculo* . . . (1885); Childs, *Umbundu Kinship* . . . , pp. 197–99; Lopes de Lima, *Ensaios sobre a statistica das possessões Portuguezas*, III, parte I, 121–23, parte II, 22–24; L. Silveira, *Un Missionario português no Congo* . . . (1943).

6 See Da Silva Correa, *História de Angola, passim,* and especially I, parte I, 1–182, and II, parte III, 48–233.

7 See De Mello, *Angola no começo do seculo* . . . .

8 See Lopes de Lima, *Ensaios sobre a statistica das possessões*

Portuguezas, III, parte I, 122–35 (*Auto de undamento*); Duffy, *Portuguese Africa*, pp. 73–76, 142–45; Egerton, *Angola in Perspective*, p. 67.

9   See Childs, *Umbundu Kinship* . . . , pp. 199–207; Duffy, *Portuguese Africa*, pp. 77–78, 150–53; Egerton, *Angola in Perspective*, pp. 67–86; J. J. Monteiro, *Angola and the River Congo* (1875); F. Valdez, *Six Years of a Traveller's Life in Western Africa*, II (1861); Felgas, *História do Congo Português*, pp. 107–14.

10   See Duffy, *Portuguese Africa*, pp. 97–99 and n8.

11   See Lopes de Lima, *Ensaios sobre a statistica das possessões Portuguezas*, III, statistical tables.

12   See Childs, *Umbundu Kinship* . . . , pp. 207–15, 226; Duffy, *Portuguese Africa*, pp. 99–102, 120–29, 152–57, 225–67.

13   See J. Cuvelier, *Relations sur le Congo du Père Laurent de Lucques (1700–1717)* (1953); L. Jadin, "Le Congo et la secte des Antoniens . . . ," *Bull. inst. hist. belge*, XXXIII (1961), especially 432–33, 444–46, 486, 589–91: De Gallo (in Jadin) comments on page 475, "Because the principals draw with them the accessories, the provinces of the kingdom have also revolted, one against the other." See also A. da Pavia, "Relation," manuscript 3165, fol. 68–132 v°; A. Zuchelli, *Relazioni del viaggio e missione di Congo* (1712); J. Merolla, *Relatione del viaggio nel regno di Congo*, English trans. in J. Pinkerton, ed., *A General Collection* . . . (1814). On the division of Soyo around 1750, see *La pratique missionaire des PP. Capucins Italiens* . . . (1931), p. 105.

14   See R. da Dicomano, "Relation 1798," ms. F.G. 8554, fol. 114 n1, on *mbanzas*. See also Da Silva Correa, *História de Angola*, II, 206, where he estimates (in 1793) the population of a *banza* at 200 huts; *La pratique missionaire des PP. Capucins Italiens* . . . (around 1750), pp. 142, 146–47, 159–60.

15   According to L. Jadin, whose monograph on Kongo in the eighteenth century is in process.

16   O. Dapper, *Naukeurige beschrijvinge der Afrikaensche gewesten* (1676), pp. 186–87, who first refers to Mosul as a smaller "principality," then as a more important one. The Dutch West Indies Company used to have a trading post there. Cuvelier, *Relations . . . du Père Laurent de Lucques . . .* (p. 193) and Zuchelli, *Relazioni del viaggio e missione di Congo* (p. 350) mention that it was still dependent on Mbamba (around 1705). Jadin, "Le Congo et la secte des Antoniens . . . ," has mentions of it among the marquisates on p. 432 (1702), p. 486 (1709), and p. 589 (1713?). It is clear that by 1709 Mosul was practically indepen-

dent. Toward the end of the century, it was strong enough to be a menace to Luanda, both commercially and militarily. See Silveira, *Um Missionario português no Congo* . . . , pp. 24–25; Da Silva Correa, *História de Angola*, II, 141, 145, 172–73, 177–80; De Mello, *Angola no começo do seculo* . . . , pp. 554–55; Lopes de Lima, *Ensaios sobre a statistica das possessões Portuguezas*, III, *catalogo* . . . , p. 123. On the broader question of trade in general, see *La pratique missionaire des PP. Capucins Italiens* . . . , pp. 24–25, 93, 105, 138–39 (for the material on trade going to the harbors north of Congo, Portuguese trade not being allowed, and the quarrels between nobles easily leading to the enslaving of many of their subjects); and Da Dicomano, "Relation 1798," fol. 111v°, 113. See also Da Silva Correa, II, parte IV, 175–233, where the trade in the Loje valley is described. See also De Mello; J. van Wing, *Etudes Bakongo*, I (1960), 74–76; A Bastian, *San Salvador* (1859), pp. 25–33, 50–51, 76–77, 107, 129–33, 190–91, 210–11; Monteiro, *Angola and the River Congo*, pp. 47–49, 57–60, 77–78, 107–12, 115–16; A. de Sousa Barroso, *O Congo* . . . (1889), pp. 28–30, 46–54; J. Vansina, "Long Distance Trade Routes in Central Africa," *JAH*, III (1962), 375–90.

17 See Da Dicomano, "Relation 1798," fol. 105v°–107v°, 110v°.

18 See J. K. Tuckey, *Narration of an Expedition to Explore the River Zaire* (1818), pp. 200, 202, 329; Monteiro, *Angola and the River Congo*, pp. 117, 119–20, 140–43. See also Bastian, *San Salvador*, pp. 49, 53, 82, 211–12; K. Laman, *The Kongo*, II (1957), 138; Van Wing, *Etudes Bakongo*, I, 44–66, 76, 105–6.

19 See above, Notes 16–18. There are probably hundreds of documents which relate to Kongo in the eighteenth and nineteenth centuries and have not yet been used. This documentation will help us to refine or discard the hypothesis set forth.

20 Loango was one of the major African kingdoms before 1700, but we have few published historical materials about it. Descriptions of the state are given by E. Ravenstein, *The Strange Adventures of Andrew Battell* . . . [around 1610] (1901); Dapper, *Naukeurige beschrijvinge* . . . ; L. de Grandpré, *Voyage à la côte occidentale d'Afrique* . . . *1786 et 1787* . . . (1801); A. Proyart, *Histoire de Loango, Kakongo et autres royaumes d'Afrique* [1776], in Pinkerton, ed., *A General Collection* . . . , XVI, 577–87; and E. Pechuel Loesche, *Volkskunde von Loango* [1878] (1907). There are, however, a number of unpublished materials, especially for the late eighteenth century and the late nineteenth

century, mainly from missionary archives, which I have not been able to consult. In addition there is a rich oral tradition which still exists but has not really been tapped. R. Lethur, *Etude sur le royaume de Loango et le peuple Vili* (1960), pp. 21–24, summarizes what he has collected. It appears that the ruling dynasty originated in Ngoy. At some time in the past (during the eighteenth century?), the ruling dynasty of the Bouvandji was replaced by two new dynasties: Konde and Nkata. A thorough investigation of the history of Loango ought to have a high priority in historical research about Central Africa.

The histories of Kakongo and Ngoy, states which existed since Affonso I at least, also remain to be studied. They were, however, of small importance until their harbors became major trade centers for slaves in the eighteenth century.

21 Jadin, "Le Congo et la secte des Antoniens . . . ," p. 540; and Bastian, *San Salvador*, p. 131.

22 For the above material, see Dapper, *Naukeurige beschrijvinge* . . . , pp. 146–47, 157–60, 216–18, for the organization of trade in Loango (see also Note 16). On Cabinda and Malemba, see G. A. Cavazzi, *Istorica descrizione de'tre'regni Congo . . .* (1687), V, Nos. 53–54, for Dutch occupation of Malemba; Dapper, pp. 182–85. For the situation in 1700, see J. Barbot, *A Description of the Coasts of North and South-Guinea and of. Ethiopia Inferior, Vulgarly Angola,* in *A Collection of Voyages and Travels,* comp. A. Churchill, V (1732), 497–522. For the situation around 1688, see Merolla, *Relatione del viaggio nel regno di Congo,* pp. 269–70, 275. For the war of Soyo against Ngoy (both helped by English traders) around 1688, see De Pavia, "Relation," fol. 95r°–96r°.

23 For the eighteenth and nineteenth centuries, see Proyart, *Histoire de Loango, Kakongo et autres royaumes d'Afrique;* J. Cuvelier, *Documents sur une mission française au Kakongo 1766–1776* (1953), pp. 21–23, 34–35, 48–50, 68, 81–82, 100, 103; De Grandpré, *Voyage à la côte occidentale d'Afrique 1786 et 1787,* I, xxii–xxvii, 21, 43, 67–69, 105–26, 136–41, 163–218, II, 5–32, 36–37; Tuckey, *. . . Expedition to Explore the River Zaire,* pp. 70, 200; Bastian, *San Salvador,* pp. 57–59; Pechuel Loesche, *Volkskunde von Loango,* pp. 154–65, 175–205, 252–57.

24 See Tuckey, *. . . Expedition to Explore the River Zaire,* pp. 152, 246; and Monteiro, *Angola and the River Congo,* pp. 47–49, for Boma. For other harbors on the lower Congo, see Tuckey, pp. 135, 180, 200–201, 210. For the external relations of the

area of Kongo with Angola, see Felgas, *História do Congo Português*, pp. 101–end.

25 See Childs, *Umbundu Kinship* . . . , pp. 167–69; M. Ferreira Ribeiro, *Homenagem dos heróes* . . . (1885), p. 29; L. Magyar, *Reisen in Süd-Afrika* . . . (1859), pp. 362–444.

26 See G. M. Childs, "The Peoples of Angola in the Seventeenth Century . . . ," *JAH*, I, No. 2 (1960), 272. L. Figueira, *Africa Bantu* . . . (1938), mentions an expedition against Bailundo in 1645, but this is no more than a geographical surmize ("the region of Bailundo"), not substantiated by texts. The references in Childs, *Umbundu Kinship* . . . , p. 194; Ravenstein; *The Strange Adventures of Andrew Battell* . . . , p. 172; and the original reference from whom all authors copy: Lopes de Lima, *Ensaios sobre a statistica das possessões Portuguezas*, III, parte I, *catalogo* . . . , p. 374, and parte 1, p. 99; is also wrong. O. de Cadornega, *História Geral das Guerras Angolanas*, II (1940), mentions the 1645 raid and there is no question of Bailundo about it. See also R. Delgado, *História de Angola*, II (1948), 457 *n*73. For the Jaga, see Childs, *Umbundu Kinship* . . . , pp. 169–89.

27 See Childs, *Umbundu Kinship* . . . , pp. 17–27, 186–88; A. C. Edwards, *The Ovimbundu under Two Sovereignties* (1962), pp. 11–14; Magyar, *Reisen in Süd-Afrika* . . . , pp. 240–64, 270–80, 323–32.

28 See R. Delgado, *A famosa e histórica Benguella* . . . (1940), pp. 1–41; Da Silva Correa, *História de Angola*, II, 35–137.

29 Delgado, *A famosa e histórica Benguella*, pp. 24–27, mentions the trip of 1795. He catalogues the other events in Ovimbundu–Portuguese relations up to the war of 1902 against Bailundo and Wambu (pp. 41–320). Childs, *Umbundu Kinship* . . . , pp. 195–232, discusses, more, the significance of the historical changes in Ovimbundu country since 1770.

30 For the following material on Cassange, see Cavazzi, *Istorica descrizione* . . . , VII, Nos. 15–39, 58, III, No. 226; De Cadornega, *História Geral das Guerras Angolanas*, III, 217; De Mello, *Angola no começo do seculo* . . . , p. 557; A. Neves, *Memorias do expedição ao Cassange* (1854); A. Verbeken and M. Walraet, *La première traversée du Katanga en 1806* (1953), especially pp. 81–82, showing Cassange's reluctance to let the *pombeiros* pass and the reasons for this attitude; H. Dias de Carvalho, *Expedição ao Muatiamvu* . . . (1890), pp. 95–97; Valdez, *Six Years of a Traveller's Life* . . . , I, 147–52; A. de Almeida Teixeira, *Lunda, sua organização e occupação* (1948), pp. 51, 154,

190–96, 189, 20–21, 3, 78; C. von François, "Geschichtliches bei den Bangala, Lunda und Kioko," *Globus,* LIII (1888), 273–76; O. Schuett, "Im Reiche der Bangala," *Ausland,* XX (1881), 381–84; Schuett, *Reisen im Südwestlichen Becken des Congo* (1881), pp. 57–110; H. von Wissmann *et al., Im Innern Afrikas* (1888), pp. 16, 48–50; H. Capello and R. Ivens, *From Benguella to the Territory of Yacca,* II (1882), 289, 320–34, 369. Nothing much is known about their history during the eighteenth century. Yet unpublished materials are available for this and a later period and should fill out the sketch given here.

31   De Mello, *Angola no começo do seculo* . . . , p. 557.

32   See J. Cuvelier, *Koningin Nzinga van Matamba* (1957), pp. 231–32; Lopes de Lima, *Ensaios sobre a statistica das possessões Portuguezas,* III, *catalogo* . . . , 117, 131–33; Da Silva Correa, *História de Angola,* I, 362–65, II, 148–49; De Mello, *Angola no começo do seculo,* p. 557; Capello and Ivens, *From Benguella to the Territory of Yacca,* II, 52–54, 71–73, 153 n3, 163, 187; "Auto de undamento e vassalagem que prestou o soba iundo aquembi em 1838," *Mens. admin.,* XV (1948), 39–40; De Almeida Teixeira, *Lunda* . . . , pp. 179–83. Especially for the trade, see M. Buechner, "Die Ambakisten," *Zeits. Ethnol.,* XLVII (1915), 394–403. As for Cassange, most documents dealing with Matamba and the Ginga are still unpublished.

33   For the following material, see M. Plancquaert, *Les Jaga et les Bayaka du Kwango* (1932), pp. 70–74, 81–99; E. Torday and T. Joyce, "Notes on the Ethnography of the Bayaka," *JRAI,* XXXVI (1906), 39–58; H van Roy, "L'Origine des Balunda du Kwango," *Aequatoria,* XXIV, No. 4 (1961), 136–41; Torday and Joyce, *Notes ethnographiques sur des populations habitant les bassins du Kasai et du Kwango oriental* (1922), pp. 238, 243–45; Capello and Ivens, *From Benguella to the Territory of Yacca,* II, 123–26. Yaka history is still largely unexplored.

34   See Plancquaert, *Les Jaga* . . . , pp. 48–49, 81–83; Torday and Joyce, "Notes on the Ethnography of the Bayaka" (they do not distinguish between Suku and Yaka).

35   I. Kopytof, "Suku Religion . . . ," Ph.D. dissertation, 1960, pp. 1–11, 16, 18; F. van der Ginste, "Anthropometric Study on the Bapende and Basuku of the Belgian Congo," *Amer. J. Phys. Anthr.,* NS, IV, No. 2 (1946), 125–52.

36   See Plancquaert, *Les Jaga* . . . , pp. 43–48, for Tsamba; p. 50 for Tiki; and pp. 78, 80–81, 83, 94–96, for Mbala. See also J. F. Colard, "Note sur les Batsamba," *Congo,* I, No. 4 (1936),

523–25; R. de Beaucorps, *Les Basongo de la Luniungu* . . .
(1941), pp. 7–13; J. de Pierpont, "Les Bambala," *Congo,* I
(1932), No. 1, 22–37, No. 2, 185–99; Torday and Joyce, "Notes
on the Ethnography of the Bambala," *JRAI,* XXXV (1905), 398–
426; Torday and Joyce, "Notes on the Ethnography of the Ba-
huana," *Man,* VII (1907), 81–84; Torday and Joyce, "On the
Ethnology of the South-West Congo Free State," *JRAI,* XXXVII
(1907), *passim,* especially 153–54; Torday and Joyce, "Note on
the Southern Bambala," *Man,* VII, No. 52 (1907), 81–84; E.
Torday, "Note on the Natives of the Kwilu, Congo Free State,"
Man, V, No. 75 (1905), 135–38; Torday and Joyce, *Notes ethnographiques sur des populations* . . . , pp. 227–50; E. Torday,
Camp and Tramp in African Wilds (1913), pp. 78, 96–102, 128–
34, 154, 173, 201–2.

37 See Plancquaert, *Les Jaga* . . . , pp. 72–74; Dias de Carvalho,
Expedição ao Muatiamvu . . . , pp. 108–11.

Chapter Eight

1 See M. Tew, *Peoples of the Lake Nyasa Region* (1950), pp. 94–
96; E. H. Lane-Poole, *The Native Tribes of the East Luangwa
Province* . . . (1949), p. 5; C. Gouldsbury and H. Sheane, *The
Great Plateau* . . . (1911), pp. 28–29; J. Coxhead, *The Native
Tribes of North-Eastern Rhodesia* . . . (1914), p. 6; W. V. Brels-
ford, *The Succession of Bemba Chiefs* (1944), p. 6.

2 See V. W. Turner, *The Lozi Peoples* . . . (1952), p. 13; D. Livingstone, *Missionary Travels and Researches in South Africa* (1857),
p. 218; E. Smith, "Sebetwane and the Makololo," *African Studies,*
XV, No. 2 (1956), 49–70; C. M. N. White, "The Ethno-history
of the Upper Zambezi," *African Studies,* XXI (1962), 14, 18, 26–27;
D. F. Ellenberger, *History of the Basuto, Ancient and Modern*
(1912), pp. 305–30; M. Gluckman, "The Lozi of Barotseland
in North-Western Rhodesia," in E. Colson and M. Gluckman,
eds., *Seven Tribes* . . . (1951), p. 2; A. Jalla, *Pionniers parmi les
Ma-Rotse* (1903), pp. 326–27.

3 See Livingstone, *Missionary Travels* . . . , p. 263; M. Richter,
Kultur und Reich der Marotse (1908), pp. 23–25; Jalla, *Pionniers
parmi les Ma-Rotse,* pp. 327–28; Ellenberger, *History of the
Basuto* . . . , pp. 331–63; White, "Ethno-history of the Upper
Zambezi," p. 19; A. Schulz and A. Hammar, *The New Africa*
. . . (1897), p. 103.

4 See A. A. de Serpa Pinto, *How I Crossed Africa* (1881), I, 317,
II, 15–17; Jalla, *Pionniers parmi les Ma-Rotse,* pp. 328–29; E.

Holub, *Von der Capstadt ins Land der Maschukulumbe,* I
(1890), 346, 350, 368, 372. Schulz and Hammar, *The New
Africa* . . . , p. 404; V. Cameron, *Across Africa* (1877), p. 353;
F. C. Selous, *A Hunter's Wanderings in Africa* (1881), p. 246;
White, "The Ethno-history of the Upper Zambezi," p. 19; Richter, *Kultur und Reich der Marotse,* pp. 25–31; A. E. Jensen,
"Die staatliche Organisation und die historischen Ueberlieferungen der Barotse . . . ," *Jahresbericht des Würtemberger Vereins
fur Handelsgeographie,* L (1932), 108–9; Gluckman, "The Lozi
of Barotseland . . . ," p. 2; E. Beguin, *Les Ma-Rotsé* . . . (1903),
p. 71.

5   See Jalla, *Pionniers parmi les Ma-Rotse,* pp. 329–32; Jensen,
"Die staatliche Organisation . . . ," pp. 109–11; Richter, *Kultur
und Reich der Marotse,* pp. 31–46; White, "The Ethno-history
of the Upper Zambezi," pp. 20–25; Selous, *A Hunter's Wander-
ings* . . . ; J. P. R. Wallis, ed., *The Barotseland Journal of James
Stevenson-Hamilton* . . . (1953), pp. v, xiv–xv, xxii; Holub, *Von
der Capstadt ins Land der Maschukulumbe,* I, 368; G. C. R.
Clay, *History of the Mankoya District* (1945); S. J. Chibanza,
Kaonde History (1961), pp. 53–67; A. Gibbons, *Exploration and
Hunting in Central Africa, 1895–96* (1898); F. Coillard, *On the
Threshold of Central Africa* (1897); A. J. Bertrand, *The King-
dom of the Barotsi* (1899), appendix I; H. Depelchin and C.
Croonenberghs, *Trois ans dans l'Afrique australe* . . . , II (1882–
83), 270–end.

6   See M. Gluckman, *The Judicial Process among the Barotse* . . .
(1955); M. A. Bryan, *The Bantu Languages of Africa* (1959), pp.
70–71, 149. It seems that the Lozi of the flood plain speak today
a form of Sotho.

7   J. R. Graça, "Expedição ao Muatayanvua," *BSGL,* IX (1890),
365–68.

8   Livingstone, *Missionary Travels* . . . , pp. 319, 327, 339–51,
456–59.

9   See E. Verhulpen, *Baluba et Balubaisés* (1936), p. 138; F. Valdez,
Six Years of a Traveller's Life in Western Africa, II (1861), 174–
211; A. C. Pedroso Gamitto, *O Muata Cazembe* . . . (1854), pp.
487–97; M. Ferreira Ribeiro, *Homenagem dos heróes que precederam Brito Capello e Roberto Ivens* . . . (1885), pp. 14, 30–
33; H. Dias de Carvalho, *Expedição ao Muatiamvo* . . . (1890),
pp. 554–80; A. Verbeken and M. Walraet, *La première traversée
du Katanga en 1806* (1953), p. 77; J. J. Macqueen, "Journal of
Silva Porto with the Arabs . . . ," *J. Roy. Geog. Soc.,* XXX (1860),

151–53; A. F. da Silva Porto, *Silva Porto e a travessia do continente africano* (1938), pp. 19–20, 69, 108–13; White, "Ethnohistory of the Upper Zambezi," pp. 19, 26. The travel accounts are precise enough to enable us to fix the limits of Cokwe settlement by 1850. Contacts between the Cokwe and European (Portuguese) culture via the Ovimbundu are obviously old and certainly date from the eighteenth century. When one examines Cokwe art, however, for example–as in M. Bastin, *Art décoratif Cokwe*, II (1961)–it seems that European influences are even older, for the typical Cokwe chief's chair has evident connections with European Renaissance chairs.

10 On Cokwe ways of expansion, see Cameron, *Across Africa*, pp. 331, 347–48; I. Struyf, "Kahemba . . . ," *Zaïre*, II, No. 4 (1948), 367, 389–90; M. McCulloch, *The Southern Lunda and Related Peoples* (1951), pp. 40–43; O. Schuett, *Reisen im Südwestlichen Becken des Congo* (1881), pp. 128–68; H. Baumann, *Lunda . . .* (1935), pp. 141–42. On similarities between Cokwe, Mbunda, and Lwena, see White, "Ethno-history of the Upper Zambezi," pp. 25–26; McCulloch, pp. 33, 36, 59–61, 70–71.

11 On assimilation of other peoples, see G. Haveaux, *La tradition historique des Bapende orientaux* (1954), p. 31 (for the Pende) and p. 29; Dias de Carvalho, *Expedição ao Muatiamvu . . .* , p. 100; H. Capello and R. Ivens, *From Benguella to the Territory of Yacca* (1882), I, 191, II, 253; M. van den Byvang, "Notice historique sur les Balunda," *Congo*, II, No. 2 (1937), 201; L. de Sousberghe, *Deux palabres d'esclaves chez les Pende* (1961), pp. 48–49, 62; H. von Wissmann, *Unter Deutscher Flagge . . .* (1890), pp. 62, 35.

12 P. Pogge, *Im Reich des Muata Jamwo* (1880), p. 50.

13 *Ibid.*, p. 47.

14 See Schuett, *Reisen im Südwestlichen Becken des Congo*, pp. 128–68, especially p. 132; H. Capello and R. Ivens, *De Angola á contra-costa*, I (1886), 16–17; Capello and Ivens, *From Benguella to the Territory of Yacca*, II, 217, I, 317, 369; L. Duysters, "Histoire des Aluunda," *Prob. Afr. Cent.*, XII (1958), 90; Van den Byvang, "Notice historique sur les Balunda," No. 5, p. 558; Dias de Carvalho, *Expedição ao Muatiamvu . . .* , p. 563. The preceding references refer to the early movements of the Cokwe in northern Angola. The route from Mona Kimbundu to Mai, and therefore the Lulua route, was known in the 1850's. See Livingstone, *Missionary Travels . . .* , p. 456. For Cokwe expansion in Kasai and Kwango and subsequent events, see

von Wissmann, *Unter Deutscher Flagge* . . . , pp. 41, 47, 44, 35, 70–106, 336–end; A. van Zandijcke, all references (see Bibliography); Pogge, *Im Reich des Muato Jamwo*, pp. 22, 50; P. Denolf, *Aan de rand van de Dibese*, I (1954), 75–91, 455; Schuett, pp. 145–56, 150; H. von Wissmann *et al.*, *Im Innern Afrikas* (1888), pp. 9, 72, 115–92; M. Buechner, "Das Reich des Mwata Yamvo und seine Nachbarländer," *Deutsche geog. Blät.*, VI (1883), 63 ff.; A. F. da Silva Porto, *Novas jornadas* (1885–86); P. Timmermans, "Les SapoSapo près de Luluabourg," *Africa-Tervuren*, VIII, No. 2 (1962), 29–53.

15   On the cruelty of Naweej II, see Valdez, *Six Years of a Traveller's Life* . . . , II, 87; Livingstone, *Missionary Travels* . . . , pp. 317–18.

16   On Naweej II and trade, see Pedroso Gamitto, *O Muata Cazembe*, pp. 482–84; Pogge, *Im Reich des Muata Jamwo;* Cameron, *Across Africa*, pp. 358, 364; Da Silva Porto, *Novas jornadas*, p. 629; Capello and Ivens, *From Benguella to the Territory of Yacca*, I, 180; Dias de Carvalho, *Expedição ao Muatiamvu* . . . , pp. 581–600; Duysters, "Histoire des Aluunda," pp. 90–92; Van den Byvang, "Notice historique sur les Balunda," I, No. 5, pp. 559–62; and Livingstone, *Missionary Travels* . . . , p. 456.

17   Pogge, *Im Reich des Muata Jamwo.*

18   See Dias de Carvalho, *Expedição ao Muatiamvu* . . . , pp. 600–634; Duysters, "Histoire des Aluunda," pp. 92–93; Van den Byvang, "Notice historique sur les Balunda," II, No. 2, 193–202.

19   Buechner, "Das Reich des Mwata Yamvo und seine Nachbarländer," pp. 137–63.

20   See Pogge, *Im Reich des Muata Jamwo*, p. 47; Schuett, *Reisen im Südwestlichen Becken des Congo*, p. 132; Buechner, "Das Reich des Mwata Yamvo und seine Nachbarländer," pp. 137–63; Da Silva Porto, *Novas jornadas*, pp. 625–29; Von Wissmann, *Unter Deutscher Flagge* . . . , pp. 35, 47.

21   For the specific events involving Mwa Cisenge, see, in the same works cited in Notes 19 and 20, Schuett, pp. 145, 156; Da Silva Porto, pp. 629, 642; Dias de Carvalho, *Expedição ao Muatiamvu* . . . , p. 100; Von Wissmann *et al.*, *Im Innern Afrikas*, pp. 58–59, 100.

22   See Dias de Carvalho, *Expedição ao Muatiamvu* . . . , pp. 634–64; Duysters, "Histoire des Aluunda," pp. 93–98; Van den Byvang, "Notice historique sur les Balunda," pp. 202–8; P. Ambrosius, "Inleiding tot de Chichoksche spraakleer," *Congo*, I, No. 3 (1935), 368–69; Verhulpen, *Baluba et Balubaisés*, pp. 331–32,

291–95; E. Verdick, *Les premiers jours du Katanga 1890–1903* (1952), p. 25; McCulloch, *The Southern Lunda* . . . , p. 30.

23 Struyf, "Kahemba . . . ," pp. 365–67; Haveaux, *La tradition historique des Bapende orientaux*, pp. 28–31; R. P. Struyf, "Migrations des Bapende et des Bambunda," *Congo*, I, No. 5 (1931), 668–69; L. Bittremieux, "De inwijking der Baphende's," *Congo*, I, No. 2 (1938), 163–65; E. Torday and T. A. Joyce, "On the Ethnology of the South-West Congo Free State," *JRAI*, XXXVII (1907), 142.

24 See White, "The Ethno-history of the Upper Zambezi," pp. 21–25; F. Grevisse, "Notes ethnographiques relatives à quelques populations autochtones du Haut-Katanga industriel," *CEPSI*, No. 32 (1956), 110–12; V. W. Turner, *Schism and Continuity in an African Society* (1957), pp. 6–7, 321, 326–27, 39–42.

25 Verbeken and Walraet in *La première traversée du Katanga en 1806*, p. 75, note traders from Garenganza, obviously Nyamweziland.

26 See E. Labrecque, "Histoire des Mwata Kazembe . . . ," *Lovania*, XVII (1950), 34; A. Verbeken, *Msiri, roi du Garenganze* (1956), pp. 1–49, and references given there. On the copper mines, see P. L. Lefebure, "Een wegstervend bedrijf: Het kopergieten bij de negers in Katanga," *Congo*, II, No. 3 (1930), 359–67; M. A. Mahieu, "L'exploitation du cuivre par les indigènes au Katanga," *Congo*, II, No. 1 (1925), 107–29; R. Marchal, "Renseignements historiques relatifs à l'exploitation des mines de cuivre par les indigènes de la Luishia," *BJIDCC*, VII (1939), 10–17; J. de Hemptinne, "Les mangeurs de cuivre du Katanga," *Congo*, I, No. 3 (1926), 371–403.

27 Pedroso Gamitto, *O Muata Cazembe* . . . (on p. 323, 338, 420), mentions the trade from Kazembe to Kilwa or Zanzibar and mentions also that he saw Arabs in 1831 (on p. 360). That the trade was well established by 1850 is also indicated by Livingstone, *Missionary Travels* . . . , p. 503; D. Livingstone, *Last Journals* (1874), p. 278; Da Silva Porto, . . . *Travessia do continente africano*, pp. 17–29 (a Coimbra was already in Katanga by 1852), pp. 108, 113. On Ibn Saleh, see Tippu Tib, *Maisha ya Hamed bin Muhammed el Murjebi yaani Tippu Tib* (he was a kinsman of Tippu Tib) (1958–59), parag. No. 19; and Labrecque, "Histoire des Mwata Kazembe . . . ," XVIII, 34.

28 See Labrecque, "Histoire des Mwata Kazembe . . . ," XVIII, 31–38; Mwata Kazembe XIV, *My Ancestors and My People* (1951), pp. 80–86.

29   See Verbeken, *Msiri* . . . , pp. 49–65.

30   See Verbeken, *Msiri* . . . , pp. 63–67; Labrecque, "Histoire des Mwata Kazembe . . . ," XVIII, 39–45; Kazembe, *My Ancestors* . . . , pp. 86–90.

31   See Labrecque, "Histoire des Mwata Kazembe . . . ," XVIII (1951), 45–53; Kazembe, *My Ancestors* . . . , pp. 90–95.

32   See Verbeken, *Msiri* . . . , pp. 67–138; Capello and Ivens, *De Angola á contra-costa*, II, 80–109; P. Reichard, "Bericht über seine Reise in Ostafrika und dem Quellengebiet des Kongo," *Verhand. Gesell. Erd.*, XIII (1886), 111–22.

33   See Carpentier, "Histoire de la souschefferie Kashobwe" (1929), unpublished manuscript; Labrecque, "Histoire des Mwata Kazembe . . . ," XVIII, 53–65; Kazembe, *My Ancestors* . . . , pp. 86–110.

34   W. F. P. Burton, "The Country of the Baluba . . . ," *Geog. J.*, LXX (1927), 332, which gives 1887 as the date for the death of Kasongo Kalombo. Verhulpen, *Baluba et Balubaisés*, pp. 103–4, mentions Yeke residents in Luba land. For the southern part of the empire, see Chibanza, *Kaonde History*, pp. 59–61; R. Marchal, "Le tribunal des Balamba," *CEPSI*, No. 2 (1946–47), pp. 86–87. About Msiri during this period in general, Matayu's and the Coimbra's, see Capello and Ivens, *De Angola á contra-costa*, II, 66–160; Capello and Ivens, *From Benguella to the Territory of Yacca*, I, 138; Da Silva Porto, . . . *Travessia do continente africano*, pp. 17–19; D. Crawford, *Thinking Black* (1912), pp. 191, 295–99; Verbeken, *Msiri* . . . , pp. 89–100, 141–59. Both wives were probably considered to be *ntombo* or tributary wives.

35   See Verbeken, *Msiri* . . . , pp. 159–end; Verdick, *Les premiers jours du Katanga* . . . ; Crawford, *Thinking Black*. Generally speaking, other sources about Yeke history are: A. Munongo, "Lettre de Mwenda II (Mukandavantu)," *BJIDCC*, XVI (1948), No. 7, 199–229, No. 8, 231–44; L. Bittremieux, "Brief van Musiri," *Kongo-Overzee*, III, No. 2 (1936), 69–83; A. Munongo, "Chants historiques des Bayeke . . . ," *BJIDCC*, XVI (1948), 280–94, XX (1952), 305–16; Munongo, "Kanoni Kasembia," *Jeune Afrique*, II (1948), 45; J. Cornet, *Katanga* (1943). For the later years of Msiri's reign, see also F. S. Arnot, *Garenganze* . . . (1889); Arnot, *Bihé and Garenganze* . . . (1893); R. S. Arnot, "F. S. Arnot and Msidi," *N. Rhod. J.*, III, No. 5 (1958), 428–34.

36   See J. A. Clarke, "Edits prononcés par Mushidi ou Msiri . . . ," *BJIDCC*, XI (1938), 259–60; G. Cuvelier (for Yeke introduction of the sweet potato), "La vie sociale des Balamba orientaux,"

Congo, II (1932), 166; for edicts, smallpox, and copper thread, see Verbeken, *Msiri* . . . , pp. 110, 47, 125. For Yeke culture now, see F. Grevisse, "Les Bayeke," *BJIDCC*, V (1937), No. 1, 43 (blood brotherhood); Mahieu, "L'exploitation du cuivre par les indigènes au Katanga," 107–29; Cameron, *Across Africa*, p. 234; Crawford, *Thinking Black*, pp. 181–82; Grevisse, p. 19 (on divination with pullets); Reichard, "Bericht über seine Reise in Ostafrika und dem Quellengebiet des Kongo," p. 117. In the political structure interlacustrine evidence is present everywhere and can be documented from the vocabulary used.

37 F. Grevisse, "Les Bayeke."

38 For Tippu Tib, see *Maisha ya Hamed bin Muhammed el Murjebi yaani Tippu Tib*, parag. nos. 1–69. For the earliest reference to Arab trade, see F. J. de Lacerda, *Diarios de Viagem* (1944), p. 189, dating from 1797. Other early references are cited in Note 25. See also Livingstone, *Missionary Travels* . . . , pp. 218, 223–28; Da Silva Porto, . . . *Travessia do continente africano*, pp. 87–93; Macqueen, "Journal of Silva Porto with the Arabs . . . ," especially p. 150; Pedroso Gamitto, *O Muata Cazembe* . . . , citing Magyar, pp. 496–97.

39 For the above section, in general, see Tippu Tib, *Maisha ya Hamed bin Muhammed el Murjebi yaani Tippu Tib*, parag. nos. 70–end; P. Ceulemans, *La question arabe et le Congo* . . . (1959), pp. 28–367; Timmermans, "Les SapoSapo près de Luluabourg," pp. 30–33, map; H. M. Stanley, *Through the Dark Continent* (1877), pp. 376, 380–452; Cameron, *Across Africa*, pp. 263–80; Von Wissmann, *Unter Deutscher Flagge* . . . , pp. 143–68; A. van Zandijcke, *Pages de l'histoire du Kasaï* (1953), pp. 26–146. Ceulemans and Tippu Tib were the main references used.

40 Verdick, *Les premiers jours du Katanga* . . . , pp. 63–69, 73–74, 118–21.

41 Cameron, *Across Africa*, pp. 294, 299, 303, 313–14, 324, 334.

42 See D'Orjo de Marchovelette, "Notes sur les funérailles des chefs Ilunga Kabale et Kabongo Kumwimba . . . ,"*BJIDCC*, XVIII (1950), 364–68; XIX (1951), 1–8; A. van der Noot, "Quelques éléments historiques sur l'empire luba, son organisation et sa direction," *BJIDCC*, IV, No. 7 (1936), 143–45; Verhulpen, *Baluba et Balubaisés*, pp. 102–4; Tippu Tib, *Maisha ya Hamed bin Muhammed el Murjebi yaani Tippu Tib*, parag. no. 104; Cameron, *Across Africa*, pp. 294–352; A. Delcommune, "Au coeur du Congo Belge . . . ," *Mouvement Géographique*, XXIX, No. 1 (1912), 7–10.

43 See M. Gluckman, "Succession and Civil War among the Bemba: An Exercise in Anthropological Theory," *Rhodes-Livingstone J.*, No. 16 (1954); and Brelsford, *The Succession of Bemba Chiefs*. According to Gluckman, the rules of succession lead to a drifting away from the main line of succession. After three or four generations the drift leads to rebellion of a junior branch which holds key chieftainships and one of the vital chieftainess titles, but sees no chance to succeed to the kingship. Cileshya's case would be a recurring event in a cyclical process. The argumentation is strong but not entirely convincing. For Bemba expansions, see Pedroso Gamitto, *O Muata Cazembe* . . . , pp. 136, 173–74, 348; Brelsford, pp. 2–5; Gluckman, pp. 11–12; A. I. Richards, "Tribal Government in Transition . . . ," *JRAI*, XXXIV, No. 137, Suppl. (1935), 12, 16.

44 Gouldsbury and Sheane, *The Great Plateau* . . . , pp. 17, 29; L. H. Gann, *The Birth of a Plural Society* . . . (1958), pp. 23–26; Coxhead, *Native Tribes of North-Eastern Rhodesia* . . . , pp. 5–7; Tippu Tib, *Maisha ya Hamed bin Muhammed el Murjebi yaani Tippu Tib*, parag. nos. 11, 18, 20, 33, 64–66; F. M. Thomas, *Historical Notes on the Bisa Tribe, Northern Rhodesia* (1958), pp. 32–49; Brelsford, *The Succession of Bemba Chiefs*, pp. 5–6.

Appendix

1 See J. Cuvelier, *L'ancien royaume de Congo* (1941), p. 253 n4.

2 See J. Cuvelier, *Koningin Nzinga van Matamba* (1957), pp. 14–17. Lists of kings are derived from G. A. Cavazzi, *Istorica descrizione de'tre'regni Congo* (1687), II, 126–38; E. Ravenstein, *The Strange Adventures of Andrew Battell* . . . (1901), pp. 140–45; and for the Pende, from G. Haveaux, *La tradition historique des Bapende orientaux* (1954), pp. 6–15. By 1519 Ndongo is reported by documentary evidence; see R. Delgado, *História de Angola*, I (1948), 134–39.

3 See J. Vansina, "La fondation du royaume de Kasanje," *Aequatoria*, XXV, No. 2 (1962), 45–62, where this date is discussed.

4 See I. Cunnison, "The Reigns of the Kazembes," *N. Rhod. J.*, III, No. 2 (1956), 131–36, for Kazembe chronology. Father Pinto wrote in 1799 at Kazembe's capital that it had been founded about sixty years ago, according to his informants.

5 O. Dapper, *Naukeurige beschrijvinge der Afrikaensche gewesten* (1676), pp. 218–19.

6 The evidence is given by M. Plancquaert, *Les Jaga et les Bayaka du Kwango* (1932), pp. 86–87. Mwene Putu is mentioned in a

written report at the Vatican before 1724/1730. A mention of war in 1657 by Nzinga against a Yaka chief would have involved not the Lunda but only the Yaka, who were there before the Lunda arrived. More unpublished documentation is probably available and additional sources will help to establish the chronology of the kingdoms in the interior of Africa. This is certain for the Imbangala, where the fair of Cassange was located, and is probable for the Yaka (Lunda) kingdom and even the Lunda homeland.

7   For Kuba chronology, see J. Vansina, *Geschiedenis van de Kuba* . . . (1963). The basic dates are a sun eclipse of 1680 and the irruption of the Jaga in Kongo in 1568 or 1569.

8   See H. van Roy, "L'Origine des Balunda du Kwango," *Aequatoria,* XXIV, No. 4 (1961), 139–41; and Plancquaert, *Les Jaga et les Bayaka* . . . , pp. 85–133, for a discussion of the Yaka case. For the Lozi, the first relatively firm date would be 1840. The kingdom originated seven generations before, and if a generation is taken to be thirty years, this would place the origins around 1610. It may in fact be later. C. M. N. White in "The Ethno-history of the Upper Zambezi," *African Studies,* XXI (1962), 11, states that the dynasty was established in the early years of the eighteenth century; see pages 26–27 for the eighteen-forty date. For the Bemba, the work of Father Tanguy, *Imilandu ya Babemba* (1949), which is the only work on which a chronology could be based from Bemba tradition, has not been available to me. I. Cunnison, *The Luapula Peoples of Northern Rhodesia* (1959), p. 40 *n*1, mentions that there were four Nkuba between the first one and the arrival of the Kazembe of the Luapula, i.e., roughly 1740. The Bemba immigration may be either somewhat earlier or contemporary with the arrival of the first Nkuba; this would give a date of 1640 if twenty years of office per Nkuba are used as a rough index.

9   If at a date x an eldest son takes over the succession of the father who died just after the birth of the youngest son, the reigns of all the sons in succession from elder to younger cannot be longer than the lifetime of the youngest son, say, seventy years (if, of course, they die in order from the eldest to the youngest). In any other case, it is the longest living brother who takes over until his death. The reigns of all the half brothers correspond therefore to the life span of the longest living (normally the youngest) among them.

10   See E. Verhulpen, *Baluba et Balubaisés* (1936), tables; L. Duy-

sters, "Histoire des Aluunda," *Prob. Afr. Cent.*, XII (1958), 88–89.
11 See H. Dias de Carvalho, *Expedição ao Muatiamvu . . .* (1890), pp. 549–54.
12 M. van den Byvang, "Notice historique sur les Balunda," *Congo,* I (1937), 556–57.
13 Vansina, *Geschiedenis van de Kuba . . .* , chapter V, discusses length of generation with the Kuba and arrives at the same mean.
14 Verhulpen, *Baluba et Balubaisés,* in his tables, applies a mechanical mean of generation and length of reign without taking into account what is known by tradition. He has Ilunga Kabale dying around the beginning of the century; E. d'Orjo de Marchovelette, "Notes sur les funérailles des chefs Ilunga Kabale et Kabongo Kumwimba . . . ," *BJIDCC,* XVIII (1950), 350, goes against all documents by placing his death from 1880 to 1885. He probably confused Ilunga Kabale with Kasongo Kalombo.
15 Tippu Tib, *Maisha ya Hamed bin Muhammed el Murjebi yaani Tippu Tib,* parag. nos. 89, 104.
16 For the lists of Luba kings, see Chapter III, Chart II.

Selected
Bibliography

Books

Abreu e Brito. *Um inquerito a vida administrativa e economica de Angola e do Brasil,* ed. A. Felner. Coimbra, 1931.

Adams, J. *Remarks on the Country Extending from Cape Palmas to the River Congo, including Observations on the Manners and Customs of the Inhabitants . . . .* London, 1823.

African Elders. *History of the Bena Ngoma.* London, 1949.

Almeida Teixeira, A. de. See De Almeida Teixeira, A.

Andersson, E. *Contribution à l'ethnographie des Kuta.* (Studia ethnographica Upsaliensia, No. 6.) Uppsala, 1953.

Arnot, F. S. *Garenganze or Seven Years of Pioneer Mission Work in Central Africa.* London, 1889.

———. *Bihé and Garenganze; or, Four Years' Further Work and Travel in Central Africa.* London, 1893.

———. *Missionary Travels in Central Africa.* Bath, 1914.

Atri, M. d'. See D'Atri, M.

Barbot, J. *A Description of the Coasts of North and South-Guinea and of Ethiopia Inferior, Vulgarly Angola.* In *A Collection of Voyages and Travels,* comp. Awnsham Churchill, Vol. V. London, 1732.

Barros, J. de. See De Barros, J.

Bastian, A. *San Salvador.* Berlin, 1859.

———. *Die Deutsche Expedition an der Loango Küste.* 2 vols. Iena, 1874–75.

Note: See List of Abbreviations.

Bastin, M. *Art décoratif Cokwe. (Subsidiós para a história, arqueologia e etnografia dos povos de Lunda.)* 2 vols. Lisbon, Museu do Dundo, 1961.

Bastos, A. *Traços gerais do a etnografia do Districtó de Benguella.* Lisbon, 1909.

Bateman, C. S. L. *The First Ascent of the Kasaï.* London, 1889.

Baumann, H. *Lunda. Bei Bauern und Jägern in Inner-Angola.* Berlin, 1935.

Baumann, H., and D. Westermann. *Les peuples et les civilisations de l'Afrique* (by H. Baumann) and *Suivi de les langues et l'éducation* (by D. Westermann), trans. L. Homburger. Paris, 1948.

Beaucorps, R. de. See De Beaucorps, R.

Beguin, E. *Les Ma-Rotsé: étude géographique et etnographique du Haut-Zambèze.* Lausanne, 1903.

Bentley, H. *Pioneering on the Congo.* London, 1900.

Bertrand, A. J. *The Kingdom of the Barotsi,* trans. A. B. Miall. London, 1899.

Biebuyck, D. (ed.). *African Agrarian Systems.* (Second International African Seminar.) London, 1963.

Bohannan, P., and G. Dalton (eds.). *Markets in Africa.* Evanston, 1962.

Boletim official do governo-geral da provincia de Angola. Parte naõ official. Luanda, 1800–.

Bontinck, F. *Jean François de Rome OFM. Cap. La fondation de la mission des Capucins au Royaum du Congo (1648).* Louvain, 1964.

Bouveignes, O. de. See De Bouveignes, O.

Bowdich, T. *The Discoveries of the Portuguese in the Interior of Angola.* London, 1824.

Boxer, C. *Salvador de Sá and the Struggle for Brasil and Angola.* London, 1952.

Brasio, P. *Monumenta missionaria africana: Africa occidental.* 19 vols. Lisbon, 1953–.

Brelsford, W. V. *Aspects of Bemba Chieftainship.* (Rhodes-Livingstone Institute Communications, No. 2.) Lusaka, 1944.

———. *The Succession of Bemba Chiefs.* Lusaka, 1944.

Bruel, G. *L'Afrique Equatoriale Française.* Paris, 1918.

Bryan, M. A. *The Bantu Languages of Africa.* (Handbook of African Languages, No. 4.) London, 1959.

Buettner, R. *Reise im Kongolande.* Leipzig, 1890.

Bulck, V. [G.] van. *Les recherches linguistiques au Congo Belge.* (IRCB, Vol. XVI.) Brussels, 1948.

Burton, R. F. *The Lands of Cazembe.* London, 1873.

———. *Two Trips to Gorillaland and the Cataracts of the Congo.* London, 1876.

Burton, W. F. *Luba Religion and Magic in Custom and Belief.* (MRAC, No. 35.) Tervuren, 1961.

Cadornega, O. de. See De Cadornega, O.

Caeneghem, R. van. *Over het Godsbegrip der Baluba van Kasai.* (IRCB, Vol. XXII, No. 2.) Brussels, 1952.

————. *Hekserij bij de Baluba van Kasai.* (ARSC, Vol. III, No. 1.) Brussels, 1955.

Cameron, V. L. *Across Africa.* New York, 1877.

Campbell, D. *In the Heart of Bantuland: A Record of Twenty-nine Years Pioneering.* London, 1922.

Capello, H., and R. Ivens. *From Benguella to the Territory of Yacca.* 2 vols. London, 1882.

Capello, H., and R. Ivens. *De Angola á contra-costa.* 2 vols. Lisbon, 1886.

Carvalho, H. See Dias de Carvalho, H.

Castello Branco, G. M. de. See De Castello Branco, G. M.

Cavazzi, G. A. *Istorica descrizione de'tre'regni Congo.* Bologna, 1687. [German translation, Munich, 1694.]

Cerqueira, I. de. See De Cerqueira, I.

Ceulemans, P. *La question arabe et le Congo 1883–1892.* (ARSC, Vol. XXII, No. 22.) Bruxelles, 1959.

Chatelain, H. *Folk-tales of Angola.* (Memoirs of the American Folklore Society, Vol. I.) New York, 1894.

Chibanza, S. J. *Kaonde History.* (Central Bantu Historical Texts, Rhodes Livingstone Institute Communications, No. 22.) Lusaka, 1961.

Childs, G. M. *Umbundu Kinship & Character.* London, 1949.

Chimba, B. *A History of the Baushi in Bemba.* Cape Town, 1949.

Chinyama, T. *The Early History of the Balovale Lunda.* (African Literature Committee, Lumbrito Series, No. 15.) Lusaka, 1945.

Clay, G. C. R. *History of the Mankoya District.* (Rhodes Livingstone Institute Communications, No. 4.) Lusaka, 1945.

Coillard, F. *On the Threshold of Central Africa,* trans. Catherine Winkworth MacKintosh. London, 1897.

Colle, P. *Les Baluba (Congo Belge).* 2 vols. (Collection de monographies ethnographiques, Vols. X–XI.) Brussels, 1913.

Colson, E., and M. Gluckman (eds.). *Seven Tribes of British Central Africa.* London, 1951.

Cordeiro, L. *Benguella e seu sertão por um anonymo.* (Memorias do Ultramar. Viagens, exploraçoes e conquistas dos Portugueses.) Lisbon, 1881.

————. *Escravos e minas da Africa.* (Memorias do Ultramar. Viagens, exploraçoes e conquistas dos Portugueses.) Lisbon, 1881.

————. *Estabelecimentos e resgates portugueses na costa occidental de l'Africa por um anonymo.* (Memorias do Ultramar. Viagens, exploraçoes e conquistas dos Portugueses.) Lisbon, 1881.

Cornet, R. *Katanga.* Brussels, 1943.

————. *Maniema.* Brussels, 1952.

Cornevin, R. *Histoire des peuples de l'Afrique noire.* Paris, 1960.

Coxhead, J. *The Native Tribes of North-Eastern Rhodesia. Their Laws and Customs.* (Occasional Papers of the Royal Anthropological Institute of Great Britain and Ireland, No. 5.) London, 1914.

Crawford, D. *Thinking Black.* London, 1912.

————. *Back to the Long Grass.* New York, 1923.

Cunnison, I. *History on the Luapula.* (Rhodes Livingstone Institute Papers, No. 21.) London, 1951.

————. *The Luapula Peoples of Northern Rhodesia.* Manchester, 1959.

Cuvelier, J. *L'ancien royaume de Congo.* Brussels, 1941.

————. *Biographie coloniale belge.* (IRCB, Vol. II.) Brussels, 1951. [Articles dealing with the different kings of Kongo and with other persons of the sixteenth and seventeenth centuries in the kingdom Kongo.]

————. *Documents sur une mission française au Kakongo 1766–1776.* (IRCB, Vol. XXX, No. 1.) Brussels, 1953.

————. *Relations sur le Congo du Père Laurent de Lucques (1700–1717).* (IRCB, Vol. XXXII, No. 2.) Brussels, 1953.

————. *Koningin Nzinga van Matamba.* Bruges, 1957.

Cuvelier, J., and L. Jadin. *L'ancien Congo d'après les archives romaines (1518–1640).* (IRCB, Vol. XXXVI, No. 2.) Brussels, 1954.

Da Caltanisetta, L. *Relation sur le royaume de Kongo (1690–1700).* (Les Cahiers Ngonge, No. 6.) Leopoldville, 1960.

Da Paivo Manso, L. *História do Congo. Documentos.* Lisbon, 1877.

Dapper, O. *Naukeurige beschrijvinge der Afrikaensche gewesten.* 2nd ed. Amsterdam, 1676.

Da Santa Maria, F. *O Ceo aberto na terra.* Lisbon, 1697.

Da Silva Correa, E. *História de Angola.* 2 vols. Lisbon, 1937.

Da Silva Porto, A. F. *Novas jornadas.* (*BSGL,* Vols. V–VI.) Lisbon, 1885–86.

————. *Silva Porto e a travessia do continente africano,* ed. G. Sousa Dias. Lisbon, 1938.

————. *Viagens e apontamentos de um portuense em Africa,* ed. J. de Miranda and A. Brochado. Lisbon, 1942.

Da Silva Rego, A. *A dupla restauraçao de Angola (1641–1648).* Lisbon, 1948.

————. *Portuguese Colonization in the XVIth Century: A Study of the Royal Ordinances (regimentos).* Lisbon, 1959.

D'Atri, M. *Relation sur le royaume de Kongo (1690–1700)*. (Les Cahiers Ngonge, No. 5.) Leopoldville, 1960.

Davidson, B. *Old Africa Rediscovered*. London, 1960.

———. *Black Mother. The Years of the African Slave Trade*. Boston, 1961.

De Almeida Teixeira, A. *Lunda, sua organização e occupação*. Lisbon, 1948.

De Barros, J. *Da Asia (Decada I)*. Lisbon, 1777–78.

De Beaucorps, R. *Les Bayansi du Bas-Kwilu*. Louvain, 1933.

———. *Les Basongo de la Luniungu et de la Gobari*. (IRCB, Vol. X.) Brussels, 1941.

De Bouveignes, O., and J. Cuvelier. *Jérôme de Montesarchio*. Namur, 1951.

De Cadornega, O. *História Geral das Guerras Angolanas*, ed. R. Delgado. 3 vols. Lisbon, 1940.

De Castello Branco, G. M. *Da Mina ao Cabo Negro*, ed. L. Cordeiro. (Memorias da Ultramar. Viagens, explorações e conquistas dos Portugueses.) Lisbon, 1881.

De Cerqueira, I. *Vida Social Indigena na Colonia de Angola*. Lisbon, 1947.

De Decker, J. *Les clans Ambuun (Bambunda) d'après leur littérature orale*. (IRCB, Vol. XX, Fasc. 1.) Brussels, 1950.

De Deken, C. *Deux ans au Congo*. Anvers, 1900.

De Grandpré, L. *Voyage à la côte occidentale d'Afrique . . . 1786 et 1787. . . .* Paris, 1801.

De Lacerda e Almeida, F. J. M. *Diarios de Viagem*. (Biblioteca popular Brasileira, Vol. XVIII.) Rio de Janeiro, 1944. [Has the best texts of *Instruções e Diario da viagem da vila de Tete, capital dos rios de Sena para o interior da Africa 1798*, pp. 175–261. Cf. R. F. Burton.]

Delachaux, T., and C. E. Thiébaud. *Pays et peuples d'Angola*. Paris, 1934.

Delafosse, M., and D. Poutrin. *Enquête coloniale dans l'Afrique Française, Occidentale et Equatoriale sur l'organisation de la famille indigéne, les fiançailles, le mariage*. Paris, 1930.

Delcommune, A. *Vingt années de vie africaine. Récits de voyages, d'aventures et d'exploration au Congo Belge, 1874–1893*. 3 vols. Brussels, 1922.

Delgado, R. *A famosa e histórica Benguella. Catalogo dos Governadores*. Benguela, 1940.

———. *História de Angola*. Vols. I and II, Benguela, 1948; Vol. III, Lobito, 1953.

Del Nino Jesus, F. *La Misión del Congo*. Pamplona, 1929.

De Mello, M. A. *Angola no começo do seculo (1802)*. *Relatorio do governo de Miguel Antonio de Mello*. (*BSGL*, IX, No. 5a [1885], 548–64.)

De Morais Martins, M. *Contacto de Culturas no Congo Portugues*. (Estudos de Ciencias Politicas e Socias, Vol. XI.) Lisbon, 1958.

Denolf, P. *Aan de rand van de Dibese*. 2 vols. (IRCB, Vol. XXXIV; ARSC, Vol. III.) Brussels, 1954.

Denuce, J. *Afrika in de XVI e eeuw en de handel van Antwerpen*. (Dokumenten voor de geschiedenis van den handel, Vol. II.) Antwerp, 1937.

Depelchin, H., and C. Croonenberghs. *Trois ans dans l'Afrique australe, débuts de la mission du Zambèze*, Vol. II: *Au pays d'Umzila, chez les Batongas, la vallée des Barotsés*. Brussels, 1882–83.

De Pina, Ruy. *Chronica del Rey D. João II*. Lisbon, 1792.

De Resende, G. *Chronica dos valorosos e insignes feitos del Rey Dom João II*. Lisbon, 1622.

De Serpa Pinto, A. A. *How I Crossed Africa*. 2 vols. London, 1881.

De Sousa Barroso, A. *O Congo, seu passado, presente e futuro*. Lisbon, 1889.

De Sousberghe, L. *Structures de parenté et d'alliance d'après les formules Pende*. (ARSC, NS, Vol. IV, fasc. 1.) Brussels, 1955.

———. *Pactes de sang et pactes d'union dans la mort chez quelques peuplades du Kwango*. (ARSC, NS, Vol. XXII, fasc. 2.) Brussels, 1959.

———. *Deux palabres d'esclaves chez les Pende*. (ARSC, NS, Vol. XXV, fasc. 5.) Brussels, 1961.

Dias de Carvalho, H. *Expedição ao Muatiamvu. Ethnographia e história dos povos da Lunda*. Lisbon, 1890.

Douglas, M. *The Lele of Kasai*. London, 1963.

Drum, H. *Lueji ya Konde*. Brussels, 1932.

Duffy, J. E. *Portuguese Africa*. Cambridge, 1959.

Dusselje, E. *Les Tegues de l'Alima*. Antwerp, 1910.

Edwards, A. C. *The Ovimbundu under Two Sovereignties*. London, 1962.

Egerton, F. *Angola in Perspective*. London, 1957.

Ellenberger, D. F. *History of the Basuto, Ancient and Modern*, trans. J. C. MacGregor. London, 1912.

Estermann, C. *Etnografia do sudoeste de Angola*. (Junta das Missões Geograficas e de Investigaçoes do Ultramar. Memórias: Serie antropológica e etnológica, No. 4.) Porto I, 1956; II, 1957; III, 1963.

Everbroeck, N. van. *Religie en magie onder de Basakata*. (IRCB, Vol. XXIV, fasc. 1.) Brussels, 1952.

———. *Mbomb'ipoku: Le Seigneur à l'abime.* (MRAC. Archives d'ethnographie, No. 3.) Tervuren, 1961.

Fage, J. D., and R. A. Oliver. *A Short History of Africa.* London, 1962.

Farinha, A. L. *Dom Afonso, Rei do Congo.* Lisbon, 1941.

Felgas, H. *História do Congo Português.* Carmona, 1958.

Felner, A., de Albuquerque. *Angola.* Coimbra, 1933.

Ferreira Diniz. *Populações indigenas de Angola.* Coimbra, 1918.

Ferreira Ribeiro, M. *Homenagem dos heróes que precederam Brito Capello e Roberto Ivens na exploração da Africa austral, 1484–1877.* Lisbon, 1885.

Figueira, L. *Africa Bantu: Raças et tribos de Angola.* Lisbon, 1938.

Forde, C. D. (ed.). *African Worlds. Studies in the Cosmological Ideas and Social Values of African Peoples.* London, 1954.

Fortes, M., and E. E. Evans-Pritchard (eds.). *African Political Systems.* London, 1940.

Frobenius, L. *Im Schatten des Kongostaates.* Berlin, 1907.

Galvão, H., and C. Selvagem. *Imperio Ultramarino Portugués.* Vol. III. Angola and Lisbon, 1952.

Gamito, A. C. P. See Pedroso Gamitto, A. C.

Gann, L. H. *The Birth of a Plural Society: The Development of Northern Rhodesia under the British South Africa Company, 1894–1914.* Manchester, 1958.

Gibbons, A. *Exploration and Hunting in Central Africa, 1895–96.* London, 1898.

Giraud, V. *Les lacs de l'Afrique equatoriale.* Paris, 1890.

Gluckman, M. *The Judicial Process among the Barotse of Northern Rhodesia.* Manchester, 1955.

Gouldsbury, G., and H. Sheane. *The Great Plateau of Northern Rhodesia.* London, 1911.

Grandpré, L. de. See De Grandpré, L.

Greenberg, J. *The Languages of Africa.* (International Journal of American Linguistics, Vol. XXIX, No. 1.) Bloomington, Ind., 1963.

Guiral, L. *Le Congo Français du Gabon à Brazzaville.* Paris, 1889.

Guthrie, M. *The Classification of the Bantu Languages.* London, 1948.

———. *The Bantu Languages of Western Equatorial Africa.* (Handbook of African Languages.) London, 1953.

Hambly, W. D. *The Ovimbundu of Angola.* (Field Museum of Natural History, No. 329; Anthropological Series, Vol. XXI, No. 2.) Chicago, 1934.

Harding, C. *In Remotest Barotseland.* London, 1904.

Haveaux, G. *La tradition historique des Bapende orientaux.* (IRCB, Vol. XXXVII, No. 1.) Brussels, 1954.

Herskovits, M. J. *The Human Factor in Changing Africa*. New York, 1962.

Hildebrand, G. *Le martyr Georges de Geel et la mission du Congo (1645–1652)*. Antwerp, 1940.

Holub, E. *Von der Capstadt ins Land der Maschukulumbe*. 2 vols. Vienna, 1890.

Hughes, J. *Eighteen Years on Lake Bangweulu*. London, 1933.

Ihle, A. *Das Alte Königreich Kongo*. (Studien zur Völkerkunde, Vol. I.) Leipzig, 1929.

Jalla, A. *Pionniers parmi les Ma-Rotse*. Florence, 1903.

――――. *Litaba za sicaba sa Malozi*. Paris, 1939. [Standard history of the Lozi.]

Jaspan, M. *The Ila-Tonga Peoples of North-Western Rhodesia*. (Ethnographic Survey of Africa, West Central Africa, No. 4.) London, 1953.

Jaspert, F., and W. Jaspert. *Die völkerstämme Mittel-Angolas*. (Veröffentlichungen aus dem Städtischen völker-Museum, No. 5.) Frankfurt am Main, 1930.

Jessen, O. *Reisen und forschungen in Angola*. Berlin, 1936.

Johnston, H. H. *British Central Africa*. London, 1897.

Kazembe XIV, Mwata. *My Ancestors and My People*. (Bantu Heritage Series, No. 2.) London, 1951.

Lacerda. See De Lacerda e Almeida, F. J.

Laman, K. *The Kongo*. 2 vols. (Studia Ethnographica Upsaliensia, Vols. IV, VIII.) Stockholm, 1953, 1957.

Lane-Poole, E. H. *The Native Tribes of the East Luangwa Province of Northern Rhodesia*. 3rd ed. Livingstone, 1949.

La pratique missionaire des PP. Capucins Italiens dans les royaumes de Congo Angola et contrées adjacentes. Louvain, 1931. [Attributed erroneously to Hyacinto de Bologna. Text from the mid-eighteenth century.]

Lefebvre, G. *L'Angola: son histoire, son économie*. Liège, 1947.

Lethur, R. *Etude sur le royaume de Loango et le peuple Vili*. (Les Cahiers Ngonge, No. 2.) Leopoldville, 1960.

Livingstone, D. *Missionary Travels and Researches in South Africa*. London, 1857.

――――. *Last Journals*, ed. Horace Waller. 2 vols. London, 1874.

Lopes de Lima, J. J. *Ensaios sobre a statistica das possessões Portuguezas*. 5 vols. (Vol. II: *Ilhas de S. Thomé e Príncipe*; Vol. III: *Angola, Benguella, e suas dependencias*). Lisbon, 1844–62.

McCulloch, M. *The Southern Lunda and Related Peoples*. (Ethno-

graphic Survey of Africa. West Central Africa, No. I.) London, 1951.
———. *The Ovimbundu of Angola.* (Ethnographic Survey of Africa. West Central Africa, No. II.) London, 1952.

Magyar, L. *Reisen in Süd-Afrika in den Jahren 1849 bis 1857.* Pest/ Leipzig, 1859.

Marquardsen, H. *Angola.* Berlin, 1920.

Marquardsen, H., and A. Stahl. *Angola.* Berlin, 1928. [Much modified version from the 1920 work.]

Melland, F. M. *In Witch-bound Africa, an Account of the Primitive Kaonde Tribe and Their Beliefs.* London, 1923.

Mello, M. A. de. See De Mello, M. A.

Mendiaux, E. *Histoire du Congo.* Brussels, 1961.

Merolla, J., da Sorrento. *Relatione del viaggio nel regno di Congo.* Naples, 1692. [English translation in J. Pinkerton, ed., *A General Collection of the Best and Most Interesting Voyages in all Parts of the World,* Vol. XVI, pp. 260 ff. London, 1814.]

Mertens, J. *Les Ba Dzing de la Kamtsha. Première partie. Ethnographie.* (IRCB, Vol. IV, No. 1.) Brussels, 1935.

———. *Les chefs couronnés chez les Ba Kongo orientaux.* (IRCB, Vol. XI, No. 1.) Brussels, 1942.

Monteiro, J. J. *Angola and the River Congo.* London, 1875.

Morais Martins, M. de. See De Morais Martins, M.

Munday, J. T. *Kankomba.* (Central Bantu Historical Texts, No. I. Rhodes Livingstone Institute Communications, No. 22.) Lusaka, 1961.

Murdock, G. *Africa. Its Peoples and their Culture History.* New York, 1959.

Mwata Kazembe XIV. See Kazembe XIV, Mwata.

Nenquin, J. *Excavations at Sanga 1957.* (MRAC, No. 45.) Tervuren, 1963.

Neves, A. *Memorias do expedição ao Cassange.* Lisbon, 1854.

Nicolai, H. *Le Kwilu.* Brussels, 1963.

Nino Jesus, F. del. See Del Nino Jesus, F.

Olbrechts, F. M. *Les arts plastiques du Congo Belge.* Brussels, 1959.

Overbergh, C. van. *Les Mayombe.* (Collection de monographies ethnographiques, No. 2.) Brussels, 1907.

———. *Les Basonge.* (Collection de monographies ethnographiques, No. 3.) Brussels, 1908.

Paiva Manso, L. de. See De Paiva Manso, L.

Pechuel Loesche, E. *Volkskunde von Loango.* Stuttgart, 1907.

Pedroso Gamitto, A. C. *O Muata Cazembe.* . . . Lisbon, 1854. [Translation by I. Cunnison, *King Kazembe and the Marave, Cheva, Bisa, Bemba, Lunda and Other Peoples of Southern Africa.* 2 vols. (Junta de investigações do Ultramar.) Lisbon, 1962.]

Pereira, D. *Esmeraldo De Situ Orbis.* London, 1937.

Pigafetta, F. *Relatione del Reame di Congo e delle circonvicine contrade, tratta delli scritti e ragionamenti di Odoardo Lopez, Portoghese.* Roma, 1591. [Translations: L. Cahun (French), Brussels, 1883; W. Bal (French), Louvain, 1963; Martyn Everart (Dutch, ed. A. Burssens), *Kongo-Overzee,* VII–VIII (1941–42); M. Hutchinson (English), London, 1881.]

Pina, Ruy de. See De Pina, Ruy.

Plancquaert, M. *Les Jaga et les Bayaka du Kwango.* (IRCB, Vol. III, No. 1.) Brussels, 1932.

Pogge, P. *Im Reich des Muata Jamwo.* Berlin, 1880.

Poole, E. H. Lane. See Lane-Poole, E. H.

Proyart, A. *Histoire de Loango, Kakongo et autres royaumes d'Afrique.* Paris, 1776. [Translation in J. Pinkerton, ed. *A General Collection of the Best and Most Interesting Voyages in all Parts of the World,* Vol. XVI, pp. 548–97. London, 1814.]

Radcliffe-Brown, A. R., and C. D. Forde (eds.). *African Systems of Kinship and Marriage.* London, 1950.

Ratelband, K. (ed.). *Reisen naar West Afrika van Pieter Vanden Broecke, 1605–1614.* The Hague, 1950.

Ravenstein, E. *The Strange Adventures of Andrew Battell of Leigh in Angola and the Adjoining Regions.* London, 1901.

Rebello de Aragão, B. *Terras e Minas Africanas,* ed. L. Cordeiro. (Memorias do Ultramar. Viagens, exploraçoes e conquistas dos Portugueses.) Lisbon, 1881.

Redinha, J. *Campanha etnographia ao Tchiboco (Alto-Tchicapa).* 2 vols. (Museu do Dundo Subsidios para a história, arqueologia e etnografia dos povos da Lunda. Publições culturais, No. 19.) Lisbon, 1955.

———. *Colleção etnografica.* Loànda: Museu de Angola, 1955.

Reeth, E. van. *De rol van den moederlijken oom in de inlandsche familie.* (IRCB, Vol. V, No. 2.) Brussels, 1935.

Resinde, G. de. See De Resinde, G.

Richards, A. I. *Land, Labour and Diet in Northern Rhodesia.* London, 1939.

———. *Chisungu: A Girls' Initiation Ceremony among the Bemba of Northern Rhodesia.* London, 1956.

Richter, M. *Kultur und Reich der Marotse.* Leipzig, 1908.

Rinchon, D. *La traite et l'esclavage des Congolais par les Europeens.* Brussels, 1929.

———. *Les armements négriers au XVIII e siècle.* (ARSC, Vol. VII, No. 3.) Brussels, 1956.

Santa Maria, F. da. See Da Santa Maria, F.

Schmitz, R. *Les Baholoholo.* (Collection de Monographies ethnographiques, Vol. IX.) Brussels, 1912.

Schuett, O. *Reisen im Südwestlichen Becken des Congo.* Berlin, 1881.

Schulz, A., and A. Hammar. *The New Africa: A Journey up the Chobe and down the Okovanga Rivers.* London, 1897.

Selous, F. C. *A Hunter's Wanderings in Africa.* London, 1881.

Serpa Pinto, A. A. de. See De Serpa Pinto, A. A.

Serra Frazão, S. *Associaçoes secretas entre os indigenas de Angola.* (Estudos etnograficos dos povos de Angola, No. 2.) Lisbon, 1946.

Silva Correa. See Da Silva Correa, E.

Silva Porto. See Da Silva Porto, A. F.

Silva Rego. See Da Silva Rego, A.

Silveira, L. *Um Missionario português no Congo dos fins do seculo XVIII.* Lisbon, 1943.

Simar, T. H. *Le Congo au XVIe siècle d'après la relation de Lopez Pigafetta.* Brussels, 1929.

Slaski, J. *Peoples of the Lower Luapula Valley.* (Ethnographic Survey of Africa. East Central Africa, part 2.) London, 1951.

Smith, E., and W. Dale. *The Ila-speaking Peoples of Northern Rhodesia.* 2 vols. London, 1920.

Soret, M. *Les Kongo nord-occidentaux.* (Monographies ethnologiques africaines.) Paris, 1959.

Sousa Barroso, A. de. See De Sousa Barroso, A.

Sousa Dias, G. *Relações de Angola.* Coimbra, 1934.

———. *A Batalha de Ambuila.* Lisbon, 1942.

Sousberghe, L. de. See De Sousberghe, L.

Stanley, H. M. *Through the Dark Continent.* 2 vols. London, 1877.

Stappers, L. *Zuid Kisongye bloemlezing. Milembwe teksten.* (MRCB. Linguistique, Vol. VI.) Tervuren, 1953.

Storme, M. *Ngankabe, la prétendue reine des Baboma d'après H. M. Stanley.* (ARSC, Vol. VII, No. 2.) Brussels, 1956.

———. *Het ontstaan van de Kasai missie.* (ARSOM, Vol. XXIV, fasc. 3.) Brussels, 1961.

Tanguy, Father. *A History of the Baushi.* Ndola, 1943.

———. *Imilandu ya Babemba.* London, 1949. [Standard Bemba history.]

Tempels, P. *Bantu philosophie.* Antwerp, 1946.

Tew, M. *Peoples of the Lake Nyasa Region.* (Ethnographic Survey of Africa. East Central Africa, No. 1.) London, 1950.

Theuws, T. *De mens Luba.* (MRAC, No. 42.) Tervuren, 1962.

Thomas, F. M. *Historical Notes on the Bisa Tribe, Northern Rhodesia.* (Rhodes-Livingstone Institute Communications, No. 8.) Lusaka, 1958.

Tilsey, G. E. *Dan Crawford of Central Africa.* London, 1929.

Tippu Tib. *Maisha ya Hamed bin Muhammed el Murjebi yaani Tippu Tib,* trans. W. H. Whiteley. (*East African Swahili Committee Journals,* Vol. 28, No. 2 [1958]; Vol. 29, No. 1 [1959].)

Tonnoir, R. *La pierre de feu.* Léopoldville, 1939.

Torday, E. *Camp and Tramp in African Wilds.* London, 1913.

Torday, E., and T. Joyce. *Notes ethnographiques sur les peuples communément appelés Bakuba, ainsi que sur les peuplades aprentées. Les Bushongo.* (MRCB, Vol. II, fasc. 1.) Brussels, 1910.

Torday, E., and T. Joyce. *Notes ethnographiques sur des populations habitant les bassins du Kasai et du Kwango oriental.* (MRCB, Vol. II, fasc. 2.) Brussels, 1922.

Tuckey, J. K. *Narration of an Expedition to Explore the River Zaire.* New York, 1818.

Turner, V. W. *The Lozi Peoples of North-Western Rhodesia.* (Ethnographic Survey of Africa. West Central Africa, No. 3.) London, 1952.

——. *Schism and Continuity in an African Society.* Manchester, 1957.

Valdez, F. *Six Years of a Traveller's Life in Western Africa.* 2 vols. London, 1861.

Vanderkerken, G. *L'ethnie Mongo.* 2 vols. (IRCB, Vol. XIII.) Brussels, 1944.

Vansina, J. *Les tribus Ba-Kuba et les peuplades apparentées.* (MRCB, Monographies ethnographiques, Vol. I.) Tervuren, 1954.

——. *De la tradition orale. Essai de Methode historique.* (MRAC, No. 36.) Tervuren, 1961.

——. *Geschiedenis van de Kuba: Van ongeveer 1500 tot 1904.* (MRAC, No. 42.) Tervuren, 1963.

Van Wing, J. See Wing, J. van.

Van Zandijcke. See Zandijcke, A. van

Verbeken, A. *Contribution à la géographie historique du Katanga et des régions voisins.* (IRCB, Vol. XXXVI, No. 1.) Brussels, 1954.

——. *Msiri, roi du Garenganze.* Brussels, 1956.

Verbeken, A., and M. Walraet. *La première traversée du Katanga en 1806.* (IRCB, Vol. XXX, No. 2.) Brussels, 1953.

Verdcourt, A. *Notes sur la population Badia. Histoire et institutions d'une population à succession matrilineale du district du Lac Leopold II.* Anvers, 1935.

Verdick, E. *Les premiers jours du Katanga 1890–1903.* Bruxelles, 1952.

Verhulpen, E. *Baluba et Balubaisés.* Anvers, 1936.

Verner, S. *Pioneering in Central Africa.* Richmond, 1903.

Walker, A. *Note d'histoire du Gabon.* (Mémoires de l'Institut d'etudes centrafricaines. Mémoire, No. 9.) Montpellier, 1960.

Wallis, J. P. R. (ed.). *The Barotseland Journal of James Stevenson-Hamilton 1898–1899.* (Oppenheimer Series, No. 7.) London, 1953.

Wannyn, R. L. *L'art ancien du Métal au Bas-Congo.* Champles (Wavre), 1961.

Ward, H. *Among Kongo Cannibals.* London, 1890.

Watson, W. *Tribal Cohesion in a Money Economy.* Manchester, 1958.

Wauters, C. *L'ésotérie des Noirs dévoilée.* Brussels, 1949.

Weeks, J. *Among the Primitive Bakongo.* London, 1914.

Westermann, D. *Geschichte Africas Staatenbildungen südlich der Sahara.* Cologne, 1952.

Weydert, J. *Les Balubas chez eux. Etude ethnographique.* Luxembourg, 1938.

White, C. M. N. *An Outline of Luvale Social and Political Organization.* (Rhodes-Livingstone Institute Papers, No. 30.) London, 1960.

Whiteley, W. *Bemba and Related Peoples of Northern Rhodesia.* (Ethnographic Survey of Africa. East Central Africa, part 2.) London, 1951.

Wilson, G. *The Constitution of Ngonde.* (Rhodes-Livingstone Institute Papers, No. 3.) Manchester, 1930.

Wilson, M. *Peoples of the Nyasa-Tanganyika Corridor.* (Communications from the School of African Studies, NS, No. 29.) Cape Town, 1958.

Wing, J. van. *Etudes Bakongo: I. Histoire et Sociologie.* Louvain, 1960.

Wissmann, H. von. *Meine Zweite Durchquerung Aequatorial Afrikas vom Congo zum Zanzibar.* Frankfurt, 1890.

———. *Unter Deutscher Flagge: Quer durch Afrika.* 6th ed. Berlin, 1890.

Wissmann, H. von, L. Wolf, C. von François, and H. Mueller. *Im Innern Afrikas.* Leipzig, 1888.

Zandijcke, A. van. *Pages de l'histoire du Kasaï.* Namur, 1953.

Zuchelli, A. da Gradisca. *Relazioni del viaggio e missione di Congo.* Venezia, 1712. [German translation: *Merkwürdige Missions- und Reise-Beschreibung nach Kongo . . .* , Frankfurt, 1715.]

Articles

Ambrosius, P. "Inleiding tot de Chichoksche spraakleer," *Congo*, I, No. 3 (1935), 366–74.

Angelo, M., and D. de Carli. "A Curious and Exact Account of a Voyage to Congo 1666–1667." In J. Pinkerton (ed.), *A General Collection of the Best and Most Interesting Voyages and Travels in all Parts of the World*, Vol. XVI, London, 1914.

Apthorpe, R. "Problems of African History: The Nsenga of Northern Rhodesia," *Rhodes-Livingstone Journal*, No. 28 (1960), pp. 47–67.

Arnot, R. S. "F. S. Arnot and Msidi," *Northern Rhodesia Journal*, III, No. 5 (1958), 428–34.

Ascenso, M. "Nel Congo indipendente. Dal Sancuru al Lago Moero," *Bollettino de la Sociedade geografica italiana*, Series IV, XL, fasc. 1 (1903), 110–17.

"Auto de undamento e vassalagem que prestou o soba iundo aquembi em 1838," *Mensario administrativo*, XV (1948), 39–40.

Avelot, R. "Les grands mouvements de peuples en Afrique: Jaga et Zimba," *Bulletin de géographie historique et descriptive*, XXVII (1912), 75–216.

Badier. "Monographie de la tribu des Batékés," *Bulletin de la société des recherches congolaises*, X (1929), 37–43.

Baesten, V. "Les Jésuites au Congo (1548–1659)," *Précis historiques* (1892), pp. 529–46; (1893), pp. 55–75, 100–22, 241–58, 433–57; (1895), pp. 465–81; (1896), pp. 49–60, 145–57.

Baeyens, M. "Les Lesa," *La Revue congolaise*, IV (1913–14), No. 3, 129–43; No. 4, 193–206; No. 5, 257–70; No. 6, 321–36.

Bastin, M. "Quelques oeuvres Tshokwe de musées et collections d'Allemagne et de Scandinavie," *Africa-Tervuren*, VII, No. 4 (1961), 101–5.

———. "Un masque en cuivre martelé des Kongo du nord-est de L'Angola," *Africa-Tervuren*, VII, No. 2 (1961), 29–40.

Beaucorps, R. de. See De Beaucorps, R.

Biebuyck, D. "Fondements de l'organisation politique des Lunda du Mwaanta Yaav en territoire de Kapanga," *Zaïre*, XI, No. 8 (1957), 787–818.

Bittremieux, L. "Brief van Musiri," *Kongo-Overzee*, III, No. 2 (1936), 69–83.

———. "De inwijking der Baphende's," *Congo*, I, No. 2 (1938), 154–67.

Boelaert, E. "Coups de sonde," *Aequatoria*, V, No. 2 (1942), 26–30.

Bogaerts, H. "Iets over stamboomen," *Congo*, II, No. 4 (1939), 410–25.

———. "Bij de Basala Mpasu, de koppensnellers van Kasai," *Zaïre*, IV, No. 4 (1950), 379–419.

————. "Un aspect de la structure sociale des Bakwa Luntu," *Zaïre*, V, No. 6 (1951), 563–609.

Bonnefond, P., and J. Lombard. "Notes sur les coutumes Lari," *Bulletin de l'Institut d'Etudes centrafricaines*, NS, I, Suppl. (1950), 141–77.

Bouveignes, O. de. See De Bouveignes, O.

Brau, C. "Le droit coutumier Lunda," *BJIDCC*, X (1942), No. 8, 155–76; No. 9, 179–203; No. 10, 205–29; No. 11, 231–52; No. 12, 255–67.

Brausch, G. "La justice coutumière chez les Bakwa Luntu," *African Studies*, I, No. 4 (1942), 235–42.

Brelsford, W. V. "History and Customs of the Basala," *JRAI*, LXV (July-Dec., 1935), 205–15.

Brohez, M. "Ethnographie katangaise: Population et colonisation; Les Balubas," *Revue belge de géographie*, XXIX (1905), 373–97, 460–78.

Buechner, M. "Das Reich des Mwata Yamvo und seine Nachbarländer," *Deutsche geographische Blätter*, VI (1883), 64 ff.

————. "Die Ambakisten," *Zeitschrift für Ethnologie*, XLVII (1915), 394–403.

Bulck, G. [V.] van. "Carte linguistique du Congo Belge et du Ruanda-Urundi." In *Atlas Général du Congo*. (IRCB, No. 522.) Brussels, 1954.

————. "D'où sont venus les fondateurs d'état dans l'entre Kwango-Lualaba? (Civilisation sud-érythréenne?)" In *Die Wiener Schule der Völkerkunde*. Vienna, 1956. Pp. 205–17.

Burton, W. F. P. "The Country of the Baluba in Central Katanga," *Geographical Journal*, LXX (1927), 321–42.

————. "L'Organisation sociale des Baluba," trans. P. van Arenbergh, *BJIDCC*, IV, No. 7 (1936), 150–53.

————. "L'âme Luba," *BJIDCC*, VII (1939), No. 2, 38–55; No. 3, 78–87; No. 4, 117–37; No. 5, 141–51; No. 6, 165-84; VIII (1940), No. 7, 193–98; No. 8, 217–26; No. 9, 241–49; No. 10, 265–69; No. 11, 293–305.

Byvang, M. van den. "Notice historique sur les Balunda," *Congo*, I (1937), No. 4, 426–38; No. 5, 548–62; II, No. 2, 193–208.

Caeneghem, R. van. "De kasalazang der Baluba," *Congo*, I, No. 5 (1936), 680–705.

————. "De kasala-zang van den Bakwanga-stam," *Congo*, II, No. 5 (1936), 677–715.

————. "De kasala-zang der Bakwa-Tshimini," *Congo*, I, Nos. 1–2 (1937), 103–33.

Chabeuf, M. "Anthropologie physique du Moyen-Congo et du Gabon méridional," *Bulletin de la société d'anthropologie de Paris,* X, No. 2 (1959), 97–185.

Childs, G. M. "The Peoples of Angola in the Seventeenth Century According to Cadornega," *JAH,* I, No. 2 (1960), 271–79.

Clark, J. Desmond. "Early Man in Northern Rhodesia," *Northern Rhodesia Journal,* II, No. 4 (1954), 49–59.

Clarke, J. A. "Edits prononcés par Mushidi ou Msiri, premier chef des Bayeke," *BJIDCC,* XI (1938), 259–60.

Colard, J. F. "Note sur les Batsamba," *Congo,* I, No. 4 (1936), 523–25.

Colle, R. P. "Origine et explication du pouvoir des chefs dans l'Uruwa," *La Revue congolaise,* I, No. 1 (1910), 58–68.

———. "Généalogie et migrations de quelques grands chefs du Haut-Congo," *La Revue congolaise,* I, No. 2 (1910), 193–207.

———. "Constitution d'un village chez les Baluba-hemba," *La Revue congolaise,* II (1911–12), 309–13.

Comhaire, J. "Coup d'oeil sur l'histoire des peuples africains et afro-américains," *Zaïre,* VII (1953), No. 7, 687–706; No. 10, 1027–51.

Cordeiro, L. "Land of Muata Yamvo," *Journal of the Manchester Geographical Society,* IV (1888–89), 182 ff.

Crine, F. "Aspects politico-sociaux du système de tenure des terres des Luunda septentrionaux." In D. Biebuyck (ed.), *African Agrarian Systems.* London, 1963, pp. 157–72.

Cunnison, I. "A Note on the Lunda Concept of Custom," *Rhodes-Livingstone Journal,* No. 14 (1954), pp. 20–29.

———. "Headmanship and the Ritual of Luapula Villages," *Africa,* XXVI, No. 1 (1956), 2–16.

———. "Perpetual Kinship: A Political Institution of the Luapula Peoples," *Rhodes-Livingstone Journal,* No. 20 (1956), pp. 28–48.

———. "The Reigns of the Kazembes," *Northern Rhodesia Journal,* III, No. 2 (1956), 131–36.

———. "History and Genealogies in a Conquest State," *American Anthropologist,* LIX, No. 1 (1957), 20–31.

———. "Kazembe's Charter," *Northern Rhodesia Journal,* III, No. 3 (1957), 220–32.

———. "Kazembe and the Portuguese, 1798–1832," *JAH,* II, No. 1 (1961), 61–76.

Cuvelier, G. "La vie sociale des Balamba orientaux," *Congo,* II (1932), No. 1, 1–21; No. 2, 161–84.

Cuvelier, J. "Traditions congolaises," *Congo,* II, No. 4 (1930), 469–87.

———. "Contribution à l'histoire du Bas-Congo," IRCB, *Bulletin des Séances,* XIX (1948), 895–921.

————. "Overzicht van de geschiedenis van het oud-koninkrijk Kongo," *Kongo-Overzee*, XVI, No. 1 (1950), 1–16.

————. "Note sur la documentation de l'histoire du Congo," IRCB, *Bulletin des Séances*, XXIV, No. 2 (1953), 442–70.

————. "L'ancien Congo d'après Pierre van den Broecke (1608–12)," IRCB, *Bulletin des Séances*, N.S., I, No. 2 (1955), 169–92.

————. "Notes sur l'histoire du Congo, spécialement du Bas-Congo," ARSOM, *Bulletin des Séances*, VII, No. 2 (1961), 211–14.

Da Silva, J. G. "L'Angola au XVIII me siècle," *Annales économiques, sociales et culturelles*, XIV (1959), 571–80.

De Beaucorps, R. "Le pouvoir politique et social dans la société indigène," *BJIDCC*, XIII, No. 1 (1945), 16–28.

De Bouveignes, O. "De Grandpré à la côte d'Angola en 1786–1787," *Zaïre*, III, No. 10 (1949), 1109–17.

————. "La traite des esclaves à la Côte Occidentale d'Afrique au XXVIIᵉ siècle," *Brousse*, No. 2 (1952), pp. 26–38.

De Bouveignes, O., and J. Cuvelier. "Jerôme de Montesarchio et la découverte du Stanley Pool," *Zaïre*, II, No. 9 (1948), 989–1013.

Decazes, E. "Chez les Batékés," *Revue d'ethnographie*, IV (1885), 160–68.

Decker, H. C. "Die Jagazüge und das Königtum im mittlerem Bantugebiet," *Zeitschrift für Ethnologie*, LXXI, Nos. 4–6 (1939), 229–93.

De Decker, J. "Contribution à l'étude du mariage chez les Bambunda," *BJIDCC*, X, No. 7 (1942), 125–46.

De Hemptinne, J. "Les mangeurs de cuivre du Katanga," *Congo*, I, No. 3 (1926), 371–403.

De Jonghe, E., and T. Simar. "Archives Congolaises," *La Revue congolaise*, III (1912), 419–39; IV (1913), No. 1, 1–29; No. 2, 85–99; No. 3, 154–74, No. 4, 207–25, No. 5, 271–87.

De Kun, N. "La vie et le voyage de L. Magyar dans l'intérieur du Congo en 1850–52," ARSOM, *Bulletin des Séances*, NS, VI, No. 4 (1960), 605–36.

Delaere, J. "A propos de cousins croisés," *BJIDCC*, XVIII, No. 7 (1950), 197–215.

Delcommune, A. "Au coeur du Congo Belge. Comment les sauvages du lac Kisale acceuillirent les premiers Blancs qui se présentèrent chez eux," *Mouvement Géographique*, XXIX, No. 1 (1912), 7–10.

Deleval. "Les tribus Kavati du Mayombe," *La Revue congolaise*, III (1912), 31–40, 103–15, 170–86, 253–64.

De Magalhães, A. A. "Origem dos Basongos," *Mensario administrativo*, XV (1948), 33–38.

De Mahieu, W. "Un cas isolé de click en langue Kongo," *Aequatoria,* XXV, No. 1 (1962), 19–20.

Denis, P. J. "L'organisation d'un peuple primitif," *Congo,* I, No. 4 (1935), 481–502.

Denolf, P. "Geschiedenis der Kasayi-stammen," *Aequatoria,* V, No. 5 (1942), 106–11.

De Pierpont, J. "Les Bambala," *Congo,* I (1932), No. 1, 22–37; No. 2, 185–99.

De Quirini, P. "Les fiançailles de droit chez les Bayansi," *Zaïre,* VI, No. 5 (1952), 499–504.

Descampe, E. "Note sur les Bayanzi," *Congo,* I, No. 5 (1935), 685–88.

De Sousberghe, L. "Etuis péniens ou gaînes de chasteté chez les Bapende," *Africa,* XXIV, No. 3 (1954), 214–19.

————. "De la signification de quelques masques Pende 'Shave' des Shona et 'Mbuya' des Pende," *Zaïre,* XIV, No. 5 (1960), 505–33.

————. "Noms donnés aux Pygmées et souvenirs laissés par eux chez les Pende et Lunda de la Loange," *Congo-Tervuren,* VI, No. 3 (1960), 84–86.

————. "Un masque Tshokwe de Cucumbi (Haut-Kwango, Angola)," *Africa-Tervuren,* VII, No. 3 (1961), 85–87.

De Vos, S. "Les Bamfunuka," *La Revue congolaise,* I (1910), 87–91.

Dolisie, A. "Notice sur les chefs Bateke," *Bulletin de la société des recherches congolaises,* VIII (1927), 44–50.

Donohugh, A. C. L., and P. Berry. "A Luba Tribe in Katanga. Customs and Folklore," *Africa,* V, No. 2 (1932), 176–83.

D'Orjo de Marchovelette, E. "Notes sur les funérailles des chefs Ilunga Kabale et Kabongo Kumwimba: Historique de la chefferie Kabongo—Historique Kongolo—Histoire de la chefferie Kongolo," *BJIDCC,* XVIII (1950), 350–68; XIX (1951), 1–12.

Dullos, H. "Monographie de la chefferie de Kisandja," *La géographie,* LIX (1933), 261–83.

Duysters, L. "Histoire des Aluunda," *Problèmes d'Afrique Centrale,* XII (1958), 75–98.

Fagan, B. "Pre-European Ironworking in Central Africa with Special Reference to Northern Rhodesia," *JAH,* II, No. 2 (1961), 199–210.

Focquet, E., and G. Vanderkerken. "Les populations indigènes des Territoires de Kutu et de Nseontin," *Congo,* II, No. 2 (1924), 129–71.

François, C. von. "Geschichtliches bei den Bangala, Lunda und Kioko," *Globus,* LIII (1888), 273–76.

Freire, B., and F. A. De Castro. "Notice of a Caravan Journey from the East to the West Coast of Africa," *Journal of the Royal Geographical Society*, XXIV (1854), 266–71.

Frobenius, L. "Forschungsreise in das Kasaigebiet," *Zeitschrift für Erdkunde*, NF, IV (1905), 467–71; V (1906), 114–18, 426–31, 493–97.

Froehlich, W. "Das afrikanische Marktwesen," *Zeitschrift für Ethnologie*, LXXII, Nos. 4–6 (1940), 234–328.

Gibbons, A. "Marotseland and the Tribes of the Upper Zambezi," *Proceedings of the Royal Colonial Institute*, XXIX (1897–98), 260–76.

Gilliard, L. "Au Lac Léopold II: Les Bolia. Mort et intronisation d'un grand chef," *Congo*, II, No. 2 (1925), 223–38.

Gluckman, M. "The Village Headman in British Africa," *Africa*, XIX, No. 2 (1949), 89–106.

―――. "The Lozi of Barotseland in North-Western Rhodesia." In E. Colson and M. Gluckman (eds.) *Seven Tribes of British Central Africa*, Manchester, 1951, pp. 1–93.

―――. "Succession and Civil War among the Bemba: An Exercise in Anthropological Theory," *Rhodes-Livingstone Journal*, No. 16 (1954), pp. 6–25.

Graça, J. R. "Expedição ao Muatayanvua," *BSGL*, IX (1890), 365–68.

Grevisse, F. "Les Bayeke," *BJIDCC*, V (1937), No. 1, 1–16; No. 2, 29–40; No. 3, 65–74; No. 4, 97–113; No. 5, 125–40; No. 6, 165–75; VI (1938), No. 7, 200–216, No. 8, 238–41.

―――. "Les traditions historiques des Basanga et de leurs voisins," *CEPSI*, No. 2 (1946–47), pp. 50–84.

―――. "Salines et saliniers indigènes du Haut-Katanga," *CEPSI*, No. 11 (1950), 7–85.

―――. "Notes ethnographiques relatives à quelques populations autochtones du Haut-Katanga industriel," *CEPSI*, No. 32 (1956), 65–207; No. 33 (1956), 68–148; No. 35 (1956), 53–133; No. 40 (1958), 57–79; No. 41 (1958), 25–68.

Guiral, L. "Les Batékés," *Revue d'ethnographie*, V (1886), 135–66.

Guthrie, M. "Some Developments in the Prehistory of the Bantu Languages," *JAH*, III, No. 2 (1962), 273–82.

Hemptinne, J. de. See De Hemptinne, J.

Hiernaux, J., and J. de Buyst. "Note sur une campagne de fouilles à Katoto (région de Bukama, Katanga)," *Zaïre*, XIV, Nos. 2–3 (1960), 251–53.

Inskeep, R. R. "Some Iron Age Sites in Northern Rhodesia," *South African Archaeological Bulletin*, XVII (1962), 136–80.

Jadin, L. "Relation sur le royaume du Congo du P. Raimondo da Dicomano, missionnaire de 1791 à 1795," ARSC, *Bulletin des Séances*, III, No. 2 (1957), 307–37.

———. "Le Congo et la secte des Antoniens. Restauration du royaume sous Pedro IV et la Sainte Antoine Congolaise, 1694-1718," *Bulletin de l'institut historique belge de Rome*, XXXIII (1961), 411–614.

Jensen, A. E. "Die staatliche Organisation und die historischen Ueberlieferungen der Barotse am oberen Zambesi," *Jahresbericht des Würtemberger Vereins für Handelsgeographie*, L (1932), 71–106.

Jonghe, E. de. See De Jonghe, E.

Kaoze, S. "La psychologie des Bantu," *La Revue congolaise*, II (1910–11), 401–37; III (1911–12), 55–63.

Kopytof, I. "Extension of Conflict as a Method of Conflict Resolution among the Suku of the Congo," *Journal of Conflict Resolution*, V, No. 1 (1961), 61–69.

Kun, N. de. See De Kun, N.

Kund. "Bericht über die Kongo-Expedition," *Verhandlungen der Gesellschaft für Erdkunde*, XIII (1886), 313–42.

Labrecque, E. "La tribu des Babemba," *Anthropos*, XXVIII (1933), 633–48; XXXI (1936), 910–21.

———. "Histoire des Mwata Kazembe, chefs Lunda du Luapula, 1700–1945," *Lovania*, XVI (1949), 9–33; XVII (1950), 21–48; XVIII (1951), 18–67.

Lambo, L. "Organisation judiciaire et procédure du tribunal coutumier de Shinkaola," *BJIDCC*, IX, No. 3 (1941), 55–68.

———. "Enquête sur le tribunal non reconnu de Mufumbi," *BJIDCC*, IX (1941), No. 4, 86–90; No. 5, 93–97.

———. "Etude sur les Balala," *BJIDCC*, XIV (1946), No. 8, 231–56; No. 9, 273–300; No. 10, 313–46.

Lanfant, R. "Coutumes juridiques des Baluba de la chefferie Mulongo," *BJIDCC*, III (1935), 51–57, 78–83.

Lazariste, J. "Les Nkumu chez les Ntomba de Bikoro," *Aequatoria*, II (1939), 10–11, 109–23.

Lefebure, P. L. "Een wegstervend bedrijf: Het kopergieten bij de negers in Katanga," *Congo*, II, No. 3 (1930), 359–67.

Lemaire, C. "Les Wamboundous. Les colporteurs noirs entre l'Atlantique et le Katanga," *Revue de Géographie*, L (1902), 499–516; LI (1903), 50–68, 134–50.

Lewis, T. "The Old Kingdom of Kongo," *Geographical Journal,* XXXI (1908), 589–99.

Liétard, L. "Etude sommaire sur la tribu des Lulua," *Bulletin royal de la société belge de geographie,* LIII (1929), 40–43.

Lisulo, B. J. W. "The History of the Barotse Nation," *NADA (The Southern Rhodesia Native Affairs Department Annual),* V (Dec., 1927), 81–84.

Looy, O. van. "La famille chez les Baluba de Museka et de Kayumba," *BJIDCC,* IV (1936), 179–84.

Lopes de Lima, J. J. "Descobrimento e posse do Reino do Congo pelos Portuguezes no Seculo XV, sua conquista por as Nossas armas no secula XVI," *Annaes maritimos e coloniaes,* V, No. 3 (1845), 93–108.

———. "Successos do Reino do Congo no seculo XVII," *Annaes maritimos e coloniaes,* V, No. 3 (1845), 194–99.

Macqueen, J. J. "Journal of Silva Porto with the Arabs from Benguella to Ibo and Mozambique through Africa," *Journal of the Royal Geographical Society,* XXX (1860), 136–54.

Maes, J. "Le camp de Mashita Mbansa et les migrations des Bapende," *Congo,* II, No. 5 (1935), 713–24.

Magalhães, A. A. de. See De Magalhães, A. A.

Mahieu, M. A. "L'exploitation du cuivre par les indigènes au Katanga," *Congo,* II, No. 1 (1925), 107–29.

Mahieu, W. de. See De Mahieu, W.

Makonga, B. "Samba kya Buta," *BJIDCC,* XVI (1948), 304–16; XVII (1949), 321–45.

Malderen, A. van. "Organisation judiciaire des Bakunda," *BJIDCC,* III (1935), 58–60.

———. "Organisation politique et judiciaire coutumières des Bazela de Kiona Zini," *BJIDCC,* IV (1936), 278–83.

———. "Organisation politique et judiciaire coutumières de la chefferie de Mufunga," *BJIDCC,* IV (1936), 174–78.

———. "Contribution à l'histoire et à l'ethnologie des indigènes du Katanga," *BJIDCC,* VIII (1940), No. 7, 193–206; No. 8, 227–39.

Marchal, P. "Sur l'origine des Bazolongo," *Aequatoria,* XI, No. 4 (1948), 121–25.

Marchal, R. "Histoire des Balamba d'après le récit de Louis Lwipa," *Artes Africanae* (1936), p. 13.

———. "Comment le clan des cheveux prit le pouvoir au clan des chèvres," *Bulletin des amis de l'art indigène au Katanga,* XIX (1938), 12–17.

————. "Renseignements historiques relatifs à l'exploitation des mines de cuivre par les indigènes de la Luishia," *BJIDCC*, VII (1939), 10–17.

————. "Le tribunal des Balamba," *CEPSI*, No. 2 (1946–47), pp. 85–93.

Mattenklodt, Von. "Die Kisama." In H. Baumann (ed.), *Koloniale Völkerkunde*. (Weiner Beitrage zur Kultur-Geschichte und Linguistik, Vol. VI.) Horn, 1944, pp. 71–108.

Meiren, J. van der. "La création du monde d'après les Baluba," *La Revue congolaise*, I, No. 2 (1910), 227–29.

Miletto. "Notes sur les ethnies de la région du Haut-Ogooué," *Bulletin de l'institut d'etudes centrafricaines*, NS, II (1951), 19–48.

Milheiros, M. "Lundas e Luenas: Posto de Caianda," *Mensario administrativo* [Angola], XV (1948), 13–20; XVI (1948), 35–43; XVIII (1949), 19–21.

Miracle, M. "Plateau Tonga Entrepreneurs in Historical Inter-regional Trade," *Rhodes Livingstone Journal*, No. 26 (Dec., 1959), pp. 34–50.

Montenez, P. "Notes sur l'identité coutumière des indigènes d'origine Lunda," *BJIDCC*, IV, No. 11 (1936), 269–77.

————. "Etude sur l'organisation judiciaire des Batemba de la chefferie Kiembe," *BJIDCC*, IX (1941), 109–15.

Mue Nlimba. "História politica do Maiombe." In J. Troesch, ed., *Portugal em Africa*, Vol. LV (1953), 19–25; LVII (1953), 187–97.

Munday, J. T. "The Creation of Myth amongst the Lala of Northern Rhodesia," *African Studies*, I, No. 1 (March, 1942), 47–53.

————. "Some Traditions of the Nyendwa Clan of Northern Rhodesia," *Bantu Studies*, XIV, No. 4 (Dec., 1960), 435–54.

Munongo, A. "Lettre de Mwenda II (Mukandavantu)," *BJIDCC*, XVI (1948), No. 7, 199–229; No. 8, 231–44.

————. "Kanoni Kasembia," *Jeune Afrique*, II (1948), 45.

————. "Chants historiques des Bayeke, traduits en Français et expliqués," *BJIDCC*, XVI (1948), 280–94; XX (1952), 305–16.

Naemen, L. van. "Migration des Bayanzi (Bayeye)," *Congo*, I, No. 2 (1934), 189–96.

Nenquin, J. "Opgravingen te Sanga (terr. Bukama, prov., Katanga) seizoen 1957," *Gentse Bijdragen tot de Kunstgeschiedenis en de oudheidkunde*, XVII (1957–58), 289–311.

————. "Une collection de céramique kisalienne au Musée Royal du Congo Belge," *Bulletin de la Société Royale Belge d'Anthropologie et de Préhistoire*, LXIX (1958), 151–210.

———. "Dimple-based Pots from Kasai, Belgian Congo," *Man,* LIX, No. 242 (1959), 153–55.

———. "Une importante contribution du Musée à la connaissance des cultures protohistoriques du Congo," *Congo-Tervuren,* V, No. 1 (1959), 1–5.

———. "Protohistorische metaaltechniek in Katanga," *Africa-Tervuren,* VII, No. 4 (1961), 97–101.

———. "Notes on Some Early Pottery Cultures in Northern Katanga," *JAH,* IV, No. 1 (1963), 19–32.

Nicolai, H. "Le Bas Kwilu. Les problemes geographiques," *Bulletin de la société royale belge de géographie,* CLXXXI (1957), 21–66.

Papy, L. "Les populations Bateke (A.E.F.)," *Cahiers d'Outre-Mer,* II, No. 6 (1949), 112–34.

Peeraer, S. "La littérature orale muluba," *Bulletin des amis de l'art indigène au Katanga,* I (October, 1937), 8–15.

———. "Gouwzang der Bene-Lupulu," *Congo,* I (1938), No. 3, 261–87; No. 4, 416–40.

Philpott, R. "Makumba. The Baushi Tribal God," *JRAI,* LXVI (Jan.-June, 1936), 189–208.

Pierpont, J. de. See De Pierpont, J.

Pirenne, J. H. "Les éléments fondamentaux de l'ancienne structure territoriale et politique du Bas-Congo," ARSC, *Bulletin des Séances,* NS, V, No. 3 (1959), 557–77.

Pogge, P. "Das Reich und der Hof des Mwata Jamvo," *Globus,* XXXII (1877), 14 ff.

Quirini, P. de. See De Quirini, P.

Rauq, P. "Les relations entre tribus au Kasai. Leurs incidences géopolitiques et économiques," *Africa-Tervuren,* VII, No. 2 (1961), 47–58.

Redinha, J. "Dumba-ua-Tembo: régulo do Tchiboco (nota historico-biografica)," *Boletim cultural do museu de Angola,* II (1960), 51–59.

Reichard, P. "Bericht über seine Reise in Ostafrika und dem Quellengebiet des Kongo," *Verhandlungen der Gesellschaft für Erdkunde,* XIII (1886), 107–25.

Richards, A. I. "Tribal Government in Transition: The Babemba of North-Eastern Rhodesia," *JRAI,* XXXIV, No. 137, Suppl. (Oct., 1935), 3–26.

———. "The Political System of the Bemba Tribe—North-Eastern Rhodesia." In M. Fortes and E. E. Evans-Pritchard, eds., *African Political Systems,* London, 1940, pp. 83–120.

———. "Some Types of Family Structure Amongst the Central Bantu." In A. R. Radcliffe-Brown and C. D. Forde, eds., *African Systems of Kinship and Marriage*, London, 1950, pp. 207–51.

———. "The Bemba of North-Eastern Rhodesia." In E. Colson and M. Gluckman, eds., *Seven Tribes of British Central Africa*, Manchester, 1951, pp. 164–93. [Reprinted with slight modifications from *Bantu Studies*, IX, No. 3 (1935).]

———. "Social Mechanisms for the Transfer of Political Rights in Some African Tribes," *JRAI*, XC, No. 2 (1960), 175–90.

Roland, R. "Récits historiques des Basanga," *Bulletin des Missions*, XVI, Suppl. 1 (1937), 9–32.

———. "Récits historiques des Basanga," *Congo*, I, No. 1 (1938), 82–92.

Roy, H. van. "De godservaring bij de Bakongo," *Aequatoria*, XXII, No. 4 (1959), 132–43.

———. "L'Origine des Balunda du Kwango," *Aequatoria*, XXIV, No. 4 (1961), 136–41.

Salmon, P. "Mémoires de la relation de voyage de M. Massiac à Angola et à Buenos Aires," ARSOM, *Bulletin des Séances*, NS, VI, No. 4 (1960), 585–604.

Samain, A. "Geschiedenis der Bena Lulua's," *Congo*, II, No. 2 (1922), 229–32.

———. "Les Basonge," *Congo*, I (1924), 48–52.

Sautter, G. "Le plateau Congolais de Mbé," *Cahiers d'études africaines*, II (1960), 123–66.

Schuett, O. "Im Reiche der Bangala," *Ausland*, XX (1881), 381–84.

Sendwe, J. "Traditions et coutumes ancestrales des Baluba Shankadji," *CEPSI*, No. 24 (1954), 87–120.

Silva, J. G. da. See Da Silva, J. G.

Simonetti, G. "Giacinto Brugiotti da Vetralla e la sua missione al Congo (1651–1657)," *Bolletino della Società geografica italiana*, VIII (1907), 305–22, 369–81.

Smith, E. "Sebetwane and the Makololo," *African Studies*, XV, No. 2 (1956), 49–70.

Sousberghe, L. de. See De Sousberghe, L.

Stappers, L. "Iets over de Ntambwe fetisj in Kasai," *Aequatoria*, XIV, No. 3 (1951), 90–92.

Stas, J. B. "Les Nkumu chez les Ntomba de Bikoro," *Aequatoria*, II (1939), 10–11, 109–23.

Stienon, L. "Note concernant la tribu Baushi," *Congo*, VII, No. 2 (June, 1926), 59–61.

Struyf, I. "De verhuizingen bij de Kamtsha," *Congo,* II, No. 3 (1936), 343–50.

——. "Kahemba: envahisseurs Badjok et conquerants Balunda," *Zaïre,* II, No. 4 (1948), 351–90.

Struyf, R. P. "Migrations des Bapende et des Bambunda," *Congo,* I, No. 5 (1931), 667–70.

Sulzmann, E. "Die Bokopo-Herrschaft der Bolia," *Archiv für Rechts- und Sozial philosophie,* XLV, No. 3 (1959), 389–417.

Swartenbroeckx, J. "Quand l'Ubangi vint au Kwango," *Zaïre,* II, No. 7 (1948), 721–55.

Theuws, T. "Naitre et mourir dans le rituel luba," *Zaïre,* XIV, Nos. 2–3 (1960), 115–74.

Timmermans, P. "Les SapoSapo près de Luluabourg," *Africa-Tervuren,* VIII, No. 2 (1962), 29–53.

Tonnoir, R. "Contribution à l'enquête de constitution du secteur des Bawumbu," *BJIDCC,* III (1935), 25–27, 47–50; IV (1936), 71–77, 95–96.

Torday, E. "Note on the Natives of the Kwilu, Congo Free State," *Man,* V, No. 75 (1905), 135–38.

——. "The Northern Babunda," *Man,* XIX, No. 26 (1919), 49–55.

——. "The Influence of the Kingdom of Kongo on Central Africa," *Africa,* I, No. 2 (1928), 157–69.

Torday, E., and T. Joyce. "Notes on the Ethnography of the Bambala," *JRAI,* XXXV (1905), 398–426.

Torday, E., and T. Joyce. "Notes on the Ethnography of the Bayaka," *JRAI,* XXXVI (1906), 39–58.

Torday, E., and T. Joyce. "Note on the Southern Bambala," *Man,* VII, No. 52 (1907), 81–84.

Torday, E., and T. Joyce. "On the Ethnology of the South-West Congo Free State," *JRAI,* XXXVII (1907), 133–56.

Trezenem, E. "Les Bateke Balali," *Journal de la société des Africanistes,* X (1940), 1–63.

Troesch, J. "Le Nkutu du comte de Soyo," *Aequatoria,* XXIV, No. 2 (1961), 41–49.

——. "Le royaume de Soyo," *Aequatoria,* XXV, No. 3 (1962), 95–100.

Vancoillie, G. "Grepen uit de Mbagani traditie," *Aequatoria,* X, No. 4 (1947), 122–29.

Van der Ginste, F. "Anthropometric Study on the Bapende and Basuku of the Belgian Congo," *American Journal of Physical Anthropology,* NS, IV, No. 2 (1946), 125–52.

Van der Noot, A. "Quelques éléments historiques sur l'empire luba, son organisation et sa direction," *BJIDCC*, IV, No. 7 (1936), 141–49.

Vandevenne. "Organisations judiciaires Bayaka," *BJIDCC*, III, No. 6 (1935), 130–34.

Vansina, J. "De handelingen der voorouders," *Kongo-Overzee*, XXII, Nos. 4–5 (1956), 257–300.

――――. "Migrations dans la province du Kasai: Une hypothèse," *Zaïre*, X, No. 1 (1956), 69–85.

――――. "Recording the Oral History of the Bakuba," *JAH*, I (1960), No. 1, 45–54; No. 2, 257–70.

――――. "A Comparison of African Kingdoms," *Africa*, XXXII, No. 4 (1962), 324–35.

――――. "La fondation du royaume de Kasanje," *Aequatoria*, XXV, No. 2 (1962), 45–62.

――――. "Long Distance Trade Routes in Central Africa," *JAH*, III (1962), 375–90.

――――. "Notes sur l'origine du royaume de Kongo," *JAH*, IV, No. 1 (1963), 33–38.

Van Zandijcke, A. See Zandijcke, A. van

Verbeken, A. "Institutions politiques indigènes: accession au pouvoir chez certaines tribus du Congo par le système électif," *BJIDCC*, III, No. 1 (1935), 1–3.

Verly, R. "Le 'roi divin' chez les Ovibundu et Kimbundu de l'Angola," *Zaïre*, IX, No. 7 (1955), 675–703.

Vervaecke, R. P. "Les Bena Lulua," *La Revue congolaise*, I (1910), No. 1, 69–86; No. 3, 325–45.

Von François, C. See François, C. von

Vos, S. de. See De Vos, S.

Watson, W. "The Kaonde Village," *Rhodes-Livingstone Journal*, No. 15 (1954), pp. 1–29.

Weekx, G. "La peuplade des Ambundu," *Congo*, I (1937), No. 4, 353–73; II (1937), No. 1, 13–35; No. 2, 150–66.

Weghsteen, J. "De toren van Babel in de overleveringen van de Watabwa (Katanga)," *Kongo-Overzee*, XXI, No. 2 (1955), 157–59.

――――. "Origine et histoire des Watabwa (Haut-Congo)," *Annali Lateranensi*, XXIV (1960), 364–75.

White, C. M. N. "Stratification and Modern Changes in an Ancestral Cult," *Africa*, XIX, No. 4 (Oct., 1949), 324–31.

――――. "The Balovale Peoples and Their Historical Background," *Rhodes-Livingstone Journal*, No. 8 (1949), pp. 26–41.

————. "Factors in the Social Organization of the Luvale," *African Studies*, XIV, No. 3 (1955), 97–112.

————. "The Role of Hunting and Fishing in Luvale Society," *African Studies*, XV, No. 2 (1956), 75–86.

————. "Chieftainship in Luvale Political Organization," *Journal of African Administration*, IX, No. 3 (1957), 129–36.

————. "Clan, Chieftainship, and Slavery in Luvale Political Organization," *Africa*, XXVII, No. 1 (Jan., 1957), 59–75.

————. "Luvale Political Organisation and the Luvale Lineage," *Proceedings of the XIIIth Conference. Rhodes-Livingstone Institute for Social Research*. Lusaka, 1959, pp. 113–20.

————. "The Ethno-history of the Upper Zambezi," *African Studies*, XXI (1962), 10–27.

Winterbottom, J. M. "Outline Histories of Two Northern Rhodesian Tribes," *Rhodes-Livingstone Journal*, No. 9 (1950), pp. 20–25.

Zandijcke, A. van. "Note historique sur les origines de Luluabourg (Malandi)," *Zaïre*, VI, No. 3 (1952), 227–49.

Other Sources

UNPUBLISHED MANUSCRIPTS

Carpentier. "Histoire de la souschefferie Kashobwe." 1929.

Da Dicomano Raimundo. "Relation 1798." Ms. F. G. 8554, fol. 103–115v°, Biblioteca Nacional of Lisbon. A typewritten copy established by L'Abbé L. Jadin was used.

Da Pavia, Andrea. "Relation." Ms. 3165, fol. 68–132v°, Biblioteca Nacional of Madrid. A typewritten copy established by L'Abbé L. Jadin was used.

Kopytof, I. "Suku Religion: A Study in Internally Induced Reinterpretation." Ph.D. dissertation, Northwestern University, Evanston, 1960.

BIBLIOGRAPHIES

Bibliographie Ethnographique du Congo Belge et des régions avoisinantes. Tervuren: Musée Royal du Congo Belge, 1925. Yearly. (Succeeds Halkin)

Halkin, J. *Revue bibliographique de sociologie ethnographique*. Brussels, 1909–25. Yearly.

Jones, R. J. *Africa Bibliography Series: South-east Central Africa and Madagascar*. London, 1961.

Walraet, M. *Bibliographie du Katanga*. (ARSC, XXXII, No. 3; XLV, No. 1; XXXIII, No. 4.) Brussels, 1954–60.

ETHNIC MAPS*

Boone, O. *Carte ethnique du Congo. Quart sud-est.* (MRAC, No. 37.) Tervuren, 1961.

Forde, C. D. (ed.) *Ethnographic Survey of Africa: East Central Africa.* London: International African Institute, 1950.

——. *Ethnographic Survey of Africa: West Central Africa.* London: International African Institute, 1951.

Soret, M. *Carte ethnique de l'Afrique équatoriale française.* Feuilles No. 1 et 2°. Brazzaville, 1955.

* No other good ethnic maps are as yet available.

Glossary of African Expressions

aamyene [Tyo], councilors

acubuung or *tubungu* [Lunda], chiefs of the land

ampat [Lunda], parcel of bush ruled by a *ciloot* (political chief)

ansiku, alternate name for Tyo, used in documents

bajangi [Bena Mushilu], ancestors appearing in dreams; part of the *lubuku* (a religious cult)

balopwe [Luba], invaders; founders of the Luba "empire"

biangu [Nsese-Bolia], strips of cloth decorated with cowrie shells

bokapa ekopo [Bolia], literally, the division of a leopard skin, but actually the division of an original lump of kaolin, which symbolized belonging to group for newcomers

bokopo [Bolia], principle of political organization; "office"

bukishi [Songye], a religious association responsible for political decisions

bulopwe [Luba], sacred quality of kingship stemming from the blood line

bungulo [Lunda-Pende], title

cibiing [Lunda], official who was a guardian of the borders between Luba and Lunda

cikolwe [Luapula], hereditary headmen of clan sections

cilool [Lunda], political chief

citentam [Lunda], national council and court of highest titleholders

citimukulu [Luba, Lunda, Bemba], second king; founder of present line of kings

ciyul [Lunda], council of elders

ekopo [Bolia], leopard skin. See also *bokapa ekopo*

elima [Bolia], power of nature spirit, given to kings

iloki [Bolia], a quality possessed by witches and attributed to kings and chiefs, implying an ability to help or harm with no outward sign

inabanza [Luba], the keeper of sacred emblems, and the most important provincial chief

iyanga [Lunda], colony of the Lunda

izule [Dia], chief

kadilu [Luba], land-owning chief

kahungula [Lunda], title

3 3 3

kakenge [Lwena], title for senior chief position

kakwata [Lunda], chiefs who traveled with military retinue to collect tribute or carry out orders

kalandala [Lunda], ruler

kalandula [Jaga], ruler

kalulua [Lunda], ruler

kambòngo, title for Suku chief in 1880's

kasala [Luba], praise name for the keepers of the traditions

katongo [Luapula], domains of clans

kiamfu [Lunda], rulers; [Yaka], kings

kilolo [Luba], chief of several villages, political chief

kimbares [Angola], African soldiers

kimpanzu [Kongo], only descent group (*infantes*) for all kings prior to 1636

kimulazu [Kongo], additional descent group for kings after 1636

kioni [Luba], title in hierarchy of kingdom

kitenta [Luba], king's capital as it was preserved after his death

kitomi [Kongo], earth priest

kolomo [Lele], system of pawnship; pawns were women who were given in marriage by clan sections or villages which had received this right as a compensation for a blood debt incurred by the original clan section of a woman

koola, word for Lunda

libata [Kongo], village in a chiefdom consisting of a maximum of fifty huts

lobolo [Lozi], bride wealth, payable in cattle

lubuku [Bena Mushilu], a religious cult

lukonkesha or *rukonkish* [Lunda], a perpetual aunt

mafuk [Ngoy, Kakongo], governor of the harbor

makoko [Vila], form of Tyo word (*ūūkoo*) for king

makumba [Aushi], fetish, charm

mambuk [Ngoy, Kakongo], minister of trade and of Europeans

mani (also *ne*) [Kongo] and *na* [north of Kongo], titleholder

mani lumbu [Kongo], governor of king's quarters in capital

mani mpanza [Kongo], an official who helped supervise the government income

mani samba [Kongo], an official who helped supervise the government income

mani vangu vangu [Kongo], first judge, specializing in cases of adultery

mbanza [Kongo], village in a chiefdom consisting of a minimum of two hundred huts

mbay [Lunda], elder of the headmen

mbyazi [Kongo], client lineages

mfutila [Kongo], set of officials who helped supervise the government income

miluwa [Mbala], name for Lunda

mindele [Kongo], literally, whales, but actually caravels

moju [Sakata], chief ruler, chosen from ruling clan

mojuiceu [Dia], head of the clan

monoemuji [Boma], *mwene mushi* [Nunu], *nimeamaya* [Nunu], sixteenth- and seventeenth-century titles applying to a chief Nunu area

mpesi [Luba], title in hierarchy of kingdom

muidzu [Tyo], one of two most important titled chiefs

mukalenge [Luba], title

mulopwe [Luba], the word for chief

mulopwe wa bantu [Luba or Hemba], chief of the people

mundequete, name for Tyo used in documents

mutiy [Lunda], war leader

mvwab [Lunda], officials who governed single villages and whose *mwaantaangaand* title had lapsed

mwaantaangaand [Lunda], hereditary headmen, chiefs of the land

mwaant yaav [Lunda], literally, Lord of the Vipers, but actually a generic title for Lunda kingship

mwadi [Luba], woman in charge of *kitenta* (king's capital, which was preserved after the king's death)

mwamba [Bemba], a major chieftainship; originally a Bemba chief of a Lunda province, the first titleholder

mwami [Kazembe], title (taken by Msiri) for king

mwana uta [Lunda], the favored son

mwangana [Lwena], incoming Lunda who became chiefs, eventually with the power of judges, able to settle feuds involving murder

mwata kumbana [Lunda], title

ndumbululu [Kongo], praise name

nelumbo [Kongo], one of the oldest titles in the kingdom. See also *mani lumbu*

ngaailiino [Tyo], one of the two most important titled chiefs

ngaand [Lunda], land surrounding a village

ngaandziyóó [Tyo], titled chiefs who had no domain or *nkobi* of their own

ngambela [Lozi], title for political minister

nganbela [Lozi], title for first minister

ngeli, a class in Boma system

ngeli Boma, title of ruler of Boma kingdom

ngola [Dembo], king of Ndongo

ngolambolo [Kongo, Ndongo, Kasanje], titleholders with military titles

nkira [Tyo (Teke)], spirit of chief's domain

nkobi [Tyo], a basket functioning as a shrine for a major *nkira* (spirit)

nkuba [Shila], rulers of three smaller chiefdoms

nkula [Bemba], a major chieftainship

nkumu [possibly of Bolia origin], Bomba chief at level above village

nkwe mbali [Tyo], hoard of sacred objects

nsikala [Luba], the king who ruled during an interregnum

nswaan mulapw or *Swana Mulopwe* [Lunda], crown prince

nswaan muruund or *Swana Mulunda* [Lunda], perpetual Mother of Lunda

ntikala [Lunda], second in command

ntinu [Bungu], the title of the first king of Kongo

ntomb [Lunda], delegates who represented the tributary chiefs at the capital

ntombo [Lunda], tributary wives

nyim [Lele, Bushoong], king

nyimi [Nunu], king

nzimbu [Kongo], shells in the royal fishery (which was owned by the king) used as currency

olusenje [Mbailundu (Ovimbundu)], council for administrative and judicial matters

ouvidor [Angola], chief justice

pumbo [Kongo], market of the Hum people at Stanley Pool

rukonkish or *lukonkesha* [Lunda], a perpetual aunt

sanama [Lunda], governor's title

sungu [Luba], third in command under king

tendala [Kongo, Ndongo, Kasanje], titleholders with military titles

tubungu. See *acubuung*

twite [Luba], chief minister of a deceased king, left in charge of king's former *kitenta (capital)* with the *mwadi;* also, a titleholder who served as a war leader and head of the officer corps

tyanza [Lunda], governor

ūūkoo [Tyo], king's title

vidye [Luba], nature spirit

yeli [Ngong], chief

yikeezy [Lunda], an official appointed to supervise a *cilool* suspected of dishonesty

Index